BROTHER BETRAYED

OF GOLD & BLOOD
BOOK TWO

Jenny Wheeler

Published by Happy Families Ltd
Copyright © 2018 Jenny Wheeler

ISBN 978-0-473-43007-8 (print)
ISBN 978-0-473-43009-2 (Kindle)
ISBN 978-0-473-43008-5 (Epub)

Print Edition First published September 2018

'No matter how big your hands may be, they can't cover the whole sky.' *Chinese proverb*

If you enjoy Brother Betrayed, get a FREE PREVIEW of the first four chapters of Double Jeopardy, Book Three in the Of Gold & Blood series.

He's haunted by war. She's searching for her twin. When a mysterious murder brings them together, can solving the case heal their broken hearts?

Double Jeopardy details can be found at the end of Brother Betrayed

Prologue

August 1868, Grass Valley, California

Comprador Chung Ting Hon sprawled across the capacious bed, patrician profile smooth and unlined against the white linen of the down pillow, his right arm flung protectively across his young wife, Beautiful Jade, who snuggled against him. The only sound the man in the doorway heard as he paused, a dark shadow backlit momentarily in the ambient light from the Gold House hallway, was his own breathing, rhythmic and deep.

The new moon was hidden below the Sierra Nevadas, magnifying the Milky Way's white light dazzle that could be seen through the upstairs windows, leaving the naked honeymooners barely visible in the dim lunar gloom. They had thrown off their bedclothes, their bodies and the heat of the night all the warmth they needed, legs entwined like the new lovers they were.

The smell of orange-blossom oil lingered, reminding the man, who loitered on the threshold, of earliest memories of his father's house. He stepped lightly in and closed the door with a barely audible click. He leaned back against it as he steadied his breathing, stroking his leather-gloved fingers from tip to base as he savoured the peaceful scene. He'd become hardened to the idea of necessary death. *Kill a chicken to frighten the monkeys. Or as the gweilo say, the end justifies the means.* He'd told himself that many times in the past months, never more so than on this night. But this one would be different from all the others.

He moved with purpose, balanced and light on the balls of his feet, going to the man's side of the bed first. *Macau's one-time merchant prince has no idea he is going to end here, in the home of a man he regards as a son.* With calm deliberation he drew a long thin blade from the sleeve of his tunic and leaned over the sleeping form. One hand tightly clasping the knife's leather handle, he placed the other on the top of the man's head and pushed the lethal tip down hard into the slight depression at the base of his neck. With a wrenching slash upwards, he severed the lower brain stem and cut off all involuntary functioning like breathing and heart beat. The compradore's face was thrust with suffocating pressure into the pillow, and he died before he could even draw a last breath. His attacker was already moving to the other side of the bed, the sharpened blade red with his father's blood. His hand closed over the woman's mouth, and in one smooth movement he wrenched her head sideways and slid the ten-inch stiletto across her throat.

A few seconds more and he was back at the door. He paused and took in the room with a sweeping glance. Blood from the woman's ugly neck wound spilled onto the hand that had caressed her lovingly minutes before. Her killer stood in the doorway, his head tipped back, exultant, face washed in an affirming starlight. Then he struck a match, cupping the flickering flame in his hands until it caught hold. It was the work of seconds to set alight the discarded sheet that lay on the floor. He allowed himself a final triumphant glance and turned and left the smouldering room.

One

Business magnate and mine owner Sir John Russell had slept only fitfully when he had retired after saying goodnight to Chung Ting Hon and Beautiful Jade, his exquisite young wife. He'd woken several times and drifted back to sleep, but this time round he knew it was hopeless to wait to fall into torpor — he had too much on his mind to slumber.

He lay curled under a single sheet in the muted midnight light and listened to the usual night noises: the whispering scuttle of ceiling mice, the creaking of the pine rafters as they cooled from the heat of the day. Otherwise a comforting silence mantled Gold House, the big villa filled with out-of-town guests, his revered Chung Ting Hon among them.

He smiled ruefully. The old man who founded Russell & Chung Trading with his father Sir Robert Russell more than thirty years ago was now eighty, but at thirty-eight he was trailing the comprador in vitality. He had been very successful at diversifying and expanding the business his father had founded, but at what cost? He had no wife, no family, and the kinship ties he'd taken for granted were disintegrating around him.

The one bright spot was his recent reunion with his half-brothers

Sebastian and Nathan: they had been separated by the Pacific Ocean since their father's death more than fifteen years ago. Nathan and Seb were just boys when Sir Robert had died; Nathan had gone with his Australian mother to Sydney, Seb to his Boston uncle, and the three brothers had not seen each other again until a few months ago.

He sighed and gave up on the idea of sleep. Instead he rolled onto his back and laced his fingers behind his head, thinking back over the evening's discussions. He had invited the comprador to stay so they could settle the dangerous rivalry boiling up between Ting Hon's two sons, the first-born Chung Ji Ming, known to him as Ollie or Oliver, the name his English mother, Amelia Russell, Sir Robert's sister, had given him, and his half-brother Chung Ji Zeng.

The Chung sons ran not just the China side of the family trading company but also headed the Black Dragon Benevolent Society — one of the six powerful organisations that effectively governed California's Chinese settlers, recruiting labor for railroad building, policing their movements and completing the essential ritual task of sending their bones back home to China if they died. Part social agency and part business, Black Dragon had grown exponentially in the two decades that men from the Pearl River delta had flooded into Gold Mountain — or Gum Saan, Cantonese for San Francisco — seeking their fortunes in gold and other commodities.

Ji Zeng had always resented his brother, the first son of comprador Chung Ting Hon. After John's own mother's death when he was four years old, his Aunt Amelia had been a mother to him as well as to Ollie. They had grown up together, more like brothers than cousins.

But until yesterday, he had not grasped the younger Chung's escalating ambition, nor his new obsession with returning to opium trading — the commodity that had got Russell & Chung started, but had long ago been discarded. John knew that Ollie would be vehemently opposed, but the discussion had never taken place because he hadn't appeared at the meeting — and that just wasn't like him. Ollie put his heart and soul into his role as his father's successor and he would never stand him up.

Even more mysteriously, no one — including Ollie's English wife, Selina — had a clue as to where he was. Ji Zeng had floated a fanciful story that he was in Hong Kong on urgent business, but John knew that was pure fantasy. Ollie would never have left without telling Selina his plans. Something just wasn't right.

He yawned, suddenly feeling weary. In a few hours he would put Ting Hon and Beautiful Jade on the San Francisco stagecoach. He still had faint hopes the patriarch could talk some sense into Ji Zeng, who was adamant that Black Dragon would be left behind unless it followed some of the other Six Societies into opium and prostitution. He rolled onto his side and hugged a pillow close. Despite his restlessness, he was on the verge of dropping off when he smelt the faintest whiff of smoke. He sat bolt upright, his senses on high alert, his eyes stinging. Then he heard a sharp crack, like the snap of wood burning. Galvanized, he was off the bed and to the door in two strides, the sheets trailing behind him.

His eyes were streaming before he got his hand to the door handle. He opened the door slowly, unsure of what lay in store. Dense black smoke was curling up from the hall. He peered down the hallway to where his guests slept, his ears singing with the unmistakable roar of fire, cheeks smarting from a wave of heat that rolled towards him. The guest room door was closed, but an eerie flickering of light from under it confirmed his worst fears.

Grabbing the sheet at his ankles as a mask for his nose and mouth, he sprinted down the passage, wrenched it open and stopped dead. Flames were already creeping onto the ceiling from the wall on the far side of the room. Through the smoke he could see two figures sprawled on the bed, the man on his front, the woman on her back, her face another-worldly white except for the bloody gash at her throat. He sprang to the bed, although instinct told him they were already dead. He had just taken hold of Ting Hon's wrist when a heart-stopping boom sounded overhead.

He dropped Ting Hon's limp hand and dodged back to the shelter of the hallway as burning ceiling fragments rained down on the bed, showering him with hot embers. He was standing gawping in disbelief at the burning bed when more debris rained down, striking him heavily down his left side. Pain shot from his knee to his groin and he staggered to remain upright.

Where was everyone? The house was full of family and friends, among them soon-to-be-married Nathan, and the celebrated Maori opera singer Pania Te Awa Hayes, a friend from New Zealand who had lived in California for some years. Where were Mrs Snively the housekeeper, and his Chinese house servants Mr and Mrs Lee?

"Wake up! Fire!" Oblivious to the pain in his leg, he staggered back down the hall, banging on walls and doors, shouting warnings. His voice, which had started as a raw croak, grew louder and more urgent with every step. "Fire!"

Two

Deputy Virgil Hale drew deeply on his cigar and blew the smoke in a continuous deliberate stream over his left shoulder, narrowly missing John's face. Jaw clenched, he turned away from the deputy's gray fumes and inhaled deep, long and slow. Air that smelt of smouldering wood filled his lungs and he willed himself to relax.

He had been awake since the fire shattered his sleep eight hours ago, and fatigue and frustration were weakening his self-control. His injured leg hurt like blazes, but he stood grimly gazing at the ruins of the house he had hoped would provide a cherished sanctuary for his future wife and family. A day ago he was a successful respected businessman with the reasonable hope that the woman he chose would accept him and his fine Gold House without hesitation. Now he stood in the eye of a maelstrom; home gone, treasured father figure dead — almost certainly murdered — under his roof, his family partners locked in a deadly feud. And this mulish lawman couldn't be less concerned.

In the dazed hours after the blaze was put out he'd tried to order his thoughts and get some plan of action under way. The first step was to get in a sheriff to start investigating the comprador's death, the ensuing arson and Ollie's disappearance. It was no coincidence

— they had to be related. Then he would move on to other urgent things, like the comprador's funeral and rebuilding his home.

The big man with a graying walrus moustache standing next to him regarding the smoking ruins was one of two deputies appointed to assist and replace Grass Valley's permanent lawman Jeb Rogerson in his absence back East on urgent family business. Hale was the senior and permanent appointment while John's brother Seb was the junior and temporary, so he'd thought it best to call Hale in, but now he was having second thoughts. It was fast becoming obvious that Hale didn't see any problem that required a lawman's intervention.

"I can understand it's a damned nuisance losing your fine house, Sir John, I really can," he was saying as he tapped on the cigar, his ash adding to the black cinders they crunched underfoot. "And of course we're lucky no one else was seriously injured. A bit of smoke to get over is all. I'm sure your housekeeper will be fine in a few days. I just don't see what you expect me to do about it."

John was about to interrupt but Hale plowed on. "It's an unfortunate fact that wooden houses burn so easily. Damn near wiped out Grass Valley in Fifty-Five, as you know. Bad luck, too, that your guests were caught in it. But we've just no way of knowing who's responsible."

John stamped on a smouldering ember with his boot.

"My stable hand being knocked out when he went to investigate a noise – that indicates intruders."

Hale grunted grudgingly. "It does. But I'm not sure we'd know where to look in finding the perpetrator. And after all . . ." His eyes flickered side ways, avoiding John's gaze. "After all, they were only Chinese."

John felt the anger that he'd been struggling to suppress boil over. For a moment he was four years old, cowering in a dark alcove, his mother sprawled across the floor of their Hong Kong house, mouth opening and closing like a stranded fish. He had been powerless to do anything then too.

"I beg your pardon?" His heart was so cold that he imagined the air temperature had dropped by several degrees. "What did you say?"

Hale stubbed out his cigar and stepped out of range of his stare. "What I mean is they're not like us, are they? For a start, they aren't Americans."

John braced himself to his full six-foot-plus height. "The man who died in my house this morning was like a father to me. He was a protector and guide." He thought of the hours, days, he and Ollie had spent tagging along as Ting Hon went about his business, hanging on every word and, most of all, feeling secure in the shelter of his eminence. He wasn't called Ting Hon, a name associated with palace rule and justice from ancient times, for nothing. He was a man of influence, from a line of Imperial counsellors, and one of the wisest men John had ever known.

Hale spread his hands wide, palms up, attempting to pacify. "I intend no offense, Sir John. It's just how it is in these parts, you know that. I can understand you've suffered a grievous loss. But there's no way we can tell how your guests died — apart from being burnt to death, I mean. And if your man wasn't up to the job of security . . . Maybe you just need to take a might more care in future."

John knew he was fighting a losing battle but persisted anyway. "And what about the disappearance of my business partner, Oliver Chung — Ji Ming? Is that of no interest either?"

The sheriff shrugged. "Like I say, it's Chinese business, isn't it. Nothing I can do about it. And I don't think it's a good idea for you to be barging into it, either. You might have been born over there . . ." He regarded John with curiosity, as if seeing him in a new light. "Yes, as I say you might have been born over there, but you're one of us, is what I mean. Them Chinamen? You've got no idea who or what you're dealing with. Leave it alone is what I'd advise." He turned to leave.

In frustration, John stabbed the toe of his boot into the ashes. He supposed he shouldn't have been surprised at the deputy's attitude. It accurately reflected how many locals viewed the Chinese workers arriving daily at Gold Mountain, as they called it, seeking to accumulate a modest fortune and return home. But he felt an impotent rage that he might not be able to get justice for the man who had been a fountain of wily wisdom when he'd needed it most. He kicked again and his boot came up hard against an object in the cooling ruins. It was the iron bedstead Ting Hon and Beautiful Jade had died on last night.

He reached out and touched the blackened frame. It was still warm. The brass headboard curliques had melted away, but the bed frame stood scorched but recognizable. He closed his eyes and pictured Ting Hon's serene face, radiant with an inner spirit that defied his years. He shook his head to clear the image, and was turning to go when his eye caught an object trapped in a corner of the iron base. Curious, he reached out and captured it in his hand. He rubbed the hard surface to clean it, examining it carefully as he did.

As his fingers traced delicate Chinese characters carved into a jade surface, a charge of heat ran down his arm. He knew what this was: the precious Dragon Seal, the chop used by Ting Hon and his sons to authorize all their major transactions. He must have been holding onto it for Ollie, who had assumed general running of the company years ago, but John couldn't think of a good reason why Ollie would have passed it back to his father.

He rolled the intricately carved block between his fingers, taking momentary comfort in the elegant detailing. Ting Hon's death, the deliberately lit fire — these alone were weird enough, but to also find this treasure in the wreckage? There was no explanation for its presence. Things had just got a whole lot stranger, so finding Ollie was now even more urgent. If the lawman wasn't going to take action, John would have to do it without him.

Three

Californian stage star Grayson 'Graysie' Travers Castellanos and her Sydney fiancée Nathan Russell stood arm in arm at the entryway to the Stockton dining room, their faces beaming welcome.

"We love having you here, Pania." Graysie's red gold hair fell around her shoulders in a shining flow. "The fire was a disaster, no one would suggest anything else. We all feel for John. You can stay here with us for as long as you like." The child of Elanora Grayson Travers, an East Coast 'prodigal daughter' who eloped at 19, Graysie had inherited her mother's well-born gentility and, by the magic of nurture, assimilated her Spanish stepfather's bravura.

Pania had always admired her optimism, but she had never seen her as glowing as she was right now. Her joy lit up everything around her, not least the lightly bearded blond Australian at her side. Pania flushed with an infusing warmth just looking at them.

Nathan and Graysie had announced their engagement three days ago and were looking towards a December wedding. They were planning to visit Nathan's mother and sisters in Sydney after the wedding, but for now were focused on business opportunities in California, including getting the Ophir, an old gold mine Graysie had inherited, up and running.

Nathan had worked tirelessly for most of the day helping his brother damp down and clean up after the Gold House fire, but you wouldn't know it from looking at him. Lean, bronzed, and brimming with vitality, he had the look of a man who had discovered heaven on earth, and wasn't about to let it go.

Despite her pleasure for them, Pania couldn't ignore the sharp twinge that dug in under her ribs. Graysie and Nathan had weathered some big storms to arrive in this safe harbour, she'd give them that. She didn't begrudge them their happiness for one moment. She just wished she could mirror it in her own life. An image of Nathan's dark, intense half-brother, Sir John Russell, floated uninvited to her mind.

"Let me get you a glass of wine, Pania." Nathan was gesturing to a comfortable arm chair. As a house guest, she was one of the first to appear for the informal house-warming party Graysie was hosting in recognition of Basil and Alycia Stockton's generosity in lending her this big, pleasant home. The Stocktons were usually based on the East Coast but Basil's business interests in California had led him to buy a home for them to use when they were here. They were only too happy to share it with Graysie and her ward, four-year-old Minette.

The doorbell chimed and for the next half hour the room was a flurry of new arrivals, greeting hugs, chatter and laughter. Last night's tragedy at Gold House underlined the talk with a sombre note, but the joy evident in the house couldn't be quelled.

Pania was settled in a corner seat next to impresario Harvey Miller, playfully discussing the pros and cons of undertaking a singing tour of Australia and New Zealand, when the room quietened and her attention was drawn to the doorway. Leaning on a cane, his dark hair looking uncharacteristically dishevelled, Sir John Russell surveyed the room with his extraordinary black eyes. They flicked from her to Harvey and back again. A brief grimace of a smile flashed across his face and he tilted his head in an ironic bow before making his way towards them with a halting gait. She could see he was trying to conceal his pain, but the leg injury he sustained last night was hampering his movement. Pania rose and caught a flick of annoyance in Harvey's eyes as she gestured to him to make room for Sir John on the sofa.

"Mrs Hayes. Glad to see the night's tribulations have not prevented you from being the life and soul of the party, as usual." Pania wondered if she was being over-sensitive in detecting a hint of acid in the lightly tossed-off remark. And then she caught the quick sharp glare he gave Harvey Miller, and she knew she wasn't imagining the barb.

She patted the vacated place beside her. "Sit here, John, and rest that leg. I really have not had a chance to properly thank you for saving my life last night. If you hadn't aroused the household . . ." She let the sentence die as he waved it away.

"We were all very lucky. Except for the comprador and Beautiful Jade, of course." His deep warm voice had a ragged edge. She studied the familiar strong lines of his face: the troughs down his cheekbones were deeper than usual. With a heart jolt she saw her debonair friend was looking haggard. His eyes were shadowed, and his dark eyebrows had sprung a few rogue gray hairs. *Did that just happen overnight?*

She had known him for nearly twenty years, since she'd been the young bride of Henry Hayes, a much older man. A singer with a pure Pacific bell of a voice, she was fresh off a boat from New Zealand then and John was desperately trying to live up to the role of young tycoon thrust on him, like the title, by his father's sudden death. The knighthood was an unusual one-off hereditary honor, not the usual baronetcy, bestowed on Robert Russell in recognition of his spectacular brave rescue of a British diplomat from an angry Cantonese mob during the First Opium War. The son wore the honor lightly, but it had its uses with bankers and others in the early days when he was setting up the West Coast branch of Russell & Chung, already a wealthy merchant house in the East. Henry hadn't minded when she'd trotted out with Sir John to public functions he had no desire to attend. He said it even added to her celebrity, and she and John had become fast friends.

The magnate was so intensely involved in his business he had little time for anything else. He didn't seem to feel the need for a wife and was happy to squire Pania — her fast-rising career managed by her astute husband — if he happened to be in town.

But Henry had been dead for nearly a year, and Pania felt restless. That was one reason for the playful talk with Harvey about touring the Antipodes. She hadn't been back to her homeland since she married Henry — who had been in New Zealand visiting his American missionary brother — and fled her family. And she wasn't at all sure she wanted to go back. Some things, she mused, were best left alone. Neither had she appointed a new manager, although Harvey was making pointed hints that he would be interested in taking her on. She wasn't even sure she wanted to continue with the old touring life any longer.

John was now fending off inquiries about his injured leg. "Just give it a couple of days and it will be fine," he was saying to mine manager Irish Red. "It's just a knock."

"Strange that the fire seemed to start upstairs in the bedroom," said Pania, "when there's no fires lit in the house at this time of year. Did someone forget a candle?"

John looked at her sharply. "We're not sure how it started," he said, giving her one of his searching stares. "Deputy Hale seems to think it was simply rotten bad joss. Nothing untoward."

She searched his eyes for what he wasn't telling her. "Harvey's been cruising the Sing Song Clubs talent-spotting. There's a lot of unrest out there. The bite is going on for protection payments." She edged forward in her seat. "It's said a Nevada City club owner who refused to pay up had his throat cut. The girls are terrified. They are reluctant to tour with Harvey even if the money is good — they're frightened of retribution if they leave. That's what they're saying, isn't it, Harvey?"

John frowned. "You haven't taken Mrs Hayes out with you, have you, Miller?"

"Not yet. But I was thinking of it. They might feel more relaxed if there was a woman present."

John gave Harvey one of his impenetrable stares. "I'm not happy about that, Miller. It could be dangerous, really dangerous. There is some sort of turf war brewing among the Six Societies, and I don't want to see anyone else hurt."

Harvey's natural flamboyance deflated under John's penetrating gaze. He was a big-shouldered man, built like a lumberjack but always dressed with understated elegance. Tonight he wore a fashionable cream mid-length sack coat over a subtle, ivory-striped waistcoat — a combination designed to be noticed but not showy. With his spiky hair, neat pointed goatee, and bon-vivant sparkle, Harvey was always the first to raise a toast.

He made a humphing sound as he cleared his throat in irritation. "Russell, you're overreacting. I've been dealing with the Sing Song clubs for years. We'll be fine." He reached out to clasp her hand. "She knows a lot of the girls, and they revere her."

Pania quietly withdrew her hand and looked up at John. "There's something you are not telling me. I can sense it. Something bad. Cough up."

He shook his head and looked away for a second. "Nothing. Nothing at all, Mrs Hayes. I just don't want you out there."

"John, have you forgotten I'm an entertainer? I work the clubs.

All right, not the Sing Song Clubs exactly, but some that are not all that different. I can't stop working because you're getting anxious in your old age."

It was meant to be a light-hearted remark, intended to break the intensity of the encounter, but as soon as she'd said it she knew she'd struck a dissonant chord.

He reared back from her as if she'd slapped him. "You never take no for an answer, do you? I don't know how Henry put up with it." He pinched the bridge of his nose, as if warding off a headache. "It's dangerous, I tell you."

A taut silence stretched between them, broken only when a buxom woman rustled up in a flurry of bronze satin skirts. "Well, my goodness, here he is! Just the man I was looking for."

The fulsome dress did nothing to enhance Huldah Wilmington's puffball profile, but she seemed oblivious to the picture she presented. She planted herself in front of John, fixed him with beady-eyed enthusiasm and reached out and pumped his hand vigorously. "Sir John. Delighted to catch up again."

She perched on the arm of the sofa beside Harvey, blithely unaware she was cramping his space, and leaned across him to engage John's full attention. "While you're laid up like this, what could be nicer than to relax at my little luncheon tomorrow? You can just rest yourself in pleasant company, no troubles. After that dreadful fire you need a break."

A German widow left a comfortable fortune by her Boston sea-captain husband, Huldah amused herself holding popular match-making events several times a year for a wide circle of acquaintances and associates. As one of the state's most eligible bachelors, Sir John Russell had long headed her list of desirables.

Pania waited for the explosion. A lot of eager women on the make? It was the kind of event John despised. But the eruption never came. The weary entrepreneur glanced around him, tossing his head like a cornered animal, and his shoulders slumped forward in defeat. "I do have rather a lot on my plate," he said weakly. He shot an appeal to Pania, willing her to come to the rescue. She raised a querulous eyebrow and played dumb.

Huldah either didn't notice the silent exchange or chose to ignore it. She nodded and smiled. "A lot on your plate. Of course you do. But you can't go far until that leg recovers. And I've got the nicest people for you to meet." John shifted uncomfortably on the sofa.

Surely not. If Pania hadn't seen the evidence with her own eyes, she wouldn't have believed it. Sir John Russell was feeling mortal. *Maybe he is fearful he's left his run too late?* Watching your youngest brother get engaged could do that to a man. That and the sudden death of someone you loved.

She felt herself blush at the direction of her thinking. John was looking straight past her, seeking who knew what? A younger woman? Good old Pania apparently didn't have a part to play in his next domestic drama. She felt herself stiffen and placed her hand affectionately on Harvey Miller's arm. The poor man had been squeezed by Huldah's generous proportions. She took a deep breath and edged even further forward, relieving the pressure of his thigh against hers.

"Time for us to go, don't you think, Harvey? Didn't you want to check out a few more clubs?"

Harvey gave her a warm smile. "I did, my dear. And I'd be delighted if you'd accompany me. With the crowd there is here, I'm sure we won't be missed."

Pania shot a quick glance in John's direction, but he was rising — leaning on his cane in obvious discomfort — to greet some new arrivals. He winced. "You're not leaving?"

"I think we are, John. Don't you worry about me. All the best with getting back on your feet — literally and figuratively. And enjoy Huldah's party."

Four

Sir John Russell's leg ached from his ankle to his groin, even though he'd spent most of the evening sitting. But his pride hurt even more. As he sipped a late-night brandy with Nathan in his rooms at the Holborne Hotel, where they had resettled remarkably quickly, he reflected on the night's exchanges.

The glimpse of Pania's turned back, the determined strong line of her café-au-lait shoulders against the ruffled neckline of her dark-blue evening gown, the diamond earrings projecting shards of silver light as she stalked to the door, a picture of composure, off to do the very thing he'd practically begged her not to do. He gave a deep sigh and dragged himself back to the present. He was brooding over his brandy, gritting his jaw in frustration.

She obviously didn't plan to take notice of anything he'd said. She appeared to be hell bent on pursuing her cozy understanding with Harvey Miller. *Miller is a nice enough chap, a very successful impresario, but he isn't the right man for Pania Hayes. I'm amazed she can't see it.*

He sighed and took another sip of liquor, savoring the radiating inner glow as it went down. How on earth had he allowed himself to be sucked into accepting Mrs Wilmington's matchmaking invitation? He must be getting addled. Or desperate.

"Can't believe he's gone," he said to Nathan, who was sprawled lengthways on the leather couch with his boots off. "I'd got to thinking he'd go on forever, he was so full of vigor."

"I know. It's impossible to take in." Nathan swiveled to place his feet on the floor and, anchoring an elbow on each thigh, hands under chin, regarded him speculatively. "You haven't said much about it, but my guess is it wasn't simply bad luck."

Russell nodded curtly. "It wasn't just bad luck. The old man and his love were dead before the fire started. And as Mrs Hayes was smart enough to ask earlier tonight, how does a fire start in an upstairs bedroom in the summer? Unless it started in the kitchen below, but it doesn't look as if that was the case."

"Beats me," Nathan sighed, and they sank into companionable silence.

John felt a lightness replacing the dead weight of fatigue that had enveloped him. "It's really good to have you and Seb around, Nat. Especially at a time like this. You understand what Ting Hon was to the family. What he still is to us boys." He raised his near-empty glass in tribute. "To Chung Ting Hon."

Nathan followed his lead. "To our mentors — Chung Ting Hon and Sir Robert, our irascible father."

John felt his chest fill with a reassuring draft of air. It was good to be together. They were the three sons of a twice-widowed Hong Kong empire-builder. John was the eldest, born to Clara, an English gentlewoman, thirty-eight years ago. When she died when he was four years old, his father wasted little time in marrying Honor, a young American, who died giving birth to Sebastian, now thirty.

He sighed. "Yes, our one-of-a-kind father. He didn't have much luck with his women, did he? Although he had enough of them."

He hadn't intended the comment to sound as sour as it did, and flicked a rueful half-smile to Nathan. The soon-to-be-wed youngest, now twenty-eight, nodded in sympathy. "I know what you mean. We were all lucky my hardy Aussie mother lasted the distance." Arabella, Sir Robert's third wife, had provided the love and emotional security their brilliant but distant father couldn't, melding the unruly Queen's Road household into a harmonious unit that occasionally had included Ollie.

"Arabella was superb." John raised his glass once more. "To Arabella." He took another sip and sighed contentedly. He was just a little bit tipsy with brandy and a deadening lack of sleep, but he felt warm inside.

John thought back to the steamy Hong Kong day of his father's funeral, with the dizzying mix of Protestant and Chinese ritual required in farewelling a merchant prince who had lived more than half his life in the Orient.

That was the last time they had been together until a few months ago. Immediately after the funeral the Queen's Road house was closed down and the family dispersed. Arabella took Nathan — then just ten — back to Sydney, and Sebastian went to his mother's family in Boston for a Yankee education. John was commissioned to take his father's place in Russell & Chung, opening the California office.

When John yawned, Nathan stood and put the glass he'd been nursing down on the side table. "You need to get some sleep. Come to think of it, so do I. But where do we go from here? You'll want to get on to rebuilding before the snow comes, I imagine."

"You're right there. But I have to get to the bottom of this mess. I have to find Ollie. Ting Hon was upset — I'd even say bewildered — when he didn't turn up for our meeting yesterday. It's so out of character. You know what Ollie's like. Punctilious and particular, just like the scholar he is. And Zeng really rubbed it in."

"What do you think has happened to him?"

He contemplated the remaining inch of amber liquid in his glass, then downed it in one swallow. He shuddered and banged the glass down. "I'm hoping he's just gone into hiding. Maybe he's been threatened and has decided to lie low for a week or two. There's some kind of power struggle going on in the Black Dragons, that's for sure. And I suspect Zeng is right in the middle of it."

Nathan put his hands on his hips and stretched. "He's standing in the opposite corner from Ollie, you can bet on that. The fires of jealousy burn strong in that one. Always have."

"You're not wrong there." He gave a second weary yawn and pulled at his silk cravat. "I suppose we should be going to bed. I've got to be on deck for the funeral tomorrow."

Nathan nodded. "Good idea. Me too."

His brother was at the door about to leave when the hotel's night manger burst into the room, breathless and red-faced. "Sir John, there's a lady insists on seeing you. Even at this hour, she won't be denied." His bald dome had a sweaty gleam. The sentence was barely out before a tall, red-headed woman loomed up behind him. She stopped in the doorway and ran one hand distractedly over her head. Her hair had fallen free of a loosely drawn chignon, but it wasn't just the unruly tresses that signaled distress. She had a wild look in her eyes, as if she was escaping — or was it pursuing? — something terrifying. In her other hand she held a rolled-up parasol. She prodded the rotund manager in the back with the pointed shaft and stepped around him.

With her flawless creamy complexion, mysteriously flecked hazel-green eyes and shimmering copper hair, Selina Hamilton Chung had been the belle of many an English ball, but she had never cared for the acclaim of the crowd. A brilliant and strong-minded woman, she fell in love with Ollie when they met at his mother's house on university holidays one summer. The unorthodoxy of the marriage, when she could have secured an aristocrat with castle and title if she so desired, perplexed society matrons, who could still be occasionally heard to mutter "Such a beauty! Such a waste!"

In her wake tripped a slender teenager with perfect Cupid's-bow lips and pretty almond-lidded eyes who was going to be a ballroom show-stopper just like her mother.

Selina strode forward, her chin tilted at a desperate angle. "John, you must help!" She looked at him with glassy-eyed panic, drawing her daughter to her side as she did. "Lily and I need your help. Something dreadful has happened to Ollie. Please! Please do something." Her voice was close to cracking.

John half-rose, leaning on his cane, and Selina drew herself to a sharp halt. "Oh, I'm sorry. What have you done to yourself? Don't get up."

She swept to his side and sank down on the sofa beside him, gesturing to Lily to sit next to her. "I went to Gold House. What on earth happened? It's a ruin." She ran her hand over her head again. "What's going on? Has the world gone mad?"

John grasped her hand with long gentle fingers and steadied her. "We'll get to that later. What's happened to Ollie? You said something dreadful?" He stared at her, his body tilted forward for her answer.

"He hasn't been home for two days. He didn't say anything about going away. You know Ollie — he wouldn't do that."

He nodded. "You're right. That is very unlike him. And I've got more bad news, I'm afraid. Tell me, have you just arrived?"

"Yes, you're the first person I've spoken to apart from the coach driver and the hotel staff."

The manager was hovering at the door, unsure whether to stay or leave. John beckoned to him. "Could we have a pot of tea and crumpets or similar here as fast as possible, Reynolds? Mrs Chung and her daughter need something to eat. And we'll need some extra rooms."

He turned and gestured to Nathan who had been standing to one side quietly observing. "Selina, I don't think you've met my younger brother Nathan, from Sydney. He's been visiting for the last month or so. Nathan, meet Ollie's wife Selina Chung and their daughter Lily. Selina, Nathan was about to leave but I think it's best if he stays and hears you out."

Selina nodded. "Of course." Nathan sank onto a chair opposite the sofa and nodded to the two women. "Delighted to meet you both. Ollie was older than me when we were growing up, but he was always John's favorite cousin, we all knew that. We might not have been related by blood but Ollie was still family."

Selina shook his hand. "Nathan, lovely to finally meet at last. Ollie has spoken of his Hong Kong childhood, and the kindness your mother showed him, many times. Have you met up with him again since you've been here?"

"Just once, when John had a big welcoming lunch. It was the first time since our father died that we've all been together. I'm hoping that won't be the last time — but we've got a lot on our minds at present." He shrugged as if to say, "We've got to take it day by day."

John said, "Brace yourself, Selina. There is no easy way to tell you what happened here last night." He tented his fingers and gazed over the top of them. He knew that Selina and Lily would be preparing themselves for bad news, but he was confident they couldn't imagine the disaster he was about to disclose. He felt the burn of acid in his stomach, and took a deep breath. "Chung Ting Hon and his new wife died in a fire at Gold House last night. They were trapped in their bed. I couldn't get to them in time."

Selina thrust her hands to her face and wailed through her fingers. "Oh no! That can't be! Not Ting Hon! There must be some mistake . . ." Her silvery voice trailed off.

John shook his head. "I'm so sorry. No mistake. I know it's unbelievable. We are preparing for his funeral tomorrow."

"How? How did it happen?" Selina's voice came out in a fierce whisper, her shock immediately transmuted to anger. "Did Ji Zeng have anything to do with it? Did he?"

John's insides cramped, and he had to take another deep breath before he could reply. "Selina, why would you think that? What possible reason could there be for him to kill his own father?"

"He resents everything he doesn't control. He's been giving both Ting Hon and Ollie a dreadful time this past few months with his plans for expanding the business. Ridiculous stuff."

She darted an anxious sideways glance at Lily, and John sensed she didn't want to say anything more in front of her daughter. He shook his head. "I know things have been rocky. But why would you suspect him of something as treacherous as that? Killing Ting Hon? I can't believe he'd do it. Be reasonable."

"Reasonable? Ollie vanishing isn't reasonable either! And what about your house? Is it reasonable that it's burnt to the ground? We can forget reasonable."

Her voice had a sharp, rising edge. She was clearly close to breaking. Selina Chung was renowned for her cool composure and in all the years he'd known her he had never seen her lose her dignity.

"John, he hasn't got you enlisted on his side too, has he? You don't agree with where he wants to take things? Your good name is worth more, surely? You wouldn't betray Ollie for thirty pieces of silver?"

He was so shocked by the challenge he could barely believe she'd voiced it. "You can't seriously think that."

She grimaced and looked past him with an unfocused, distant stare. "I don't know what to think any more, I really don't. I just know something is seriously wrong and we cannot afford to ignore it . . ." She shot a quick sideways look at Lily, who sat beside her, tight mouthed and white faced.

She had intended to finish the sentence with "or else", John was sure of it. "Or else we won't see Ollie alive again." "Or else we'll be too late." But a quick glance at her grieving daughter had silenced her.

Selina patted Lily's hand and attempted a reassuring smile. "I know it's terrible news, darling. But we must try and get some sleep. We won't hold up tomorrow if we don't, and we don't want that. We have to be at our strongest to farewell your darling Yeh Yeh, your grandad."

The mention of her affectionate nickname for her grandfather Chung Ting Hon shattered Lily's fragile composure. She turned her head into her mother's shoulder and her slight frame shook with sobs.

Five

"I will not hand over the Dragon Seal. Now just cut this rubbish and let me go!"

Oliver Chung stood angrily a table width away from his half-brother, his lean body tensed, intelligent brown eyes flashing. He waved his handcuffed wrists in front of his seated brother's nose, and Ji Zeng felt the familiar burn of hatred flood his solar plexus. The bitter taste of bile rose in his throat, and he spat on the floor at his brother's feet to rid himself of the foul taste.

Ji Ming had always assumed he had the right to command, just because he was the eldest. He would always be First Son by accident of birth. Not that he'd ever done anything to earn the status. Ji Zeng always suspected it was because his father valued the foreigner who was his brother's mother above his own — one of the comprador's concubines — and that suspicion festered in him. The haughty gweilo who was Ji Ming's mother hadn't honored Ting Hon as a dutiful wife should. She fled back to England and took her son with her. He leaned back, arms crossed, and regarded Ji Ming in cold silence.

He pictured the jade chop, sinuous characters finely carved into the circular face, nestled in a golden silk wrap in a leather pouch and locked away in a place known only to the one authorized to use it — the Dragon Seal. Once that person had been his father; now it was the right of the brother in front of him, infuriatingly blind to the jeopardy he faced. Ji Ming thought the old rules still applied — that he could still call on his father as the final arbiter in tough decisions. Zeng had to suppress a triumphant laugh at the thought.

"You're not going anywhere, dear brother mine, until you hand over the chop. I need it to do the day-to-day business, that's all." He threaded his fingers and flexed them back, making his knuckles crack.

Ollie leaned into Zeng's face. "You need it to milk millions from the accounts for some malodorous personal whim!" They were arguing in furious, guttural street Cantonese. He shrugged and clasped his hands tightly in front of him as he turned towards the huge stone fireplace that took up two thirds of one wall in the underground room. "It's damn cold in here. Where are we, anyway, and how long are you planning on maintaining this damnable charade?"

"Where we are is none of your concern. You won't be leaving."

Ollie looked at him sharply. "You really have gone mad, Ji Zeng. Do you think you can just make me vanish off the face of the earth because you don't like having me around? Has that old hag you're selling women to turned your head so far it's stuck up your backside?"

Zeng jumped to his feet and lashed out across the table with a jabbing fist, snapping his brother's head sideways and back. Ollie staggered, tipping over the chair he'd been leaning on, his cheekbone patterned with an angry red welt. "You really do not get it, do you?" Zeng dropped his voice to a menacing hiss. "You have been replaced. I got tired of waiting for you to grab the gigantic opportunities we have right under our noses. I'm in charge now, and under me, Black Dragon will be invincible. Unstoppable. And *very* rich." Ollie smashed his hands palms-down on the table that separated them. The handcuff chain rattled loudly against the wooden top. "And *very* dead. You'll destroy lives, and very likely end up destroying yourself and the Black Dragon. Can't you see how it will end?"

Zeng sneered. "You can be sure of one thing, our rivals in the Six Companies — the Sam Yups and the Kong Chows and so forth — aren't holding back. If we don't move, by the end of the year they'll control the vice business. There will be no room for anyone else. Black Dragon has to step up now or be left behind." Hands braced on the table top, he glared into Ollie's face, nose to nose.

"Then let them." Ollie edged closer, jaw jutted defiantly.

Zeng could feel Ollie's breath on his face. "The decision has already been made. And even your fine cousin Sir John Russell agrees. He's ready to do a deal whenever we want."

Ollie's shoulders jerked in shock, and his throat flushed a patchy red. "You're lying! John would never get involved with something so shady. He might be ruthless in business, but he would never go into trafficking. Apart from anything else, he couldn't stand to have his reputation sullied."

Zeng threw back his head and roared with laughter. "No one will know. It's all 'mysterious China business', so who cares? Russell recognizes a good deal when he sees it. No risk to him and a great return on investment."

His brother stared back at him. "I don't believe you. I want proof. In fact, I want to ask him myself."

"That won't happen. You need to get a grip on your change in status, brother. You are no longer the boss. I am. You can accept that and move over quietly, or not. Choose the 'or not' and it will go badly for you. You *and* your precious daughter."

Ollie looked up sharply and his wrist irons rattled. "What are you saying? You leave my family out of this. It's a business dispute. Lily and Selina have nothing to do with it."

"That's where you couldn't be more wrong. There is a fortune at stake and I need that seal. I can't clear the shipments coming next month without it, so I'm willing to go to extraordinary lengths to get it. Extraordinary. I bet I know more about where Lily goes and what she does than you do. I've made it my business to know. Call it my guarantee."

Zeng sat back in his chair, legs crossed, heels on the table edge, and rocked it on two legs, his arms behind his head, a study in languid arrogance. "I'm sure there's a rebel general somewhere in our benighted homeland who'd pay big money for an English-Chinese concubine. Quite a commodity when you think of it. It's not unthinkable she'd fetch $5000 or more. There was a pretty girl — a dancer with a theatrical bent — who went for $3000 last week, and she didn't have anything like Lily's fatal charm. For a start, she wasn't a virgin."

His brother's face glistened a sickly white. "You wouldn't sink that low!"

"You have no idea how far I'm ready to go to build the empire of my imagining," Zeng replied. "No idea." He was back in the Gold House bedroom, slicing across Beautiful Jade's throat. His nose filled with the hot metallic smell of blood, overriding the acrid scent of fear that reached him from the other side of the table, where Ji Ming sweated.

Ollie crumpled onto the floor, his face in his hands. "I don't have the seal," he rasped through his fingers. "I couldn't give it to you even if I wanted to. I have no idea where it is."

Six

Chung Ji Zeng felt nothing except a prickly irritation at the two coffins laid out before him. Did he really have to go through this charade when there were so many more urgent things he could be doing? Like organize the finance for the opium shipment arriving on the *White Cloud* clipper next week.

The comprador and his wife lay wrapped in anonymous shrouds in sweet-smelling camphor wood coffins in the front room of Grass Valley's most celebrated herbalist and apothecary, Dr Wau Kee. The walls and windows had been draped in white cotton sheeting, the Chinese color for mourning, the bodies wrapped in blue and white cotton. Under more normal circumstances, his father's young wife would have been decked out in her bridal dress, and the bodies displayed, but the fire's total destruction had made that unthinkable.

It was easy to spot the sombre figure of Sir John Russell, who stood taller than every man in the room except his brother Sebastian, paying his respects at the foot of the bier, flanked on either side by professional chanting mourners. A lightly fragranced, pale blue smoke coiled from copper dishes set out on side tables in which burned 'hell money' — the paper money the couple would need to negotiate their way in spirit realms. Off to one side, a tailor sat stitching white mourning garments, and a number of those present were already decked out in traditional simple mourner's gowns from his hand.

John Russell wasn't one of them. He stood out in a dark, perfectly tailored suit which emphasized the rugged power of his frame, poised in what to Zeng felt like a threatening silence before the comprador's casket. Then he raised his eyes and his hawk-like gaze met Zeng's own, and it felt as if he was penetrating his soul. He shivered. Russell had acquired a reputation for a preternatural ability to read minds, but Zeng reminded himself it was nonsense.

An acid contempt rose in his throat. For someone who prided himself on always being up on the latest business intelligence, Russell had been remarkably dumb when it came to his own family. The comprador's Second Son coughed and quickly masked the scowl he knew had settled on his face. Let them think he was lost in grief. Now was not the time to let his true feelings show, but inwardly he sneered.

How he despised men like Russell who saw nothing wrong with manipulating the share market or extorting lucrative mine claims from drunken miners but drew the line at drugs and women. Sir John had been one of the most ruthless, acting as if it was his God-given right to trample on others, but hiding behind the cloak of respectability. He was just like Ji Ming — too worried about public opinion to do what was needed.

He looked at the coffins lying next to one another and had to suppress a smile. Funny that Russell, who thought he knew everything, didn't have a clue that he'd got away with murder.

He saw the big man coming towards him, offering an outstretched hand which Zeng took reluctantly. "Second Son, my condolences. We had to move on with the funeral preparations — I hope that isn't causing offence. But with Ollie away and you . . .

Well, I wasn't sure where you were. We had no choice but go ahead and start organizing. It's important not just to honor Ting Hon but also to protect the status of the company."

Zeng felt his annoyance rising at Russell's easy assumptions, as if the public ritual of mourning had any point or meaning as far as he was concerned. As for the fine reputation of Russell & Chung Trading? His big plan was all he cared about and this man Russell stood in his way. But he said, "I am glad you were able to act in our stead. I had important business that couldn't wait. I'm sure the Old Man would understand." His mouth was dry and the traditional plaited queue hung heavy down his back. How was it Russell was practically the only American in the room and yet it was he, Ji Zeng, who felt out of place? He pulled at his hair to ease the uncomfortable heat on the back of his neck, and then thrust his hands into the side pockets of his changsan tunic. Russell assumed control wherever he went and he hated him for it, but this was one occasion he had no desire to attend, let alone organize.

John continued, too preoccupied by the occasion to notice Zeng's discomfort. "The astrologer picked noon today for them to be brought out in their coffins. Two hours later for the funeral procession and burial at four this afternoon. The grave has been dug. Is there anything else you want done?"

Zeng shrugged and looked around the room. The musicians, hired to lead the funeral parade with a loud noise which would frighten off any wayward spirits, were gathering. Song fragments floated from the flute players as they tested their tunes, rehearsing riffs for the coming event.

John raked him with another penetrating look. "It's tragic that Ollie is missing all this. I assume he doesn't even know his father is dead, but I've no idea where to find him to tell him. You've heard nothing?"

Zeng shrugged. "Nothing. Who knows? Not me, I'm afraid. You were always the one closest to him. Thought you'd know what was what if anyone did."

Russell spread his hands in an empty gesture. "It appears not. In fact, there's a lot going on that I don't understand." As he spoke he was following Zeng's progress towards an open tiled courtyard, where an altar for receiving gifts had been set up.

Zeng turned to face the bigger man. "I wanted to ask you a few things about the business." He shuffled his feet uncertainly. "With Ollie away I need a bit of help. Like where he keeps the Dragon Seal. Ting Hon must have passed it on to him, but none of Ollie's book-keepers seem to know anything about it. I don't suppose he's ever mentioned it to you?"

John shook his head vaguely. "No, he's never said anything. It isn't critical, is it? I mean, Ollie must surface soon. There's nothing so urgent it can't wait till he gets back?"

"Well, there is actually—"

There was a clatter at the courtyard gate: the musicians were lining up ready to start in earnest. One had dropped a brass trumpet which rattled on the cobblestones. They were like a rainbow flock of chattering birds, their bright gowns in imperial scarlet and Ming blue making a startling contrast to the white cloud of mourners. More people were arriving in a steady stream, kowtowing and leaving offerings of food and other essentials for the couple's soul journey. Sweetmeats, fruit, dragon incense and candles nestled around a centerpiece pavilion of rice.

In a room off the courtyard a book keeper was listing the mourning gifts in a volume of record. Zeng was hit by a bolt of hot energy as the crowd grew and he realized with a shock that this was turning into a historic moment — the largest and the most celebrated Chinese funeral ever seen in the town.

John's attention had been distracted by the arrival of the musicians and swelling crowd, but he turned back to Zeng with a questioning look. "You say there is a reason you need the chop? Sorry, I won't be able to stay here talking much longer, but what's the problem? Is it affecting trading?"

Reluctant to confide the full extent of his ambition, Zeng said tentatively, "We've got the chance to buy into a big shipment of opium. Arriving next week. It's going to be huge."

John frowned and shook his head. "We're not—"

Zeng interrupted. "It's already happening. If we don't join them we'll be left behind."

"Ting Hon would never—"

Again, Zeng cut him off. He was talking louder than he intended, in an excited Cantonese that John still understood from his Hong Kong days. Mourners were turning to look. He could feel his rage burning hot inside. "Well, he's not here is he? It doesn't matter what he thinks. Thought."

John ran his hand through the dark line of his jaw, his eyes narrowed. A muscle below his eye flickered involuntarily. He was clearly holding himself in, as tight as a drum. "Ji Zeng," he said, "as long as I'm here, we'll honor the values set by our fathers. I'll allow they dealt in opium thirty years ago, but that's ancient history. Times change and we've long ago given up on it. You know that."

"You're wrong."

A loud gong struck up and a repetitive chiming and high pitched wailing rose above the chatter. The professional mourners were about to begin. The procession would follow. Zeng shouted over the noise, "If we don't get into this trade now we'll miss out altogether! Can't you see that?"

"I told you, Russell and Chung don't deal in that commodity. And I doubt that Ollie would want the Benevolent Society involved.

But that's for the two of you to work out."

"You don't get it, do you? That won't be happening."

Zeng fought to conceal his contempt. He made a quick calculation. *What is the oldest Russell brother's weakest point? Where is he most likely to compromise?*

"What do you mean it won't be happening?

Zeng gazed into John's angry face with a bland smile. "As they used to say in the old taipan days, it is easy to dodge a spear you can see, difficult to guard against an arrow shot from hiding."

John's gaze froze to ice. "I don't know what you're playing at, Zeng, but if you want to talk in riddles then how about the old proverb 'When a tree falls the monkeys scatter.' Your father was an almighty tree."

Zeng felt his cheeks flush red. *How dare he?* Concealed in the folds of his gown he squeezed both his hands into tight balls. He wished he could place them around Russell's neck and finish him off right now. "If you are suggesting I'm a monkey, you'll live to regret it — and sooner rather than later, I wager."

He swung on his heel and walked away. *If I continue this conversation any longer I'll say something I'll regret. Much better to keep cool and live to fight another day.*

Seven

Lunch was served to the swelling throng in the courtyard: the musicians, professional mourners and ritual keepers were quickly outnumbered by a throng of townspeople who had come to pay their respects. Along with crowds of local Chinese, John could see that many of California's leading citizens — the mayor and prominent businessmen such as Hector de Vile and Basil Stockton — were there along with his brothers, Sebastian with deputy Hale and Nathan with his betrothed, Graysie. Selina Chung and her daughter Lily hovered close to Nathan and Sebastian. Both had the dazed, startled look of someone in shock. The only notable absentees were the comprador's two sons, Chung Ji Ming and Chung Ji Zeng. He couldn't spot Zeng in the crowd, and he was sure Ji Ming wouldn't be there.

He felt a stab of heart pain at his absence. It could only mean something drastic had happened. Ollie would move heaven and earth to be here if he knew his father was dead. The farewell rituals were about to begin.

Zeng had vanished after their earlier discussion and John was wondering whether they should start without him when he glimpsed him. He had changed into a finely worked white brocade changshang tunic, with a high mandarin collar and toggled front, and a white band tied around his forehead. As he passed through the throng, Zeng handed out pieces of white paper with holes cut in them which people clutched at gratefully. It was believed that evil spirits had to pass through all the holes before continuing to their intended destination, so they became confused and distracted from discovering where the dead were to be buried.

With Zeng's return, John realized there was no further reason to delay. The mourning gown he had slipped aside to change into felt strangely foreign, but he ignored his discomfort and gave a mute nod to the chief announcer. Three horn blasts and nine strokes of the gong signaled the start of the graveyard procession.

On cue, everyone began making a big racket, with screeching wails, incantations, and loud laments accompanying the cacophony of banging of drums and cymbals. John's ears were ringing when the silence following this ritual cleansing finally dawned. Then, with leaden feet, he stepped forward to lead family and friends out to the graveyard. Zeng slipped in beside him as they bowed formally to the coffins and made their way out.

The bearers swarmed in behind them and, at the blare of another horn, hefted the two coffins onto their shoulders and carried them to a horse-drawn hearse wide enough to allow the comprador and his wife to lie side by side for their final journey.

Many of those present would walk to the graveside behind the hearse, but for those who were too frail or elderly to walk in the hot afternoon sun, a procession of wagons and buggies were lined up in the street, many bearing banners marked with good-omen characters to ward off evil spirits. John had insisted that Selina and Lily should use a wagon, and asked Pania and Nathan's soon-to-be-wife Graysie to accompany them. He was intent on walking, although his leg hurt like hell and he still needed a cane to lean on. Other wagons were loaded with offerings of food — whole roast pigs, chickens, soup, rice, cakes and sweets — and liquor, which would all be presented at the burial mound and remain at the graveside until evening for the spirit's delight.

He gritted his teeth against the pain and allowed himself a grim little smile by imagining Ting Hon looking down. He was sure the Old Man would have been gratified. No one appreciated the value of presenting the right image more than Hon, and it was especially important now with Ollie's absence casting a pall. Many Chinese would consider his failure to attend a gross insult to his father's memory and a sure sign that the company would reap bad fortune.

He glanced to his right and left to see if Zeng was anywhere near. He was following the crowd with a blank, shut-down face, like a mechanical soldier from a child's toybox. Strange for a man who had been raised in a traditional Chinese family to be so resistant to communal values. Everyone here knew without a shadow of doubt that making sure your ancestors were buried with honor and favor helped settle the volatile spirits of the recently dead. They knew, too, that providing them with food, money and goods for their transfer to the netherworld would help bring good fortune, wealth, and many children to the family left behind.

John shivered inside the hot folds of his mourning gown as his last bloody sight of Hon and his delicate wife flashed into his mind. They were certainly grievously murdered. If any spirits had reason to be angry and disoriented, theirs would.

As the procession reached the graveside, the man who had led the riderless saddled horse at the back of the procession moved forward and began giving out gold coins and sweets. As the coffins were lowered into the holes already dug for them, the dusty smell of burning paper rose in a cloud. The attendants had set fire to paper representations of clothing, houses, and money that flared into brief, dancing, orange flames as the patriarch and his treasured wife were lowered to their final resting place, showered with coins and sweets as they went. Zeng's light caramel complexion and dark, shining river of hair attracted admiring glances as he confidently cast gold paper coins onto his father's bier.

The food wagons were unloaded and their contents spread around the grave site under a cloth canopy out of the direct sun. John breathed in the mixed fragrance of fermented fruit, smoke and roast pork and for a moment he was back at his father's funeral. There was no other smell like it, the aroma of a Chinese farewell to a loved one.

The gathering lingered, the wails and laments now replaced by story-telling and reminiscences. As the afternoon faded into early evening, and the grave attendants began their work of spading soil to complete burial, a satisfied silence fell over those who were left. John sidled up to Zeng, who was standing to the side, some distance from the graves. "Everything okay?" he queried.

Zeng looked up in thinly veiled surprise. "Yes, fine. You gave the Old Man and Number Five Wife a good send-off."

"I hope you see it's for our benefit as much as anything else. It's important to be seen to be doing the right thing."

Zeng shrugged. "Not back on that old song, are we? You know what I think. There are times you need to be fearless and subtle. Times when what others think doesn't matter — especially if they don't know your business."

John gave him a probing look. "Oh? I'm starting to wonder just how far you would take that."

Another nonchalant shrug. Zeng was outwardly calm and unbothered by the questions, but John sensed that his smooth exterior concealed a tightly coiled inner spirit, which would be dangerous when unleashed.

"I'm not sure what you're getting at."

John glanced around the funeral clearing and motioned to Zeng to follow him away from the graveside. They drew up a small distance off, in the shadow of an old white pine, their steps muffled by a carpet of rusty red needles that spread in a wide circle from its base.

"Ji Zeng, have you asked yourself how a fire started in a bedroom with no lit fireplace? Has that struck you as a strange thing to happen?"

Zeng picked at his gown as if searching for extra air, even though it was cooler under the tree than it had been away from it. "Strange? Not really. Just joss, isn't it? Good luck. Bad luck. Everyone's luck runs out sometime." His gaze darted towards the graveside, where the lamentations were finally quietening. He pulled at his left ear and looked into John's eyes, challenging him to differ. "You don't agree? You're thinking — what?"

"I'm thinking that it's very unusual joss which decrees that a father and First Son are both taken out of commission at the same time. Unusual — or unusually convenient."

Zeng stepped back and the lines around his eyes tightened. "Oh? Convenient for who?" He made a gesture of open appeal with his palms out before him, a model of impeccable conscience.

John sighed. This conversation was going nowhere. "That's what I ask myself. Who has the most to gain from Ollie's absence?" He shouldn't indulge in sarcasm, he knew that, but he couldn't restrain himself. During the strangely intimate walk with the coffins, things had started to drop into place. He might even think that the comprador was whispering to his spirit, demanding justice.

Zeng took another step back, and appeared to be steeling himself. "You want some suggestions? Funnily enough, No Cousin of Mine, I just might have some. Though I doubt you'll like them."

"Oh? Please, fire away. I can't wait to hear."

"Hasn't it occurred to you Ji Ming's disappearance is very 'convenient', as you put it, for the bully boys in the Sam Yup

Company?" His eyes flicked to John's, but he couldn't hold the contact and looked away.

"What aren't you telling me?" John demanded. Zeng was hiding something — he could see it in his face.

"The *White Cloud* is docking in San Francisco this week."

"Go on."

"Well, what's to stop the Sam Yups abducting Ji Ming to stop us from muscling in on the opium shipment? I've heard whispers they've got him and they'll release him 'for consideration' — but not until after the *White Cloud* docks."

John hissed his response: "How long have you been nursing these 'whispers', Ji Zeng? How long?" He wanted to grab him by the neck of his robe and shake him like a French hound shaking a rabbit. "And when were you proposing to tell me?"

"Calm down, old boy. Calm down. Isn't that what you Englishmen say?" Zeng waved his hand airily above his head, as though he was a conductor leading an orchestra. "They're just rumors. I don't know for sure."

John took a step towards him and grabbed him hard by the shoulders. Zeng's face folded and he grunted in pain. "What the—?"

"Don't mess with me, Zeng. I warn you. Where did the rumors come from?" He tightened his hold on Zeng's shoulders, triggering a sensitive meridian point to increase the pain level.

"Let me go." Zeng ground out the command in a low rasping voice which could only be heard by the two of them. "*Now.*"

John released him and he stumbled backwards, arm outstretched to brace himself against the pine trunk. He leaned there in the shade, breathing a fraction harder than normal, but otherwise seemingly unruffled. "You're the one with the spy network, Sir John. Don't tell me you've missed something as important as your own dear cousin being taken hostage? My my, what has happened to Sir John Russell with the army of spies? Losing your touch, old boy?" The cool nonchalance had vanished, replaced by angry determination.

"Ji Zeng, if I find out that what you're saying is true . . ." John took a deep breath to steady himself and thrust his right hand through his hair, at a loss for words. "So help me, if I find out it's true I'll—"

"You'll what? Tell the comprador?" Zeng sneered. "Can't go running to him any more, can you, old boy — and neither can Ji Ming. But if you want to see your cherished cousin again, you'd better think about putting something up in payment. I'm not sure I'd bother myself, but without access to the Dragon Seal I can't raise the funds anyway. So if you want to see him again, you'd better cough up. Otherwise he's on his own."

Eight

"I've got to get out. I'm suffocating."

Pania Hayes rose from the sofa, fiddled with one of her long ruby earrings and swished her deep carmine skirts around her. She knew she looked every inch the commanding diva, her dark hair tumbling in controlled waves from the top of her head, the ruby earrings and matching necklace setting off the smooth line of her neck. She might convincingly play the diva, but inside she felt strangely adrift.

She strolled towards the open windows of the Stockton House dining room, fanning her face with her hand, casting her voice back to the table as she moved. "The funeral went very well, John, but now I need some light relief!"

John, Nathan, Sebastian and Harvey were still sitting over an end-of-meal coffee at a table where they had dined well on vegetable souffle filled with spinach, carrots and minted peas, all picked from the Gold House garden. John had his injured leg resting on a chair, taking up one side of the table.

Graysie, Selina and Lily had been sitting with Pania on a large comfortable sofa and matching armchairs at one end of the room. "Anyone else up for some fun? What about it, Selina? Would you like to join Harvey and me as we make another talent trawl through the Sing Song clubs? He still has some gaps in the chorus line for his fall tour, haven't you, my friend?" She flashed an apologetic look at John. "You need to rest that leg, I know. And Graysie, I'm sure you're content to stay home with Lily and Minette? Play Happy Families with Nathan?"

Graysie patted Lily's arm. "Yes, of course. Lily's most welcome to stay if Selina wants to go out. I know Minette would love to have her read a story." Graysie looked fondly to the huggable, curly-headed child who sat playing quietly with a doll's house in the corner. "You'd be happy to have Lily here, wouldn't you, poppet?"

The four-year-old got up and danced across the room to take hold of Lily's hand, giggling as she went. Since her mother, Graysie's best friend, had died several months ago, Graysie had become Minette's mother in all but name. The two were inseparable.

John cleared his throat. "Mrs Hayes, I've said before, I'm not sure it's safe for you to be trawling the clubs, even with Miller's protection."

Pania nodded, then looked back out the window. "Sure, sure. But we'll be fine."

Selina rose gracefully, smoothing down the gentle fall of her skirt. "You know, John, I think Pania is right. I'd love an evening's distraction. I'm so sick of worrying about Oliver. The only thing I can think about is where he is, and if he's all right. I feel so helpless, unable to do anything." She glanced over to Lily, her lips drawn down in a contrite smile. "Sorry darling, but you would be happy to stay here with Graysie and Minette, wouldn't you?"

Lily smiled. "Yes, if that's okay with Miss Castellanos.'

Graysie bubbled with laughter. "Graysie please, Lily. No need for formality. And I won't be Castellanos for too much longer anyway." She patted Nathan's shoulder.

"That's decided then." Pania glanced at John with the hint of an apology in her dark eyes, then took Selina's arm and walked out, Harvey Miller trailing behind them.

An hour later they were stepping out of the Stockton carriage and making their way in the dimming twilight to a cellar door guarded by a tall broad-shouldered Mongolian. "Here we are. Sam is expecting us." Miller gathered the women lightly about the waist, one on each side of him. "Come my princesses, the night is but young." He was looking especially confident and dapper tonight, pointed beard neatly trimmed, in a black sack coat over loose dark-gray trousers, his white shirt highlighted at the throat by a light-gray patterned necktie Selina had said was all the rage in Paris. "Let's see if we can find someone or something to awe and amaze."

The What Cheer House America on Nevada City's Pine Street had accommodation and meals at all hours on offer upstairs. In the downstairs brick-lined cellar — built after earlier premises had twice been destroyed by fire — businessmen sipped brandy delivered to their tables by Chinese attendants wearing elegant traditional tunics in all the colors of the rainbow.

The stage talent reflected What Cheer's joint ownership, backed by a wealthy local investor and fronted by Sam Ah Choi, a Hong Kong-born Eurasian with the drive to rise to the top in any situation. The What Cheer was known for its eclectic reach: on any night there might be blackfaced minstrels, barbershop quartets, Parisian magicians, the latest sensation in popular ballads, or opera singers wanting to be the next Jenny Lind, the 'Swedish Nightingale'.

Miller had been drawn to What Cheer by one of its most popular shows — a local talent quest where hopefuls from far and wide lined up to compete for a $50 prize and the chance to turn a lucky appearance into a fulltime career. "Good chance to discover the next Lola Montez — or Pania Hayes," he'd told Selena with a smile.

Sam Ah Choi led them to a prime table close to the front but a little off to one side. "So as not to give the performers stage-fright," he joked. As they settled in and the staff organized green tea, the rustle of whispers around them showed many of those already seated recognized their local celebrity — the famous impresario with the celebrated diva on one arm, and a beautiful and obviously important unknown woman on the other.

They settled in to be entertained by girls performing Irish and topical songs, dances and operatic burlesques. They were being charmed by a "genuine chanteuse from Paree" when Pania spotted a brilliant young Chinese entertainer she had seen a number of times before at What Cheer standing in the shadows near the backstage door. She gestured to Sam Ah Choi the next time he appeared near their table. "Would you ask Fan Bo Fan if she would like to come and sit with us for a time?"

Sam Ah Choi nodded, but Pania got the impression he was reluctant to comply; unusual for a proprietor who was always keen to seek opportunities for his staff and his business. Some time later, when the performers took a short refreshment break, he led Bo Fan to their table and quickly rustled up a chair for her.

"Not singing tonight, Bo?" Pania asked.

With her teardrop-shaped face and fine bones, Bo Fan was breathtakingly beautiful, and Pania knew she had a pure, bell-like soprano voice. The young woman shook her head and the side curls that corkscrewed down her cheeks bounced. She shot a quick glance at Sam Ah Choi and said quietly, "Not tonight."

"And I notice you're not alone. Quite a few of the What Cheer girls don't seem to be performing tonight." Pania drummed her fingers lightly on the table edge. "I'm wondering why, Sam Ah Choi? With Harvey here I'd have thought they might have wanted to show what they can do. He can do big things for their future careers, I'm sure you know."

Sam Ah Choi shrugged. "Maybe they are happy being at What Cheer," he said with a fleeting smile. "We treat them well."

"I'm sure you do. Of course. But to make a career as a singer you must sing on many stages."

Sam Ah Choi glanced across at Selina, who was chatting with Miller, and then said something unintelligible under his breath in Cantonese.

Pania looked at him from beneath raised eyebrows, and he leaned even closer. "Perhaps this is not the time for standing out from the crowd. Perhaps Bo Fan understands the saying, a thousand friends are too few but one enemy is too many." He came closer until he was whispering into Pania's ear. "Something Chung Ji Ming might have benefited from understanding." He drew back to a proper formal distance.

Pania fingered the ruby earring Henry had given her on their tenth wedding anniversary. She had noticed herself doing that more frequently since his death, seeking reassurance when she got anxious. She wished Sir John was here. He would be able to conduct this conversation in Cantonese, and no doubt discover a lot more than she could. Her head buzzed, and she was glad to sit aside from the table talk as she settled her thoughts, Bo Fan silent beside her. Sam resumed his role as convivial host, making small talk with Selena, sending a clear message that any private confidences were over.

There was nothing for it. If someone here knew anything about Oliver's disappearance, it was up to her to find out. She thought of Lily, a fine-boned, trusting young woman waiting for her dad to come home, and her stomach curled. She had been that young girl once. But her father had never returned.

She stood with such vehemence she set the glasses on the table rattling. "Sorry, everyone. Just thought I'd say hello to the musicians backstage while they're on their break. I've worked with many of them and it would be nice to catch up. Will you excuse me? And Bo Fan, why don't you come too? You can introduce me to the ones I don't know."

They carefully made their way to the stage door at the back of the room, each a presence that could not be ignored, watched by every man in the room. As soon as they were out of sight of Sam Ah Choi, Pania turned to face the younger woman. She put her hands on her shoulders. "Bo, what's going on here? The last time we talked it was your dream to get a booking with Harvey. To sing at as many clubs as you could. What's changed?"

Bo Fan's eyes jittered. She couldn't look her straight in the eye. She shook her head. "Nothing. I am just happy where I am." She cast her eyes down to the floor.

Pania laughed out loud. "Oh, happy. Yes, I can see that. Very happy."

The younger woman flashed her a wan smile. "You can laugh." She glanced behind her. "You don't know . . . Things are not safe." She wrung her hands together. "Let's go to the women's changing room and I will serve you more green tea. Will your friend be all right for a few minutes?"

"She will be fine. Sam and Harvey are both charming hosts." They edged along a narrow corridor to a room reserved solely for the use of the women singers, and Pania sat and waited for the tea.

What was going on? The What Cheer House had a tense atmosphere she had never felt here before. She had noticed a couple of heavies, both dressed in black, one with a tattoo disappearing from his wrist up his sleeve. Security, she supposed, but this club was usually frequented by wealthy types who didn't brawl like the miners. Tonight it had the buttoned-down feeling of a bar about to explode. And what of Sam's warning? What was that about? She couldn't imagine where to begin.

Bo Fan brought the tea and they sat in tense silence, sipping the hot calming potion from exquisite porcelain cups. Pania was savoring the last dregs when a girl burst into the room and grabbed her hand. "Mrs Opera, please help! I want to go away from here!"

Bo Fan jumped up and put a restraining arm on the newcomer. "Not now, Wai. Not now."

The girl had deep brown eyes that flashed with desperation. "No, no! I go! Go now."

Pania placed her hand on the girl's shoulder. "Please, please, calm down. What's wrong?"

The Chinese girls fell silent, each looking to the other, waiting for the other to speak first.

"Ngo Wai does not know what she is saying," Bo Fan volunteered. "To leave now, very dangerous. Best to stay."

The other girl began sobbing. "I can't. I can't stay." Tears trickled down her cheeks, leaving a wet trail on her emerald silk tunic. "Bad things. Bad things happening. You tell the lady—"

There was a loud knock at the door and the newcomer jumped back from Pania's touch. In a second she slipped through a curtained gap on the back wall. The woman the girls all answered to, Madam Wong, stood glowering in the doorway. She was a full-figured, coarse-featured woman with prominent teeth that dominated her face. She was plainly outfitted in black taffeta, the only embellishment a gold hair clip on the top of her head, holding a dark, coiled bun in place. Pania had met Madam Wong numerous times, but had never warmed to her. The girls were terrified of her.

"What are you doing here, Bo Fan? Why are you not attending to our guests?"

The young woman cast her eyes to the floor, chastened. Then she took a deep breath and stood taller. "Madam Wong, I am just paying my respects to Mrs Opera. We are just finishing." She collected the cups with a rattle.

Pania bowed towards the Madam. "I was just renewing my acquaintance with some of the musicians. I am delighted to enjoy your wonderful hospitality, Madam Wong. I know Mr Miller appreciates it."

At the mention of Harvey's name the overseer's stance softened. Harvey often brought top talent through What Cheer House America and enjoyed a good relationship with Sam Ah Choi and his partner.

"Thank you, Fan Bo, for your kindness. You've been a shining star. It won't be forgotten." She nodded first to Madam Wong and then to the girl. "Mr Miller will be most impressed to hear how well you run this house, Madam Wong. Now, don't let me take up any more of your time."

Back at the table Harvey and Selina were reminiscing about great operas they had seen in Paris and New York. *No need to worry about them missing my company.* She thought of Bo Fan's distress and glanced casually around her. The men in black still skulked at the back, practically invisible in the dim light unless you were looking for them. She was certain they would be armed and dangerous. *What's going on? And why the veiled reference to Ollie?*

She felt hollow inside — the vacuum she knew that Sir John Russell's counsel would fill, if he was here. He was such a wise, strong presence in her life. Her husband had been a dear man and a savvy stage manager, but John had a breadth of understanding she'd seen in few other men. He would know what to do if — when — she told him about tonight's conversation.

She waited for a lull in the easy chatter between Harvey and Selina. "Madam Wong sends her compliments, Harvey."

He grinned. "So she should. I give them a pretty good deal." He ran his hand through his spiky hair, making precisely no difference to his appearance. "We might call it a night. What do you think, ladies? I've pretty much seen all I need to see."

Selina smiled. "I've had a lovely night. It's so good to pretend things are normal, even if only for a couple of hours."

They were rising from their seats, and Sam Ah Choi was crossing the floor to escort them out when Pania sensed a disturbance across the room. She scanned her surroundings as Selena and Miller bantered on, oblivious to the tension. The tattooed heavy remained in place at the back of the room, but the other man, gun drawn, was advancing on a woman cowering near the door, her arms held by two men who flanked her. She was whimpering and trying half-heartedly to pull away. Pania saw with a jolt it was the newcomer, Ngo Wai. She tapped Miller's arm. "Sam Ah Choi—" She got no further.

The What Cheer America boss backed away, apologizing, and started for the door, giving urgent orders in Cantonese as he ran. The men holding Wai let her go and glowered at him, arguing and gesticulating. Pania had no idea what they were saying, but they did not like letting the girl go, that was clear.

"We'd better go," said Miller. "I don't like the look of this."

The dark feeling inside her deepened. If John were here, he would step in and issue orders. He would understand what was going on and know what to do about it.

Miller put his arm around Selena's back and they started for the door. The room had fallen silent. The crowd that had been enjoying the music now watched the door.

Ngo Wai's face was drained of all color. Her teeth were chattering as if she was very cold, although Pania was perspiring from the heat in the poorly ventilated room. She took a step towards the girl, reluctant to abandon her, uncertain if getting involved would put her in even more danger.

Before she had taken two steps she felt her elbow gripped by iron fingers. Her heart jumped. A man pressed firmly against her right shoulder blade, leaned down and positioned his mouth close to her ear. "Just keep walking. Don't look around. If you interfere now she's dead meat."

She glanced down at his arm. A tattoo curled up his wrist and into his shirt sleeve. The man she'd been seeing all night. He smelt of eucalyptus, a fresh slightly tarry smell. His hold was steady and purposeful, but not threatening. She straightened her back and regained her poise, allowing him to stroll with her to the exit as if he were an attentive aide.

They were a few steps behind Selina when Miller paused to exchange pleasantries with Sam Ah Choi, who had returned to the door. He looked up at Pania in surprise, but she raised an eyebrow to command his silence. *Don't say anything. Act normal.*

They were turning to leave when a band of men clad in traditional black Chinese tunics and trousers pushed into the bar, shoving Miller aside. Eyes darting, they fixed on Wai, who still stood bowed and shaking, the man with the gun standing over her. As they passed Pania she saw their tunics were emblazoned with a gold embroidered dragon from hip to shoulder.

The man at her side hissed, "There's trouble. Big trouble. You need to leave now." He propelled her towards Miller. "Time to go, sir."

Miller needed no second invitation. With Selina tucked at his side, they slipped out and were in the street, the last summer twilight fading into true darkness. Their coach man was waiting. The door of the carriage opened. Angry voices rose from inside What Cheer House America, then abruptly stopped.

Pania peered out of the carriage window for one last look. She heard a gunshot. A woman's scream. Then silence. As the horse pulled away, she looked for the tattooed rescuer, but he was nowhere to be seen.

Nine

"Selina, think hard, very hard. When was the last time Ollie was home?"

Selina Chung leaned forward in her chair, elbows on the dining room table, her speckled hazel eyes alert, intelligence undimmed by the late hour. "The last time he slept at home in Sacramento was on Thursday night — a whole week ago. On Friday he was going to San Francisco on business. He was only supposed to be away a couple of days. Back on Monday, he said."

"Do you know what he was doing? Who was he planning on seeing?" John sat with Selina and his brother Nat around a dining table at the Holborne, set up in the rooms he and his staff were occupying as a temporary home away from home. It would be months before Gold House would be rebuilt, so they were making the best of things. John's bustling housekeeper Mrs Snively had concocted a very pleasing light dinner of rabbit and oven-fried potatoes.

"Ye'd be wanting coffee and apple pie to finish," Mrs Snively said as her solid, square form bustled into the room, carrying a hot pie-dish in an oven cloth before her. On her heels followed Nelson, the groom turned personal assistant, with custard in a jug in one hand

and a coffee pot in the other. Anna Snively's freckled face and simple, open manner declared her to be the countrywoman she appeared: honest, capable and willing to work as many hours as were needed to get the job done. "If that's all, Sir John, I'll be off for the night. If you want for anything, ask Nelson." She beamed at him and left the room on the same gust of energy on which she had entered it.

Nelson and Mrs Snively had come with John to the Holborne; the Lees, the Chinese husband and wife team who ran Gold House, had gone to stay in Chinatown. John felt himself relax and settle, getting grounded again after the see-sawing emotions that had assailed him during the funeral.

The fact that Ollie had not been there — clearly was not in a position to travel, almost certainly had not even heard of his father's death — sealed for him as nothing else could that his cousin was in serious trouble, if not already dead. As an eldest son who ably and honorably ran the family business, Ollie would have attended if he had been physically able to do so. Anything else was unthinkable.

Selina toyed with the coffee that Nelson had served and shook her head. "Ollie usually did not go into details about his work. I knew he was concerned about a faction in the Black Dragons who were creating mayhem. Fighting with the other gangs like the Sydney Ducks. There'd been deadly feuds. Armed robberies. Abductions. Women sold. Even cold-blooded assassinations if they couldn't get what they wanted any other way. The numbers involved weren't large but they were causing a lot of trouble. And it was escalating. The others were arming themselves in defense so the problem was growing."

"And how was Ollie going to sort this out?"

"I thought it was by talking with Zeng. A lot of these troublemakers seem to look to him as The Man. But I don't really know — maybe one of Zeng's henchmen?"

John nodded. Zeng's smooth, nonchalant attitude at the funeral yesterday was hard to interpret. He had only once shown his obvious dislike. And he didn't seem to be mourning his father too deeply.

Selina took another sip of coffee. "When he didn't come home on Sunday night I thought he must have just been delayed. On Monday I went to the office and asked Zeng's man if he had heard from him, but he said he knew nothing. I had a very bad feeling about it, which is why I came to ask your advice. I couldn't just sit there doing nothing."

"And what credibility would you give to Zeng's suggestion that Ollie has been abducted by the Sam Sungs?"

"There's no doubt that violent minorities in the Black Dragons has caused a lot of problems for the Sams. They killed one of their most popular leaders. I guess it could be a revenge thing. But my instincts point in another direction — straight back to Zeng himself. There's a lot of anger festering there."

John nodded. "What about you Nat? You saw Second Son more than me when we were kids. Do you have anything in common these days? Got any idea what makes him tick?"

Nathan shook his head wearily. "I did little more than nod at him today. He wasn't in a talking mood. I suppose that's quite normal when you're burying your father. I could ask around."

Nathan had picked up a lot of Cantonese as a boy, and then refreshed it more recently on the Australian gold fields. He had also helped some local Chinese women escape abusive treatment at one of the town's hotels and enjoyed unusual trust in the Chinese community as a result.

"Good idea. Ollie's value as a bargaining chip will disappear as soon as the opium shipment arrives. We may only get one chance at this."

"How's it going to work? The mechanics of it, I mean." Nathan frowned. "Who delivers the goods? And who do they go to?"

"That's the part I'm most uncomfortable about. Zeng insists he's the only one they'll deal with. He'll take the money to the kidnappers."

Selina hammered her fist on the table top, rattling the cups in their saucers. "You can't do that. That money will never be delivered, even if Ollie is being held. It's all just a fancy extortion attempt." She held her head in her hands and wailed in protest.

John waited until she had quietened. "And you're so sure of that you're willing to take the risk? Have you got proof, or is this just the bad blood there's been between you two ever since you married his half-brother?"

Selina blushed. "I don't have proof, I admit it. I just know in my gut. He wouldn't deliver it even if Ollie was being held against his will. All you'll be doing is funding his secret — or not-so-secret — ambitions. Maybe even hastening Ollie's death. If Second Son gets that money, he'll spend it on opium, not on a ransom."

A grandfather clock chimed midnight from a house on a side street and John shivered even though it was a warm August night. He had been standing in the shadows on the edge of town for thirty minutes or more, waiting for the witching hour. The only sign of life had been a couple of caterwauling tomcats, and he couldn't suppress a feeling of anti-climax. He didn't know what he'd been expecting, but it wasn't a deserted street blanketed in silence.

The gold for Ollie's release hung heavily in a satchel that bumped against his thigh, and he could believe, if he glanced down, he might see hot vapor rising from inside the cool, neutral, leather casing. Roughly a thousand dollars' worth of gold ingots as a payoff. Yes, he was going crazy, but everything about this night was crazy.

They had broken up after their dinner: Selina went to comfort Lily while Nathan slipped out to check with the fixers in the Chinese community. It had been a brief trip, and he came back with nothing; if Ollie was being held by the Sam Sungs, word had not leaked out. Nathan was finishing relating this news when Zeng turned up and told them the cash delivery had been set up for midnight. John had raided the safe — the one thing that had survived the house fire intact — to put it together.

Now here he was alone on the edge of town, waiting for Zeng and the Lord knew who else to turn up to collect. He heard the slightest of noises to his right and Zeng slid from the shadows into full view, dressed in a simple pair of dark blue Chinese trousers and traditional Mandarin collar tunic. John's stomach quivered with last minute doubts. What if Selina was right? What if this was blatant extortion? "How do we know Ollie is still alive?" he demanded.

"We don't. We have to take their word for it."

"And how do we know they can be trusted?"

Ji Zeng looked at him hard and then laughed. "As the saying goes, even the most vicious tiger won't devour his cubs."

"I'm serious. I want them to produce something Ollie always has with him. That might not prove he's still alive, but it would prove they actually have him."

Zeng looked dubious. "Like what?"

"Like his wedding ring."

Zeng laughed. "You want them to bring his wedding ring from wherever he is, which could be San Francisco or even farther away, and bring it here before you pay up?"

John realized how unrealistic the demand was. He flexed his hands to try and reduce his rising tension. He was just so damned unused to not being in control. "It could work. Depends how much they want the money." He hugged the satchel closer and let out a long sigh. "It will be good to see the end of all this."

"All what?"

John opened his mouth to speak and felt cold metal against his neck. He sensed a big man behind his left shoulder, but couldn't turn to check. Big or not, he had moved soundlessly, giving no warning of his approach.

"Give the bag to Chung Ji Zeng." The man spoke Cantonese with a provincial accent. John lifted the bag gingerly with his right hand, held it aloft and addressed the gunman in passionate Cantonese: "It's all there. You can tell your bosses if anything happens to Ji Ming, if he is not returned unharmed, I will search for them to the gates of Hell and beyond and make them pay. Do you understand?"

The gun pressed harder against his neck, as if the hitman was tempted to finish him here and now, but then he eased back. He pulled the gun away and gave him a hard shove on the shoulder. "Big talk." He cleared his throat of phlegm, hoiked it, and said, in perfect English, "Get lost. Go on, git." He waved the gun to emphasise the point. "And if you go to the sheriff, Ji Ming is dead."

John backed away gingerly, his hands raised in surrender. Zeng leaned down to pick up the satchel, and then the enforcer put the gun in his back and marched him off in the opposite direction.

Ten

John looked around the room with a sinking heart and asked himself for the umpteenth time why he had allowed himself to be persuaded to attend the Saturday match-making luncheon put on by Constanza Huldah von Werden, otherwise known as Mrs Huldah Wilmington. Nor could he recall how he'd ever got to know Huldah's full name before she married her Boston sea captain.

To many she was the Dowager because she rode roughshod over others to get what she wanted, barely noticing the embarrassment she left in her wake. And of course she had been Mrs Wilmington from the day she married her sea captain. A sea captain who also owned the line. Huldah had always been socially ambitious.

John was jammed beside her on a couch in the Holborne Hotel reception room, which hummed with excited but muted chatter. Well-dressed women and elegantly suited men nodded in conversation while surreptitiously scanning the crowd with an expectant air, as waiters circulated with trays of hors d'oeuvres.

Several times a year Huldah hosted these events where she brought together worthy and attractive women with some of the region's most eligible men. John knew that some of the guests had paid a handsome fee for their invitation — Huldah was nothing if not canny. But she also had a remarkable network of friends, business contacts and acquaintances that spread across the state — indeed, the world — and she attracted some interesting guests.

John's injured leg ached as he rested it against the cane he still needed to stop himself toppling off-balance. He shouldn't have gone gallivanting off last night, for all the good it had done. Was Ji Zeng now a victim of a rival Society as well as his half-brother? He seriously doubted it, but his head whirled. He shouldn't be here. He should be doing something proactive in tracking Ollie's kidnappers down. His world was all upside down.

Where was Ollie? Who had dared to kill the comprador? All his previous certainties were crumbling around him, and for the first time in many years he was at a loss for what to do next.

Huldah cast a satisfied look in his direction and patted his thigh in a motherly fashion. He had no idea how old she was: quite a bit older than him, he thought. He gave her a brief polite smile but inwardly seethed. This was all Pania's fault. If she hadn't provoked him so brazenly by cavorting with Harvey Miller, he wouldn't have been remotely tempted to come. What with Graysie Castellanos marrying his young brother, Pania thumbing her nose at him, and Huldah patronizing him — the picture of a battered old suitcase rose to mind. He'd been around too long.

He felt a pressure against his ribs. Huldah was saying something and digging him in the side to draw back his wandering attention. He checked himself, ran his other hand down the side of his leg to ease the pain. "Sir John, I'd like you to meet Mrs Adeline Baker. Mrs Baker, Sir John Russell." Huldah paused as their eyes met. "Mrs Baker's husband died some time ago and she's spent the last year and a half in Europe. Now thankfully returned, I believe, to settle in our beautiful state."

The woman who stood in front of him was of medium height and had a pleasing rounded figure. She had attractive gray eyes, dark hair with a deep rust sheen, and the quiet composure of someone who knew she was right most of the time. When she spoke her voice was warm and engaging, with a clipped intelligent ring. "Sir John, delighted I am sure. Please don't get up." She glanced at the cane. "I understand you've recently suffered a terrible misfortune. My sincerest condolences at your loss."

Huldah stood and indicated the spot she'd vacated. "Mrs Baker, please join Sir John here. As you so rightly see, it is difficult for him to move freely at present. His loss is our gain. Please excuse me — I have other guests to see, but I'll be sure to send some refreshments your way."

John nodded and turned his full attention on Mrs Baker. "In Europe, as Mrs Wilmington says? Tell me, where have you been?"

For the next half hour Adeline Baker gave him an entertaining account of her adventures and misadventures in London, Paris and Berlin, and her life before her recent travels. Born and educated in a well-to-do Boston family, she married a banker and life had followed the path her station set out for her until the family asked her husband to take over their banking interests in California. She found San Francisco's melting pot of sophisticated strivers unlike anything she'd encountered at home, and she loved it. When her husband had died suddenly she knew just one thing: she did not want to return to her old life in the East.

"So here I am. It's been a wonderful interlude. Of course I still miss Clayton fiercely, but I want to re-establish my life here, where we spent our happiest times." She looked up at him with a direct open gaze. "Does that seem strange to you?"

He felt an admiration for her strength, her honesty. "Not at all strange. Admirable. I imagine it's difficult for a woman to make her way alone anywhere, but perhaps more so in California. It can be a pretty rough and ready place."

"Maybe, yes. But also very freeing. After the life I've enjoyed here, I really couldn't settle for the confines of the Boston set." Mrs Baker gave a light laugh. "Enough of me. What about you? I can hear in your voice that you are probably an import too. Where did you grow up?"

It surprised him that after nearly 20 years in California she could still pick up the slight nuance of an English — or Hong Kong — accent that made him different. Observant too, he thought approvingly. He gave her a brief resume of his family. Three half-brothers born in Hong Kong to a Scottish taipan with a ruthless appetite for business and women. His younger brothers each sent back to their mothers' families after his father's sudden death 18 years ago — one to Australia, one to Boston — and only very recently reunited for the first time.

"I was about to start work here in the family company in San Francisco when my father died, so I just continued on with that and set up here. I was the oldest and my mother died when I was very young. I barely knew her."

Mrs Baker listened. Really listened. And appeared to be genuinely intrigued. For a few seconds he entertained the thought that there was nothing as appealing as a woman who listened — and then banished it.

He wondered what she would think about the things he wasn't telling her — about his mother's death which he remembered far more vividly than he ever wanted to, about Ollie and Zeng and Ting Hon's death. He would wager that she'd find it hard to handle all that.

He thought of olive-skinned, sloe-eyed Pania Hayes, and of the trusted minder he'd sent to keep watch over her in recent days. Pania, who could bring any song to life, the high-born daughter of a New Zealand Maori chief who had been killed in a family dispute. She had seen things in her young life that made her pretty well unshockable. He didn't know whether her fierce need to protect the vulnerable came from her experiences then, but she was a force of nature when aroused. And she had given him a clear message to butt out of her life.

She seemed pretty set on this new thing she was onto — working with Miller. Maybe he'd be wise to look elsewhere. He glanced at the attractive, responsive woman sitting next to him, her hair caught in a sweeping whorl at the back, her slender throat laced with an expensive pearl choker.

A longing for someone to hold and love rose and hit him in the back of the throat so sharply he coughed. He really did need to do something about this new thing that was stalking him — a hot desire for wife and family. But first, he must find Ollie and get his other family on an even keel. After that? Well who knew?

Eleven

"You what?"

"I went backstage with Bo Fan to find out why the place was more tense than normal. Something was going on there, John."

Pania lounged comfortably on a settee with a coffee cup nestled in her lap. She had slept surprisingly well and felt rested after her narrow escape last night. Now in the early afternoon had called on John at the Holborne Hotel to tell him about Sam Ah Choi's oblique reference, and of Ngo Wai's desperation. She put the cup to her lips, sipped briefly, and put it down again. "They know something we don't. I'm certain of it."

"Pania, the thing that concerns me more is the idea of you putting yourself at risk. We don't need any more bodies."

"I didn't put myself at risk. Besides, there was some man in black there who seemed to be detailed to look after us. Maybe one of Sam Ah Choi's men." She looked at her magnate friend seated opposite her, his be-socked shoeless foot once again resting on an ottoman. After several days of looking exhausted and disconsolate, today he was in one of his elegant business suits and looked energised. His leg must be coming right.

"You're not listening to me," he said. "It's dangerous. Some kind of gang rivalry is probably brewing. You don't want to be caught up in it." He ran his hand down his thigh and massaged around his knee cap.

"I'm not. I'm trying to tell you something. From what Bo Fan said, Selina needs to make sure Lily is well protected. And Sam Ah Choi seemed to know something about Ollie. At one stage he said something about how Ollie had not taken notice of warning signs and now he was paying for it. I couldn't understand what he was driving at."

"Exactly my point. Please, just leave it alone."

Pania put her coffee cup down abruptly. She leaned back against the fat bolsters of the settee. They were firm and unyielding, not like the comfortable ones up at Gold House that John had made specially to fit the room. His suite here at the Holborne was comfortable, but it lacked any of the personal touches he had so carefully cultivated in his own home. She thought of the greenhouse where he painstakingly cared for his orchids, spending hours cross-pollinating them. Thank goodness they hadn't been destroyed in the fire. John was a man who took great care of the things he valued. Personal care. So why was he ignoring the warnings she was trying to give him about Ollie and Lily?

It came to her in a flash: *He already knows. This isn't news to him.*

Her stomach lurched, leaving her feeling hollow inside. *How much more is he keeping from me?* "You knew about this last night. You didn't need me to come here and tell you. You already knew."

He gazed at her with a bland expression, neither confirming nor denying.

"So why not just be upfront and tell me? Why all the secrets?"

She felt anger building up inside. She was known for keeping her cool when most others lost it, but something about this situation really got under her skin. They had been friends — close friends —

for how many years? And here he was patronizing her. Treating her like the little woman. All she could think about was that he didn't trust her with the information he'd already gleaned. Didn't he understand how important it was to her to do everything she could to protect Lily? Even after all these years, the pain of losing her father when she was about Lily's age resurged, like a knife in her chest.

John was looking at her with a bemused expression, his hands spread out before him, palms upwards, as if he had no idea of the problem. "Where were you earlier today?" she demanded. "Around lunchtime? I called and your man said you were out at lunch?"

A secretive flicker crossed his face, and he sat up a little straighter in his chair. "Lunchtime?" he said vaguely.

"You went to Huldah's match-maker! Your best friend is missing and his daughter is in danger and you were chasing skirts."

"No, Pania, you've got it all wrong. I . . ." His protests died away as she slowly rose and picked up the shawl she had thrown down beside her when she came in. "Where are you going?"

"Me? I'm going to try and find someone who takes my concerns about Lily seriously. Maybe Nathan will listen. I just can't believe we're having this conversation."

"No, Pania. Stop. You've got the wrong end of the stick. It's not like that."

He struggled to stand up and interrupt her departure, but she drew herself up to her full regal bearing and glared at him, brows drawn down, dark brown eyes flashing. When she stood straight she could almost match him eye to eye. "No? So what *is* it like, then? Tell me you didn't go to Huldah's pitiable little golddigger's lunch. And that you didn't know anything about what went on at What Cheer last night until I got here. Look me in the eye and swear it."

He remained silent, his lips pursed. He was still looking faintly amused, as if this was some mysterious women's game. As if he didn't understand why she was so upset. Well he'd just made one of the biggest mistakes of his life. To think she'd even harbored secret hankerings that he might, they might . . . She didn't want to think about it. She was so lucky she still had Harvey Miller to keep her company. Because there was no way after this display that she would bother Sir John Russell with her concerns ever again. And she sure as hell didn't love him.

Twelve

Isabella Wilmington stood mesmerized as Lotta Crabtree, the variety star a New York critic had recently dubbed the 'California Diamond', demonstrated the steps of her Lotta Polka — the dance that was being copied by everyone. She fought the impulse to pinch herself to prove she was really here, watching her hero. Lotta Crabtree was here in Grass Valley. And not just in town, but right in front of her, chattering and laughing, demonstrating little dance steps, singing snatches of her most popular Irish songs.

The 21-year-old performer had got her start in this very house, which had once been owned by the notorious Lola Montez, Countess of Landsfeld. And it was Lola who, more than a decade ago, had taught Lotta her first songs and dance steps and set theatrical ambition burning in the formidable Miss Crabtree's breast. Her mother had proven herself a redoutable promoter. With Lotta's talent and her mother's ambition, they'd made an unbeatable team.

Isabella's attention flickered away from Lotta for a moment as her eyes searched out her own mother in the crowd clustering in the Mill Street house lounge room. Shame she didn't share Mrs Crabtree's passion. Huldah Wilmington was standing front forward, right at the head of the group of mothers and others who were gathered around, entranced or shocked by Lotta's routines. The expression on her face was stony.

Isabella sighed. She was only three years younger than Lotta, but by the time Lotta was seventeen she had been touring and performing in mining camps all over the state. She was a seasoned entertainer, whereas Isabella had appeared in only a few school musicals. And she'd had an almighty argument with her mother to even get here.

Huldah's attitude was that Isabella most certainly could not go anywhere unchaperoned, and she was not at all sure the stage was a suitable place for a young lady to be seen even if she was accompanied by her mother. She certainly did not want to encourage any mad ideas Isabella might have of a singing career, no matter how much natural talent she had.

"You've nearly finished with school here in California. It's just the prime moment for us to go off to Europe, and for you to spend some time in a Swiss finishing school," she had insisted. Finishing school? Isabella couldn't abide the thought, and yet she had cravenly agreed on a compromise: if Huldah would let her come to see Lotta, she would agree to go to Europe, no arguments.

How she was going to get out of that one she had no idea, and she wasn't worrying about it now. Lotta (short for Charlotte, of course) was back in California for a brief tour and repaying the generosity Lola had shown her by doing the same for the next crop of stage hopefuls. She had announced she was holding an afternoon gathering for all the youngsters who had hopes and dreams of making a career on the stage, to give them advice, demonstrate some routines, and generally show everyone a good time.

A dozen or so young hopefuls of all ages clustered around Lotta when she finished the dance, every one of them wanting to catch her eye, be somehow magically touched by her success. Lotta sank onto an old wooden bench, and clapped her hands for them to gather around her.

Her flat-heeled leather boots were intricately laced to halfway up her calf. She showed a few daring inches of shapely leg and then they disappeared into black taffeta breeches that were gathered into a band below her knee. Isabella thought she looked like some rakish cowgirl with the white jerkin hanging below hip level over the lighter blouse and perky plumed cap clipped over her dark curls.

"Come on now. Who'd like to sing for me? I've done my part — now I want you to do yours." She laughed a soft musical laugh and clapped her hands. "If I like you, I'll give you lessons."

A murmur rose around her but Isabella was the only one to boldly step forward. She raised her arm high. "I can! Let me'" She snatched up Lotta's banjo which lay on the seat beside her. "May I?"

Lotta nodded. "Of course. Go ahead!"

Avoiding looking to the section of the room where she knew her mother was standing, Isabella strummed a few chords to get her ear tuned to the instrument and launched into 'Oh! Susanna', Stephen Foster's popular song. As soon as she got through the first verse she forgot about the people watching. She was so completely caught up she felt a little charge of surprise when it ended.

There was a stunned silence and then Lotta stood up and gestured to her to move alongside her. "Come and sit with me."

Others followed with a range of song-and-dance routines. A couple tried out comedy or burlesque turns. But Isabella sensed that none of them had won as much attention from Lotta as she had. When everyone had done their stuff Lotta turned to her and grasped her hand. "Isabella, you've got something there. Would you like to have some lessons while I'm here? I'd be more than happy to spare the time."

"Lessons? With you? That would be wonderful!" She grabbed Lotta's forearms and squeezed lightly in gratitude. "I can't—"

She didn't get a chance to finish. "What is going on here, Isabella? And when are you going to introduce me?"

Her mother loomed over them, like a Spanish galleon under full sail in a massive magenta crinoline with yards of lace flouncing and wide pagoda sleeves. Everything about her was overstated, and she should have looked ridiculous, but such was the force of her will and the set of her jaw that she was still intimidating.

Isabella jumped up, clumsily knocking the banjo sideways and only just catching it before it crashed to the floor. "Mother. Of course. Lotta, I would like you to meet my mother, Mrs Huldah Wilmington. Mother, Miss Lotta Crabtree, who of course needs no introduction. Everyone knows who she is."

She looked up into her mother's blotchy, red-faced scowl. She knew her own face was shining with excitement and didn't feel like trying to hide it just because her mother didn't approve. "Miss Crabtree has kindly offered to give me some lessons while she is here in Grass Valley."

The atmosphere was icy as the seconds ticked by and her mother stood glaring, an odd, cold smirk on her lips. Isabella pulled her shoulders back, braced herself and asked, "Mother? Did you hear what I said?"

Her mother took a step towards her and grabbed her by the elbow. "If your father could see you now!" She was hissing, actually *hissing* in her ear. "You are coming home now, young woman, and no more of this nonsense. And as for more lessons!" For the first time in her life Isabella saw her mother lost for words, fighting to keep control of her temper.

Huldah gave a slight nod to Lotta. "Miss Crabtree, it's not that we don't appreciate your kind offer. Of course, we are violently appreciative of your kindness. But Isabella's future does not lie on the stage. That is not what I have raised her for, and it is not where she belongs. No offense, of course. You have created a remarkable career." She seemed to conclude she'd be best to leave it at that. "Now we must go."

Gripping Isabella in an iron clasp, she propelled her briskly out of the house and onto the street. Outside she came to an abrupt stop and rounded on Isabella, still clutching her elbow. "I have had entirely enough of this nonsense!"

At least that's what Isabella thought she said. Huldah was clenching her jaw so tightly it was hard to hear. She cast her eyes to the street so she didn't need to look her mother in the eye. Taking a deep breath, a wave of faintness passed through her, and she swayed slightly, but her mother didn't seem to notice. She felt light-headed, almost hysterical, as a capricious thought surfaced. *What a great skit this would make.* The aspiring maiden singer and her jail-keeper mother. And it ends with her wearing pantaloons like Lotta's and smoking the same cheeky black cigar.

An unruly tidal wave of giggles launched itself from deep within. She clamped her lips together to stop them escaping, but she needn't have worried about her mother noticing. Huldah was already turning towards their waiting carriage, pinning her to her side as she strode forth. As far as she was concerned her word was law. If she said it, it happened.

But not this time, Isabella vowed. *I am eighteen. Nearly nineteen. Nearly as old as Lotta Crabtree. No, I'm not going to give in this time.*

Thirteen

Huldah sat down to breakfast alone the next morning. Isabella had complained of a headache and begged off rising at the normal time. She was sick, she said. She needed to rest. She pulled the fine-thread cotton sheet over her head and moaned, "Go away, Mama. I want to sleep."

Huldah banged her cup down too sharply and coffee sloshed into the china saucer. Sleep indeed! If she hadn't got herself caught up in that ridiculous farce at Lotta Crabtree's yesterday she'd be just fine — ready to talk seriously about their plans for next year.

She idled at the table rethinking her approach. With Isabella unwell she couldn't go shopping for new dresses for the girl at Cressida Washington's as she had intended. She pictured the rapturous reception they would receive back home in Germany in a few months. Isabella's many cousins would be charmed by the girl's grace and beauty, of that she was sure.

She examined the hand that held her cup. Dark liver spots showed up dully through the wrinkled skin and she sighed. At Isabella's age she had only ever rated as a pleasant enough girl, if a bit bovine, and even that slight attraction had vanished before she reached her mid-twenties. She tweaked the flesh that folded uncomfortably under the waistband of her full-paneled burgundy silk with a flounced hem and thanked her lucky stars that Isabella was nothing like her. But then, why would she be?

Her musings were interrupted by the squeaking hinge on the garden gate. The baker, delivering today's fresh German loaf. Elbows on the white linen tablecloth, she slumped over her cold sausage and fried potatoes. She was pleased to hear her housekeeper's footsteps in the hall. She had obviously heard his arrival as well.

She pushed her plate aside. She had no appetite. She felt the lump of undigested food at the back of her throat, a hard mass that made it difficult to swallow. *For goodness' sake, woman, she scolded. Pull yourself together. Everything's going to be fine. Didn't Sir John and Mrs Baker hit it off nicely yesterday?* She'd be seeing more of that pair, she felt confident. And the stubborn chit upstairs? She'd come around soon enough with a bit of coaxing and bribing. She always did.

She heard the light murmur of voices at the front door, and then the door shutting. She rose from the table and pushed back her chair ready to leave the room. She was standing there when the housekeeper came in, moving faster than her usual measured gait, brown frizzy curls hanging over a frown on her freckled face. "Something for you, ma'am. Left at the front door it was." She had a broad Cornish accent, and as she spoke she handed over a small basket such as you might use for collecting flowers from the garden. There was something in it that looked like a Chinese silk of some sort.

Huldah raised her eyebrows in a query. Mrs Williams gave a slight shrug. "No idea, ma'am. Was just sitting there, it was, when I got the bread from the baker." She held out a couple of brown rye loaves wrapped in muslin as evidence.

"Odd. Well, thank you, Williams. Clear these plates and you can go."

She sank back down into her chair at the table and examined the basket. She had never seen it before, of that she was certain. The fabric was a finely embroidered scarlet brocade and carried a familiar faint scent of carnations and light incense. Huldah paused, her heart in her mouth. A softly oriental fragrance, like a Chinese medicine shop, with sandalwood added. She hadn't smelt it in years, but she remembered exactly where that was and who she was with when she'd breathed it last.

Her sister Bertha. The last time they'd spoken. It was some expensive perfume Bertha affected wearing — Lubins Bouquet or some such name, as she recalled it. Bertha always did have big ideas, and she'd found some fancy male protector willing to buy her costly perfume. Huldah slowly unwound the fabric. It appeared to be a woman's shawl or scarf. She had a wild idea that it might once have belonged to Bertha — but why on earth would anyone bring it here? Bertha was dead six months now, and they hadn't spoken in years. As far as she was concerned, no one even knew they were sisters.

Strange shivery sensations rippled up her arms as she fingered the shiny material. She had a peculiar sense she was handling something holy, anointed, somehow. As she unwrapped it she became convinced the scent was getting stronger. Swaddled in the center was a black jeweller's box, bigger than a ring box, but not big enough for a necklace. Scarcely trusting herself to breathe, she bent forward and carefully opened it.

Nestled inside was a delicate gold chain, making a tiny circle on the white satin lining, the sort of chain wealthy families sometimes gifted to small children with a nameplate on it. This one had no nameplate, though. Instead, a tiny gold-plated acorn dangled from a gold link, a good-luck charm from the heady first days of the Gold Rush. The sort of acorns Huldah knew early gold miners often had dipped in ore to celebrate their first big strike.

Her hands were trembling as she picked up the finely wrought piece. Why had it been delivered to her? And what did it mean? She draped it over her opened palm and looked back down into the brocade wrapping. Lying hidden right at the bottom lay a tatty piece of rag paper. It had once been white, but now carried light, rust-colored stains like watermarks.

She drew it out and rested it in her hand. Nothing but the staining pattern on one side. She turned it over. The other side was covered in some kind of scribbled drawing.

Her heart contracted as she held the scrap up for a closer look. The drawing was actually a cartoon — a savage cartoon in black ink. And she recognized its subject. Sir John Russell's exaggerated profile was unmistakable. He was leaning over a baby's cradle in a predatory lurch. A baby's foot protruded from the end of the cradle, its dainty ankle plainly encircled by a delicate chain.

A crude X-shaped symbol had been drawn along the bottom of the caricature: as she looked more closely she gasped. The X was made up of two crossed Chinese axes, heavy iron hatchet heads hefted onto brutal wooden handles. She had seen the same crude symbol in newspaper cartoons about the crime wave in San Francisco's Chinatown.

Her head swam and she clutched at the table edge to stay upright as a wave of dizziness engulfed her. *What is going on? It's too weird.*

She looked around her with a sudden wild thought. *No one must know about this. It could ruin Isabella's reputation.* She didn't understand the meaning, but her face burned with secret shame at the conviction it was intended to threaten Isabella. She knew it in her bones.

Her brain seemed to kick into action. She was clear what her next step must be, and she felt a surge of galvanising energy. With panicky fingers she stowed the keepsake box and rag missive back in the brocade, then fled upstairs. At Isabella's door she steadied her breathing and gently tapped. No response. *She's probably asleep.* She waited a few more seconds and then slipped into the room. The bed lay empty, the sheets stripped back to the footboard.

"Isabella! Isabella, where are you?" She tried to keep the sharp edge of hysteria damped down, but she wasn't doing it very well. No answer. She held her breath, waited a few seconds more, but no one replied, nothing stirred.

She whirled out and ran down the stairs, taking them two at a time, holding her full skirts high in front of her, forgetting about decorum in her panic. She reached the bottom and stopped, drew herself together, told herself to calm down. She strode to the kitchen where Mrs Williams was preparing a slow stew. "Have you seen Isabella? She doesn't appear to be in her room."

"Not recently, ma'am, no. I took her up some warm milk an hour or so ago, but she was fast asleep so I didn't disturb her."

"Well, she's not asleep any more." Huldah felt despair grip her insides like a vice. "I have to go out. If Isabella returns while I'm away, please make sure she stays."

She hurried to the breakfast room and snatched up the brocade wrap containing the bracelet and cartoon. She had no idea why Sir John was included in this, but he must have some idea. He was the only one she could confide in. Nothing good would come of it. Of that she was certain.

Fourteen

Oliver Chung lay on the narrow iron bed and counted the days on his fingers. Five nights. Six days. He'd been in this cell that was not much better than a cave for a week. A changing rota of Black Dragon enforcers brought him the meanest gruel and dry bread twice a day. There was a bucket in the corner that was rarely emptied, so the air was acrid with stale urine and worse. He recognized none of the surly silent men who served him, and there had been precious few clues to tell him where he was being held.

It felt as though it was deep underground. No outside sounds penetrated; the silence was muffled and wadded, as if even whispers had to pass through hard rock and empty air to reach him. He ran his hand over his stubbly jaw. He hadn't had a wash or a shave since he'd been here.

This must be what it feels like to be awaiting execution.

His stomach cramped, and he rolled over and clutched his knees to his chest. The certainty of his fate was settling on his shoulders like a cold black fog, increasingly real and burdensome with each successive day. Ji Zeng would never release him. He had taken things too far, and couldn't go back now. He would have to kill him.

He jolted to a sitting position. He'd spent these last days going over and over everything in his mind, trying to work out the whys and the hows of his half-brother's murderous ambition. He felt as if he'd just been hit by a lightning bolt that brought with it a new sharp clarity. *I once was blind but now I see.*

He didn't have to understand any of it. He just had to get out of here before he was killed. And that could be any time soon. Second Son would not have second thoughts. Ollie had been hoping — desperately wanting to believe — that John Russell would work some magic on his behalf to get him freed, but that showed no sign of happening.

He heard the rattle of a key in the door. It wasn't the usual time for the guards to bring him his meager provisions. He slid off the bed and stood as straight and strong as he could, facing his adversary.

Fifteen

Huldah Wilmington followed the hotel manager up the stairs to Sir John Russell's Holborne suite at a gallop, her steps thumping on the risers as she stayed right on his heels. She had emphasized to him she had an emergency and needed Sir John's help this instant. She could feel cold sweat pooling at the base of her throat, running down the gully between her breasts.

A gale of naked fear propelled her forward. She was moving faster than she ever had done before in her fifty years of life. The blast of panic was so real she wanted to turn around and check if anyone was behind her, but a rising superstition prevented her from doing it.

If I look back, the bad thing pursuing me will know I'm terrified.

Keep facing ahead and she could preserve the myth that she was in control; not needing to show any concern about the thing that was lurking, watching, following, waiting to make some blackmail demand.

She didn't know what terrified her more — the implications of the bizarre cartoon she carried like a scorpion in her purse, or Isabella's absence. As soon as she reported in to Sir John she'd be straight on to the Mill Street house where Lotta Crabtree was staying. She'd be furious with Isabella if she found her there, but compared to the alternative it was a minor infraction. She didn't even want to contemplate the other option.

Sir John was reading the *Marysville Chronicle*, his injured leg stretched out on an ottoman before him. He looked up in surprise as the hotel manager led her in. He nodded his dismissal to the clerk and gestured to a seat on the sofa. "Mrs Wilmington! This is a surprise."

Huldah had no time for niceties. She dropped down on the settee and rested the brocade wrap on her lap. "I've just had a very unusual delivery, Sir John. You need to see it because it concerns you." She unfolded the faintly scented brocade, delicately drew the ragged cartoon from it, and without further explanation handed it to him. He looked at it for what seemed a long time without saying anything.

She could hear the grandfather clock on the far wall ticking, the brass pendulum swinging back and forth in a reassuring rhythm, as if the world could be depended upon to remain stable and regular. Except now she knew for sure she couldn't rely on anything any more. She studied his expression as he looked at the communication which could only be interpreted as a threat. Because that was certainly what it was, even though she had no idea who had sent it or what they wanted. It was some sort of subtle threat that perhaps only Sir John would understand.

His fingers on the page were steady, but she detected a quickening in his breathing. Otherwise, his expression was masked, his handsome features bland and his eyes distant. After several minutes he placed the drawing on the table by his coffee cup and looked at her. "When did this arrive? And how was it delivered?"

She explained how it was left in the basket, wrapped in the brocade fabric. She didn't mention the lingering perfume that so reminded her of her sister. That must be just a coincidence. He nodded occasionally as she talked, still the tycoon in control of his world. There was another long silence.

Then she added the unthinkable: "And the other thing is, Isabella has gone." She gasped the words out, fighting against even acknowledging their reality.

"Gone? What do you mean?"

"She said she was feeling unwell and wanted to stay in bed and rest, but when I went up to check on her after this arrived she wasn't there. She wasn't in the house anywhere."

"And you've no idea where she could have gone?" Sir John looked worried, and Huldah felt her face color up. "I have a thought that she may have defied me and gone back to Lotta Crabtree's studio. Lotta offered to give her lessons and she's infatuated at the prospect."

Russell let out a relieved breath and his lips curved in a small smile. "The allure of the stage. Highly likely, I'd say. But this cartoon is another matter. Have you shown it to anyone else?"

"No. No!" Her voice rose in protest. "Of course not."

"Good. Just asking. Have you any idea what it's supposed to mean?"

She shook her head. She didn't even want to think about it. She didn't know why, she honestly didn't.

She delved her hand into the silky shawl and brought out the keepsake box. "This was with it as well." She handed it to him, and he opened it with long fine fingers, a musician's fingers.

"The chain looks like it's the same as the one in the drawing. They're linked, don't you think?" Huldah knew her voice sounded anxious.

Russell picked up the drawing again and examined it carefully. Then he draped the gold chain across his hand and fiddled with it for what seemed like a long time. Finally he sighed wearily. "Used to see a lot of these in the early Fifties. Miners got sentimental about big strikes. They often had one of these cast as a kind of good omen to signify the big finds would keep rolling in. Of course, mostly they didn't." He looked sadder and older than she had ever seen him, as he sat still, caressing the charm.

"Isabella's never had one of these?" He asked the question casually, but Huldah wondered what was hidden behind his eyes as he looked across at her. He held it up so it dangled above him, twirling it in the midday light. "No one has ever given her one?"

She hesitated. Her throat was very dry. "No." She thought his line of questioning was a bit strange. Off the point. What significance could a gold charm possibly have? *This stupid drawing has nothing at all to do with Isabella. Nothing!*

Maybe Sir John could feel her rising irritation at his questions. He shot her a quick glance. "Mrs Wilmington, Huldah, I'm wondering if there is some link going back many years — maybe even to Isabella's birth — that's behind this odd delivery. Would you mind my asking, where was Isabella born? And when exactly?"

Her heart skittered in a panicky irregular beat. "I can't see . . . How is that relevant to anything?"

After all these years, surely Isabella's birth isn't going to become an issue. She willed herself to calm down. She had nothing at all to fear. She had done nothing wrong. "Isabella turns nineteen soon. She was born in San Francisco. But why that has any relevance I can't imagine."

Russell shrugged. "It might not have any significance at all. Maybe whoever drew this just wanted to frighten us with wild fancies. I've never had children, or had anything to do with children. So picturing me bending over a cradle is an aberration for a start. But obviously someone is suggesting a link. And threatening Isabella's safety, by the looks of it. We can't just ignore that."

Huldah leaned across the gap between them and grabbed Sir John's hand. "Please! You can't let anything happen to Isabella. You — we — just can't. I've got to get her away from here, as soon as possible."

She was clutching his hand tightly, vaguely aware that hers were icy cold and locked onto his, as if her life depended on keeping hold of him. She had felt anxious and frightened when she came here, but now she felt a terror like she had never known. She could hear her heart thumping in her ears, and briefly saw black spots before her eyes. If she tried to stand up, she doubted her legs would hold her. She let go of Sir John's hand and sank back into the sofa cushions, taking deep breaths to calm herself as she did.

"I've been intending to take her to Europe to further her education—"

"That may be a very good idea." Sir John's piercing stare made her uncomfortable. The man had a presence that made you feel he could see into your soul. "One problem I see with it, Mrs Wilmington. At this precise moment, you don't have a clue where Isabella is."

Huldah's hands flew to her face, and she shook her head, wanting to contradict him. A sob caught in her throat. *What is going to become of us?*

She thought of all the years she had carefully maintained the story of Isabella's birth. That was for the child's own good, no question. Was she going to have to ruin seventeen years of happiness trying to save her daughter's life from some madman? Destroy their past and present to try and protect her future? What sort of a best bad choice was that? Her eyes searched the still, controlled face of the man who sat calmly beside her. This was all his fault. It must be. His fault. It was nothing to do with them.

"What have you done?" She rose to her feet before she'd registered her own intentions, and grabbed him by the shoulders. She was a big woman, and he was caught totally by surprise. She rocked him back and forth like a mechanical dummy, screaming at him, "What have you done? It must be something bad. Something really bad. My Isabella is a child, an innocent. She's done nothing to deserve this."

She fell back into her chair weeping. "Nothing. She's done nothing," she whispered to herself.

Sir John rose and limped across the room to a sideboard that held a tray and water carafe. He returned with a glass of water in one hand and a table napkin in the other. "Take this, Mrs Wilmington. You need a moment to catch up with yourself."

They sat in silence. Sir John's face as closed and composed after her outburst as it was before, but she saw his chest rising and falling rapidly. She drank the water in one draft and dabbed at her sweaty hairline and wet cheeks with the napkin. "I have to find Isabella." Her voice was croaky, in danger of cracking completely. "I've got to. And I need your help."

It was a fierce statement of fact. She wasn't here to plead or beg. Her determination came rushing back in like a flood. She was going to find her daughter. And this man, for reasons she could not yet fathom, had to help. There was something deep and dark here, going back years maybe, but whatever it was, he owed her.

Sixteen

Oliver Chung waited for the door to open. His heart was hammering in his chest, but he pulled his head up, planted his feet down hard and hauled back his shoulders. If he was going to face an executioner, he would do it standing strong and proud. Was this the violent end he had feared ever since he was locked up? The door would open and one of his brother's goons would be there, holding a deadly cleaver in his twitching hand?

The key turned and the door slowly creaked open. No one entered, but the big-shouldered guard with his front teeth missing stood in the doorway. The key he used to unlock the door was dangling from one finger but he wasn't issuing his usual brisk, flat commands. He was looking at the floor, not at Ollie, and he was blank-faced and disengaged.

Behind him stood an older man dwarfed by the guard's bulk, his dark hair pulled back off his unlined face in a traditional queue. The tidiness of his hair didn't fit with the ragged clothes, the dirt-streaked cheekbones. Ollie's stomach lurched — the face looked vaguely familiar. He took a step back as the older man prodded the guard in the back and he stumbled forward into the room.

The second man had a gun at the guard's back. A Remington. He waved the barrel and shouted to the guard in Cantonese, "Get in the corner! Face the wall and sit!" He waved the gun around again. "Do as I say and you've nothing to fear."

What was going on? Ollie couldn't believe his eyes.

The old man lowered the gun and gazed into his face. "Ji Ming . . . Ou Lee Fu."

Ou Lee Fu. Oliver. Oliver in Chinese. He was a boy in his father's library, listening to a long story about emperors and armies — and this was the man who had been reciting it.

He gazed at the lined, bland face again, disbelieving. Leong Sing Pak. A young clerk in his father's merchant house who had become one of his most trusted administrators. *Sing Pak has found me!* He dropped to one knee, and clasped Leong's bony hand. His throat was dry. He croaked out his name, kissing his hand.

Sing Pak gently tugged on his fingers. "Come and stand over here with me." He spoke softly in English. "We don't have much time." He cast a glance towards the guard. "Chung Ji Zeng has a system where there are always two of them on duty. This thug's compatriot will be back checking the route soon. And we have a lot to talk about."

He perched on the edge of the table, facing the guard. "Firstly, Ji Ming, brace yourself for bad news. There is no easy way for me to tell you what comes next." His eyes raked Ollie's face, and he gave a heavy sigh. The gap between his eyebrows pinched in pain. "I am grievously saddened to be the one to tell you that your father and his young wife are dead. They were burned to death in a fire at Gold House nearly a week ago. But they were almost certainly dead before the fire started."

A stunned silence expanded in the gap between them. A high-pitched screaming sounded in his head, yet no sound emerged from his mouth. Ollie clenched the sides of his head and his heart faltered, as if it could not continue beating.

"No! I can't . . . It can't . . ." He was mumbling and gasping and shaking his head to get rid of the terrible image of his father in a burning house.

He tried again. "Sing Pak, surely not. He was so full of life." The words sounded lame and hopeless, even to him. He put his head in his hands and struggled to hold onto his self control.

Sing Pak waited. "I fear your half-brother has more in mind than pushing you aside and assuming control. He wants to be emperor. And anyone who stands in his way is in danger."

Ollie nodded. This part was no surprise. But to arrange, to contrive the death of your own father, a man like Chung Ting Hon?

His insides contracted. He was going to be sick. He got up and stumbled away from the table, swallowing back down the nauseous reflux as he moved. His throat burned. He stood bent, sides heaving, and waited for the attack to pass. When he turned back to Sing Pak, the nausea had gone. In its place was a roaring, rage. "How dare he? How dare he? For this there is nothing but revenge."

Sing Pak sat, his elbows on the table, his chin resting on one hand. "An understandable reaction. But now is the time for strategy, not righteous retribution. Many lives are at stake. If a gang war breaks out none of us will be safe."

A gang war? The rage fizzled and died. *Has it really come to that?*

Sing Pak seemed to read his thoughts. "Ji Zeng has been enlisting a secret army within the Black Dragon company for some time, planning for it. That's one reason I can't free you now. If I did, we both would likely die."

Aeyee ah. The final blow. *He can't free me. I'm not getting out. I'll die in this hole.*

"I see. So why are you here?"

"I'm here, Ji Ming, my commander-without-peer, to make sure you are still alive. To tell you about your father — I guessed no one else would have done that. And to find a way to ultimately get you out. Not now, I am sorry, but very soon."

Sing Pak nodded at the guard. "He can't speak English, so has no idea what we're saying. He'll be terrified he'll be the next one dead if Ji Zeng finds out he allowed himself to be taken, so he won't talk. And we'll use that to our advantage. You're being held in the tunnels under Nevada City. Zeng's house has a cellar that opens onto them. He built this jail to deal to people who don't see things his way. Entry through his house is impossible for us — but there are other entries from other places. That's how I got here."

"So what's the plan?"

The back of Ollie's neck was tingling. He put a hand over his shoulder to massage the skin and ease the prickles. If anything the itchiness intensified. He darted a glance across at the guard in the corner. He was getting up from his stool, turning towards Sing Pak, waving his arm to get attention. Ollie grabbed Sing Pak's hand. "Someone's coming. I can feel it — and so can he."

"The plan is to sit tight. Don't do anything to help him, but neither do anything to inflame him."

Sing Pak jumped up, grabbed the guard's arm, and made for the door, giving him quiet instructions. Ollie picked up a few phrases. Sing Pak was going to let the guard go, he told him to tell no one of what had happened. And in return the guard was going to let him melt into the dark of the tunnels. Playing 'Three Monkeys': hear no evil, see no evil, speak no evil.

Ollie called after him. "Tell John on no account give away the seal. And to guard Lily and Selina with his life!"

He was still shouting his instructions as the key grated in the lock, and he was once again alone.

Seventeen

"Came by to see how that leg is, brother." Nathan helped himself to fresh coffee from the pot sitting on a silver tray on the dining room table. "You're still looking a tad peaky, old man. But I suppose that's understandable with what you've got to deal with. How are the house plans coming along?"

"Sebastian's dealing with a lot of that for me, thank goodness," said John. "Today's drama just arrived in the person of Huldah Wilmington. Her daughter Isabella has gone missing. She's just checking she hasn't returned home in the last half hour. If she's still absent, then I'm taking her out to see if she's absconded to Lotta Crabtree's."

He gestured to a chain and a scrap of paper that sat on the dining table.

Nathan raised his eyebrows. "What's that? And why Lotta's?" He put down his coffee and picked up first the chain and then the cartoon. "Looks very much like a caricature of dear brother mine. Is this some kind of bad joke?" He laid on an Australian twang, and grinned at John, still not catching the full import of what he was seeing.

"You can laugh, old chap. You'd be the only one who is. Look closer."

Nathan peered at the paper and let out a low whistle. "Crossed hatchets?" He waved the paper in front of his face. "What on earth is it all about?"

John shook his head. "Wish I knew." *Wish I could tell you.* Much as he valued Nathan's support, he could not bring himself to reopen a chapter of his life he had been so sure was closed forever.

Nathan wasn't to be nudged away. "What's it got to do with the Wilmingtons? It sounds like you were linked to them somehow."

"This got anonymously delivered to Huldah's doorstep this morning. Leaving the insinuation the baby in the cradle is Isabella . . . Naturally Huldah felt perplexed by it. We all are. And then when Huldah went to check on her, the girl wasn't in bed sick as she'd claimed to be. Huldah suspects — even hopes — the girl played sick and then sneaked off to Lotta's. Apparently she was furious when Huldah said she couldn't take the free singing and dancing lessons Lotta offered."

Nathan ran his fingers through the light blond beard that followed the neat curve of his jaw — one of his habits, John had noticed — when he was mulling over something. "So what's the significance of the cradle and the gold acorn charm? I mean, what have you ever had to do with Isabella and the Wilmingtons?"

Always one to get straight to the point, thought John. "Good question. I don't have a clue. I'd never laid eyes on the girl until very recently. Well not that I know of." *I guess I should say, "Not that I remember." If she's who I think she is, the last time I saw her was the cataclysmic night Elanora died.*

Nathan watched him steadily. "Not that you know of?" he echoed. "What exactly does that mean?"

Russell felt boxed in. "It means just what I say. I don't recall having anything to do with any babies ever. So why am I pictured leaning over a cradle? Well, Jove only knows. Whoever drew this crude threat is obviously trying to frighten Isabella and Huldah and implicate me, but to what purpose I have no idea."

Nathan set his coffee down with an abrupt rattling of the cup on saucer and slumped into an armchair. "That silky shawl thing has got a faint whiff of something Oriental — sandalwood or something. Reminds me of Hong Kong. This couldn't be mixed up with the China stuff, could it? With the comprador's death and Ollie's disappearance?" He picked up his cup and wandered over to the window that looked out onto the main street. "You don't recognize it?"

"The fragrance? Not really."

"Did Mrs Wilmington?"

John's palms felt sticky. "Stupid of me — I should have thought of that."

"Do you think she's told you everything she knows?" Nathan turned back from the window and came and sat at the table next to Russell.

"No. No, I don't." John remembered the way Huldah frowned and her shoulders lifted in challenge when he asked her where Isabella was born. *Definitely got her hackles up.* But he was just as bad. He could take a very good guess at why she was so defensive, and he wasn't talking either. What had Huldah muttered? "The best bad choice." Exactly what he was facing.

Nathan sat and gazed into space. John imagined the wheels and cogs turning in his young sibling's lightning-fast brain. Any minute now he was going to challenge him. Ask him if he was coming clean with everything.

John hauled himself to his feet and took up his cane. "I'm still feeling like an old cripple." He laughed, but it sounded hollow even to his ears. "Hope this knee gets better soon."

Nathan tailed him out without another word, but he knew he'd left too many questions unanswered. His brother wouldn't be inclined to let them go.

Eighteen

"Isabella?" Lotta Crabtree was stretched on a recliner, her neck wrapped in a warm scarf, a hot toddy of black tea and whiskey in one hand, a slim black cigar resting in a crystal dish that served as an ashtray. John breathed in the spicy fragrance of the toddy, which together with the faint smell of earth and leaves from the cigar's wispy curling smoke gave the room the pleasant smell of a gentleman's club.

"She did come to visit, but I'm not up to giving lessons today. I've got a bit of a throat coming on, and I have to be fit for Sacramento in another few days." She dipped her toddy glass in a mock salute. "You're most welcome to join us if you wish."

She gestured towards her companion, a man with a walrus mustache who was perched on a chair close to her recliner, giving every appearance of being the star's attentive lackey.

His stomach knotted as he recognized acting deputy sheriff Virgil Hale was perched beside the California Diamond. His eyes had an oily, eager-to-please sheen.

"Afternoon, Sir John," Hale said, raising his toddy glass.

"Deputy Hale." He nodded curtly, and drew Huldah Wilmington into the circle. The muted light gave her skin a sallow hue which emphasized the anxiety lines around her eyes.

"Mrs Wilmington is sick with worry about her daughter. It seems she went out without permission and her mother is looking for her. When was she here?"

Lotta gestured to them to sit. "When was it, deputy? About an hour ago?" Hale nodded. "When I explained I wasn't able to give lessons today she said that was fine and left."

Huldah gave a strangled cough. "You let her just walk out without any chaperone?"

Lotta looked at her in astonishment. "It's Grass Valley, Mrs Wilmington. And she only had to walk a few blocks to get home. A little over-protective, aren't you?"

Huldah's puffy cheeks flushed a mottled red. "Over-protective? Well, as it happens, no I'm not. You have no idea of the threats that have been made against my child."

At the word threats Hale straightened. "Threats, Mrs Wilmington? What threats? Have you reported them to the sheriff's office?"

Huldah flicked an uncertain glance at John and shook her head. "No, I haven't had a chance. It only happened this morning."

"What happened?" Hale fixed her with an attentive stare. "Tell me."

Again Huldah looked towards John, as if inviting him to take the lead.

"Mrs Wilmington is referring to some items that were left on her front door step this morning," he said. "One of them appeared to make a threat against Isabella's person."

"What kind of threat?"

"It was a drawing which included a sketch of the long-handled machetes used by the Chinese gangs." Even as he was speaking he realized how ridiculous it would sound to Hale. Some crazy scribble. Easily dismissed as a practical joke or childish prank.

"A drawing? With some murderous Chinese weapon? Surely you

don't take something like that seriously, Sir John? Maybe Isabella has some female rivals and they're being nasty. I hear she did rather eclipse all the other contenders at Miss Lotta's impromptu talent show."

Huldah began to protest. "No, you don't understand. It wasn't like that."

She cast a despairing look. "Isabella has been here. That's good. She isn't here now. That's bad. We had better hope she's gone straight home. That somehow we just missed her."

She rose from the couch with dignity and gave Lotta Crabtree a courteous nod. "Thank you for your help, Miss Crabtree, but we really must be on our way."

John followed her out. This time, he didn't blame Hale for dismissing the idea some kind of crime had been committed. A threatening caricature? And don't even mention the gold chain and acorn emblem. A lawman certainly had better things to do with his time than chase dragons.

Except John knew better than anyone there was reality to the threat. And he knew just where he needed to look next if he wanted to track down its source.

Nineteen

"Ever seen this before?"

John perched on a stool at Ji Zeng's Sing Song Bar in Nevada City and eyed Oliver's half brother coolly.

Ji Zeng's eyes widened in undisguised shock and just as quickly he masked the surprise with a bland gaze. He picked up the rag paper item with one hand. "What is it?"

"A little something delivered to Huldah Wilmington earlier today. Recognize anyone?"

Zeng examined the drawing, his lips pursed in a tight line. He let out a long whistle. "Is that meant to be you?" He gave a deprecating laugh. "They could have done a better job of it, I must say. What's it all about? Don't tell me you're next?" He laughed again, this time with a disbelieving note.

"The very question I've been asking myself all day."

"And you think I've got the answer? Flattered to be considered such a mine of information, I'm sure, but sadly, no. Never seen it before."

John knew Zeng was a consummate liar, but the way his eyes skittered away as he was speaking confirmed what he'd already suspected. He *had* seen it before, was probably its architect. That meant he also knew something about Elanora's death. And he also knew that Isabella was not Huldah's daughter by blood.

He marvelled at the reach of Zeng's information. The number of people who knew of Isabella's origins must be tiny — less than a handful, for sure. Even he hadn't known it — well, still didn't beyond an educated guess — and he would have thought he was closer to Huldah's inner circle than Zeng was.

Zeng shook his head as if to emphasize he was totally in the dark, and cleared his throat, signaling a change of topic. "Just wondering if you've come across that Dragon Seal in the clean-up? It's getting very hard to run our side of the agency without it. How is everything coming along, by the way?" He leaned on the bar, resting his head on one elbow, displaying a vague interest.

John struggled to suppress a laugh at the falsity of it all, and then gave tit for tat, responding with the same hazy dimness. "Clean-up's going well. And sorry, no sign of the seal. Wouldn't Ollie have it?" He tried to look wide-eyed and confiding. He would hazard a thousand-dollar bet Zeng was no more taken in by his little act than he had been. But he had a deep certainty in his spirit. *Give up the seal, and you're signing Ollie's death warrant.*

Zeng regarded him with an amused smile. "Pity. Good luck with your search for the author of that jape. I guess you'll be hoping nothing more comes of it. Reputation once destroyed is so had to restore, don't you think?" His eyes shone with mischief. He savored the look on John's face for a moment, then slid off the stool. "Gotta go."

John put out an arm to detain him. "Just before you do, what happened the other night? I haven't seen you since they took you away at gunpoint. Don't tell me that was just another 'jape'. And have you had any word on Ollie? Where did they take you?"

Zeng waved a hand, as if dismissing his questions. "It was the Sam

Yup's insurance policy, nothing more. They're laughing at us now, but I'll get my revenge."

"What do you mean?"

"Oh, they're not saying, but they'll release Ollie when the *White Cloud* docks and the opium is landed. Don't worry about it. They've got Ollie and they've got our money, so just for now our hands are tied. Not forever, though. And if they don't release him, they know what will happen."

"Oh? And what's that?" Prickly irritation hit the back of John's throat at Zeng's slippery nonchalance.

"War. Outright war, of course." Zeng's humor vanished, replaced by a dark determination. "No one crosses me and gets away with it."

For a long time after Zeng walked away, John stayed on his stool, slowly sipping his drink, going over the conversation. He had just been given a warning, and he knew it. *Forget about Ollie and get me the seal, or suffer the consequences.*

The ransom payment he made a few nights ago was a setup, just as Selina predicted. It was Zeng's convoluted way of extracting money from the company in lieu of the Dragon Seal. It was very likely he was using it to buy into the *White Cloud* shipment. No wonder he thought it a big joke. *Well, the joke's on me. If I give him the seal, I'll be signing Ollie's death warrant. If I don't give him the seal, I'm risking my reputation and my life.*

He glanced up from his reverie as one of Zeng's exquisite Chinese girls stopped by to offer him a fresh drink. She was beautiful, no doubt about it, but she didn't come close to Pania's allure. Proud, statuesque Pania, with a queenly command of herself and her milieu. He imagined her turning to him, eyes sparkling, café au lait skin highlighting her high cheekbones, and he felt as if he'd been punched in the gut.

He still had hopes of something more with Pania. Would they

survive Zeng's implied threat to destroy his reputation? His heart lurched. He had done things he couldn't forgive himself for — would she understand?

He could bury his head in the sand, hand over the seal and play dumb to Ollie's plight. Or he could fight for Ollie and do something to scrabble back his own integrity.

He waved away the young woman who had been patiently waiting for his response on the drinks. "No thanks. M'sai m goi."

He stood slowly and stretching his shoulders in his sticky shirt turned slowly for the door. The entertainment was just beginning, the chatter gradually fading as the crowds at the tables recognized that the music was about to begin.

As he stepped into the hot evening he smiled grimly. He was going to risk everything for a gamble that might already be lost. Ollie might already be dead.

Twenty

Crowds of visitors filled Chinatown's main street, clustering around the Hou Wang Miao temple and the dozen or more small enclosures and altars that had been set up around it. It was a brilliantly lit festive scene, priests in white robes and light blue satin caps carrying lighted tapers singing incantations as they followed a clamorous group of musicians under trees hung with bright red lanterns.

It was Day Six of the two-week festival. Pania was here with Nathan and Selina to honor the comprador and his wife, but she was also hoping to find some snippet of information that would help Selina find Ollie. With Nathan's help, surely they might find someone who knew something? She tried not to think of John Russell, who though still limited by his injured leg, had disappeared off to Nevada City on some urgent business earlier in the day.

The noise of the Chinese instruments — a mix of a bagpipe-like reed instrument, cornstalk violins, muffled small drums and loud cymbals — rose in a weird but strangely harmonious cacophony into the still night air. The smell of incense, pork fat and a myriad of spices enveloped the crowds. They had come from as far as San Francisco to take part in Grass Valley's vibrant Hungry Ghost festival, but under the noise and color there was a dark undertone.

She felt herself shiver in the late afternoon sun as she strolled up Bank Street with her friends. They were entering the last week of the festival, which would end with fireworks and even more energetic celebrations on the last night, when Chinese followers believed the gates of hell would be shut for another year.

For the previous two weeks, however, they were open, and there was a manic edge to the need to drive out or appease the hungry spirits of the dead who were roaming the earth, so they wouldn't plague those left behind with bad fortune in the coming year. And the way the comprador and his young wife had died, without warning in a fire, set up the perfect circumstances for mischievous, lost or disconsolate spirits to be stirred up.

Zeng showed no inclination towards filial duties, and Ollie was still missing, so at John's behest Nathan had worked with temple director and Chinese doctor Dr Wau Kee to set up a small altar, arrayed with two finely wrought large urns containing greenery and flowers, lit up on either side by perfumed candles and smoking red incense sticks. On display in the center were two objects Chung Ting Hon used daily: an old Russell & Chung ledger filled with his exquisite spidery calligraphy, and his reading glasses, symbolizing his earthly stay.

They had come like all the others, to pay their respects to dead family and friends, by offering food — fruit, rice, and small pieces of dried meat — as well as burning money in a silver tray. These ministrations would satisfy the spirits until the end of the week, when the offerings would need to be repeated.

All around them similar stalls and pavilions, some dedicated to different deities or reflecting various religious themes, were on display. Nathan hung close on their heels as they paused in front of Ting Hon's altar to make their presentations. As they wandered he gave a quiet commentary on what they were observing and its significance, and Pania looked at him in gratitude as they concluded the formalities by setting fire to the paper money with a lighted taper.

"Can we wander a little more?" Pania asked, gauging the others' willingness to stay and soak up the exotic surroundings.

"Certainly." Selina took her arm affectionately. "We aren't in any danger here, are we Nathan? Not with so many people around."

Nathan shrugged. "Can't ever be certain, but it should be fine. It's very well-lit and there are plenty of good folk here."

"Is there anyone here who'd be likely to know anything about Ollie?" Pania kept her voice low and squeezed Selina's hand to reassure her. "I mean, anyone here who could shed any light on what might have happened to him?"

Nathan looked around him. "Who knows? Quite possibly. There are a lot of out-of-towners here. Getting them in a quiet corner to talk? Not so easy. And knowing just where to start? More difficult still."

They continued a slow aimless stroll through the pulsating rainbow crowds. A few yards ahead a firework crackled along the ground, scattering people in its path, and they paused to allow room for the people pushing past. Through a gap in the wall of people, Pania caught sight of a familiar face, hovering at the front of a crowd, transfixed. She followed the girl's gaze and saw a seated woman, her face partly concealed by a fall of long black hair, who appeared to be weeping blood. Her beautiful young face was made up in a heavy theatrical Chinese style, and red paint streaks ran from her eyes down her cheeks. She was wailing and shrieking, waving her hands in agitated circles, while a crowd gathered around her enclosure joined in her chorus of lament.

"If they weep and wail loud and long enough, the hungry spirits will be either satisfied, or driven off," Nathan explained as they watched.

Pania, though, was more interested in the girl watching from the crowd. It was Ngo Wai, the young woman who had been so frightened the other night in the club, and she looked to be in some sort of religious ecstasy. Pania quietly filtered through the constantly shifting people until she reached her side. Wai wore the same emerald silk tunic she had when she'd seen her last, and apart from the strange glazed look in her eyes she was as luminously beautiful as ever.

"Ngo Wai, are you all right?"

The girl looked up and her eyes gradually focused on Pania's face.

"I was worried after the other night . . ." Pania tried again to focus her attention.

"You. Mrs Opera?" Ngo Wai looked around wildly, as if terrified to be seen talking to her. "No. I can't. Trouble, big trouble if I talk to you."

She backed away, staring into Pania's face.

"No, wait! I could help." Pania put out her hand to restrain the girl, but she slipped out of reach and was gone. Right then the bleeding woman gave a piercing shriek, and the crowd surged in.

"There's something very wrong," Pania told Nathan. "I saw that girl at the club the other night. Not long ago, she was desperate to join Harvey's chorus and come on the road. Now she's terrified to even be seen talking to me."

She cast a wary glance around the surrounding street. The crowds ebbed and flowed like waves hitting a beach, some sweeping this way, some off in another, each intent on their own mission. No one was taking any notice of them. Except . . . She felt a sixth-sense prickle at the back of her neck and whirled around, looking to the far edge of the mass of people. Did she catch a glimpse of a black figure, the keeper who'd mysteriously seen them out of the club? She couldn't be sure, and when she looked again, if there had been anyone watching, they'd gone. No one she recognized, just a colorful surge of anonymous people.

Selina took her arm to comfort her. "That girl's weird but harmless. Let's keep wandering a while longer. And, Nathan, please try and keep your eyes and ears tuned for any sign that could help us find Ollie."

They wandered for another half hour or so, sipping yet more of the iced drinks that were dispensed free to the crowd as they watched some San Francisco entertainers who had been brought in for the week. Nathan stopped and talked to a number of acquaintances, but gleaned little that was of use in their quest for information.

Eventually the crowd began to thin out and Pania felt herself dragging behind. It was getting late. "Shouldn't we go? We've accomplished what we came for, haven't we? Part of it anyway."

"I guess," said Nathan. "Pity we couldn't pick up anything new." Taking Selina by the elbow he began steering her gently up the street away from the temple, to where Bank Street merged into Mill Street

Their carriage loomed out of the twilight and Nathan gestured to the ladies to get in while he unhitched the horse which was chewing twigs from the tree it was hitched to. Pania pulled open the door, indicating to Selina to get in ahead of her. Selina stepped forward and then uttered a little cry and fell back.

Pania looked at her stricken face. She was shaking her head wordlessly, uttering little gasping moans. Pania briefly drew her to her shoulder. "What is it? What's wrong?"

White-faced, Selina continued to shake her head, swallowing hard, saying nothing.

Pania gently let go of her and stepped around her, to pull open the closed carriage door. Sprawled on her back across the seat, arms and legs spread wide, her blue-green tunic stained red, lay Ngo Wai. Her mouth was open in a frozen 'O' of protest, a jagged cut across her throat leaking blood.

Pania leaned over and felt her wrist, although she already knew what she would find. No beating pulse, however fluttering and fragile. Only a void that would last into eternity, in her rapidly cooling body.

Twenty-One

Pania slept badly, and the last thing she felt like doing on a Monday morning was going to a frock-fitting session at Cressida Washington's. As she tossed and turned she tried to decipher the riddle of Ngo Wai's ruthless murder. What had anyone to gain by slaughtering a frightened girl? Was this some convoluted revenge killing, a merciless warning to Black Dragon families who were resisting Ji Zeng, or was it a personal message directed at her? If it was the latter, at what cost? Had Ngo Wai even told her anything important?

She lay awake at Stockton House, hearing the quiet murmurings in the hallways and kitchen from the household's early risers. High-pitched childish giggles floated from the kitchen. Minette pestering the cook for a cookie, no doubt. Everything seemed so normal, but she couldn't get the image of Wai's defiled form from her mind.

What had Ngo Wai told her that night at the club? She thought back. She gave vague warnings about Lily and Selina. Very vague. That was it. And she said nothing last night, she'd been too terrified. Pania rolled over and sighed. Trying on dresses was the last thing she wanted, but she knew better than to let her emotions rule.

What was it Henry always told her? "It is easier to act your way into a feeling than feel your way into an action." A second stab of loss pierced her, not as keen as what she was feeling for Ngo Wai, but it registered. Her husband had been a wise man and she missed him.

She was in Cressida's welcoming salon by ten o'clock, ready to try on the gowns she would take on tour with Harvey in a couple of weeks. After all the confusion she had been feeling about John it was good to simply settle down to her work, one thing she could understand and control.

Cressida had set aside an hour for a private consultation and the time flew by as her confident fingers adjusted the seams, taking an inch in here, letting an inch out there, ensuring a perfect, comfortable fit. As they chatted and joked, Cressida's mouth was set in a firm line. Pins sticking out from between her lips, she shook with mirth at Pania's naughty gossip, but never let a single pin escape.

"And what about that Adeline Baker?" Pania pitched the inquiry with a mischievous twitch of her right eyebrow. "Reckon she's got her hat set at Sir John?"

The bi-racial widow who'd come out West to escape the Civil War after her black soldier husband's death took the last pin out of her mouth and regarded Pania with frank curiosity. "And we're interested, Missus Opera." She camped up the nickname "We're interested because?" she said teasingly.

Pania felt herself blushing. Darn it, the warmth was creeping into her cheeks. She knew that her natural olive complexion would be deeper, brighter than usual. Talk about shining like a Christmas tree, and it was only August.

"He's an attractive man. I guess it's natural he'd be on Huldah's list of most desirable bachelors. Never thought he'd stoop to attending one of her little match making soirees, though."

She tried to make it sound like a light, tossed-off remark, but could see that Cressida wasn't taken in. The dressmaker flashed a skeptical grin and stepped around her to begin unfastening the back of the hot-pink finale number.

"Attractive, no argument. But perhaps the poor man has spent so much energy making money he's woken up and discovered time is passing him by. Especially with his young brother appearing out of nowhere and stealing the bride from under his nose. When you see who he's marrying, well, let's just say Miss Graysie Castellanos is no small catch as it's turned out, her inheriting that gold mine and all. Maybe your poor old Sir John is feeling a bit overtaken by events. I wouldn't blame him."

Pania was momentarily dumbfounded. Then she felt like a fool. Why hadn't she seen what had been so obvious to Cressida? John might just be suffering from a temporary loss of confidence for the first time ever in his life. And it hadn't occurred to her. *I've let it become personal, let it needle me. Like an unruly petticoat, my insecurities are showing.*

She stood with her arms hanging at her sides, fidgeting her fingers as she absorbed Cressida's commonsense comments. If the sensible mama was right, where did that leave her? Before she had any chance of answering that for herself, the doorbell sounded. Cressida looked up expectantly and her housekeeper popped her head around the door post.

"Mrs Wilmington wishes to call, ma'am. Is it all right to show her in?"

"Give us a few minutes for Mrs Hayes to change. You can show her in then. I think this session's finished. We'll have these all completed and to you by the end of the week?"

Pania nodded. "Fine, thanks."

Ten minutes later Pania and Huldah sat either side of a small occasional table sipping coffee as Cressida looked out some fabric samples for Huldah to take home to show Isabella.

The girl had turned up at home, as Lotta Crabtree had suggested she would, and Huldah was so relieved to have her safely back she hadn't made a big fuss about her disobedience. She'd merely tried to impress on her that the world was a dangerous place and she shouldn't wander off alone again. Isabella appeared to be willing to stick to that understanding, but she was still resisting the idea of going to Europe.

"She wants to do what you're doing" Huldah said, her mouth drawn down at the corners. "Is there any chance you could talk to her? She thinks it's going to be one great big adventure." She sighed. "You've reached the top, Mrs Hayes, but I am sure there were times when you were coming up that were far from pleasant."

Pania took a sip of coffee and put her cup down. "Most certainly. And remember, I had Henry to represent me, work on my behalf. That was a tremendous advantage. I don't think I could have done it without his help."

Huldah nodded. "Lotta Crabtree's mother does the same thing for her. I've heard she's a very canny manager. We're just new chums by comparison. I'm afraid I could never match her."

Pania fiddled with the marcasite ring on her left hand, which was coming loose. "Mrs Crabtree is one of a kind — very hard to copy. She's born to the role."

"Could you talk to her? Isabella, I mean."

Pania considered the request. What could she say that would be of any help? What would a star-struck girl like Isabella be open to hear? Was it all a waste of time?

"There could be a compromise," she said tentatively. "There are some very good singing teachers in Europe. Maybe you could take her to the Continent on the promise of getting her more professional training. If she still wants to go on the stage when she's completed that, you agree to try and find her an agent?"

Huldah clapped her hands together excitedly. "What a great idea! I'll have to get some names from you."

"I'm curious. Where did this love of music come from, do you think? Are either you or your husband musical?"

Huldah's demeanor changed so sharply it was as if a candle had been blown out. Her expression went from bright anticipation to a faint scowl. Not a question she welcomed, Pania could see. "No. No neither of us." Her answer was faltering. "Just one of those things, I guess. A throwback."

Cressida returned with the samples. "Here we are. The blue and gold would look especially fine, but Isabella's such a beautiful girl she'd be lovely in any of these." She handed the swatches to Huldah. "Anything else?"

Huldah jumped up so fast you'd think she had sat on an ant's nest. "No, that's everything. I'd better be going." She gave a brief bow and turned and headed for the door without another word.

Pania collected her reticule and parasol. As she sauntered up Main Street in the sunshine, she reflected on the abrupt end to her chat with Mrs Wilmington. *So unlike her. She usually likes to hang around and gossip. But not about who Isabella takes after, though. That innocent little question was about as welcome as a skunk in the drawing room. I wonder why.*

Twenty-Two

Why hadn't she noticed before? Pania Hayes sat across from Sir John Russell in the shaded hotel courtyard and studied her friend as he finalized the orders of the timber and bricks needed to get the rebuild of Gold House under way. They had just finished a relaxing lunch together when Nathan arrived with the Gold House work supervisor to discuss progress.

She sat and observed the men talking, sipping the last of her coffee and daydreaming. Cressida Washington's words echoed in her head: "Maybe your poor old Sir John is feeling a bit overtaken by events." She regarded the proud profile she knew so well, and noticed salt-and-pepper shading in the dark beard that hugged his firm jawline, and a network of tiny worry lines crowding the outside corners of his eyes.

When did they appear? Chung Ting Hon's death and the loss of his magnificent home had left deep marks on him, she could see that. But she sensed it was more than the calamities of the last ten days that weighed on him. He was carrying a deep weariness she'd hardly noticed before. Her heart softened as she gazed at him. The poor dear man. He was carrying the cares of the world on his shoulders. And here she'd been, accusing him of only being interested in himself.

They had managed to confine their lunch chat to safe topics — what Graysie and Minette had been doing, how her plans for the next tour were progressing, the Gold House blueprint — and fallen into their familiar comfortable rhythm. She was reminded all over again what a precious friendship they shared.

But now that her husband was no longer alive, she saw for the first time that friendship would inevitably change. Henry had been like a protective dyke — a safe wall that had fenced off the possibility of her relationship with John ever being anything more than one of shared intellectual interests in art and the theater. Now that he was gone, the protective wall was no longer there. She and John would have to build a new set of parameters. And she was afraid to consider what they might look like.

With a rush she recognized that if either of them embarked on something new — if she got closer to Harvey, for example, or John took up with Adeline Baker — it would change the whole basis of their friendship. They'd have to start over. Her stomach felt peculiar as she tried to imagine what that would be like. Her insides went light and fluttery. A sick churning.

Him with Mrs Baker, her with Harvey, meeting at the opera? Sharing a box? She suddenly understood she had lost far more than a husband when Henry died. She had lost the protector who had also given her a safe best friend. When he died, she lost both husband *and* best friend. The loss of one was hard, but the loss of both . . . She shook her head.

"Something wrong?" John's warm baritone cut across her reverie. Nathan and the workman were picking up their plans and lists and departing.

Pania shook herself and tried to snap back into the present. "All fine," she said with a smile. "Thank you for a very pleasant lunch."

"My pleasure." He had been able to stop resting his injured leg and start moving more freely, and seemed more cheerful now he was on the move.

"Are they meeting the deadlines you wanted?"

He nodded. "It's still probably going to be next summer before I'll move in — we won't be able to get a lot done over the winter — but at least we're getting started."

"I saw Huldah at Cressida's this morning."

He cocked his head to one side, immediately wary. "Oh? What was she doing there?"

"Picking up some fabric samples to take home and show Isabella. She was complaining about the fascination the girl has with Lotta. Asked me if I could talk to her, tell her some of the hard facts of stage life."

"What did you say?"

"I said I doubted I could break through the stardust to show her the sawdust. She's probably not ready to see it just yet."

"Think you might be right there. I'm just very glad she turned up safely. You know she went off to Lotta's against Huldah's wishes? Huldah was beside herself."

"No! I didn't know that. No wonder she was so riled up. I suggested she sell her on the idea of Europe by finding her a good vocal coach. That way you're buying time, hoping she'll see sense, but not killing the dream outright."

"Clever lady. I always have appreciated your ability to see around corners." Pania felt an unreasonable warm glow. He'd complimented her, and she loved it. "Really? Well, how about we apply some wide-vision thinking to that terrible murder last night. Have you any idea why that poor girl was killed like that? And why she was left for us to find?"

John hesitated and rubbed his forehead, gently massaging between his brows out to his temples. "I suspect it's to frighten Selina and generally intimidate anyone who wants Ollie found."

Pania nodded. "Makes sense. Wai was acting a bit frantic and crazy. Maybe she'd become a liability. She didn't say anything last night — she was too terrified. But as I told you, she did vaguely hint at the club she knew something about the whole family — Ollie, Selina and Lily — that she was too frightened to go into."

"I've got security on Selina. Any time she goes out. Trying to ensure it's harder work for the ruthless devil, whoever he is, to wreak his havoc."

Pania's mind flicked to the man with the tattooed hand at the club. She suspected he was there last night too. "This man, the security, doesn't have a tattooed hand, a tattoo that disappears up his shirt sleeve by any chance?" She spoke softly, and held her breath for the answer, knowing the tenderness she felt inside showed in her eyes.

John gave a brief laugh and moved forward to the edge of his seat. He took her hand in his and gently massaged the back of it between supple fingers. "I believe he might, Mrs Hayes. Why do you ask?"

It was a simple gesture of affection but it made her heart roll over. "I saw a man just like that at the club. The night I went out with Harvey. And I'm certain he was there again last night, though I never really sighted him. Just felt him. That was your doing?"

He looked deep into her eyes. "It was. Losing Ting Hon, the house, it makes a man realize what he values most."

There was a long silence between them. Pania was holding on tight, scared to breathe, searching his face.

He let go of her hand and pushed back in his chair. "I don't want to lose you, Pania. You may find me an impossible beggar, but I don't want to lose you."

She stared at him, wishing he still held her hand, missing his warm touch. Maybe they could find a way to be together without Henry's sheltering wall. If they held hands and held on, maybe they would make it.

Twenty-Three

I did all this a week ago. I really don't want to have to do it all over again, especially for someone so young.

John Russell fingered his beard — it needed a trim — and placed his offering of fruit and burning incense on the altar set up in the thoroughfare outside the temple. With the Hungry Ghost Festival building to its climax there were hordes more people than usual milling around, wanting to farewell the beautiful young woman who had died so violently right here.

The immediacy of it all was irresistible. He sighed. *I wonder how many of them ever met her. I wonder if we will ever learn the truth about what happened. Why she was killed.*

He moved on, threading his way through bands of musicians, mourners, solo entertainers, and dancers to Ting Hon's memorial, where he lit more paper money and incense. The comprador's altar was overflowing with gifts. He ran his hand lightly down the spine of the leather-bound volume, Hon's accounting book, that was on display. How many days and weeks had Hon sat inscribing pages like these with his immaculate tallies? He was a man who noticed the smallest detail, and valued every nuance. A tide of sadness rose from within him, and he had to squeeze his eyes shut to ward off surprise tears. He owed it to Hon to uncover what happened in his final hours.

He turned away from the memorial and scanned the pulsing, noisy throng. The air was heavy with the thrumming of drums and shrieking of horns.

The woman with the bleeding eyes Pania had described was still shrieking and wailing and leaking red fluid, attracting a big crowd, including a gang of ragamuffin urchins who loitered on the periphery begging for sweets and coins from the high-spirited festival goers.

As he stood and watched, one of the boys slipped away from his friends and veered towards him. He made as if to go past him, then hesitated and placed his hand on the side seam of his trousers. He gave a light tug, and hopped from one foot to the other as John bent down to him. The boy looked around as if on a danger alert and said, "A man wants to talk to you. Watch where I go and follow me." John made a show of giving the boy some sweets and turned to walk on, as if their transaction was complete. But he watched as the lad slid into the tiny corridor between the Chinese medical store and the temple and disappeared.

He hovered, making a show of giving some of the other boys coins and sweets and after several more minutes he followed the boy's path. It was quieter and cooler away from the crowds where pine trees shaded a narrow walking trail that led into an area of rough parkland. He paused and glanced around. What if this was some kind of trap? Was he designed to be the next casualty? Was he crazy to be thinking like this, or just being careful?

His soft leather boots made no sound on the needle-strewn path. He slipped his hand into his jacket pocket and stepped forward, moving carefully, stopping to look around him every few yards. Thank goodness his knee was back to normal. The trail forked up ahead, and he was wondering which path to take when his young guide slid out from behind a tree trunk, pointed to the left-hand fork, and danced on.

The festival noise had faded to a distant hum, the only other sound a whispery sighing high up in the pines. At ground level the air didn't move, and even in the shade it was still hot enough to make him sweat. He was just beginning to ask himself how much further he would allow himself to be led when the boy stopped and motioned to a natural craggy outcrop.

Several big boulders leaned into one another, creating a natural cavern. The boy stood aside and gestured to him to enter. As he peered in he saw an older Chinese man in traditional navy-blue trousers and tunic perched on a flat-topped rock. His face was smooth and unlined, his posture erect. He carried with him an aura of deep calm, despite quicksilver flashes that lit up his sparkling, deep-set eyes. John paused at the entry to the cavern, letting his eyes adjust to the shaded light, and his mind scramble to grasp what he was seeing.

He clasped his hands in front of him in the steepled gesture of greeting suitable for honoring an elder, and bowed over them. "Leong Sing Pak."

"Sir John Russell."

Sing Pak. Chung Ting Hon's right-hand man before he and Ollie were sent off to boarding school. As far as he knew, Sing Pak still worked for Chung Trading in Hong Kong — or was it Macau? That was Ollie's side of the business, and he hadn't needed to know. *What is he doing here in California? Surely he isn't working with Zeng?* Sing Pak stepped forward and took his hands in a firm, confident grip.

"Greetings, Sing Pak. This is a surprise."

Sing Pak smiled. "Even an ill wind will bring something good." He indicated a flat rock. "We've little time and I have much to relate."

John and Sebastian wanted to remain anonymous and invisible so they dressed accordingly. Loose black trousers, similar to those worn by Chinese railway workers, soft-soled boots, faces obscured with cotton shawls. They hoped to spring Ollie out of jail without firing a shot by approaching through the back tunnels Sing Pak had told them about.

John's fingers and toes tingled with a heightened sense of alarm that told him Ollie's guards would not leave themselves vulnerable for a repeat of Sing Pak's earlier visit, but he suppressed it. This was the best option. At the moment, it was the only option apart from brazenly fronting up to Ji Zeng's house and demanding Ollie's release, and he couldn't see Zeng capitulating to any kind of standover tactic.

As Sing Pak recounted the details of his visit with Ollie in the park earlier that day, John boiled over. It confirmed his deep suspicion that the comprador's second son was behind the mayhem, but he still found it inconceivable that a son would attack his own family. He had to be stopped, and it was pointless trying to get Deputy Hale to act. Sebastian had official standing as a temporary deputy, and was a battle-hardened Civil War veteran. He hoped that would give them an edge.

Sing Pak had tried to insist that he lead them in, but John point-blank refused to let him put himself in danger. He told him he'd already achieved a great feat in finding and talking to Ollie. Now it was their job to free him.

He'd left Nathan and the tattooed enforcer in his employ to keep watch back at Stockton House, with strict instructions to ensure the womenfolk of the extended family — including Pania, Huldah and Isabella — did not stir until he and Sebastian returned. He didn't want to risk anyone else becoming a revenge target if they freed Ollie. If they failed . . . Well, they *couldn't* fail.

Sing Pak had led them to a mining hut on the edge of Prospect Hill, a simple structure that provided basic cover for a set of steps leading down to a battered trapdoor, their alternate entry into the gold tunnels. He carefully drew them a detailed sketch of the way he'd gone, and talked them through it step by step before they set out. They waited until midnight and now this was it. Time to get moving.

He motioned to Sebastian to raise the trapdoor. The hinges creaked as Sebastian pulled on a big brass ring fastened to the top. A stray beam of moonlight from the small window glinted on the barrel of the gun in his hand. They wanted to come and go without being seen, but had to be prepared for anything. As the heavy boards lifted, a musty damp underground smell hit him, as he followed a few steps in behind his brother. A hint that these tunnels were deep and ran for miles in all directions.

Sebastian made his way down six steps and paused to let his eyes adjust to the dim light. They had brought a flint and lantern for emergencies, but agreed not to use any light going in which might tip someone off they were there, so they had to rely on night sight to move. Behind him, John drew the trapdoor down. It was dark, no doubt about it, but after a few minutes he could make out the dim outline of the dark rock walls and sensed rather than clearly saw the vacant tunnel space they enclosed. Sebastian turned and he nodded his encouragement. Onward and upward.

He had Sing Pak's sketch in his pocket but memorized its details. In the darkness there could be no stopping to check they were on the right path. They moved in slow, careful steps, Sebastian setting a steady measured rhythm. Every dozen or so strides he'd stopped to check whether his brother was still there and comfortable with their progress.

The tunnel went downwards, at first on a gentle slope and then more steeply, until it crossed a shallow stream and started to ascend again. Just what Sing Pak had described. So far, so good. John's hand on his gun relaxed. His jaw softened from a rigid clench. They were on their way and making good progress.

They continued at their stealthy prowl for another ten or fifteen minutes. Sometimes their feet dislodged rocks or pebbles which set off a metallic scuffle and they would halt, barely breathing, half-expecting to be called out by Ollie's keepers, but they continued unchallenged. One section they passed through smelt of human urine, another had the unmistakable stench of decaying rodent, but otherwise the tunnel was empty.

They came to a junction Sing Pak had described where the underground pathway forked. Take the left-hand branch, he had instructed. John sniffed the air. A rocky dust caught in his nostrils and settled at the back of his throat. He caught a sulfurous whiff of black powder in the dust.

Someone had detonated rock here recently — within the last couple of hours. He peered down the right-hand arm: the way was blocked by jagged lumps of rock. He strode forward and grabbed Sebastian's arm, arresting his movement and pointing him towards the fall. Not natural, but a detonated rock dump. So what was that about? What purpose could there be in closing that underground arm?

"Any idea what's going on here?" he whispered. How close were they to Ollie? He had no idea.

Sebastian shrugged. "Maybe to close off escape?" They shared a dirty frown. Not a good sign. What if the tunnel was collapsed around them, or before they could leave?

John shivered. *Please God forbid.* They looked at one another and nodded in agreement. They needed to be extra wary, but they had to go on.

John took the lead from Sebastian, slowing their pace by half, frequently pausing to listen for any sound of Ollie or his guards. All was still and silent, but his skin was twitching. Something felt off. They had gone on for another ten minutes and were beginning to wonder if Sing Pak's sketch was confused in its detail when he saw lights shining dimly up ahead. Sing Pak had said the tunnel immediately around Ollie's cell was minimally lit. Had they got to him? John waited for Sebastian to draw alongside.

Without speaking he pointed to the dim glow and mouthed, "Ollie's cell?"

Sebastian nodded and mouthed. "Maybe." He waved his arm forward as if to say, "There's only one way to be sure." They continued in silence, gradually entering into light cast by a few lanterns hung on hooks on the timber tunnel supports.

They came to a door. The door Sing Pak had described, God willing. Sebastian stood to one side, gun raised, back to the tunnel wall, in a defensive posture, and gestured to his brother to go ahead and open up.

John tried the door. It was locked. He pulled out the key Sing Pak had taken from the captured guard, which dangled on a cord around his neck. The lock stayed rigid, unresponsive to the key shaft turning. What now? Had they changed the lock since yesterday? They stood and glared at each other, and then at the solid wood barrier blocking them.

Sebastian raised his gun in a wordless question: *Shoot it out?*

John hesitated. Gunshots would bring the guards running, but how else could they gain entry? He nodded. *We have to take the risk. We've come this far, we can't stop now.*

Sebastian placed the barrel close to the lock and fired. The boom in the close tunnel made their ears ring. A jagged hole about the size of a child's fist opened up where the keyhole had been, and the door swung open. John gave Sebastian a thumbs-up and widened its opening further, sheltering along the door jamb as he did. Total silence. Not a thing moved. John and then Sebastian stepped into the room, Seb closing the door behind them.

The only light in the room came from a single lantern that sat on the bare table. A chair lay overturned, as if someone had left in a hurry. Heart in his mouth, John surveyed the room from left to right, taking in every small detail as he swiveled on his heels. Ollie's cell — if this was Ollie's cell — was empty.

They must have got to him and moved him. So what now? As the brothers stood contemplating the vacant space, a thunderous charge echoed down the tunnel from outside. A detonator, going off with a mighty roar. Then the clatter of showering rock fragments, reverberating down the tunnel and through the closed door. The floor vibrated under their feet.

In unison, they turned to the door, guns raised, one moving to one side of the room, the other the opposite. The shooshing sound of smaller rock fragments, falling like fine dust, continued for several minutes after the heavier clatter of rock ended.

Then came shouts and the tramp of running feet. It sounded like men, running from the blast up the tunnel towards them. John looked wildly around the room and saw something he hadn't noticed before. A door. Another door. On the opposite wall. He stood guard and gestured to Sebastian with his gun barrel. "Go. Now." Sebastian backed to the door, gun still cocked. He opened it without any difficulty and was through it instantly. John followed right after him.

Twenty-Four

They found themselves in a rickety stairwell similar to the one they had come down to get in here, but with more height. Several flights of steps teetered above them. They plunged up the first set, rounding the corner to the next level in a frantic energy surge.

Just as they got into the second set John heard the door below them crash open, and a bullet pinged off the banister and plugged into the rock wall in a trajectory of fire just above his shoulder, sending up a spray of stone fragments. He felt the sharp sting of debris hitting his face. He flung his hand up for protection and pulled it away covered in blood.

He spun around and fired back down the stairwell in one swinging movement before charging on after Sebastian. Someone howled from below. *Good, that might slow them down. Make them less determined to keep up the chase.* He turned and fired again.

Two more flights and another wild shot came from behind that he once again returned. His knee was screaming at him to ease up and sweat dripped from his hair into his eyes. He had to keep squeezing them shut and then blinking to be able to see. The steps exited into a mining locker like the one they'd come through forty-five minutes ago. As they burst out into the clear night air he could still hear the thud of their pursuers' feet on the stairs behind them.

They came out at the top of one of the seven hills Nevada City was built on. The waxing crescent moon sailed through the open dome of stars overhead. After the dimness underground the light from the sky was dazzling. A night breeze dried his sweaty face within a few yards of getting into the open. They plunged on down a rocky tree-stripped hillside. He could hear the tinkling sound of a stream to his right. His brain worked overtime to calculate their location. They were on a hill with the town below them and a stream to their right. Almost certainly Deer Creek, he guessed.

That meant they had exited on Prospect Hill and were fleeing into the town's central business district. Another shot hit the dirt behind his feet. Ollie's guards were determined to run them right off the hill. He wondered how much further they would continue to chase them. He tried to keep up with Sebastian as he dodged and weaved, using boulders for cover wherever he could. And then his feet hit a wooden boardwalk. He heard faint music from a nearby bar. Surely now their pursuers would give up and go home? He was at the end of his strength.

He paused to catch his breath and saw Sebastian's back disappear through a narrow doorway. Ignoring the pain in his knee he pounded after him. They couldn't afford to get separated now. More stairs led into a bare corridor smelling of stale tobacco and sour beer. He frantically filtered the possibilities. They appeared to be in the back of an old music hall or pub, so must be somewhere near the National Hotel on Lower Broad Street. They might even be in the annex attached to the hotel that had been temporarily closed by fire six months ago. Somewhere in that vicinity, anyway.

Ahead of him, Sebastian waited for him to catch up. A door behind them burst open and ricocheted against the wall. *Damn.* At least one of their pursuers was still there. As he caught up with

Sebastian they both turned, raised their guns and stood their ground. The man who was following them — there was just one — slowed the instant he saw them facing up to him. He too raised his gun, and continued advancing on them, but now more cautiously, his eyes fixed on their faces. Sebastian backed down the corridor with John following, also stepping backwards, eyes fixed on their pursuer. Sebastian's steps stopped so suddenly he backed into him. His hot breath warmed the back of John's neck. He leaned in close and rasped, "Door at my back, exiting now."

A hot gust of air carrying the scent of warm bodies and floral perfume filled the corridor. The faintest tinkle of a piano came with the aroma. John held position in the corridor, staring down the gunman. He cocked his gun and took aim. The man stopped dead.

The hesitation gave him the moment he needed to back through the gap and slam the door shut behind him. *Let him try to enter a room where he knows two armed men are waiting. Surely he'll give up now?* He leaned against it hard and waited for his vision to adjust to the dim lighting.

They stood in a luxuriously furnished room: puffy velour-covered couches piled with cushions in a rainbow of colors, silver-tray bearing waiters in dark evening jackets who appeared to glide from station to station, intent on satisfying their customers' needs with a minimum of disturbance. And in the center of it all, Second Son Ji Zeng sat in a peacock chair in a mandarin-collared turquoise jacket with gold brocade trim, sipping a cocktail.

"I've been expecting you," he said. "What took you so long?"

The door from the outside hall opened and the gunman who had tailed them showed in silhouette, his gun at the ready. Zeng set down his cocktail glass and glanced over to him. "I might need to call on your services later. But for the time being, well done."

He looked up at John and sneered, "You didn't think you'd get in there undetected, did you? I'll deal with Leong Sing Pak later. Now sit down and listen hard." He indicated two hard spindly chairs set up opposite his peacock throne. "This won't take long."

John felt strangely off-balance, uncertain of what had just occurred. Had he just been set up, played as Zeng's dupe? He didn't believe Sing Pak would have been in on it, but the back of his neck prickled with irritable rising heat as he considered that possibility. How had they managed to fall so completely into the lure set for them? He shook his head in disbelief.

The piano man kept up a flow of melodic romantic melodies from a baby grand in a far corner. Well-heeled businessmen sat around on couches, arms draped over beautiful Chinese girls dressed in jewel-colored, high-collared silk tunics; one or two got up to dance a slow waltz. Ji Zeng's Sing Song girls. Ngo Wai's friend was among them, the illusion of flawless elegance dissolved by her nervy, high-pitched giggles.

Six years, John thought. That was all that separated the Chung brothers in the line of inheritance growing up. Chung Ji Zeng was the comprador's second son, to his second wife; but in his first year he was sent to Ting Hon's childless brother, as was sometimes the custom. They had seen him at family gatherings, but he'd never been close to Ting Hon or John the way Ollie was. He thought of the years spent in English boarding schools, or on the ship to and from Hong Kong and England. It was the tradition for powerful Hong Kong families to get their sons —at least their first sons — a Western education. After the age of eight he and Ollie were each other's family: together at boarding school during term; staying with Ollie's mother Amelia, his father's sister, some holidays; and returning to Hong Kong once a year for the long break. He had lost touch with Zeng and was now paying the price.

Zeng was a good-looking man, with fine features and a square jaw, his dark hair shining like satin in his lightly oiled plait. Dark brows over penetrating deep brown eyes. *But what cold eyes.*

"I'm surprised. I didn't expect you to be so picky in the face of certain profit." Zeng linked his fingers together. "It's time you understood very clearly what is happening here. "These are the 'not negotiables' for Russell and Chung Trading under my control. The company will be moving into new lucrative areas of business. Ollie will no longer be involved. You will find and convey to me the Dragon Seal by Friday. That is two days from now. That should give you plenty of time." He raised an eyebrow, challenging disagreement, but neither of the brothers responded.

"If you refuse to meet these demands, you will never see Ollie again. Bring me the seal and I'll give you Ollie. A fair trade. No seal, no Ollie. I'm capable of being just as ruthless as you've been to get where you are today. Do we understand one another?"

John regarded him with rising irritation. *Who does he think he is, making these demands?*

"And one more thing. Give up this farcical quest to find Ollie. You're wasting your time." Zeng looked them over like they were schoolboys caught trying to cut classes.

John took a deep breath. "I'd say if you want to talk about farces, that episode the other night when you extorted funds from me under false pretences would rank right up there. Why go to the bother?"

"It suited my purposes at the time. It kept you guessing, so I'd say it worked."

"So now you're admitting you had Ollie all along. What about Ting Hon's death? Did you orchestrate that too?"

Zeng glared at him, his eyes never flickering. "Ollie, Ollie, Ollie. That's all I ever hear. Honorable, upright, never-can-do-wrong Ollie. Ollie who had an inheritance in his own right, but ensured he doubled it by marrying a rich heiress. Ollie the English half-breed, who uses his mother's name in preference to his honorable father's."

John assumed he was referring to Ollie's use of Pakenham as a middle name — a family name going back generations on his mother's side.

Zeng spat into a spitoon at his feet. "The world doesn't start and stop with Ollie."

"What's wrong with you, Ji Zeng? This is your brother you're talking about."

"Half-brother. And I couldn't care less. He's never acted like a brother. He wasn't even around. Too busy being the perfect little Englishman." Ji Zeng's eyes glittered.

"You're so wrong!" John clenched his fists and fought the urge to drag Zeng off his fancy perch. "At school he was always bullied because of his Chinese heritage. He never disowned it —he always stood up for it proudly. And his mother, my aunt, was the reason we spent so much time in England. She was determined to take us both under her wing and ensure we got a decent education after my mother died. She was never going to be the submissive little wife and your father understood that. He might even have liked it."

Ji Zeng put his hands over his ears. He did not want to hear. When he seemed confident he wouldn't be interrupted again he dropped his hands to his knees. "He's always been in my way." His voice was low, intense, the words coming out with a hissing sibilance. "Now he isn't in the way any longer. Nor ever will be again."

John folded his arms. "Look, I don't have the Dragon Seal and I don't know where it is."

"I don't believe you. But if that is true, you'd better find it damn quick. I won't stop at Ollie."

Sebastian, who had not said a word until now, interjected. "Hey, Ji Zeng, slow down here. No point in making silly threats." He rose from his chair and melted across the space to Zeng. He leaned into him and said softly, "It's getting late. Best we conclude this discussion for now. We'll come back to it another time." He had a soothing smoothness to his voice, the product perhaps of being tested in battle as a Union soldier during the Civil War. He had learned to talk down overwrought men.

But it failed to work any calming magic on Ji Zeng, who bristled as Sebastian towered over him, his six foot two dwarfing Zeng's five foot eleven. "Sit down, Sebastian," he hissed. "You'll go when I say you can go. I haven't finished yet."

He waved Seb back to his seat and glared at John. "I won't stop at Ollie," he repeated. "I'm warning you. What would you pay to get back, say, the haughty Selina Chung? Or the delectable Lily? Now there's a piece to make someone a great Substitute Wife. Maybe even me. Wouldn't that thrill the snobbish Selina? Her precious daughter wed against her will to the wicked uncle?"

He stared at John, a calculating half-smile on his lips. Then, stabbing his index finger towards him: "Find the Dragon Seal by the end of the week or live with the consequences."

The room had gone deathly quiet. Without having raised his voice, Zeng had established a sense of deadly threat, even the piano player had stopped his continuous tinkling. John was glued to his seat, Zeng's demands sparking shock rather than fear.

"Or else, do you hear me?" Zeng's voice was quiet but deadly. "You think you're untouchable. Your precious reputation can't stand being involved in opium and vice, but how about kidnapping and murder? Oh, yes. The righteous Sir John's early career as a highwayman and kidnapper. I bet you'd love *that* little tale to be told around town."

The piano player resumed his playing, thumping out a faster and louder military sounding march and the Sing Song club's clientele went back to drinking and canoodling as if they hadn't heard Zeng's threats, but John was certain they would lose no time in repeating the accusations everywhere they went.

The vile charges hung in the air, and John braced himself for what was coming next. Sebastian shot him a confused, questioning look, then leaned towards Zeng, staying seated this time, but speaking in the same quiet, not-to-be panicked deep bass. "Chung Ji Zeng, it's getting late and we've all had a busy day. Let's call it quits for now. I for one don't have a clue what you're referring to. We can always resume in the morning if you've got more you want to say." He regarded Zeng with an open genial expression, his light freckles and sandy red hair giving him a boy-next-door cordiality few could resist.

Zeng was one who could. He simply smirked. "Tell him, Sir John. What am I referring to?"

John leaned back in his chair and let out a long sigh. His heart felt like stone, and he dreaded whatever it was Zeng was determined to disclose next. "Why don't you tell both of us, Ji Zeng? You obviously know more about it than either of us."

There was a long silence. Zeng appeared to be calculating how best to press the advantage.

Sebastian interjected again in measured tones: "Come on, Zeng. what's so important we have to be here discussing it after midnight?"

"More importantly," John chimed in, "who did you hear it from?"

At that Ji Zeng threw back his head and laughed. "Where did I get it from? Let's just say the source no longer walks this earth, so it hardly matters, does it?"

"That depends," said John.

"Depends on what?"

"On how reliable that person was known to be in life."

"What's all this about?" Sebastian asked, finally sounding slightly exasperated. "Will someone please tell me?"

John took a deep breath and resisted the urge to make a special appeal to Seb for understanding. "It appears that Isabella Wilmington, Huldah's daughter, may be a lost child whom she adopted and has raised as her own. There's no crime in that, it happens in hundreds of families, but Huldah herself won't confirm it, or say how she came by the child. I wonder if Ji Zeng intends to explain what he knows."

He looked at Zeng, who was lighting a cigarette. Clouds of blue-gray smoke formed around him as he sucked and exhaled.

Seb broke in again, sounding increasingly bewildered. "You've lost me. Why should we be concerned?"

Zeng smiled. "Tell him, Sir John. Tell him how Huldah Wilmington got her grubby old hands on the beautiful Isabella? That's if you know."

"I'm waiting with bated breath for you to tell me." John glanced at Seb and shrugged

"The part I like best is your part in Isabella's 'disappearance' in the first place. Is that what you'd call it, *Sir* John?" He put an ironic emphasis on the honorific.

"I wouldn't call it anything except a very nasty accident," he replied.

"Not what I hear," Zeng taunted.

Sebastian, exasperated: "Will someone please tell me what we're talking about?"

Zeng turned to him with a triumphant air, steepling his fingers in front of him as if embarking on telling a long tale. "Your brother was involved in a fatal stagecoach crash years ago where two children vanished. They were searched for high and low, never found. Sir John was present, so no doubt he can tell us what happened. One of those children is Isabella."

"And you know this exactly how?" John's voice rose to a sharp edge. "It would be more than irresponsible to promote this information unless you are absolutely certain it is true."

"Oh, I know it's true all right, but I don't have to tell you how I know it. All you have to know is if you don't find me the Dragon Seal by Friday not only will you never see Ji Ming again, but everyone — and I mean everyone — in this town will hear how Sir John Russell abducts children. Just think how that will go down on your white-as-white reputation."

John thought with a shudder of Pania. He had been close to her practically all his adult life, but he'd never told her about this terrible episode. Would she be able to accept his keeping something so important from her all those years? And what about the woman Nathan was going to marry, Grayson Castellanos? His hands went cold and clammy as he pictured Graysie, her red-gold locks, her vibrant demeanor. If Ji Zeng's information was right, Isabella was Graysie's half-sister.

From his recent re-engagement in her life — she stayed with him at Gold House for a few weeks when she first arrived in Grass Valley — he knew she'd suffered life-long anxiety over the stagecoach crash that had taken her mother's life. Worse still, her twin siblings — a boy and a girl, just toddlers at the time — vanished before the rescuers found the wreckage.

Would Graysie, would anyone, understand how the craziness of that night started out as a juvenile escapade pulled off by a love-mad twenty-something guy and his reluctant friend? He cursed Eustace Mountfort, the best friend who'd drawn him into what had started out as a mad-boy escapade. *What were we thinking?* he asked himself for the thousandth time.

Like a firebrand at his back, he felt the heat of Zeng's pitiless strategy. Make it impossible — make it a triple jeopardy — for him to refuse. If he continued on with his determination to find and free

Ollie, he faced the possibility of losing Ollie, as well as his own life and reputation. He felt sick inside at the prospect of it all. Crushed, destroyed, ridiculed, he would never again be able to command the prominence he had now.

He felt as if he was lugging his own cross up the Gethsemane mount. His feet dragged under the weight of it, but he didn't flinch. *I will not make a pact with the devil,* he promised himself. *No matter what the cost, I will find Ollie. And I won't relinquish that seal. I owe it to Ting Hon not to give in.*

He glanced across to Sebastian. "I think it is time for us to get moving, brother mine," he said. "Let's not worry about this tedious tale now. I'll tell you what I know of it later."

As John made to leave, Zeng jumped up and snarled, "Friday. No later. Get me the seal or else."

Twenty-Five

"Oh look!" Lily Chung pointed to a tiny peachy-ginger colored kitten which gamboled on a pile of hay at the edge of the stagecoach yard, chasing its own tail, rolling over to punch its paws at nothing Lily could see, and then pausing to stretch luxuriously in the morning sun. She glanced over her shoulder. Selina was too busy supervising the loading of their luggage aboard the early morning Sacramento coach to hear or notice. Her bag with her precious drawing pencils, along with her mother's trunk and jewellery case, all needed to get stowed.

They had arrived in the yard with time to kill, and as far as seventeen-year-old Lily was concerned the kitten was the best thing that had happened since she woke up. She kicked a stone with her dusty shoe and clenched her teeth. She couldn't fathom why her mother had decided they had to go back to Sacramento.

She felt in her bones that if they left here they were moving further away from her papa, but Mother had insisted. Selena feared someone may be trying to contact them at home, to give them intelligence about Oliver Chung's whereabouts, and they weren't there to receive it. "Besides," she'd argued, "we can't presume on other people's hospitality indefinitely."

Lily didn't see why not. She loved being around Graysie and Minette, and relished the bustle of people coming and going. Graysie rehearsing around the piano with Mrs Hayes — it was all so much more interesting than home.

She glanced back to her mother and saw she was deep in conversation with the driver. Kicking another stone, she hesitated and then wandered across the yard towards the kitten. It was so cute! Wriggling on its back with its four paws in the air, inviting her to tickle it. She leaned across the bale and lightly ran her forefinger along the center of the kitten's tummy, where the fur was thinnest and you could see the delicate pink skin underneath. The cat responded instantly, clipping her finger with its paws, but very gently, no claws out, as if to say, "Yes! You noticed! Playtime!"

For the next ten minutes, maybe longer, Lily played with the kitten. She immediately christened her Peaches because of her gorgeous pale-watermelon color. Resting in the sunshine, teasing the little will-o'-the-wisp creature with a hay stalk which she chased obsessively. Lily felt the dark cloud, which had rested on her ever since her father went missing, begin to lift.

She giggled: Peach's exploits were so ridiculous. How did the little thing manage to flip in the air, land on its feet, and wriggle with delight, all in one second?

Finally the fluff ball tired. Its movements slowed and it began to slowly lick its paws. She picked it up and nestled it under her chin, stroking it gently along its silky back. The kitten purred for a minute or two and then fell asleep. Its sides flickered with slow little breaths, and sitting there holding it made her so peaceful she was in danger of falling asleep herself.

"Really, Lily! What are you doing?" She looked up and her mother stood over her, hands on hips, her face scrunched up in an angry frown. "What is that . . . that thing? It will certainly have fleas."

Selina shuddered at the thought. "Dirty thing! Put it down. You'll get ringworm. Anyway, the coach is leaving any minute."

Lily's pulse raced, the drowsy peace she'd been enjoying shattered. Why did her mother always do that? Make a drama out of everything. She could never just ride with it. No wonder she was a poor horsewoman as well. She just couldn't go with the flow. Always had to be interfering.

The dark cloud settled back over her. She looked up at her mother. "This is Peaches. My new kitten. I'm taking her with me."

"No you're not." Her mother would never make a scene in public, but her outward calm didn't fool Lily. She was furious. Her neck was mottled pink, a sure sign Lily would be in trouble as soon as they got somewhere private.

"Mother, for just this once can you let it go please? We don't have to pretend we lead perfect lives. It's pretty obvious we don't, with Papa gone." She felt her voice crack. "If she's got fleas we'll find a treatment, but I don't see any."

The conversation was abruptly interrupted by a stirring around the stagecoach parked across from them. The driver was standing at the coach door, consulting a passenger list. "We can't continue this discussion now," her mother hissed. "Put the kitten down and come."

Lily stood up and began to walk towards the coach carrying the warm soft bundle of fur, which slept on.

Her mother trailed behind her. "Lily . . ."

They got to the coach door. "Were our bags loaded without problems?" Lily asked the driver. "Can I just check to make sure?"

He looked surprised, but gestured to the top rack of the coach. "Up there, madam. Three, no sorry, two bags as you can see."

Selina stopped sharply behind her. "Two? No, driver, there should be three. Definitely three." She looked up at the luggage rack, her face drained of color, the kitten forgotten. She ran her hands distractedly across the top of her head. "I can't . . . It's not . . . Where is it, the third item, driver? My jewellery case?"

Deputy Virgil Hale looked up from the report he was filling out to regard the fuming woman at his side. She was the sort who thought they ran things, but not on his watch. "Please, Mrs Chung, take a seat. This won't take long."

"I can't believe it. Can't believe it. All my jewels! The Hamilton Diamonds. Things that have been passed down the family for two hundred years!" She twisted her hands together and paced back to the door, then swung back to face him. "And we've missed the coach home! On top of everything else! I don't believe it!"

Virgil had been called to the scene of the robbery at the stagecoach office. The coach's departure was delayed as the luggage was unloaded and checked, but no jewellery case was found. The yard was searched. Nothing. Nor had anyone seen anything unusual. The coach departed without them. And now here they were, in the sheriff's office, reporting a robbery.

Virgil had picked up the tension between mother and daughter. The mother had railed about how the robbery was the cursed kitten's fault. If her attention hadn't been distracted by the flea-ridden mongrel, she might have noticed what was going on and stopped someone robbing her. That's why Lily was in the sunny courtyard outside the deputy's office, the kitten with her.

"Calm down, madam. The sooner we get the details, the sooner we get a chance to find your property."

Twenty minutes later, the deputy and the gentlewoman stumbled into the courtyard where Lily was playing with the cat, momentarily blinded by the dazzling sunlight after the dim room. Except there was no Lily. And no cat. Selina squeezed her eyes tight, as if to clear her vision, and opened them again. She turned to Virgil. "Where is she?"

He shrugged. *How should I know?* That's what he wanted to say. Instead he considered his words carefully. "Would she have gone for a walk anywhere?"

"Most certainly not. She knows better than that."

"Perhaps she got too hot and she slipped into the waiting room for more shade." He ducked his head through to look at the waiting room, which stood silent and deserted. "She's not in there. Well, I'll be blowed. I really can't say . . ." Hale knew he sounded weak and ineffectual, but what could he do? Perhaps the silly girl had just wandered off.

Selena drew herself up so straight and imperious you'd think she was the Queen of England. She looked him straight in the eye, her face thunderous, and in a voice that brooked no contradiction she demanded, "Get Sir John. Get Sir John Russell right now!"

Twenty-Six

"Thought you might like some roast pork and wontons for lunch." Pania spun her parasol gleefully and pointed it to a makeshift table which had been set up in the yard of the Gold House stables. Nelson, John's man of all tasks, dutifully deposited a cloth-covered basket down on the rough-sawn pine planks set on trestles where the carpenters working on the new Gold House took their breaks.

John had endured so much ill fortune recently she wanted to do something to cheer him up. That's why she was here, she told herself. To offer her old friend moral support.

He looked at her quizzically and smiled a tired smile. "Very thoughtful of you, Pania, I'm sure. Completely unnecessary, but much appreciated."

The old house site was a hive of activity. The foundations were completed, and the carpenters were busily working to get the timber framing that would support the ground and upper floors in place. The rhythmic back and forth buzz of metal handsaws and the knock of the mallet as joints were knocked into place rang around the site. The new was rising from the old, Pania saw with satisfaction.

She inhaled a deep breath of pine. The fresh-sawn logs gave off an invigorating resinous smell that smothered the lingering odor of charred remains. And John, in an open-necked checked workman's shirt and heavy working boots, exuded an energy and purpose she hadn't seen in him since well before the comprador's death.

He should shed those stuffy business suits for this casual attire more often, she thought approvingly. He looked years younger and, well, the word that came to her mind was 'irresistible'. John Russell, irresistible? She must have been out in the sun too long. She centered her parasol so she stood in complete shade and sank onto a bench seat with a sigh. "Sit down and have something to eat while it's still warm," she called to no one in particular. She swept her arm across the table in a gesture that might have included John, or might not. She skewed herself around to seek out Sebastian and waved for his attention. "Refreshment break," she called. "Come and have something to keep your energy up."

Minutes later they were gathered around the feast she'd organized from the Chinese stores in town, together with lemonade from the housekeeper. All talk ceased as the men tucked in and Pania watched, darting secretive little looks at John whenever his attention was distracted. *Has he always been this attractive?*

"This is so good." Sebastian gave a satisfied sigh and put his fork down. "A man could get used to this." He gave Pania a big grin and a thumb's-up sign. "Wouldn't you agree O brother mine?"

John nodded. "Mrs Hayes has always been a very good friend."

The conversation lulled, the sound of crickets in the grass under their feet and of workmen at their backs the only accompaniment to their private thoughts.

"No word of Ollie I suppose?" Pania looked from Sebastian to John and back again.

Sebastian looked to his brother, as if seeking guidance. "No. Not for want of trying."

Pania's brow furrowed and she caught herself: frowning was so unattractive. "I don't understand. Has something happened or not?"

John shot his brother a look that clearly said *Why did you have to open your big mouth?* then shrugged. "We went with Sing Pak last night to try and free him, but they'd moved him before we got there."

Pania could see he was trying to play down whatever had occurred the night before. "You knew where he was?"

"We thought we did, but plainly not. He wasn't where we were told he should be."

"So what's next? We can't do nothing."

He gave her a hard look. "I thought we'd had this out once before, Mrs Hayes." He always seemed to default to her married name when he was annoyed with her. "*We* can't do anything. I don't want you involved. It's too dangerous."

She ignored him. "It's Ji Zeng, his half-brother, that's behind this thing, isn't it? It has to be."

He hesitated, as if reluctant to confirm even that much, then nodded. "Yes, I think we can say categorically Ji Zeng is the instigator after what happened last night." Again the brothers glanced at one another, but remained silent.

Pania put her hands on her hips and took a deep breath. "Please. It's more important to me than you'd ever know. What is going on?"

Sir John gave a quick — and, she was sure, heavily censored — account of the previous night, and they sat in silence once more, staring at the table, at the flies looking for crumbs, each lost in private thoughts, only vaguely aware of their surroundings.

Pania stirred and pulled her shoulders back. "I never told you. I never talked about it. But this last week I've hardly thought of anything else." She sighed. "When I was Lily's age — well, actually when I was fourteen — a few years younger — my father was killed by a mad hothead from another village intent on kidnapping some of our women. He came with a small war party, posing as peaceful visitors." Her voice slowed. Her stomach quivered. It was a long time since she'd allowed herself to recall the events of that night.

"We knew them, they were distantly related. We had no reason to suspect them. But in the middle of the night they rose up like treacherous traitors. Tried to abduct me and some of the other young women. They saw it as justified 'utu', our Maori word for revenge, because they'd lost a whole lot of their own young women in a typhoid epidemic. Typhoid — one of the diseases, as they argued, brought by the Europeans. And because our people in Te Arawa had cooperated with the missionaries and the white settlers more than most, they blamed us for their loss. Said we'd let in the White Peril."

The carpenters had stopped eating. They watched her with widened eyes, engrossed in her story. She cleared her throat, which had suddenly closed up. "You know there's an old Maori saying: 'He wahine, he whenua, e ngaro ai te tangata.' It means that wars are fought over women and land. It was certainly true for us."

She glanced at Sebastian and John, whose faces were set. "I never felt safe after my father died; he was my defender. Silly, I know. But when Henry asked for my hand and said he was planning to live here in California, I was ready. I married at seventeen and I've never gone back."

She roused herself from her reverie and took a deep breath, felt new energy flow through her. "I've no regrets, but if there's one thing I want to do, it's ensure Lily doesn't have to experience the desperate emptiness I felt when my father was killed and there was nothing I could do to bring him back. To have to see his abused body, the wounds they inflicted . . ." She shuddered. "I'd do anything to ensure Lily doesn't face that."

John gave her a fleeting smile and gestured with open hands. "I had no idea. I'm so sorry."

She shrugged. "No reason why you should know. I've never talked about it. But hopefully now you'll understand why this is so important to me. I know you don't approve, but can you understand?"

He gazed at her for what seemed like a long time. Then he nodded, as if he'd made a decision. "I don't want you getting mixed up in this, and I particularly don't want you endangered. But it seems as if we're both caught on the horns of fate. We have no choice. There's an imperative neither of us can refuse."

Pania raised an eyebrow teasingly. "My, you're suddenly waxing eloquent, John." She shot him a half-mocking and half-apologetic smile. "So what exactly are we going to do?"

He tugged at the neck of his shirt. "I suppose you go fishing for clues among your Chinese friends, like you did before. I don't like it, though, not one bit. Whenever you're faced with a choice, think of Ngo Wai."

She nodded. "I can't forget her. And it's not as if she told us anything." She stood and began packing up the lunch remains. "I've delayed your work long enough. Back to it, chaps."

The two men rose from the table and stretched and shuffled, hesitating to farewell her before returning to the house building. They were lightly hugging and saying their goodbyes when they were interrupted by the loud drum of horse's hooves. In unison they turned to the source of the noise. Nathan Russell was pulling up, jumping from his horse, leaving the reins trailing as he sprinted towards them.

"Emergency, guys. Selena is hysterical. Lily's missing, maybe abducted. You need to come. We've got no time to lose."

Twenty-Seven

Hector de Vile was a tall, lean man with a sandy beard and piercing blue eyes. He laughed a lot, but his temperament could change to stormy without warning. Second Son Ji Zeng couldn't hear the laugh, but he had plenty of time to study de Vile's strong profile in the large daguerreotype that hung above him as he waited to see the man in person. At first sight he gave the impression of some jovial *gweilo* Father Christmas, but anyone who mistook him for St Nicholas was making a dangerous mistake, Ji Zeng knew.

They had agreed to meet at noon and de Vile's assistant, a thin nervous man with brown hair that frizzed out around his ears, had apologized profusely for his master's absence when Zeng had arrived at his Nevada City rooms ten minutes early. The yet-to-be inducted Senator de Vile had been called out to an emergency at one of his mines, he explained, an unavoidable crisis, but he was due back very soon. If Mr Ji Zeng would courteously agree to wait? The Senator was very keen to talk with him.

Hector de Vile's business empire stretched from the Sierra Nevadas to San Francisco; he had a finger in most expanding ventures where there was big money to be made. He also had an unerring sense of where the next big thing was coming from, and

Zeng knew he wouldn't be going to Washington unless he saw a dollar in the move.

He had got in on the railway boom after the initial visionaries had lost their shirts, but in time to cash in on a steady profit stream. He owned a lion's share of the silver being mined in Virginia City and had positioned himself with controlling interests in two of the most productive gold mines in Grass Valley. But he was a man with a restless drive for more; he took it personally if someone beat him to a business opportunity and he wasn't a good loser, as many a competitor had discovered to their cost.

Just the sort of business partner Black Dragon needed, Zeng thought, if it was going to leapfrog out of small-time importing and trading and into big-time capital development with California's expansion from Wild West backwater to the richest state in the Union. And to get the money he needed to match it with de Vile, he required the sort of big injection of funds that opium importing and women would bring. De Vile need not know about the details, but he would understand the necessity of the trade.

Zeng's mind flicked to his meeting a few hours ago with his brother. Ollie would never understand, but a part of him was pleased he was so obdurately opposed. He didn't want to share roles in the company, the way his father had devised — with him handling the importing from China and Ollie heading the benevolent society side of things as well as developing new Gold Mountain business. He wanted it all, and now he was on a fast ride to getting it.

They had already agreed on terms for what he hoped would be the first many future joint ventures, but de Vile had unexpectedly called him to a second meeting. Zeng was offering to supply one thousand able-bodied Chinese workers for his latest railway project. He was looking at a profit of $100 on each man, and with the contacts he had back in his homeland he had no worries about being able to recruit good men. Yes, de Vile would love him. The Chinese workers were proving so much tougher than the Irishmen or, God bless them, the home-grown Californians. Zeng smiled with satisfaction.

The *White Cloud* shipment that should arrive in the next week promised to be the best Patna opium from India, so much better that the acrid-tasting Persian or Turkish stuff which gave smokers headaches and skin rashes. Refined by experts in Hong Kong, it was packaged all ready for sale — a dark, molasses-like syrup in five-tael tins (about six and a half ounces) which sold in San Francisco for $8 each. He slid his palms together in suppressed glee.

As for the millions to be released when he got his hands on the Dragon Seal: well, he was confident he could still terrify or torture his brother into telling him where it was. *Whatever it takes. Now I'm free of family, the sky is the limit.*

Zeng heard the heavy tramp of feet on the stairs at the end of the long hallway and de Vile strode forcefully towards him, hand outstretched in greeting. He rose and just as quickly deflected, palms pressed together in deference. His chest was light, his breathing easy. The light picked up the sheen on his black satin high-necked changshan. He felt the warming surge of being in the presence of power in his tingling thighs, his warm belly. He was glad he'd chosen to wear a traditional Chinese tunic. De Vile wouldn't see him as American, so he intended to make his difference work for him.

He saw de Vile check himself and start to withdraw his hand; Zeng stepped into the space between them and with perfect timing completed his traditional greeting and then presented his hand to be shaken, American-style. De Vile gave a low chuckle, as if to acknowledge he'd been bested.

"Mr Chung," he said expansively. "My heartiest apologies for the delay. We had a collapse in a new area we are working in the Rose

Dawn Mine so of course the men expected me to be there to take an interest. Not too many deaths, fortunately. Mining is a dangerous business — it's inevitable we'll lose a few."

The nervous assistant had rushed up as he was speaking and de Vile now turned to him. "Jitters, can you get refreshments brought to my office? You will have some green tea, Mr Chung?" Zeng nodded his assent and followed de Vile into his office. The big man flopped into one of two large chairs positioned either side of a sweeping mountain-oak desktop which was clear of anything except a silver-topped ink stand and pen, and gestured to him to sit. "Everything set for the railway workers? We need them here before the winter closes in." He lit a fat cigar and settled back in his chair.

Zeng put his elbows on his knees and leaned forwards as if sharing a valuable secret. "All organized. They will be landed by November the sixth. We will accommodate them at the Benevolent Society hostel and make sure they don't get lost or sick. They will be divided into small teams based on family or village connections, each with basic provisions — tent, food, suitable clothing. You will be very happy with them. Chinese workers don't give up." He sipped the tea the assistant had poured them, trying to ignore de Vile's noxious cigar smoke. *Give me the sweet, almost sickly, smell of opium any time.*

De Vile blew out a long stream of smoke and nodded happily. "Good, good. But I asked you here today to discuss something else entirely. The Sacramento Council is letting a contract for the rights to the state-approved gambling they're introducing. It will require a substantial investment to get the Governor and public officials onside, and then an army of assistants, shall we say, to enforce it. I've got the contacts to ensure we are at the front of the line for getting the concession. It seems to me your Black Dragon associates could be ideal troops to help run it. I'm happy to cut you in on, say, thirty-five percent of the profits if you come on board." He tapped the ash from his cigar into a waste bucket at his feet. "What do you think?"

"I'm most honored that you would consider me as a possible partner in a venture like this." Zeng spoke slowly and deliberately, carefully calculating the risk and the opportunity as he did. "It would be a goldmine in its own right for sure — and no need for deaths along with it!" He shot de Vile a wry smile. "However, I am thinking that fifty-five percent might be a fairer share for all the work involved state-wide. And also there's the unwanted attention it will bring. You know there are some vehement opponents of gambling out there and we always prefer to keep a, shall we say, low profile. Visibility can have a high cost."

De Vile shuffled in his seat. "If you want to go up to fifty-five, then I suggest you should help pay the expenses to persuade our legislators it's a good idea — say, put up a stake of a hundred thousand dollars."

Exactly the amount I hope to make out of the worker consignment, Zeng thought grimly, *and doesn't he know it.* "How about we settle on fifty thousand dollars and fifty percent?"

De Vile gazed at him through narrowed eyes. "Sixty-five thousand dollars and fifty percent. And I need it right away."

Zeng felt a tightness in his chest. As well as the opium he had a shipment of women on their way from Canton. He didn't have enough coin to cover opium, railway workers, women *and* bribes for Sacramento bureaucrats, not without getting access to the Trading Company's deep bank reserves. Not without the money released by possession of the Dragon Seal.

Damn his brother. Or was it Sir John Russell he should be stalking? One thing he knew — he had to get his hands on that Dragon Seal sooner rather than later. He had to stop boxing with shadows and make a serious bid to locate it. He felt a confident wave rise within him. *Just as well I already have my insurance plan in place.*

Twenty-Eight

John lifted his head from the dining-room table and rattled his empty coffee cup irritably in the saucer. Mrs Snively appeared as if guided by sixth sense and poured him and Sebastian refills. Spread at his elbow was an array of the week's papers, some open, some creased and discarded in untidy stacks beside them. The brothers were sharing an afternoon break while catching up on the week's news.

"Seb, what on earth am I going to do?" John ran his fingers through his hair and massaged his temples. "I've got to find Lily — I've just got to — and I don't have the faintest clue where to start." He shot Seb a look of desperate appeal, as if willing him to produce something from a hat. "Zeng's deadline is Friday. If I don't produce the Dragon Seal, goodness only knows what he's capable of. And if I *do* produce it, I'm probably writing Lily's death warrant. Hers and Ollie's."

Sebastian's head jerked up. His eyes narrowed and he fixed his brother with a frustrated glare. "You mean you've got the seal? *Now* you mention it."

"Complete chance. I found it in the ruins." John rubbed his index finger under his nose, pondering. "Ting Hon must have had it." He returned his attention to the paper in front of him and flicked over a page. "Best no one knows."

Sebastian shook his head in disbelief. "Your secret's safe with me. It's not as though I'm going to advertise it in the paper," he chuckled.

Street sounds floated in from the windows at the far end of the room: the graunching of cart wheels on the wooden boardwalk, the high-pitched wail of the afternoon newsboy. . . Also floating in was the odor of damp horse droppings.

"*Grass Valley Union*! See what Lying Jim's got for you todaaay . . ." The paper boy's voice tailed off in a lament.

John thumped his feet on the floor and jumped up, galvanised. "That's it! We'll call on the services of Lying Jim." He grabbed his broad-brimmed hat off the chair beside him and made for the door. "Come with me for a stroll down to the *Grass Valley Union*, Seb. I've got some business to do there."

Seb trailed after him, catching up as they stepped onto Main Street boardwalk. "What kind of business? And what's Lying Jim got to do with it?"

Union editor 'Lying Jim' had ridden into town four years ago and started the newspaper to support Abraham Lincoln's re-election and the Union effort in the Civil War. A drinking companion of Mark Twain's, and a great storyteller, James 'Lying Jim' Townsend was known from the San Francisco coast to the Rockies for putting entertainment ahead of the facts, and his audience relished his nerve.

"It just came to me — why not post a reward for information leading to the whereabouts of Lily Chung and her father Oliver Pakenham Chung? What do you reckon would bring the whisperers out of the woodwork? A hundred dollars? A thousand dollars?"

Lily had been missing for a day, and all their attempts to poke into seedy corners had not produced any leads. They fell into step, pausing to dodge shoppers as they talked. The lunchtime crowds had gone and Grass Valley's merchants were winding down for the day. Outside the timber yards a burly assistant was sweeping up a pile of steaming horse dung. Further up the street a man with a cart laden with bags of flour whistled through his fingers to attract the attention of a loitering odd jobs boy. The yeasty smell of freshly baked bread and coffee overlaid the smell of horses. For most of the town, it was a day like any other.

"What sort of bribe would bring out new information? That depends," said Seb. His serious hazel eyes settled on John's face.

"Depends on what?"

"Anyone with any clue knows that talking to you carries the risk of being hacked to death by Ji Zeng or his men. How much money would tempt them to take that risk?"

"Good point. And how much is it worth to me to get this thing done with? It's not just Ollie and Lily's lives we're talking about. Russell and Chung Trading won't survive Ji Zeng's greed. I see that more and more clearly. He'll destroy what we've spent thirty years building up." His hands hung like heavy lumps at the ends of his arms. *This is what being hamstrung is like. I've never felt more useless.*

"And not just that. I've got to do something to keep Selina's hopes up. Not to mention head off Mrs Hayes from another fishing expedition in the Sing Song clubs. That can only be a good thing. The girls in those places will be terrified to be seen within five yards of her after what happened to Ngo Wai."

"Ah yes, the alluring Mrs Hayes." Sebastian darted him a curious look. "That was certainly an extraordinary story she told about her father's death. You can understand why it's cutting deep with her."

"I'd never heard any of that before either, and I know her pretty well." He thought momentarily of the things Pania did not know about him, and flexed his hands uneasily. He slowed his pace. "There's no doubt death makes you think about life. Certainly brought me up short. Made me think I need to hurry up and get on with the whole wife-and-family thing myself."

He twisted his mouth in a self-conscious wry line. He hated admitting something that personal to Sebastian, but he suspected his brother had already guessed it. Nothing much escaped his reticent, deep thinking notice.

Sebastian chuckled. "And it's no coincidence you admit that immediately after Mrs Hayes's name pops up," he said with a grin. "Funny that."

John gave him a reluctant answering smile. "It's early days." He paused at the *Grass Valley Union*'s double doors. "I'm thirty-nine next birthday. Don't they say you're an old man at forty? Suddenly I'm a lot more aware of legacy. I guess it was brewing anyway, but it's become so much stronger with the comprador's death. We don't have long here, and I've already wasted too much time." He put his hand on the brass door knob. "I guess this is all familiar stuff to you, as a war vet. Must have been damned hard."

Sebastian levelled his gaze, then nodded. "Yep. Certainly makes you think." There was finality in his tone that didn't invite discussion.

John realized he knew nothing about his brother's wartime experiences. He hung back, unsure of his ground. "What about you? You haven't thought about marriage?"

Seb took a step back, then shook his head. "I've got a lot of time to make up before I think of marrying — if ever." He shrugged his shoulders, as if deflecting a heavy load, and grinned. "Don't let that deter you, though. Mrs Hayes is a pretty woman."

John drew an arm around his half-brother's shoulder and pulled open the office door so they entered together. "Let's get this done, old chap. As for Mrs Hayes, I may have already damned my prospects there. If we manage to sort out this other mess then maybe I'll have a chance to find out."

Twenty-Nine

Ji Ming was sitting on the floor on a dirty blanket, his back braced against the wall, his cuffed hands hanging limp on his knees when Zeng returned, flinging the door open with a ferocity that told him he was all roiled up. Whether Zeng's excitement was triumph or fury, he couldn't tell, but either way it could only mean bad news for him.

Zeng's cheeks were flushed pink, and he swayed arrogantly as he leaned over him in the cold bare room. There was no bed or chair; the blanket was the only additional item in a dusty windowless cube.

Ming let his eyes slide over Zeng's shoulder to focus on the rough stone wall behind him. He gazed into the middle distance, sending the message: *Nothing you say is of any interest to me.*

Zeng's voice dripped contempt. "I hope you've had time to reconsider your position." He planted himself squarely in his brother's line of sight. "I'm running out of time without the Black Dragon money to draw on. And I'm running out of patience, waiting for the Dragon Seal."

His brother shuffled his behind on the hard packed floor and gave him an unyielding stare. "And I don't know how many times I have to tell you, I have not got the seal. I cannot help you."

"Pity you're so stubborn." Zeng moved back to the door and

leaned against the jamb. "But then, you always did think you knew best. Ah well, you've only got yourself to blame."

He saw a flicker of uncertainty in his brother's otherwise stony glare.

"To blame for what?"

Zeng didn't answer. He rapped on the door and called, "Bring her in."

There was a thunderous noise outside and a panicked voice cried, "Don't push me! Don't push!"

The rough wooden door banged against the wall with a violent crack, and a woman pitched over the threshold and fell to her knees, sobbing, her face buried in one bare arm. Her clothes had been cut away from one side of her body, exposing her breast and thigh; both sides of her head were shaved bare, leaving just a ridge of dark ebony across the top of her skull, her untrimmed locks flowing on down her back.

It was Lily, his enchanting daughter Lily, humiliated and mutilated in a fiendish parody to demonstrate that Zeng ruled. Ji Ming lunged up, crossed to her in two urgent strides, and fell to his knees beside her, shielding her nakedness with his body, his cuffed hands inhibiting his movement. "You bastard! What has my daughter got to do with anything?" He struggled up and leapt at Zeng's throat, grabbing his shirt at the front in his cuffed hands. "You will pay for this."

Zeng went rigid, but didn't flinch. They stared at one another in unveiled hatred for a few seconds, and then Ji Ming turned back to Lily. She was curled up on the earth floor, clutching her ripped clothes tightly to her slight form. He lurched on the discarded blanket and, holding it up like a cloak, drew it around Lily, covering her nakedness.

Zeng sneered, "The great Chung Ji Ming. Helpless to save his precious daughter. A rat-chewed blanket the best he can do."

The furious silence that stretched between them was broken by the rustle of cloth. Lily scrambled to her feet, reed-slim body securely wrapped in her father's blanket which she held up against her throat with one hand. The other she stretched out to her father, her long fingers cupping the side of his face lovingly, her finely drawn lips in a radiant smile. "Papa! You are alive! I can hardly believe it!" Her voice cracked, and she drew her hand back for a moment to dash a tear away. She took a big breath, stepped right up to him, and wrapped her arms around his neck, pressing her body and the blanket against him. He felt the warmth of her breath on his face. "I love you, my darling father. I love you. It is so good to see you." She was whispering and crying, and her face shone with joy. "We've missed you so much." She smothered his face with butterfly kisses.

Ji Ming's face was wet — from her tears or his, he couldn't tell. They stood like that for a few seconds, and then she calmed her breathing and stepped back, grabbing the blanket around her as she let go of him. "Don't do anything because of me. Just seeing you is reward enough. But don't change anything because I'm here."

Zeng stepped forward and struck Ji Ming across the face with the back of his hand. He stumbled sideways, his cheek stinging, but he did not collapse. "Father and daughter reunion," Zeng snarled. "How touching. All I can say is, don't get used to it. You're going up for sale. One for the block. I'm sure a Boxer warlord would drop a lot of gold coin for you. There's no accounting for tastes." His smile stiffened and he spread his arms wide. "I need to raise funds one way or another, and if the Dragon Seal isn't found …" The threat hung in the stale air.

"You're such a fool, Chung Ji Zeng." Ji Ming's chest filled with air. He stood erect, leaning into his daughter, offering her protection, hobbled as he was. "You killed our father — our venerable, wise and good father — and for what? Not for any great cause. Just out of sick greed."

Zeng stood staring, an ugly twist to his mouth.

"The truth of it is, our venerable father had the Dragon Seal. I know this because I gave it to him. So I wasn't lying when I said I had no idea where it was. He had it."

He thrust his face closer to Zeng's. With an icy, deadly control, he said, "I don't know where the seal is, you imbecile, and you killed the only person who knew. No doubt he put it somewhere no one was likely to look for it. So when you murdered him — and I have no doubt that is what you did — you destined it to be a mystery forever. Isn't that what the *gweilo* call poetic justice?"

He drew his daughter to him, turned his head to the heavens and laughed. A response fuelled not by mirth but by marrow-piercing pain it might be, but as he held Lily close a bubbling defiance welled up from deep down inside. With his daughter alive in his arms, it felt good to stand and laugh, however bitterly.

Thirty

"What was my father like? You never talk about him." Isabella looked up from the lemon meringue pie on her dessert plate and her rosebud mouth twisted into a questioning curve. "Am I like him? Because you'd have to agree, you and I aren't very alike, are we — in looks or interests."

Huldah Wilmington was momentarily blindsided by the hint of challenge that underlay the query, and the implied criticism it carried. For a moment her tongue knotted. Isabella was right. Even as a young girl she had been thick-set with stumpy legs, a female with a biggish nose and broad jaw who regarded the world with suspicion. Nothing like Isabella, with her tall, slender grace and captivating gaiety.

Isabella had never asked about the family before, and without warning she fell into the yawning thirty-year age gap that separated them. Huldah was in her mid-thirties when Isabella was born; she was now almost old enough to be her grandmother, and at this moment she felt every day of those eighteen years.

They were breakfasting together, finishing up the leftover pie from last night's dinner, and had been chatting happily about the daily gossip, what Isabella's school friends were doing over the holidays, how delicious last night's roast pork was, whether today would be as hot as yesterday. Huldah had been steeling herself to introduce the sensitive subject of their European trip, and Isabella's possible singing lessons somewhere on the Continent, when the girl had launched her inquiry.

She glanced down at her own plate, where the pie sat uneaten. "Your father? He was a good man. A very good provider. He would have been so proud of you." Her voice wavered, and when she looked up she saw a shaft of irritation cross her daughter's lovely face, momentarily darkening the flawless, light-gold complexion.

She shook her head, a quick impatient little flick, like stamping her foot. "No, I mean what was he really like? Did he like music? Was he fun to be around?"

The truth was Huldah's husband was a hard-driving merchant who was impatient with anything that took his time and attention away from business. He had never seen the child; he was lost at sea not long after her birth, leaving a void that the new baby filled so satisfyingly. Huldah blushed to admit she hadn't really noticed his absence.

"He was . . ." *How to explain he was a taciturn man who worked hard? That's the beginning and end of it.* "Not exactly fun to be around, no. He was a serious man. Didn't talk a lot. And as for music, I never saw him show any particular interest in it. But he loved us, wanted to do the best for us."

It sounded lame, coming on the end like that. She took a deep breath and tried again. "He loved the sea. Loved going to different places. Trading was his big adventure. Speaking of which, have you given any more thought to the idea of going to Europe? If you're interested we might even visit your father's hometown."

Isabella let out a dramatic sigh. "Mother, you know I don't really want to be away from home for too long. I've got everything I need here. I want to start establishing myself right now. I don't want to delay."

"Isabella, I thought we'd agreed—"

"I just don't understand what the fuss is about, Mother. Look at Graysie Castellanos and Mrs Hayes. And Lotta. Oh, and so many others. California is the place to be. Don't you see that?"

"Isabella, it's just not the right thing."

"Oh you and your 'right thing'. Stop being such a stick in the mud. I'm nearly eighteen. I want to start making plans. The world's not like it was when you were a girl. That was a long time ago. It's changing."

Huldah grabbed the edge of the table with both hands and held on tight. She was overcome with dizziness as fear washed over her. Fear and frustration at all the reasons she couldn't explain for why it would be best for them to go away.

"It's not changing all that much, young lady." She had found her voice and it came through, loud and strident. "And as long as I'm your mother, you'll do what I say. Your father would be shocked to hear you speak to me like that!"

"My father? Pah! You can't even tell me what the man was like. Why should I care?" Isabella thrust the gold-rimmed dessert plate, which had been part of Huldah's wedding trousseau, into the middle of the table where it clanged against the water jug. Huldah winced at the sound, and started to protest but Isabella swept her chair back and stood, glaring. "I'm going to Maria's. She's asked me to stay the night." Maria was her best friend, who lived a few streets away. She glared at Huldah, hands on hips. "You just don't understand!" With that she stormed out of the room.

Huldah sank back into the chair she had half-risen from and listened as Isabella thumped up the stairs in a rage and slammed her bedroom door.

It reverberated with Huldah's racing heartbeat, as she sat, head in her hands, shedding the pent-up tears she had been holding back for days. Years, maybe.

What was she going to do, short of kidnapping the girl herself?

Thirty-One

"Sir John Russell. Where is he? I have to talk to Sir John immediately." Huldah stared at the Gold House foreman, who stood in the midst of the rising framework of the new house, and squeezed her eyes tight. Until last night, she had been a woman whose composure rarely cracked. But she'd never been as frightened of anything as she was right now. The thought that she might lose her darling Isabella, never see her sweet smiling face again — well, it just didn't bear thinking about. She couldn't countenance it.

Her hands were fluttering at her side like wounded birds. She stiffened them and looked back up at the carpenter, hammer in hand, who was gazing at her, waiting for her to explain. When she'd gone into the village this morning to do her usual grocery shop and seen all those reward posters calling for information about the missing Lily Chung she knew she couldn't hold out any longer.

"Please. It's urgent. Where can I find him?"

"Why, I believe just over there." The man pointed to a milling pit where workmen stood around a long two-man saw. She heard the screech of the metal teeth in the fresh wood and realized they were milling the timber for the house on-site. John Russell stood supervising the work, while his brother Sebastian and Pania Hayes rested on a couple of cut stumps off to one side watching the action. Pania sat on a canvas cover, probably from the stables, protecting her dress from the sticky resin which filled the air with a green, fresh perfume.

Lifting up her skirts, Huldah picked her way carefully across the sawdust-covered site, taking care not to trip on the scattered lumber debris. Pania looked up in surprise as she approached and jumped to her feet. "Mrs Wilmington, what a surprise." Pania's eyebrows were raised as much in concern as surprise. "Is something wrong?"

Huldah tensed. She hated going to anyone as a supplicant, and realized she was giving off an anxiety Pania had immediately picked up on.

"I need to see Sir John urgently." Her voice sounded higher than usual, and had a desperate edge.

Pania took a step back. "Why, yes, of course. He's working with the men. Seb, could you see if John has a minute? Mrs Wilmington, come and sit here." She gestured to the stump she had vacated and saw Huldah's hesitation. "It's fine — the canvas keeps your frock protected. He shouldn't be long."

Seb made his way to where John stood with his back to them, in conversation with a couple of workers. He glanced back in surprise when Seb tapped him on the shoulder and spoke in his ear. Then he made a small gesture with his hand — I'll be with you in a minute — and turned back to the business at hand. Getting this house completed before the winter freeze made the work more difficult was obviously a high priority.

Pania made no attempt at small talk. For that Huldah was grateful. Her head raced with a disorganized jumble of thoughts. What to do next? Who to talk to? She could think of nothing except her beautiful Isabella.

She'd waited for Isabella to return from Maria's and when she had not turned up by morning coffee time she'd gone to her friend's house to check she was alright. That's when she discovered the girl had never been there. Maria was surprised to learn she'd said she was going to visit. She had probably gone and chased after Lotta Crabtree again, but Huldah couldn't just brazen it out and hope everything was going to turn out all right. Isabella's life was far more important than her reputation.

She sat on in the sun, the sounds of the saw and hammers drowning out the faint sounds of birds in the distant trees. Her fingers were clasped in a tight knot, and her head was beginning to ache. She stood up abruptly and felt herself swaying. She squeezed her eyes tight and when she opened them Sir John was striding over the grass towards her. Dressed in casual workman's shirt and riding boots, he tipped his hat informally. "Sorry for the delay. Had to ensure the men knew what I wanted. How can I be of assistance?"

"It's Isabella," said Huldah. "I'm so worried! She's gone again. When I saw all those reward posters around town for that lass Lily Chung I had to come to you. She said she was staying with a friend but when she didn't come home this morning I went to see where she was. Maria says she never went there. I suppose there's a good chance she has gone chasing after Lotta Crabtree — but what if she hasn't? What if something has happened to her like seems to have happened to Lily?

Sir John was looking at her with a slightly bemused expression, as if he wasn't sure where this conversation was heading. She was gabbling, she realized, the words all tumbling out breathlessly, with no stops, all her fears pouring out in one great gale of dread. "You see. . . Well, I wasn't completely candid when we spoke last."

It seemed to her as if all activity stopped around her. She knew she was being overly self-conscious. The men's saws had stopped, but their hammering continued. Sir John tipped his head back and looked skywards, and then nodded in her direction, as if he anticipated what she was going to tell him.

He took her gently by the arm and guided her towards the stables, some distance from the workmen. He called to Pania, "Mrs Hayes, would you be so good as to organize some water for Mrs Wilmington? I fear we need to take better care. The lady is in extreme distress."

Someone had left a tray with a large stoneware pitcher of water and beakers on a tackle bench next to where the horses were watered, and Pania quickly gathered it up and returned to where a red-faced Huldah was seeking shade in the stable entry.

She sipped the cool water in little gulps and within a few minutes her breathing slowed and her face dimmed from bright red to a light pink.

Once Pania had assured herself the stout matron was not in danger of fainting, she felt awkward about staying. Obviously Huldah had something private to discuss — and she should just make herself scarce. She stood to go, reaching out to take Huldah's hand and give it a comforting squeeze. "I'd better be getting on," she said. "Lots to do."

"Please, stay if you can." Huldah's voice was wobbling and reedy. "I would appreciate your advice — and support. When word gets out, well, it might make life difficult. You know how people talk. It would help to have an ally. Someone who knows the facts, not just gossip."

Pania involuntarily shuffled back a step or two, caught off-guard on the rough ground by Huldah's unexpected appeal. She recovered her balance and stood firm. "Why, of course Mrs Wilmington. Anything I can do to help."

"Huldah, please. You're about to hear my most intimate secrets,

I think first names are in order." Huldah shot her an apologetic smile. "I appreciate your willingness to be drawn into this mess."

John had been out in the yard giving the groom instructions about watering the horses, and now returned with a stout wooden stool in each hand. "You're staying?" He looked from Pania to Huldah uncertainly.

"I'd prefer she does, if you don't mind," Huldah said. "Thank you for the water." She took another long draft. "I guess I'd better get started."

Pania could almost feel the woman's heart rate increasing under the stress of whatever it was she was about to disclose.

"One thing no one ever knew — and one thing I wasn't keen to have known — was that I had a sister, Bertha. A sister with a notorious reputation. My husband didn't want her in the house, so I only ever got to see her when he was away at sea. He was away a lot, so I did see her from time to time — for better or worse." She took another sip of water. "Jedidiah and I dearly wanted a family, but for whatever reason, it didn't happen. It was a bitter thing. A husband away a lot at sea providing handsomely for my needs, and me at home alone, not doing my part. I felt useless, like a hen with its head cut off. The pain of that lack ran deep, though we avoided talking about it."

Huldah chewed her lip nervously, as if steeling herself to continue. She put down the beaker and folded her arms over her ample bosom. "Sixteen years ago, almost to the day, Bertha arrived unannounced with a small child. She was about one year old, a darling little bundle, on the verge of walking. Bertha said the child had been orphaned in a stagecoach accident. She said that for a payment, the only relation — a drunken uncle with no inclination to take the child in — was willing to see her placed in a good home, no questions asked."

She picked up the beaker, took another sip. "Of course I suspected the story. It was just like her to get mixed up in something nefarious. But I thought, what good would it do to challenge it? She'd just look elsewhere for another buyer. And I desperately wanted a child. I knew we could provide her with a good life. I accepted her story without question and took the baby girl in. Jedidiah was away at sea.

"I told everyone I was going to stay with an aunt in Sacramento and I moved somewhere where no one knew me. Was I going to tell Jedidiah the truth when he returned, or pretend I'd finally fallen pregnant and had the baby while he'd been at sea? I truly don't know what I would have told him, but as it happened, we never had that conversation. His ship was lost in a storm and I did not get word of it until months later. It was simplest just to carry on for all the world as the sea captain's widow with a baby daughter. No questions asked.

"Isabella has no idea of her origins. My sister died last year — murdered over some deal gone wrong. I never thought any harm was done, not really, until that cartoon turned up on my doorstep a few days ago. That's when I realized that Bertha must have tattled to someone. I hate to say it but she got involved in some nasty things in later life — one reason we drew apart."

Silence fell. John was perched on a bale, legs out in front of him, hands clasped on his knees, gazing at the straw-covered ground. He didn't seem to have been listening to Huldah's tale. A nearby horse snuffled and munched, releasing musky smells of rotting hay as it shuffled in its stall.

Pania cleared her throat. "I feel for you, Huldah, but I don't understand why you are so fearful. Don't misunderstand, I know it's worrying that Isabella has disappeared, but isn't there still a very good chance she's safe with Lotta? Why this sudden anxiety over her being linked to Lily? I'm baffled. Have I missed something?"

John was still gazing at the ground, as if he was reluctant to enter the conversation. Then he lifted his head and looked straight at her. "I think Mrs Wilmington is trying to tell us that her sister was the matron who ran the old Exchange Hotel. Madam Ring, not so affectionately known as Madam Moustache. Is that correct, Huldah?"

Huldah nodded and sniffed miserably.

Pania still didn't get the point. "What's the significance of that?"

"Madam Ring was almost certainly getting the women she used as cleaners and other things from Ji Zeng," John said. "Slave labor indentured to the gangs. And she was implicated in Minette's brief disappearance — remember that? It doesn't take much of a leap to see it was likely to be Zeng who was threatening Huldah last week. Looks like Bertha did tell him about Isabella." His shoulders sagged. "And it's not a big stretch to see that Huldah wasn't the primary target for the threat. I was."

Pania stood and took a step towards him. The only person she was aware of was John Russell. The muscles along his jawline flickered. The skin around his eyes tightened and he gave her a pained stare. She put her hand out to touch his arm, as if to offer comfort. "I don't see. . ." The words died away.

"No reason on earth why you should, my dear Pania." He gave a bitter, hollow laugh. "I had no idea until Huldah brought me that drawing, but I knew for sure the minute I saw it. You remember back all those years ago, our early days in San Francisco, when we fleetingly knew Graysie's mother Elanora Castellanos, the Spanish photographer's wife?"

He looked to Huldah, including her in the reminiscence: "For a few months there our little group took Elanora under our wing while Rafael was away on a long photography trip. Eustace Mountfort was the instigator. He was my best friend and Elanora was an old sweetheart of his, so it kind of fitted together." He nodded to Huldah again. "Eustace and I were in business for many years, right up until when he died six months ago."

Pania watched a little olive-green feathered finch hopping on a nearby sawdust pile, its pointed beak probing for insects, as the memory of those carefree days flooded back. It seemed then as if the sun shone all the time. And then Elanora had been killed in a horrible stagecoach crash when she was going to Sacramento to rejoin her husband.

It came to her in a rush — weren't there two other children lost? Just a few months ago Grayson had discovered that Eustace was her father — but didn't she have twin siblings, a boy and a girl?

John was speaking slowly and clearly, addressing his words to Huldah. "I don't know how much your sister told you about Isabella's background."

Huldah was shaking her head, mute, one hand covering her mouth as if she didn't trust what might come out of it. She dropped her hand from her mouth and brought both hands to her ears, as if she couldn't handle hearing anything more.

Pania's skin tingled; John's voice sounded very far away. She glanced back at the little bird, but it had gone. She took a deep breath and focused her attention. The sunny afternoon, the sharp pine scent, the sound of the workmen's hammers, everything came rushing back into focus, brighter and more dazzling than before, and John's baritone sounded louder as well.

"You need to hear this, Huldah. . .Isabella. She must be Elanora's child." He stepped up to Huldah and gently dislodged her hands from her ears. "It is the only conclusion to draw. She is Elanora's and Rafael's daughter. And I swear, until I saw that drawing, I had no idea."

Huldah withdrew her hands from his grasp and clutched the stall rail as if she was in danger of being swept away in rough seas. Her face was a chalky white, her jaw set tight. "I feel dizzy. Just a minute." Her face was slack and vacant as she waited for the spell to pass. Pania handed her some more water, and after a few gulps she resumed. "Bertha never told me who the baby was and I never asked. I thought it best if I didn't know. That is the truth. I can't believe it. What am I going to tell Isabella?" She was whispering, but it came out like a desperate wailing.

"Hang on, Huldah, I don't think the story's finished." Pania couldn't be patient any longer. "I seem to remember that Elanora had three children. Graysie was a few years older than the twins, if I recall. So if Isabella is Grayson's sister, or half-sister, what happened to the other twin, the boy? How do you know it's the same family, John? How can you be so sure?"

In the silence that followed she was aware of the busy, engaged sounds of the workmen hammering away on the new Gold House. The birds could still be faintly heard beyond the sounds of hammer and saw.

"I know, Pania, because I was there. Huldah's sister Bertha was too. Elanora had engaged her as a temporary nanny, a sort of paid travelling companion, to help get the children to Sacramento. And Ji Zeng obviously knows it.

"As for what happened to the little boy, I wouldn't have a clue. Until a few days ago I thought they were both likely dead."

Huldah Wilmington dissolved into loud wails.

Thirty-Two

Pania's head was buzzing with a high-pitched, nerve-piercing whine, as if a wasp's nest was lodged right behind her eyes. The excruciating noise drowned out all sense of time and place. She was only aware of the hot dusty air and John's white, stricken face gazing at her.

What was he telling her? That all those years ago when Elanora was killed, he was involved? They were good friends — she had imagined very close friends — and he had never so much as hinted at anything like this before. She, John and Eustace had been like the Three Musketeers, practically inseparable when she wasn't touring. She remembered she had noticed an unusual tension between the two men around the time of the crash, but she'd put it down to Eustace being so deeply upset about Elanora's death. He had faded out of the threesome around that time, she recalled, and she and John continued socialising without him.

She thought of all the nights at the opera, of the balls and supper evenings they shared, the happy camaraderie. She thought she knew Sir John Russell. She had trusted him as a straightforward, honorable man. A hard-driving businessman, yes, but basically decent. Did righteous men get mixed up in the death of a young mother, the loss of young children, and keep quiet about it? Continue their lives as if nothing had happened? Not in her view.

What had she repeated to Graysie once, that phrase she'd thought she'd overheard? "I'm sure they were alive when we left them." She was puzzled by it but concluded she must have heard wrong. What kind of men would leave children at the scene of an accident and run? *Men who would find it very difficult to explain why they were there at all.*

She stood just feet away from John, but they hardly occupied the same universe. He was ramrod-straight, his posture unnaturally stiff, his face a mask drained of life. She took a step backwards. "What do you mean, you were there? What are you saying?" Her voice sounded rusty, as if she'd had to force the sound out of her throat. "Why have you never mentioned this before? All those years . . ."

The corners of his mouth came up in a wry grimace and his eyes narrowed. "It's hardly something you want to broadcast. I curse the night I ever allowed Eustace to persuade me to accompany him."

"But you did. And then you left little children unprotected—"

"We weren't thinking. We believed rescuers would be along in a short time. Don't you see? We couldn't afford to be seen there. We had no idea what the coach driver, what the other passengers, would recall. We had to get out."

She stared at him, wanting to deny what she was hearing.

"I know it's unforgivable. I'm not making excuses." He was rooted to the spot, unbending, proud, refusing to ask for any special understanding.

She searched his face, and saw not shame but weary resignation. "It was always about the money, wasn't it?" She whispered the words, gazing into his dark eyes. "Always the money that came first?"

He shook his head. "No. It wasn't like that. But Eustace, well, it's distressing to admit it, he couldn't afford to be ruined by a scandal and neither could I. We were both just starting out." He flashed a look of appeal and then gave a long sigh. "I don't expect you to understand."

Huldah stood with a rustling of skirts. "Sir John, please. Whatever's gone before, can you do all you can to find Isabella now? I am sick with anxiety. I can't think of anything else."

Pania stepped aside, giving Huldah room to move into the space she'd vacated. John maintained her gaze for another second or two, then looked pointedly at Huldah. "I will do everything in my power to make this right," he said. "Everything. And I think the place to start is to confirm whether Isabella is with Lotta Crabtree's troupe or not. That is still is a possibility. Maybe even the most likely explanation." He took Huldah's arm and began to gently guide her towards her carriage.

Pania sank back down onto one of the stable stools. She thought of the times the three of them — she, John Russell and Eustace — had entertained one another, the laughter, the jokes. Young and free as birds, she had thought them to be, when the other two were always carrying a guilty secret.

The dynamic between the two men had shifted after Elanora's death, she remembered. It seemed even more significant now. John had become the lead partner in their business dealings, Eustace the follower.

She shivered, even though her skin was moist with perspiration. A picture of Eustace, looking glum and reluctant, flashed to mind. John was always pushing him to introduce him to the 'right' people, the East Coast merchant circles which were his family's established world. *It was always about the money, whatever he says.*

She heard the rumble of coach wheels and looked up, expecting to see Huldah's coach rolling away. Instead, she saw a smart cabriolet drawing up at the roadside and a driver in a navy blue jacket and trousers jump down to hand down Adeline Baker. She descended, stately and serene, shaded from the scorching rays of the sun by a pink parasol.

Pania watched the scene unfold as if it was a play. Her world had tilted on its axis so sharply she wasn't sure whether the ground under her feet was stable, what was truth and what lies.

"Sir John," Adeline Baker said, stepping forward confidently and offering her right hand. "I do hope you don't mind, but I thought it would be fun to see what progress you are making on this exciting new build. Such a beautiful day, I thought I'd come out for a drive."

John responded in the same courtly manner. "Mrs Baker, you're most welcome. Come and take a look."

So that's how it's going to be. Business as usual. He really hasn't changed in all these years. Pania clasped her hands together and gave a bitter little laugh. *Why should he change? What he's doing seems to be working for him just fine.* She felt the doors of her heart start to close, like the yellow-and-orange California poppies which open in the sun and close when it gets cloudy.

It might work fine for him, but it wasn't how she wanted to live. Honesty and trust were essential pillars in any friendship that she valued, and she couldn't count on them here.

She braced herself and took a deep breath. She was the stage star, preparing to front up to her most difficult role of her life. She started her proud promenade towards John and his new guest, who were approaching from the road side.

Seeming to sense the awkwardness of the moment, John turned to her. "Mrs Hayes, I believe you've met Mrs Baker?"

"Oh yes, good afternoon." Pania stopped in front of the visitor standing before her in a full-paneled skirt in magenta, the latest fashion color. "Enjoy your tour. Sir John certainly is very popular with the ladies today."

She made a slight bow, fleetingly catching John's eye as she gathered up her skirts and continued in full flow to her carriage. She really had wasted enough time here. She'd been taken for a proper fool, and that stopped right here and right now.

Thirty-Three

Graysie Castellanos leaned comfortably into her fiancée Nathan Russell as they nestled into the Stockton House drawing-room sofa. John had asked them to come for a mysterious meeting — but so much strange stuff had been happening lately she had learned to take extraordinary events in her stride.

Four-year-old Minette, her recently acquired god daughter, played happily in the corner with a large fully outfitted doll's house. The curly-headed moppet had the tiny pieces of furniture and fittings — beds, chairs, tables, sofas, lamps and plates — spread out on the floor around her and was humming an old French folk song under her breath as she played. The songs were part of her babyhood, a comforting reminder of the mother who had died six months ago. Graysie still sang them to her every night at bedtime. She smiled. Plenty there to keep her occupied for a while.

Beside her Nathan took her hand and squeezed it gently. "Everything OK, sweetheart?" Her insides lit up as she looked into his loving, mischievous face.

"Perfectly wonderful," she said. "Couldn't be better." Astounding to think how much life could change in a short time. It wasn't much more than six months ago that she'd been a rising singing star traveling the concert circuit throughout the Western states, a single girl pursing a rapidly burgeoning career. And then disaster struck: her closest friend Francine Dubois was killed in a gambling-hall fire, leaving a small daughter behind. Minette's father might still be alive somewhere — who knew? He disappeared around the time of her birth and hadn't shown any interest since. Francine had been adamant she didn't want him in control of Minette's life, even if he could be found. She made Graysie promise she would care for her daughter if anything happened to her, and Graysie accepted the commitment without hesitation.

She shivered as she reflected on what had happened next. Traveling on the concert circuit with a four-year-old proved unworkable, and in a funny serendipity she'd been contacted out of the blue by a Sacramento solicitor advising her she was the beneficiary in an old mine left by a Eustace Mountfort, a friend of her mother's. She barely remembered the name, but he initially represented himself in the beneficiary documents as her 'uncle' — not by blood, but by association through her mother.

She'd grabbed at the idea of the gold mine — perhaps in the same mad way the early Forty-Niners had been lured by gold fever — because she so desperately needed an alternative to the concert circuit. She gave up the touring and focused on making money out of the inheritance — either by selling it or by working it, whichever proved most practicable.

If only it had been that straightforward. It had been a rough ride, but it was over now. And the best of it was, she'd met Nathan through it all. She had never imagined herself married, and here she was about to take the big leap.

She gazed up at the man beside her and counted her blessings all over again. She'd gone from being alone in the world — her mother died when she was about to turn four, and her father when she was twelve — to discovering new family ties through Eustace. She wriggled in her seat and sighed as she thought of Eustace Mountfort, Sir John's long-term business partner, her mother's first love and, to her consternation, recently revealed as her father — an identity which, as stipulated by Eustace, had not been declared when she was told of the bequest.

It still made her stomach churn when she dwelt on the circumstances of her conception — an out-of-wedlock tryst between two young people certain they were going to wed and spend their lives together, only to be thrown apart by the unexpected death of Eustace's mother, and his punitive father's reaction to the son he considered spoiled. By the time Elanora realised she was pregnant, Eustace had been banished to the West Indies, his father determined he would learn the family business the hard way. Another suitor who'd been patiently waiting his chance — the Spanish photographer Rafael Castellanos, madly in love with the gorgeous Elanora — had chivalrously wed his expectant bride.

That's how Graysie hoped it had happened, anyway. She had no way of truly knowing if her mother had confided her enceinte condition to her new husband, or just hoped he wouldn't notice and ask awkward questions. What Graysie did know was that when her mother's family got wind of her state they disowned her and she and her knight in shining armor eloped to South America.

The life they built together came crashing down sixteen years ago when a night stagecoach rolled and Elanora was crushed in the wreckage. Graysie remembered how excited she had been at the prospect of seeing her father again after he'd been away working. He had secured a partnership in a Sacramento daguerreotype studio, and they were traveling out to join him — her mother, her, and the two-year-old twins, Alejandro and Gabriela. When the rescuers arrived at daybreak the next morning, Graysie was the only one alive. Her mother was dead and the twins were nowhere to be found. The speculation was that they'd been taken by predators — wolves, bears or mountain lions. She had felt the guilt of her survival almost every day since.

But she had no reason to question her parenthood until the bombshell was dropped by Eustace Mountfort's solicitor a couple of months ago. Rafael was passionate, a loving father, and a gifted artist. She cherished her memories of him. One of the earliest was when she was a tiny tot, sitting on his knee laughing uproariously as he leaned playfully into her ear and whispered to her in Spanish. But after Elanora's death he was never the same. He took a second wife, but Humpty Dumpty couldn't be put back together again.

She stood and stretched her arms over her head, suddenly feeling hot and cooped up in the stuffy room. "Sir John's taking his time. Are you sure he said one o'clock?"

Nathan smiled at her affectionately and drew her down beside him. "He'll be here any minute, I'm sure."

"Any idea what this is about?"

Nathan's open expression clouded with a flicker of doubt. "I don't. I've had the impression he hasn't been telling me the full story lately."

"The full story about what?"

"Think we'd better leave him to tell us that. Here he is now."

Graysie looked up as John slid into the room. He greeted them warmly, but he wasn't his usual confident self, she could feel it. His hand jerked on the glass of water he'd picked up from a tray on the table as he came in, sloshing it down his trousers. He brushed at it with clumsy strokes. Sir John Russell was definitely out of sorts.

Graysie looked at Nathan uncertainly and he shrugged and settled back into the sofa, placing his arm companionably around her shoulders.

John sat down opposite them and lifted his shoulders, as if steeling himself to convey bad news. "There's something I need to tell you both. Particularly you, Graysie. It can't be delayed any longer and I'm afraid it will come as a big shock."

John could barely remember a time he'd felt more at odds with himself. As he sat across from his youngest brother and the woman who was soon to be his wife, the warmth and joy that overflowed from them as they sat close on the sofa reached across the room. And he was about to shatter that contentment with his news. Would either of them want him in their lives after this disclosure?

They made a handsome couple, his tanned brother with his sun-touched hair, and the fine-featured, graceful young woman who sat next to him. Strange to think he'd recently imagined Graysie as a possible wife for himself. He leaned back in his seat, increasing the distance between them imperceptibly, and acknowledged his mistake. He'd been thinking as a businessman again, weighing up the pros and cons and seeing it as a sound proposition.

Nathan and Graysie had followed their hearts. Truthfully they'd each been willing to give up everything for the other, rather than calculate what they were going to get out of it, and look how it had turned out. Nathan was now a partner in the promising Ophir Mine project, overseeing new developments in the mine Graysie had inherited from Eustace. It galled him that Eustace had kept the whole transaction secret. The least he could have done was warned him. He ground his back teeth. He'd been well off-target there.

His musings were interrupted by Graysie's dulcet voice. "Please, John, do go on." With a quick start he realized he'd slipped off into his musing, avoiding the task ahead.

Graysie's blonde-red hair caught the rays of the afternoon sun and added to the aura that surrounded her. "I can't imagine what can be so important as to bring you here at short notice. Do tell." She smiled directly at him, open, fresh and guileless.

If only . . . He cut off the thought before it went any further. "Graysie, I'm afraid this will be part-confession, part-revelation. Some of it I have hidden for many years. I've not been honest with those closest to me. And some of it I genuinely had no clue about until a few days ago."

Nathan grinned. "Fire ahead, old chap. I'm sure we can handle whatever you're about to tell us. After all, no one's died, I hope." He glanced at Graysie fondly. "We can manage it, can't we, sweetheart? Together we can climb mountains."

Russell cleared his throat. It felt closed and dry. His chest tightened. What these people thought of him mattered. It came to him in a rush that he didn't want to lose their respect, or their affection. "Graysie, I think I've indicated to you before — and I admit probably not in the most generous spirit — that there were some details about Eustace's relationship with your mother that I hadn't come clean on. Some of those you've now heard from others like Eustace's lawyer. I had no idea he was your father, I can assure you of that. But there were other secrets known only to a very few people, who chose to remain silent."

Graysie nodded sympathetically. "Of course. Discovering Eustace was my father was a complete shock but now I think of it, it makes sense. So what else is there?"

John took a deep breath. "You know from the details Eustace left for you that he was there the night your mother was killed. It was an awful mistake, a stupid action, but one with no malicious intent. He was desperate to try and talk Elanora out of rejoining Rafael. What I've never admitted is he persuaded me to go along. So I was there that night. I shared in the dreadful choices we made. I don't want to make excuses, but he minimised the risk. 'Boys being boys,' he said.

He'd heard some story in a bar about a chap who abducted his sweetheart and wed her to save her from being forced to marry someone else. He admired his audacity."

Graysie's face was pale and blank. Nathan was frowning. John pulled a handkerchief out of his coat pocket and mopped his hot face. "It's very painful to admit that when everything went horribly wrong and we saw that your mother was dead, we fled. We just wanted to get away."

As he'd been talking, Graysie's open serene expression had become pinched; her eyes widened and her brows furrowed. The color drained from her face and she released her hand from Nathan's and brought it up to her throat, as if she were having trouble breathing. John grimaced and stared straight at her, as if unwilling to dodge the shame.

"We couldn't reasonably explain why we were there. We were out in the mountains, miles from anywhere. We didn't know how much the coach driver would remember. He was alive but badly dazed. Would he recall Eustace sitting on his horse in the middle of the road holding up the coach like a highwayman? Would he admit that he'd foolishly tried to run him down rather than pull up, as Eustace expected him to? Would he admit that the horses shied and he'd lost control? If he remembered what really happened, he wouldn't have come out of it looking so good either. But we couldn't count on him being honest about what did happen. So we ran for it. Eustace saw instantly that Elanora was dead. We left you and the twins there and ran."

The three of them sat in silence for several minutes feeling no need to speak, each digesting Sir John's bombshell in their own way. Then Nathan drew Graysie closer and looked at his brother with an expression more serious than John had ever seen. "So that's the part you've been hiding. What about the new details you mentioned?

That you've just discovered. Where do they fit?'

John felt a surge of warmth towards his youngest brother. Never deflected by unnecessary drama. "You recall a few days ago I showed you that strange cartoon that was left on Huldah Wilmington's door step? As soon as I saw it, I recognized its significance. I just had no idea who had put it all together."

Nathan's brow furrowed. "You're not making sense, John. I need the jigsaw pieces laid out more clearly."

"A caricature of me with a small child? That could only be pointing to Elanora's accident. The missing twins? Believe me when I say the disappearance of the twins has been a knife in my ribs from that day to this. The only logical conclusion I could draw was that Huldah's daughter was one of the twins."

He paused to let Graysie register the full impact of what he was saying. "Graysie, Huldah had no idea of the full story either. The only thing she knew and kept secret was that Isabella was adopted. Until she was ready to be open about that, I felt I couldn't do anything."

Graysie jumped up as he spoke, and paced the room, her gait agitated, her expression distant. She reached the end wall lined with its windows that looked over the garden, swung back and clasped her hands together. "I can't believe it. I just can't believe it.' She shook her head. "Please. Do carry on."

"This morning Huldah came to me in great distress," John said. "She'd seen my reward posters for Lily, and her resolve to keep silent snapped. It seems Isabella has run off again. Huldah is terrified that whatever has happened to Lily might also have happened to Isabella. She was so desperate she was ready to tell all. And it seems that yes, sixteen years ago, her sister brought her the toddler we know as Isabella.

"Huldah's sister Bertha — none of us had a clue they were related — was the woman we knew as Madam Ring, the hotel manager who died a few months back. In those days she was pretty, young, and reckless. She thrived on excitement. Elanora took her on the Sacramento trip as a nanny cum companion, to help her with you three children. She was keen to get to Sacramento, and your mother provided the means.

"But when the stagecoach crashed, she scarpered before help arrived. How she got out of there I don't know. Maybe she hitched a ride with another wagon. And turned up at Huldah's with Gabriela — your mother called the girl Gabriela, didn't she? Offered her to Huldah 'for a sum'. She had some story about her being an orphan that Huldah chose not to question too closely. She knew Huldah was desperate to have a family."

Graysie had resumed her seat next to Nathan, her eyes sparkling with tears. "So she's alive? Gabriela's alive. And she's here." She whispered the words to herself, savoring each phrase, digesting the momentous news. Then she turned her head into Nathan's shoulder. Her muffled sobs were the only sound in the tense silence. Nathan stroked the back of her head consolingly and waited. No one else spoke or moved.

After several minutes she broke away and gave John a wan smile. "I'm happy. Very happy. I'm crying because I'm happy. Crazy isn't it?" She laughed, a light gasping snicker, and her breath caught in more sobs.

Nathan drew her back to his shoulder. "So Gabriela — now called Isabella — is alive, but we don't quite know where she is. That's the guts of it, isn't it?"

That's what he loved about this pair, John thought. Always quick to get to the point. "Quite right. There still is a decent chance she ran off with Lotta's troupe, given how besotted she was with them. If she's not with them then it's of more concern, but we'll find her. I make that my pledge."

He looked from Graysie to his brother and back again. "I hope you'll believe me when I say I've been over and over that night in my head and wished I'd acted differently. And I still know nothing about what happened to your brother Alejandro. Did Bertha take him as well? She never mentioned another child to Huldah."

Graysie gulped, deep dry mouthfuls of air, and nodded. "There's just one thing now, and that's to find her. Gabriela, Isabella, whatever she's called. After all these years!"

Russell felt the weight on his heart get heavier. Now that he had opened up this long-held secret, his burden hadn't lightened but intensified. He pressed his hands into both sides of his face to stop his jaw from trembling. Shame. He felt a core-deep shame at the devastation his actions had caused.

He knew that, come what may, he was going to do whatever he could to right that wrong. And it began right now, with searching out the Crabtree show.

Nathan withdrew his arm from around Graysie's shoulders and stood up slowly. "You're going looking for Lotta?" He turned to Graysie. "You can spare me for a few days, sweetheart? We've got to go and find your sister."

Graysie threw her arms around his neck and broke into fresh sobbing. John waited until the sobs had quietened and she pulled back and wiped her eyes. He gave Nat a long, grave embrace "You are champions, you two. You've been far more accepting of me than I am of myself. Give me a chance to earn that grace. That's all I can ask. I hear the Crabtree outfit was heading for engagements in Marysville. Let's get going before dark."

Thirty-Four

They had been riding for four hours and were getting saddle sore. Nathan, who was much more road-hardened than John was, slowed his horse to a walk and gestured to a pretty vantage point, a rocky spur protruding out from the main range offering great views over the valley below. To get to it they had to cross a small stream where the horses could drink.

"What do you say, brother? I suggest we give ourselves and the horses a short rest and brew a billy. I'd say we're a couple of hours away. We should get there before full nightfall, even with the rest."

John was glad of an excuse to dismount. He'd got too soft with town living. He tried to muffle the groans as his feet hit the ground and his buttocks protested at the unusual exercise. He used to be on a horse every day, he reflected. Now it wasn't unusual for it to be once a month.

A short time later they were sprawled in the warm afternoon sun, sipping hot tea while their horses contentedly cropped the green grass that grew streamside. He thought ahead to their mission. Graysie had been amazing. No recriminations about his behavior, just a forward-looking determination to find Isabella. He was determined not to let her down.

It seemed he'd just made that vow to himself when he felt a hand on his shoulder, gently shaking him awake. He came to consciousness in a second, his hand automatically going to his hip, then relaxed and he remembered. He was on this mission with Nat to find Isabella, and they'd stopped for a break.

"Time to move again, Sir J. Prefer not to be out here at nightfall." Nathan easily hauled himself up and got moving.

Up ahead the trail narrowed into a track over a steep gully crossed by the miner's answer to a bridge — full logs felled and roped together to form a rustic platform. The horses hated being wrong-footed, and they would need to take it very cautiously to prevent injury. He sighed. There was always something.

Nathan turned and gestured towards the structure, indicating to him to take care. They were just entering the uncomfortable channel-like thoroughfare — once you entered, it would be difficult to turn back — when his eye caught a flicker of movement on the ridge above them. He slowed his horse and glanced up just in time to see two horsemen, both clad in black with dark hats pulled down low, coming up behind them fast. His senses went on high alert. He didn't like confronting anyone unknown in the mountains. Mules laden with miner's supplies, no problem. Lightly provisioned, fast-moving horsemen were another matter.

He called to Nathan to alert him. "I'm probably being unduly cautious here, but we've got company closing in on us fast." He pointed up the mountainside. "I don't like it."

Nathan followed the direction of his outstretched hand, but the riders were no longer visible. "What do you want to do?" he asked. "We can draw aside and set some sort of ambush. Or wait for them to pass us and see if they're harmless." His mount, maybe sensing the approach of strange horses, raised his head, upper lip exposed, sniffing the air. Nathan leaned forward and patted its neck. "Or we could just try and move along at a reasonable pace and get across this river. Once across, we'd be in a lot stronger position to regroup and face them on the other side."

John nodded. "Yes, let's settle for that option. The other one is too dicey. There isn't a lot of room for setting any sort of ambush."

They moved on across the log bridge, conscious of maintaining a good pace while not unsettling their horses by pushing too hard. They were onto the section that spanned the river a hundred feet below when the riders emerged from the trees. John was very aware of them at his back.

"Uh-huh. We're pretty much at the point of no return," John muttered to no one in particular. "Here goes." He had a very uncomfortable feeling of being forced down a chute. Hopefully they would pop out the other end unscathed.

Nathan was continuing his steady clip ahead of him. He set his eyes on his brother's back and increased his own pace. Without looking back he could sense the men were gaining on them. Could these be Ji Zeng's men, sent to silence them a long way from where anyone could see what happened?

A sixth sense told him to pull his rifle out of the slot behind his right hip where it was stowed. He controlled his horse with his thighs, reached around to get hold of the rifle, and rested it across the front of his saddle.

Completing that movement he had fractionally taken his eyes off Nathan. They'd crossed the expanse of river and were moving into the bushes flanking the other bank, and when he glanced back up his brother had disappeared. Then he heard a high-pitched squeal and Nathan's horse reared up into view. Something had spooked it. Nathan was fighting to stay mounted. He gradually reined it in and brought the frightened mare under control.

John grinned at Nat. "Doesn't like the company we're keeping."

They wheeled around and faced the oncoming horsemen. Nathan hauled out his rifle and the two of them stood their ground, guns aimed straight back down the bridge. The snuffling of their own horses, the clip of the approaching horsemen, the chatter of the small river a hundred feet below, were the only sounds.

They sat on their horses for what seemed like an age, the approaching horsemen slowing to a walk and then stopping entirely. Even at a distance John imagined they regarded them in sullen insolence. Killers they might be, but were they willing to hazard their chances in a situation like this? The sweat on his chest and arms was cooling, sending little shivers all over. He watched as the anonymous black riders came to a sudden conclusion. They wheeled their horses around and rode back in the direction they had come from.

John lowered his gun. "Seems like round one to us. It's nice to win for a change. Don't seem to have been doing much of that lately." He turned his mount towards the Marysville road. "We can't afford to be casual about it, but I think we live to fight another day. Let's get going. No time to waste."

They entered Marysville on nightfall, just as they had anticipated. The throng amassed around an open-air stage left no question as to where the Lotta Crabtree Troupe was performing, and as they slipped off their horses and joined the throng they could see the show was well under way.

The crowd was gathered in front of a temporary bare-board stage where a group of blackface minstrels, Lotta leading in an intricate soft-shoe shuffle, were in the middle of a rousing rendition of 'I Wish I Was in Dixie's Land', the minstrel song that had become the Confederate anthem. Most Californians had been staunch for the Union, but the song was still a miners' favorite.

John leaned against a hitching post at the back of the arena and breathed in the mingled smells of kerosene from the stage lights and the yeasty serge twill of trousers.

A few women and children were squeezed in up the front, but the bulk of the crowd was male: muscular, hearty working men with rough dirt-ingrained hands, intent on enjoying a break from hard labor.

He glanced around. Moths dive-bombed the lanterns set at irregular intervals around the arena, striking the hot flames with a spluttering *pfft*. Not enough light to pick out Zeng's Black Dragon killers, if that's who they were, he thought. Or anyone else. If Isabella was loitering in the shadows, she'd be hard to see.

Lotta laughed as she danced, touching off what were usually seen as masculine steps with quick little grotesque rhythms of her own fancy which were greeted with delighted cheers. She had a special genius that sparked a rapturous response. The men stamped and whooped and yelled "Encore!" and showered the stage with money and gold nuggets as she danced on. It was intoxicating, he had to admit. A scene like this would be irresistible for a young woman like Isabella. Was she watching, wishing, dreaming of what if, somewhere in the darkness?

The minstrel numbers were coming to an end. Lotta was well into 'Oh! Susanna', the Stephen Foster tune that had become the Forty-Niners' anthem. Instead of coming to Alabama with a banjo on her knee, as in the original, Lotta came to California with a washpan on her knee.

Amid rapturous applause she kicked off one of her dancing slippers and ran around the stage, picking up her booty, bowing and curtsying as she went. The slipper was soon filled to overflowing, nuggets spilling everywhere, which gave more fuel for her highly individual comedy. A boy came on stage and passed her an old hat which she held at a rakish angle on her elbow. When she put the gold into it, it turned out to have no bottom; more nuggets hit the deck, and the audience went wild.

A small break for a baritone gave Lotta time for a quick change out of blackface to a long-tailed, Irish-green coat. She bounced into jigs and reels with her characteristic lightning-quick footwork before segueing into a series of Cockney ballads where she could send herself up — one moment the bumpkin sailor singing a ridiculous love song to his Mary Ann, and then pantomiming 'I'm A Covey What Sings', straight from the London docks. Barely a man among them had been born in California, and wherever they hailed from, they drank it up.

Still no sign of Isabella. It was highly likely if she was here that she'd just have a small turn here and there in a chorus line, or playing Lotta's stooge, and they arrived halfway through the show so they might have missed her. He resolved to tackle Lotta's mother after the show and challenge her outright. Were they sheltering a runaway?

He knew he'd have to move fast. It was likely the company would exit straight out the back onto waiting horses and ride a dark trail to the next engagement. He'd heard the stories of how Lotta, dressed as a boy, asleep in the saddle, the halter of her horse held by the rider in front, had on more than one occasion narrowly missed death from boulders loosened by mining or a stumble of a horse on a steep ravine as they journeyed from town to town.

For the final number what looked like the whole troupe — about a dozen performers and musicians — assembled on stage for another favored miner's melody, 'To the West, To the West'. With a wild energy the men joined in and sang, "Then hurra! hurra! for our pine-clad hills, where the ruddy miner works by gushing rills, He knows no cares — he knows no ills, but laughs Ha! Ha! Ha! Ha! as his purse he fills," roaring defiance at their rough-and-ready lives and the dreams that propelled them.

And then it was over. Men faded home to sleep, or migrated to the gambling dives which remained open late into the night, and John's heart quickened. He tapped Nathan on the shoulder. "Got to try and catch Mrs Crabtree. I didn't see anyone who looked like Isabella."

They slipped around the back and sure enough, the troupe's support crew were already waiting in line, horses loaded with baggage, ready for the performers to get in the saddle and start riding. He searched in the dim light for Lotta's formidable mother. He spotted her, a handsome ruddy-complexioned woman, standing beside the front of the line, preparing to depart. She was talking with a stocky man in a cowboy jacket who looked as though he ran the transport.

John quickly stepped up and presented himself. "Mrs Crabtree, Sir John Russell at your service. We met in Grass Valley a few days ago. Great performance tonight by the way. You certainly won hearts in Marysville!"

Mary Anne Crabtree looked up, brows raised. "Sir John? Yes, of course. How can I be of help? I'm sure at this time of night this isn't a social call."

He nodded and hoped his face registered mild concern. "You may recall we came to you seeking out a young woman, Isabella Wilmington, one of your daughter's stage struck devotees? With her mother?"

Mrs Crabtree nodded vaguely. "Yes, I think I recall."

He glanced around the backstage area, where actors stood around obviously waiting to mount and move on. He turned back to Mrs Crabtree, who'd been distracted by the man in the cowboy jacket. He waited till they'd finished talking and tried again.

"I regret to say that Isabella has gone missing from her home, and we wondered if she'd come to you. Maybe she even made it sound like her mother approved." He gave an apologetic smile. "She hasn't tried to join your ranks, has she? Her mother is desperate to find her."

"I don't recall any Isabella. Young women who think they want to be on stage come and go, but I don't recall an Isabella." She pressed her lips together in a tight line and added, "Sorry," before turning back to the road manager.

John screwed up his face in disgust. "Seems we've traveled all the way here for no purpose. She's not here."

Nathan rubbed his nose. "Maybe. Or maybe she isn't calling herself Isabella. Maybe she isn't even dressing as a girl. I wondered about a couple of those 'men' in the chorus line for that final number. It might pay to hang around a little longer." He kicked at a grass root with his boot.

John beat an impatient tattoo on his thigh, waiting for what was coming next.

Nathan glanced up with a piercing, direct look. "I do see someone else you'd recognize, however." He wheeled on his heel and cast a seemingly casual glance over the backs of the lined-up horses to the alley beyond.

John followed his gaze. Standing with his hands in his pockets, his back partly turned towards them, stood Grass Valley's deputy, Virgil Hale. And standing beside him were two big men dressed all in black.

Thirty-Five

Isabella ripped off her curly black wig with a sigh of relief and dropped it on the small performer's dressing table set up in one of the caravans. She peered in the mirror. She still found it hard to recognize herself in the reflection that stared back. She had chopped off her long blonde hair, and the big blue eyes that looked back from under the jagged short locks didn't look like hers.

"What's wrong?" Rosie bumped down onto the stool beside her and also dragged off her wig. "Phew, hot isn't it? Two down, five more to go." The plump, red-headed Irish girl had become her best friend at their first meeting at Lotta's studio a few days ago. Practically every day since, she'd slipped out to watch Rosie rehearse while letting Huldah believe she was at her schoolfriend Maria's house.

Rosie nudged her along the bench, bumping hip to hip. "Make room for one more, Californio." Her Irish lilt broke up in peals of laughter.

Rosie's star turn was a sparkling rendition of 'The Girl I Left Behind', an old Irish ballad that had been another Civil War favorite. Every time she sang it she got a chorus of encore calls. Isabella dreamed of having a solo item like that someday. She hid a yawn behind her hand and dug her friend in the ribs. "My turn to sleep tonight. Your turn to lead."

"Isabella!" Rosie tried to sound indignant, but she always dissolved into good-natured giggles. She picked up a hairbrush from the dressing table and playfully brushed Isabella's boyish locks. "You don't look much like a minstrel with this." She plucked out a short blonde lock.

Isabella laughed. "Just as well I've got this, isn't it?" She picked up the black wig and waved it in the air in front of them. "I'm not exactly going to make a name for myself when no one can even recognize me, but I guess it's all part of learning the business."

The show was over, but Isabella didn't have the sense of euphoria she'd anticipated from being on stage with Lotta's crowd. For one thing, it took hours to get her face cleaned up. She had to apply the blackface cream so heavily to mask her fair complexion that it was a nightmare getting it off.

And then there was the little matter of traveling every night. She thought wistfully of her soft featherdown bed at home in Grass Valley. What she would give to be able to slip into it tonight and sleep right through till cock's crow.

Rosie stilled the hairbrush and gave Isabella a light pinch on the arm. "Take care out there, acushla." Rosie peppered her talk with Irish endearments, but she sounded unusually serious tonight. Her gaze drifted to the mirror in front of them.

Isabella glared back at her in the mirror. "Is something wrong?"

"No, not really." Rosie shrugged lightly. "Well, probably not."

Isabella dug her in the ribs again. "Rosie! Tell me. What's wrong?"

"Well, I was out the back just now watching Eddie bring round the horses and there's this fellow hanging around out there. Shifty-looking fella. Wearing a deputy badge, with a long gray moustache. Asking questions."

"Questions? What kind of questions?"

"Questions about a girl he was looking for. Said she'd stolen jewels from a rich lady in Grass Valley. He had reason to believe she might have joined Lotta's gang. And if we didn't give her up we'd be harboring a fugitive."

Isabella could feel the blood draining from her face. She knew that under the blackface cream her skin would be even whiter than usual. "What happened?"

"As far as I could tell no one was too impressed. They were all too busy getting the gear loaded, ready to move out. But there aren't too many young ladies who've joined us in the last week or so." Rosie looked somber.

"I didn't steal anything!" Isabella spoke much louder than she intended, and she smothered her mouth with her hand. She repeated the phrase, but this time in a whisper. "I did not steal a thing." She looked at Rosie directly now. "You do believe me, don't you?"

"I do, acushla, I do. But proving it to that lumbering lawman might be another story."

Isabella looked at her friend, who was only a few years older than her — she said she was twenty but she seemed much older sometimes — and wished she had her foxy wisdom. "What do you think I should do? What would you do in the circumstances? Not that I'm saying I'm that girl, mind."

"Not that you're saying that for a minute." Rosie smiled into her eyes and squeezed her hand encouragingly. "Maybe the folks back home are worried and have set him on this girl's tail. Or maybe he's got his own reasons for being here. I didn't like the look of him, that's all."

"What if he blames me for something I didn't do?" Isabella felt herself shiver in the hot night. "It would be my word against his."

"Honestly?" Rosie squeezed her shoulder. "I know you love the roadshow, but this guy's bad news. Is there anyone who could protect you from him? I wouldn't try to take him on alone."

Isabella thought back to Huldah, to Sir John Russell, to her mother's frantic efforts to stop her from doing exactly what she had done — run away with Lotta Crabtree. Her mother would be frantic with worry. And Sir John would almost certainly stand up for her if this deputy tried to make trouble. She nodded. "There is someone, more than one, who'd help." The path she should take was now so clear when before it had been misty. "I need to make sure I'm with them if he comes looking again."

"The Marysville night stage comes through in an hour or so." Rosie began tugging the hairbrush through her own red curls and gave Isabella a bright smile. "You need to be on it. I can lend you the money for the fare if you need. You can repay me when you join us later on."

Isabella smothered her in a hug which sent the hairbrush clattering to the floor.

"Watch it," Rosie said in a schoolmarmy voice. "And you'd better get that blackface properly cleaned off before the stage comes."

Isabella glanced in the mirror: she still had streaks of dark makeup around her nose and under her eyes.

"You can hide in here until Lotta's crowd are pretty well moved out, and then slip across and wait. Stay in the shadows till the very last minute. I'll cover for you. Lead your horse out and make it look as if I'm getting ready to depart."

Rosie shot her another bright smile, but Isabella could see her lower lip trembled slightly. She enveloped her in another warm hug. "Rosie. You know the answer to everything! Thank you! I will make it up one day."

Rosie gave her blonde locks another tweak and rolled her eyes. "The sacrifices we make! Now get that face cleaned up."

Thirty-Six

"To what do I owe this pleasure?" John looked up at Deputy Virgil Hale over his warm buckwheat pancake. He wasn't going to get up from the breakfast table to greet the man. His hair was still damp from cleaning up after the tense ride back from Marysville, and he'd just sat down to eat. "Pull up a chair. I presume you've had breakfast, but I'm sure cook can find you a coffee." As if on cue, Mrs Snively bustled in with a fresh coffee pot.

John and Nat had made excellent time back to Grass Valley, but his stomach had clenched every time he thought of Zeng. Today was Zeng's deadline, the day he expected the seal to be delivered — or else. Or else what, John wondered. Was Isabella already the next casualty, or had they just failed to find her?

He'd hardly noticed the translucent dawn light on the ridges or heard the chorus of birdsong that heralded the first rays of the sun on the peaks. Nat, no doubt sensing his preoccupation, was also lost in thought.

The deputy, by contrast, gave off the confidence of a man who knows he can't lose. He proffered his hand in a firm shake, his broad, sun-scorched face overflowing with bonhomie. "Just a routine call, Sir John. Wondered if you've had any response to that reward you posted a day or so ago. I know you don't agree with the way I handle things, but thought I'd check on your progress."

"Fair enough." John sipped his coffee, savoring the jolt of energy that radiated from the base of his skull as the hot black liquid went down. "A bit too soon to say, I think. We're still assessing the results."

Hale settled back in his chair with deliberate casualness. "Not surprising, if you don't mind me saying." His dark eyes gleamed with information he was keeping to himself. "I do have a piece of news you may find of interest, however. Given your complicated family, that is."

He dipped his head as he said 'complicated' and the dislike John felt for the man rose again to stick in his throat. This was the lawman who didn't think Ting Hon's death was worthy of investigation. "Oh really? And what's that?" John took pleasure in turning the phrase with his haughtiest English accent, and saw dislike flicker in Hale's eyes.

"I hear on the grapevine that Ji Zeng — what is he, your half-brother? No, that's the other one. Sorry, it's all rather confusing. Your cousin, or whatever he is. I hear Zeng is planning to marry Lily Chung."

John tamped down his disgust and raised one eyebrow. "Yes? And you know this how?"

Hale gulped his coffee. "Oh, I believe the source is highly accurate. Afraid I can't divulge who."

John fought hard to contain his anger. "You haven't any leads on where she actually is, I suppose? You do understand she's a sixteen-year-old who's been abducted.? So strange the way she disappeared when she and her mother were in your care."

Hale's face flushed a deep red. "Strange? I wouldn't say that. The girl was having a sulk, that's all." He fingered his empty cup, hinting at a refill.

"Then how do you explain that she seems to now be in Ji Zeng's hands? You think she ran into his arms? And Mrs Chung's jewelry? Any sign of that?" He smiled. "Just checking, as you say. These people are all members of my 'complicated family'. This wedding — where is it to take place? And when? Did your informant tell you that?"

Hale's walrus mustache drooped as the corners of his mouth turned down. "No, it pains me to admit they didn't. Of course, even if I knew, I've got no cause to be stepping in and stopping things. It's purely a private matter as far as I'm concerned."

"A private matter. A young girl is abducted and it's a private matter. I fear once again Deputy Hale, our views of what constitutes justice are wildly divergent. He pushed back his chair from the table and threw down his table napkin. "But don't let me hog the discussion with my concerns. I gather you've been seeing action over in Marysville?"

Hale's bushy eyebrows shot up and he shook his head. "Don't know where you heard that. No, no. I've got plenty to keep me busy much closer to home."

"I see." John was momentarily caught off-guard. Why would Hale lie about something like that? They had seen him with their own eyes. He let it drop. "Someone got the wrong idea then."

"Must have," said Hale. He stood as if ready to go, then said, "Goodness, I forgot. One of the young lads was cleaning out the sheriff's office yesterday and they found this."

He reached into his back pocket and handed over a grubby envelope. "I've no idea how it got there or who left it. Jake said it was just lying on the desk. Most odd. It's got Chinese writing on the front so I guessed it must be for you. Seeing as you have a lot of high-up Chinese friends."

John's name was written across the front in Chinese script. As

Hale spoke, his blood surged and his heart pounded in his ears. He opened the envelope carefully, fearful of what it might contain. Inside lay a long dark tress of hair and a gold wedding ring.

Only a few nights ago, he recalled, he had told Zeng he wanted Ollie's supposed captors to produce his wedding ring. *And this is the proof that Zeng has Ollie and Lily, and their time is running out.*

When he looked up, Hale had gone.

John sat slumped in his chair for a long time time after Hale departed, fighting to marshall his thoughts into an orderly plan. Any orderly plan. If Zeng really was planning to marry Lily, he had to do something.

A picture of father and daughter the last time he saw them together flashed through his mind. Lily's exquisite profile, dark hair cascading around her face, leaning over her father as he labored over a crossword puzzle. She was pointing to the page and making solution suggestions. Ollie had dropped a butterfly kiss on Lily's cheek and laughed, "What a champion! Atta girl," and Lily, plainly basking in her father's love, had rolled her eyes and said, "Dad," in affectionate exasperation.

He sighed, and stood, poised to do something, go somewhere. Anywhere. His hands felt tied behind his back. This had become about so much more than business for him. When had winning at all costs started taking second place?

He tapped his foot awkwardly as he recalled his dealings with Eustace. He had always held the Elanora disaster over his head to extract maximum financial advantage, considered it his reward for the reckless risk he'd been placed under.

And Pania? He had treated her in the same way, yet another tool to assist his rise to the top. Having a beautiful, classy woman as a companion was never a hardship, but really he'd exploited her contacts and access to business intelligence with little consideration for what he might offer in return.

He reached for his hat. It was only after Graysie Castellanos spurned his clumsy offer of marriage — and what was that but another advantageous business proposition? — that he'd begun to rethink his priorities. Why had he toyed with the idea of marrying Graysie? To get his hands on the mine Eustace had left her, because he was peeved he'd kept it a secret from him, and because he thought it would be a good trade — her beauty and lure as a hostess for his money and protection. He had expected her to leap into his arms, grateful to be rescued from a life of penury. Instead, she moved out to stay with the nuns.

Graysie might be years his junior, but she had the discernment of someone twice her age. He chewed his lip. *What was I thinking?* Graysie had proven herself far more astute than he was, capable of bedrock integrity. She had sacrificed a rising career to care for her best friend's daughter; she'd moved from his capacious Gold House into a bare room at the convent to care for an old prospector she'd conceived responsibility for.

He had hurt Pania's feelings and maybe irrevocably damaged their friendship with his clumsy maneuvering; he hadn't understood how much he'd used and abused Eustace's goodwill until after his death; and he'd been blind to the deadly rivalry between Ting Hon's sons building right under his nose.

He ran his tongue around his lips. The roasted flavor of coffee was still there, but it couldn't mask the taste of ashes. He had put value on the things of least worth. He'd committed to finding Ollie out of a sense of familial affection, as well as to promote his own business advantage. But now something had changed inside him. It wasn't just about doing the right thing any longer.

He pushed his hat hard down on his head and stepped out into the hotel hall, his hands tightening into fists. A surging determination flooded into him so powerfully he felt the tips of his ears warm. He was going to find and free Ollie and Lily because what was happening to them was wrong and had to be stopped. He was possibly the only one who could do it, and he vowed he would, whatever the cost.

Thirty-Seven

"Whose silly idea was this anyway?" John leaned back in his chair and glared at his younger brother. His mood hadn't improved in the hour and a half since Virgin Hale had delivered Zeng's threat.

His mind was still frantically scrambling for a way to find the Chung father and daughter, but everywhere he turned he was pestered by tipsters eager to collect the reward for information about Lily's whereabouts. He ran his hands up and down his arms and shifted his weight testily. He was irritable and antsy and scratching wasn't helping.

He and Nat were lounging in the sun at the back of the Gold House stables. It was a beautiful still morning, and the position of Gold House on the crest of a rise gave them rolling views over the valley below. The hillsides were colored lemon-yellow and coppery in the summer dryness, and everywhere there whirled a velvet ocher dust from the rocky hillsides. Now and then he caught a flash of indigo as blue jays rose on spreading wings. But the peace of the scene hadn't done anything to quiet his soul.

He had barely stepped out into Main Street before Ernie, the lanky, half-baked odd-jobs man had grabbed him, insisting he'd seen Isabella in one of the bars in town with a cowboy. Ernie was tall, one of the few men who could look down on him. Tall and very enthusiastic. He leaned over him, full lips eager and shining, his breath smelling faintly of whiskey although it wasn't yet ten o'clock, as he went into excited detail of his sighting.

John had just sent Ernie shuffling off when he was accosted by Mrs Sweet Jessamine Charters, the rancorous old gossip who, with her husband, ran Charters' Supplies, one of the provisioning merchants in town. She was certain she'd seen Lily riding out of town in a buggy with good-looking young Jethro Thomas, the doctor's son. Probably eloping, she'd volunteered. "Ask Dr Thomas, he'll know." And so it went on, one wildly inventive suggestion after another. Each seemed more far-fetched than the last, but John had to remain restrained and receptive through every account.

"I should've known. The promise of money brings out midsummer madness." He ran his hand through his hair and gave a long sigh. "I could be more forgiving if I didn't have this dreadful feeling of time running out. The token delivered by Hale this morning is all the evidence I need." He shook his head. "The Dragon Seal is probably the only bargaining chip I've got for keeping them alive."

Nat was sprawled in a resting posture similar to his own. His long legs stretched in front, heels down, hands linked at the back of his head, he rocked with minute movements back and forth on the back legs of an old stable chair. He was lost in his private reverie.

"Are you listening?" John said sharply. "Or am I talking to the air?"

Nathan gave a big swooping movement and sat upright, feet slapped down to arrest his momentum. "I called down at the stables to check on Antonio while you were talking to Ernie and the others."

Antonio was a young Mexican Nathan had befriended after his prospector father was killed. He now worked at Grass Valley's central stables to help support the family — his Aunt Anna Maria and his five cousins.

John felt his irritation levels rising. "Oh? And how is talking to Antonio going to help my current problem?"

"In your current mood you mightn't want to hear how," Nathan said, standing and stretching his arms over his head. Deliberately avoiding eye contact. "Please yourself." He picked up his hat, making as if to go.

"Okay, okay. Settle down. What is it you want to tell me?"

Nathan sat back down again with a thump and skewered John with a look. "Antonio is a very smart kid. He misses nothing. He's had to be smart to stay alive."

Russell decided it was worth listening to whatever was coming next. What did he have to lose? He seemed to be going nowhere fast as it was.

"We saw Virgil last night. You know that. But exactly what was he doing over at Marysville with those two hoods? We have no idea. So with that in mind, is it just coincidence Antonio reports that Virgil's also been taking long rides on other nights this week. Staying out much longer than planned. He says the horse Virgil normally uses out of the deputy's station has gone lame, he's ridden it so much. That's why he's had to hire extra mounts from the stables. You'd wonder where he's going all the time."

Nat gave an extra push on the chair legs. "Anyway, Antonio has to wait up for the horse to be returned so he can wash it down, and on Thursday night he had to sleep at the stables all night because Virgil didn't return till morning. That just happens to be the day Lily disappeared. Antonio says when he did bring it back, it was hobbling. He had to take extra care when he was cleaning up. That's how he came to find an odd little memento caught up in the girth ring. It's a bit of a fluke it didn't drop out."

"Oh?" John's curiosity spiked despite his low mood. "What kind of odd little memento?"

"A gold locket." Nathan fished inside his jacket and drew out a small shiny object. "A yellow gold locket. It's a very fine piece with a delicate spray of flower diamonds across the front. And I've a strong inkling if we show it to Selina she'll recognize it."

He handed the piece to John, who examined it in minute detail then prised it open. "Two locks of hair, entwined together. My guess would be they are Ollie's and Selina's. Willing to place a bet?"

Nathan threw back his head and laughed. "Not likely. I'd bet it would be a certain way to lose."

John smiled. "Let's go and visit Selina and see if we're right."

John wouldn't have believed it if he hadn't seen it with his own eyes. Selina Hamilton Chung, who let the whole world know all cats were filthy, flea-ridden mongrels, greeted him in the Stockton House drawing room with a tiny, ginger-peach kitten perched on her shoulder, purring amazingly loudly for something so tiny and delicate.

"She's Lily's."

John raised a questioning eyebrow. "She?"

"Yes. We've settled it conclusively. She. We found her wandering in the yard near the deputy's office. I think that's the surest evidence you'd need that Lily didn't leave of her own free will. She'd never have just dumped the kitten. I'm looking after her till Lily comes home." Her voice cracked slightly and she glanced away.

John didn't miss the sparkle of tears in Selina's penetrating, hazel-green eyes. This was the woman who was usually the model of upper-class composure. He had never seen her show emotion, not even towards Ollie who, he had no doubt, she loved deeply. He held her gently by the shoulders and searched her face. "I understand this is a great trial, and on top of Ollie's disappearance . . . I know, it's too much."

He led her to the sofa and sat down beside her. She cupped the kitten protectively against the curve of her neck, careful not to disturb her as she sat down. He turned to her, willing himself to infuse her with a calmness and confidence she obviously wasn't feeling. Her normally self-assured bearing was fraying at the edges; some strands of auburn hair had escaped from her normally immaculate chignon and her eyes were lined and weary.

"Selina, I have something to show you. It's going to be a shock, so brace yourself. It's not bad news, not bad at all, it might even be good news, but it's likely going to surprise you. Are you ready?"

She looked into his face with a desperation that touched him to the core. Any news, but especially good news, was better than a vacuum. She dropped her eyes to her lap then gave him a quick smile. "Please, go on John. I'm ready."

He reached deliberately into his jacket and drew out the locket, which he had wrapped in a crisp white handkerchief. "Nat and I found something we have reason to believe might belong to Lily. Can you take a look at it and let us know if it's hers?" Very slowly he unwrapped the locket and placed it in her upturned palm.

Like a bird starving for any crumb, Selina had not taken her eyes off his hands through the whole procedure. "Oh . . ." The word came out in one long-drawn sigh. She stared at the locket without touching it. Then with her free hand she gently lifted the kitten off her shoulder and placed it on the sofa next to her. Cupping the locket in one palm, she caressed it with the fingers of the other hand.

"This is Lily's locket. It was her sixteenth-birthday present. We gave it to her earlier this year. It was mine before it was hers, and she's not taken it off since she got it. With my jewelry gone it's the only piece that remains from my personal collection. I'm certain. I know it well. Where did you find it?"

Nat quickly outlined his conversation with Antonio. "The only explanation we can see for it being there is if Lily was on that horse and it somehow became unfastened during the ride. It's just a miracle it got caught in the girdle ring and held fast. If it had been stolen then perhaps it would be more likely to be in the saddle compartment. We're hopeful where it was found gives reason to believe Lily is alive and was wearing it when she was taken somewhere. Maybe she even deliberately left it as a clue. Now we just have to find out where she was taken." He sighed. "That won't be easy — but we're not giving up."

Selina tilted her head to one side. "So wait a minute," she said, looking from Nathan to John and back again. "You believe Lily was taken away somewhere by that deputy on the same day she disappeared? You did say the horse had been used by the deputy?"

They both nodded.

"Doesn't that mean he colluded in her initial removal? Could it even mean the whole burglary thing at the stagecoach station was a set-up to distract me and get us to the deputy's office?"

She's always had a razor-sharp mind, I'll give her that. In his own fuzziness, maybe because of lack of sleep, John hadn't taken it that far, but as soon as she suggested it something in his spirit chimed in. Hell and damnation, she was almost certainly right. Find where Lily was, and you'd have a better than fifty percent chance of finding her mother's heirloom jewels as well — or if not, at least the person who took them.

The kitten stirred on the sofa, rolled over onto its back and stretched its paws out luxuriously. Selina turned to it and tickled it gently around the neck. "Don't worry, little Peaches, your mistress will be home soon." She gave John a strained smile. "Now all you've got to do is find her. Hopefully, the trail will lead us to Ollie as well. You keep looking and I'll keep praying."

John stood with his back against the top rail of the fence that ran between the stable yard and the coach station next door. It was a sleepy hot morning; a cockerel and chickens scratched in a haystrewn corner, but other than that the ground was flattened into submission by the heat. The only sounds came from the grinding of the horses' big jaws on their morning grain, and the occasional squawk of protest from a hen when another stole its rations.

He might be clutching at straws, he conceded, but Lily's locket was the closest thing to a lead they had. He wanted to pump this boy Antonio for every minute detail he might know. Coax out of him stuff he didn't even know he knew.

They had interrupted Antonio in his chores, and he was edgy, glancing over his shoulder as if expecting Virgil or his boss Hank to descend and reprimand him for talking when he should be working.

"The lawman?" The boy's nose wrinkled. His father had been shot dead by persons unknown less than two months ago, and Virgil hadn't made much of an attempt at catching his killer. He darted a look sideways, as if checking he was in the clear. "He never used to come in much at all, but they're short of horses over at the deputy's office and since his own mount went lame he's been coming in a lot more. "Seems to be going on a lot more long trips too — that's one reason his horses are getting injured. Rides them too hard, I reckon."

Nathan pivoted and parked his butt on the edge of the trough. "Could you get word to us if he does come in? We'd pay you for your trouble."

Antonio fidgeted with his hands, running one down his pants leg as he squinted up at them in the bright light. "I don't know. I mightn't be here when he comes in."

John could sense the boy's uncertainty and he didn't blame him. "We might just come and hang out here a bit more than usual," he said. "Would you be okay with that?"

Antonio shot him a relieved grin. "So long as Hank doesn't mind and you don't get in the way."

Nathan reached over and ruffled his hair affectionately. "Cheeky pup," he said.

John laughed and the tension in the air eased. They'd better let the kid get back to his work before he did get into trouble. He was turning to go when he noticed a small crowd gathering outside the Wells Fargo station next door. Just another day in a small Sierra Nevada town, with folks waiting for the coach from somewhere to arrive or depart. A couple of dogs snarled at one another, standing nose to nose, hackles raised, a scrap of refuse on the ground between them.

He heard the familiar rumble of coach wheels and was enveloped in a dust cloud that floated across from the street as a big vehicle rolled in. "Must be the Nevada City flyer," he remarked. The Nicolaus to Nevada City stagecoach made the ten to twelve-hour trip day and night in season, going via Marysville, Johnsons Ranch, Rough and Ready and Grass Valley. "It's usually here about eleven. Let's get moving old chum. Can't stand around all day. Things to do."

Nathan put his hands on Antonio's shoulders. "We'll be back, son. Take care. And if anything happens in the meantime, well, you'll know what to do. Just take care."

John was striding out ahead of him when Nathan grabbed his shoulder hard and leaned his mouth next to his ear. "Check out the young woman who's just got off the stage and tell me that's not Isabella Wilmington."

John froze mid-stride. A young woman with a slightly dazed air was standing beside the open coach door, clutching a soft carpetbag to her chest as people surged around her, uttering greetings or sorrowful farewells. Her white dress was modest and crumpled and she looked tired and overwhelmed. She swung around uncertainly as if deciding where to go next. Under her straw hat her hair looked short and wispy, emphasizing her winsome innocence. Travel-worn she might be, but her luminous beauty shone through. John admired her finely arched brows, bright blue eyes, and sculpted rose pink lips.

"Well spotted," he said. "I'm certain you're right. Let's go see." He strode out of the stable yard with the air of a man who was simply taking in the morning air, Nathan trailing behind him.

They wandered into the stagecoach yard and stood a few yards away from Isabella, watching. She looked as if she was about to step away from the coach when a tall, lean man with a long nose and prominent teeth sidled up to her. "Looking for someone, miss? Can I be of assistance?" He placed a hairy arm on the bag she was holding. "Here, let me take that for you." He grinned, and big teeth flashed white in the sun.

John was across the gap between him and Isabella before the stranger had the chance to say another word. "Miss Isabella!"

She looked up sharply, caught between panic and shock. "Oh, Sir John. How wonderful to see you. Did my mother send you?"

Well caught. At least this one's got her wits about her. "She most certainly did. She is so delighted you're coming home."

The grafter who'd approached her melted away, leaving an uncertain threesome — John, Nathan and Isabella — in the midst of the chattering crowd.

"Please," he said, taking Isabella's bag from her with one hand and gently guiding her by the elbow with the other. "Let me take you somewhere to catch your breath and perhaps have some breakfast. Then we'll take you home to Huldah. You have no idea how elated she'll be."

Isabella's face lit up with excitement at the mention of Huldah, then clouded over as quickly as it had brightened. She looked around her nervously, surveying the crowd, seeming to search the faces for someone in particular.

"What is it?" John said, holding her arm a little more firmly than he would usually to try and communicate security. "Are you worried you're being followed?"

She gave him an incredulous stare. "How did you know?"

"How did I know what?"

"Why, that the deputy — the one with the long mustache — was looking for me. He was apparently telling everyone I'd stolen some jewels or other and was on the run." Her voice rose in pitch. "I was so scared. That's why I came home. I didn't want him to find me before I had a chance to clear my name."

Thirty-Eight

"Easy on him, Pania! He's had a lot happening the last couple of weeks, wouldn't you say?" Graysie looked at Pania over the top of the coffee pot she was holding. "Another one? Seems to me you could use it."

Pania laughed and passed her cup to her friend. They were sitting in the garden at Stockton House, enjoying the shade of an apple tree that hung heavy with unripe fruit, watching Graysie's ward Minette gambol with Peaches.

"I know this hasn't been his greatest time, of course. But I feel as if the ground has been cut away from under me. How much of what I've believed existed between us actually did? Honestly, Graysie, I would have thought you of all people would understand."

Graysie's attention was momentarily captured by Minette, her cascading curls falling over her face as she played a boisterous game of hide and seek, jumping out on the kitten from hiding places. "Careful, Minette," she called. Her voice had a light gay note to it. "You don't want to frighten her, or worse still, trip with that hair over your face and fall on her. You might hurt her."

She turned back to Pania. "Sorry. Where were we? Oh, yes, that I of all people should sympathize? By that do you mean now I've discovered John always knew a lot more about my mother's death than he let on? That I should be mad at him?" Graysie raised her eyebrows and spread her hands wide, palms facing upwards. "I guess if I'd known two months ago what I know now, I would have felt upset with him. But I've got a new perspective. They were young and stupid. I believe John when he says Eustace was the main instigator, and he got caught up in it.

"And I can see why he'd feel it was best to let sleeping dogs lie. He didn't know what happened to the twins and there was nothing he could do to bring my mother back or make amends. Since I've met him in these recent times he has been very generous in helping me in one way or another. And of course now he's going to be family. I just don't believe in wasting energy lamenting the past when we can't change it."

Pania frowned. "I see what you're getting at, but I lived right through all of those years alongside him. I thought we had an open, frank, friendship. I can't believe he'd conceal something so important from me for so long. And he seems to have a bee in his bonnet about getting married and starting a family. He's completely changed from the man I thought he was — even being willing to go to that matchmaker event. The old John Russell would never have done that."

Graysie nodded. "So he's changing. Is that so bad? Let's walk and talk a little. I'm feeling very lazy." They rose and set off at an ambling pace down the garden path to the extensive vegetable gardens Basil Stockton's man kept at the back of the house.

"I think John might be feeling vulnerable," said Graysie, "and who could blame him? A man he revered is killed in his home. His cherished Gold House burnt to the ground. The cousin he regards as a brother disappears without any explanation. Isn't that enough to start on, without all the rest?"

Pania sighed. "He won't let me into any of that. I know it must be hard — but he won't let me in to help. I don't know, maybe he's decided he prefers Adeline Baker." She paused to smell a rose that grew by the path, putting on a good show of nonchalance. "Maybe he thinks her social contacts will help him pick up again where Eustace's death forced him to leave off. That's another thing — the way he exploited Eustace's family connections. It came close to extortion. Eustace felt he owed him."

"Oh Pania, bitterness does not become you." Graysie took Pania's hands and drew her towards her, looking into her eyes. "Give him another chance, that's all I'm saying. Isn't that what you told me once in regard to Nathan — and see where that's ended up. Which brings me to a completely different matter, my forthcoming wedding. Would you give me the pleasure, the sheer delight, of being my matron of honor? There's no one I'd like better to do it."

Pania's face was suddenly hot. It was so sweet of Graysie to ask her, but playing at being all bright and cheerful at a wedding was the last thing she felt like. Then the little voice inside chimed in. *You've enjoyed immense blessing. Don't begrudge others their moments of joy.* "Graysie, that is too kind," she said. She thought back to her own wedding day in New Zealand — a brief exchange of vows under the disapproving eye of her husband's brother Edward, who had come as a missionary to her home region of Rotorua and as far as she knew lived out the rest of his life there. Edward wasn't comfortable with the age gap between her and Henry or, if she was honest, the fact that his brother was marrying a native Maori girl. But their marriage had worked out happily. She would bet, though, that whatever she wore as Graysie's matron of honor would be a hundred times more lavish than the simple dress that had been her own wedding gown.

"You're got such a generous spirit, Graysie," she said. "You deserve every minute of happiness this marriage promises to bring you."

Would John be the best man? Would she be forced to go through a charade of standing at the altar with her old friend, knowing they had no future? Her stomach flipped at the thought. When it came to it, she wasn't sure she could face it.

She really had to get all her defenses set up if she was going to survive this next season with her pride intact. She smothered a sigh. She didn't want to diminish Graysie's joy at the coming nuptials.

They watched Minette standing halfway down a row of flourishing peas, tearing open the fresh pods with her sharp little teeth and devouring their contents with giggling relish. Pania heard quickening footsteps coming down the path behind her and turned to see Nathan coming up to them with a sense of urgency. "You're looking for us? For Graysie?"

He nodded. "We've got visitors. Huldah's just arrived, and she's got someone unexpected with her. You'll want to see them."

Graysie looked up at him, her eyebrows raised in surprise. "Unexpected? Who?"

He shot her an adoring look, but Pania sensed tightness around his eyes. "Isabella. She's returned. And she has quite a tale to tell. You need to hear it."

Thirty-Nine

Nathan drew his arm protectively around her lower back as they approached the drawing room where John, Huldah Wilmington and Isabella stood in a tight cluster. Isabella's face was flushed and she was examining her fingernails with an uncertain, slightly dishevelled air. And her hair! Her beautiful long blonde mane was now a boyish short cut that framed her elfin face and made her blue eyes appear even bigger and bluer than before.

Graysie felt a sudden clench in her stomach. Was this girl really her sister — or, rather, half-sister? She didn't know whether to feel exhilarated or cautious. What if it was all a big mistake? She silently signaled to Nathan with her eyes: *Is it going to be all right?* He drew her briefly closer in a comforting gesture, before stepping aside to make way for her to precede him into the room. "You go first," he whispered. "I'm right here behind you."

She acknowledged her future brother-in-law with a nod. Funny how this was her house but he seemed to have once again assumed natural command of the situation. But he looked nettled and liverish; the skin around his eyes and mouth was drawn tight, and his collar was grimy.

Her voice had a challenging ring: "Sir John, Mrs Wilmington,

Isabella. Welcome." She smiled at Isabella and Huldah. "I can hardly contain myself. Please sit down."

She caught the quick look of understanding that passed between the brothers. John said, "I'm just going to explain . . . Why don't you sit here?" He indicated one of the big sofas that filled the room. "Huldah and Isabella can sit opposite you. Mrs Hayes?" He gestured to a single armchair set opposite his own.

Rather like a maitre d', thought Graysie. She tasted sourness in her mouth. John gave her an inquiring look, and she guessed her resentment had shown on her face.

Nathan gently held her hand as John began speaking. "We all see, and wonderful it is too, that Isabella has come home to us unharmed. That's a miracle, for which I know Huldah will be saying Hail Marys for a long time to come — and she's not even a Catholic." He smiled around the circle, pacing himself and the message he was about to deliver. "Isabella can tell you more about the details of how she came to return. She did, as we suspected, run off with Lotta Crabtree's players, but that's not our primary focus at this moment."

Nathan glanced apprehensively at Graysie, who'd never felt more grateful for his strong hand holding hers. "I think I can take up the story from here," he said. "It goes back sixteen years to that dreadful night and the accident that killed your mother, Graysie."

At the words "dreadful night" an iciness inched around her heart. After all these years of trying to put it behind her . . . She stared at a spot on the carpet where someone had dropped a candied cherry from the fruit cake she'd served at afternoon tea and for a few moments wished she could float away.

Nathan turned to Isabella. "Graysie already knows some of the details about that night, Isabella. We're here to let you in on the secret as well."

At the word "secret" Huldah reached over and squeezed Isabella's hand. "You're going to be surprised, Izzy. But in a good way." She gave her a funny little half smile and her gaze was warm.

Nathan spoke up again. "Huldah's right about that, Isabella. Really, I can only tell it like it is. I think you've been feeling curious about your early days, about your father? That story is quite a lot more complicated than we ever knew. And we've only just discovered the full truth of it."

He paused and glanced across at Isabella, whose face was screwing into an anxious frown that deepened the longer he went on.

"What? What is it?" She gazed at her mother. "Mother? What is it?"

Huldah glanced at Nathan. "I suppose . . ."

He nodded. "Go ahead."

"The thing is, dear Izzy, I'm not your mother by blood. Just by heart. I adopted you seventeen years ago, after your own mother died. I never knew who she was until very recently. But now I do, and I want to tell you too."

Isabella gasped, and threw her arms around Huldah's neck, half laughing, half crying. Gradually she calmed down and pulled back to gaze around the group.

"With all of you here, I can only think you are somehow involved. Tell me. Where did I come from?"

Nathan smiled at her. "Your mother, Isabella, was Elanora Castellanos." He paused as Isabella's mouth gaped open. She darted a nervous look at Graysie.

"Elanora? But that means . . ." Her words trailed off.

"Yes, Isabella." Nathan smiled again, this time more broadly. "That means you and Graysie have the same mother. You are the daughter of Elanora and Rafael Castellanos. And Graysie is your half sister."

Isabella was regarding her with a pinched, nervous expression, as if she was unsure how she would be received.

"Isabella." Graysie's throat closed up and she had to clear it loudly before she could continue. "Isabella . . . After all these years I can't believe . . ." Tears sprang to her eyes, blurring Isabella's anxious grimace. The girl looked as if she was holding her breath, waiting for a blow to fall. *The poor child is preparing herself for rejection.*

Graysie groped and stumbled around the low table that separated the two sofas. Isabella jumped to her feet. They met in a collision of arms and tears and hugs, Graysie sobbing, wrapping her arms around Isabella's slim shoulders.

Isabella's head pressed into the dip of her collarbone and the shoulder of her dress grew wet with the younger woman's tears. Graysie patted her on the back gently, just as she did when Minette was upset.

They stood like that until Graysie started to feel dizzy. She drew long shuddering breaths to try and re-stabilise and laughed into Isabella's chopped hair. "I guess we'd better sit down again before we fall over." She sank back into the soft cushions, drawing Isabella to sit beside her, smoothing her cheeks in both hands as they settled.

"What have you done to your hair?" She sounded like a bossy older sister and they both broke into bubbling laughter. Huldah had got up and quietly moved to the other sofa to make room for them, and Graysie shot her an apologetic look, but the older woman sat and beamed broadly at them both. "What a sight," she said. "Never did I expect to see this day." Her eyes sparkled. "I'm so sorry I didn't tell this story earlier, but of course I didn't dream it could have such a happy outcome. I was frightened I'd lose everything. Isabella is the most precious thing I have."

Graysie nodded. "I understand." She turned to the trembling young woman beside her. "Isabella, we've got a lifetime to catch up on. But I'm so glad it isn't too late."

She turned back to Huldah. "I know you've shared this with the others before, but could you repeat it for me now? I really do want to hear it from you."

Huldah briefly outlined the story of her sister's sudden arrival with a baby girl, and her story that she was orphaned. "I chose not to ask too many questions," Huldah said, shamefaced. "I knew Bertha was trouble, and it was very odd that she'd suddenly have a child to farm out. But then again, I knew I could give that baby a better life than most — and I think I did that." Graysie and Isabella murmured their agreement.

"You know, I barely remember that Mother had a friend traveling with us," Graysie said suddenly. "I guess my memory of that detail was wiped by the shock of the accident. All my life I've wondered, are the twins alive somewhere? And I've blamed myself. I've told myself I should have saved them. I didn't even remember there was another adult there."

"You and everyone else," John said. "Sadly she had a reputation for being feckless, so when she disappeared from the accident scene no one thought too much of it."

Huldah nodded. "You're so right. Taking the children? It was a terrible thing to do. But it's blessed me my whole life since."

As tears spilled down Huldah's cheeks, Graysie gave her a sympathetic smile. "I think Isabella had a much happier time with you than she'd have had with my stepmother," she said. "Take that as a consolation." She turned to Isabella. "So you ran away to join Lotta Crabtree. Naughty girl!" She gave Isabella a quick hug to show her she was half-teasing. "I can understand why — but not the best choice."

Isabella nodded in vigorous agreement. "I know that now, truly." She turned to Huldah. "I promise never to do anything like that again. It was so stupid."

"And so what brought you home? How does that little chapter end?" Graysie realized with a shock that the set of her half-sister's mouth — the perfectly chiseled, determined tilt of her jaw, the up-turned corners of her lips — were exactly like their mother's.

The tips of Isabella's ears were turning red and she was swallowing nervously. "That deputy, the one with the gray walrus moustache. He frightened me."

Graysie moved a little closer to Isabella, snuggled up to her so their thighs touched. "Frightened you? How?"

"One of my friends overheard him making inquiries about a runaway who he claimed had stolen a lady's jewelry. From the description he gave she guessed it was me and thankfully she didn't believe I'd have done something like that. But I was scared. What if he found me and planted something on me? It might sound far-fetched but I just didn't want to risk it." She glanced sideways towards Huldah. "Besides, I missed home dreadfully." Huldah gave her a grateful smile.

"I hid and waited for the night stage to come through Marysville. I crept on board — and here I am. I'm never doing anything like that again."

Pania broke the silence that followed Isabella's vow. "Nathan, John. It's wonderful that Isabella is returned to us safe and sound, but what about Lily? Do you think Virgil Hale is involved? If he is, what can we do about it?"

Good old Pania. Graysie slipped forward on her seat and waited for one of the Russell brothers to respond. Her dear New Zealand friend was never one to miss a trick.

John was the first to reply. "In a word — well, a few words actually — Pania, yes we can and yes we will. Do something about it, that is."

Selina came into the room and he flashed her a quick smile. "Just working out our next step, Selina. We're not giving up on anything." He sighed and stood up. "The question we really need answered is why Deputy Hale is always popping up in unexpected places. If we knew the answer to that, I'm betting we'd be close to finding Lily and Ollie."

Forty

John was short-tempered and ankle-deep in sawdust when a carriage pulled up outside the Gold House site. Mrs Adeline Baker slid out and began to pick her way on cautious tiptoes across the bumpy ground. His heart slumped to his mud-caked boots. She wore a vibrant blue ankle length walking dress in the new short style over buttoned up boots with broad square toes. On her head she had a black velvet bonnet — Pania would know what the style was, he was sure — trimmed with feathers and fastened under her chin.

"Sir John. Delighted, I'm sure." She had a faint hint of a Southern accent that hadn't been so evident before. She fluttered her eyelashes and twirled her gauzy white parasol. He guessed the accent was all part of a come-hither scene she was staging, with herself cast in the lead role of desirable heiress.

He hadn't realized until that minute how much he disliked the studied manner she adopted when seeking approval. Come to think of it, he'd never seen her do anything spontaneously. Everything was calculated for maximum effect, and mostly she succeeded. He, in contrast, was tired, sweaty, and no doubt had stray bits of straw in his hair. He ran his hand across the top of his head and ruffled it self-consciously.

"Good afternoon." He attempted to inject some enthusiasm into the greeting. "Excuse my appearance — we're hard at work here." He shot her a rueful look.

"Sorry to disturb. I won't stay long. I've come with a very special request. But first, how is progress? Weren't you hoping to move in by Christmas?"

"I'm sorry. Forgive me. We're not exactly set up for guests. I'm afraid your dress will get dirty out here but the stables aren't much better." An image of Pania at their last meeting here with Huldah flashed before his eyes. Pania, her bottom parked on a wooden stool, elbows on her thighs, feet tucked up on an upturned feed bucket, perfectly balanced and at home. She'd plucked some straw from the barn floor and held it out to one of the horses that hung its head hopefully over the railing. Without hesitation the mare had stepped up and began pulling on the sheaf, while Pania stroked its neck as it chewed, the hint of a satisfied smile on her lips.

Mrs Baker cast a quick glance around her surroundings and barely concealed her distaste. She made a quick flicking gesture with her finger, as if getting rid of a spider or ant that had crawled in from the field, and flashed him a look intended to appeal to chivalry. "Oh dear, I so hate creepy-crawlies," she said, with another little flutter of her hands. "Perhaps we could perch in my carriage to talk for a minute or two? I won't detain you long."

John closed his eyes for a few seconds then nodded in silent consent. She turned and retraced her path to the carriage, the blue skirt swaying from side to side, one hand clasping it at the front to lift it off the ground as she moved. Her coachman stood at attention at the carriage door as she stepped in and gestured to John to sit next to her.

She looked just as attractive as she had when he'd met her at Huldah's little soiree, and she was just as flatteringly attentive. But somehow the charm wasn't working on him today. She leaned towards him. The fingers of her gloved hands were laced together in her lap, her lips slightly parted.

She took a quick, short breath and the tip of her tongue flicked to the middle of her lip for a millisecond. "Sir John, I hope you don't mind, but I wanted to ask a favor of you." She flashed a brief smile. "I wondered, would you be willing to accompany me to the Black and White Ball in San Francisco next month? I'm sure you will have been before. Everyone who is anyone will be there, and of course I always get tickets." She glanced out the open carriage door, onto the sunlit house site, with its resinous odor. "Clayton and I used to always go. He used to say he'd chased down many a good deal there between dances. . ." Her voice died away and momentarily she faltered. "I haven't been since he died. I thought it might be useful for your business interests, as well as simply being wonderful fun."

John found himself struggling for the right response. He'd gone to the Black and White Ball with Eustace and Pania more than once, and Adeline Baker was right. Everyone who was anyone would be there, and it was a great gathering for deal-making and breaking. But chasing deals now was like dust in his mouth. Freeing Ollie and Lily was the only thing dominating his thoughts, and he had no idea how long that was going to take, or whether he'd be available for any ball anytime soon.

More importantly, he saw in a lightning flash that if he escorted Adeline Baker the gossip-mongering matrons would assume they were seriously courting, which was just what the canny Mrs Baker intended. *Spider, spider, catch your fly.* Mrs Baker was spinning her web.

"Mrs Baker, that's a wonderful offer. A most generous offer." He pinched the bridge of his nose, suddenly aware of a thumping headache. "I am mortified to have to refuse it, but I'm afraid it's impossible. I have some very urgent business I must complete, and I've no idea how long it's going to take. I can't make any commitments until it's settled."

Adeline Baker shuffled slightly in her seat and the yards of fabric rustled around her. "Oh," she said in a shaky soft voice. "Urgent business? I didn't realize there was anything untoward—" She broke off, and twisted her hands in her lap. "Well, of course, with the death of the comprador and the fire I knew there were exceptional circumstances, but I thought that was all behind us." Her words were halting, uncertain.

John gave a weak smile and leaned in closer until their thighs were almost touching in the confined space. "Don't worry, Mrs Baker, I understand what you are saying. The matter that is unresolved is the whereabouts of my Russell and Chung partner, Oliver Pakenham Chung, and his daughter Lily. It's urgent that I get to the bottom of what's going on, and it spares me little time for anything else at the moment. I am sorry."

Adeline Baker's face had flushed bright pink. Her chest rose and fell in quick distress. John reached out and took her hand gently as he looked solemnly into her eyes. "I am very sorry, Adeline. The last thing I want to do is cause you discomfort."

She let her hand lie in his for a few seconds, then quietly withdrew. "No discomfort at all, Sir John," she said brightly. "I fully understand your priorities." Her clipped tone echoed in the carriage space.

In response he inched back and half-rose, ready to leave. "Perhaps another time?" He didn't know why he'd said it.

"Perhaps." She gave him a stilted smile and called to her driver that she was ready to depart.

As he backed out of the cozy little compartment and took a relieved breath of forest air he heard the rumble of wheels. He turned and saw Pania had arrived. She was driving the Stocktons' smart little sulky dressed in a black-and-red riding outfit, and came striding across the grass to meet him in sensible flat-soled black boots, her glorious dark eyes flashing. For the second time that morning, John's heart dropped. This was the woman he wanted by his side for the rest of his life. He felt her allure even as she glared at him stormily across the grassy space. *What have I done wrong now?* He crossed the grass to meet her and said, "Hello, my dear Mrs Hayes. It's a beautiful morning, and lovely to see you too. How can I be of assistance today?" He shot her an ironic grin, unable to resist the urge to tease.

She'd paused and folded her arms as he approached, and she now tightened her stance and swayed back on her solid soles. "What was she doing here?" She drilled him with her gaze, and it dawned on him she wasn't playing games. She wanted answers, and he didn't know what she expected him to say.

"Mrs Baker? She wanted me to go somewhere with her, that's all. Nothing more to it." He rubbed the back of his neck and swiveled on his heel to look across to the house site. "Want to come and see how we're going?"

Pania hated herself for grandstanding, but she remained planted where she was. She'd arrived just in time to see her rival getting into her carriage, and she didn't know if it was the stylish Mexican Blue dress or the Russian bonnet that irritated her the most. "And you said?"

"I said I couldn't make any commitments just now. I declined.'

He gestured for her to precede him across the grass. They fell into step as they strolled across to the source of the loudest hammering. "I didn't know she was coming." He knew he sounded defensive. "And she probably won't be coming again."

To Pania's ears that sounded pretty lame. "Oh? Might I ask why? You seemed to be getting along rather nicely."

John shrugged. "What is this, Pania, the third degree?" When she didn't respond, he sighed. "She's nice enough, but I have stuff I need to be doing."

"Like Lily. And Ollie. I know." The heavy feeling in her chest was replaced by a tightness, as though her heart was shrinking. He had set Mrs Baker aside temporarily, perhaps, while he sorted out the mess in the Chung partnership. But he was still all about business, and she didn't appear to figure in his calculations.

She swallowed. "I just can't get Lily out of my mind," she said. "Is there any news?"

"Not beyond what we told Selina about the locket. She told you about that?"

Pania nodded. "So what's the next step?"

"We're keeping a close tail on Hale. He knows where Lily is, I'm sure of it. If he makes any move we'll know."

"That seems pretty passive." The heavy disappointment in her chest crept into her limbs. Her arms tingled. She stamped her feet to shake off a leaden feeling that went right to her toes. She'd have thought he could come up with something a bit more adroit than that. "Actually I came by to say that I'm leaving town for a few days. I'm accompanying Harvey on his next talent circuit to some of the neighboring towns."

John glanced away. One of the carpenters was backing down a ladder from the second story of the new Gold House, which was starting to take shape before them. He was signaling for attention, waving one arm while steadying himself on the ladder with the other. "Sorry, Pania. Can you wait just a mo?" He waited at the foot of the ladder until the man reached the ground, and they engaged in an animated conversation — something to do with floor joists. Pania had no idea what it all meant.

She felt the warm sun on her back, breathed in the menthol-tinged air, and for a moment let her mind flick to the fantasy she'd returned to more often than she liked to admit recently, of living in this new house with John, being his wife. What an idiot she was. If he'd had anything like that in mind he'd had plenty of chance to indicate it. Really, business was all he'd ever really cared about, and Adeline Baker would be the perfect match for an ambitious man desiring social status. She herself would be best to settle for companionship over love and see where her friendship with Harvey Miller might lead.

John had completed his exchange with the workman and turned to rejoin her as she slowly moved in his direction. "Sorry, Pania. Where were we?"

"I was just letting you know I won't be around for a few days. I hate to leave without hearing that Lily's safe, but if I hear anything that's useful I'll let you know."

John took a sharp little step back and jerked his head, as if he'd received unwelcome news.

"You've no objections? I mean, you seemed to be concerned about security a while ago, but those concerns have eased?" She felt uncomfortable seeming to seek some kind of approval from him. Why would where she was spending her time interest him?

John frowned. "Honestly, Pania, I don't know. But yes, you should be fine, especially if you're with company, if you're not traveling alone. Stay close to Miller." His eyes searched her face, looking for she knew not what. His expression was almost wistful. Not a look you saw on his face often. He sighed and reached out and gave her right shoulder a light squeeze. "Do take extra care."

She gave him a quick embrace, dipping her chin briefly on his shoulder. "You too." She swung back across the grass to the buggy. *It's time for me to move on. And to do that I need to get Sir John Russell out of my mind.*

Forty-One

John straightened his leg to ease the cramp in his thigh and squeezed his eyes tight. He pressed the bridge of his nose hard between his thumb and forefinger to ease his brain fog and cursed silently.

It was one o'clock in the morning and he and Seb had been keeping watch on Virgil Hale's house all evening. It opened to a street at the front and a rough lane next to a children's play area at the back, so was accessible from both sides. John was at the street side, masked by a large tree whose trunk hid his profile, keeping watch for any visitors or other activity. Seb was around the back, making sure Hale didn't make a quiet exit that way.

His neck was stiff from being stuck motionless in one place for too long and he had a headache coming on. He gritted his teeth at Pania's retort this afternoon. Passive? *Well yes, it is passive, Pania, but what else do you want me to do? Got any ideas for flushing him out?*

He posed the silent question and knew he wouldn't get a reply from Pania. When she left this afternoon she looked thoroughly brassed off, and he still didn't have a clue why. When he got through all this stuff . . .

He was contemplating calling it a night and going home from yet another failed mission when he heard a low whistle to his left. Seb appeared from the back of the house and beckoned to him. He stole through the garden to his side and whispered, "What? Is something up?"

"Movement out the back," Seb replied. "A covered wagon's coming down the lane. Looks to me like Virgil's got a rendezvous planned." Seb ducked down low. "Come on."

Bent double in the dark, hugging the house's stone wall as partial cover, they crept to a hiding place under the eaves of a rotting garden shed, its roof partially caved in. Loose tiles littered their feet and were stacked around the sides.

They had to be careful not to knock anything over, but it was a good vantage point from which to survey the back of the house. No sooner were they settled in their new lookout than the wagon pulled up and the driver sat waiting, a cigar tip glowing in the dark the only sign that anyone was there. They sat like that, the driver smoking, Seb and John squatting in the shed, for fifteen minutes or more.

Except for a flurry from a pair of fighting toms, the street was deathly quiet. No lights on anywhere. Everyone was asleep. The cigar had been smoked and stubbed out and John was beginning to wonder if anything more was going to happen when the back door of the house squeaked open and a figure made its way hesitantly down the path towards the waiting wagon.

The flicker from the lantern the figure carried rested briefly on gray hair, and he made out a walrus mustache. Hale, lantern in one hand and what looked like a fully loaded-up carpet bag in the other, slunk from back door to carriage door. The driver saw him coming and got down from his front seat to meet him.

The men shared a low garbled exchange the watchers couldn't hear, and the driver opened the wagon door.

John nudged Sebastian's foot. "If he gets in we'll lose him," he mouthed. They'd been forced to leave their horses at Gold House, because they were too hard to hide from view in Hale's close-knit neighborhood Were they going to get this close to finding out something — God knew what — have to let him get away?

"Yeowww." The warring cats set up a renewed round of caterwauling and Hale's head snapped up, his eyes searching out the source of the noise. He was clearly jumpy, which gave John an idea. He picked up a pine branch with immature cones still attached that lay on the ground by his boot and shoved it at his brother. "Create a diversion," he hissed, the sound masked by the wailing felines. Seb nodded. John slid back behind the garden shed and, sticking as close to the far wall as possible, crept closer to the wagon.

As he slipped along, bent low so as not to be seen, he heard a violent crash behind him, and then a man's voice: "Bloody hell!" He smiled. It sounded just like the racket a pile of tiles would make falling from a good height. Then silence again, followed by another crash as more tiles came down.

Hale was searching the darkness with his eyes, his back to the wagon, gun in hand, when John emerged behind him, ten feet away. The deputy and driver stood fixated on the disturbance, facing away from him. He'd have to be careful. Very careful. He slipped his Remington pocket revolver with its neat little three-inch barrel out of his jacket and stole up to Hale.

He'd just placed the barrel hard up against his neck when Sebastian stepped out of the darkness, deputy badge displayed on his shoulder, his gun trained at the driver. "Stand still and you won't get hurt,' he said in a steady voice.

Hale froze. "What the devil?"

"Drop the gun," John said. "Drop it. Now."

Hale let the gun drop to the ground and John eased the barrel's pressure back. "Well, well, Virgil. Out late? And with a bag stuffed with goodies. Mind if I take a look?"

He reached around to grab the bag, but Hale held on tight. "Damn you, Russell. It's none of your business."

His fingers slipped, John tugged, and the latch popped and burst open. A cascade of sparkling gems fell to the muddy ground: pearls, diamonds, emeralds. He had only ever seen one collection like it, and he knew whose it was.

Sebastian had tied up the driver and was turning towards them as the bag disgorged. "Oh my, Virgil. Quite a haul you've got there."

"It's not what it looks like," said Hale. His voice had a hysterical edge. "I'm looking after them for someone."

"I can imagine. Well, we can relieve you of the responsibility. No trouble returning them to their rightful owner. I think we all know who that is, and she'll be delighted to have them returned."

He dropped the bag handle and gestured to Hale with his gun hand: "Pick them up." Hale fell to his knees and grovelled in the dirt, scooping up the gems along with dead leaves and grunge in reckless haste. He was terrified, and John realized with a jolt it wasn't fear of him.

"Seb," he said, looking around wildly. He didn't have a chance to say anything more. He sensed rather than saw someone in the lane approaching from the direction the wagon had rolled in from, and he just had time to shout a warning before a gun cracked close by. He dropped to the ground as he cried out, the taste of cordite thick at the back of his throat. Seb fell to the ground as well, rolling away from the wagon, but his left hand clasped his right shoulder and blood was streaming through his fingers.

John kicked out at Hale's lantern which had been left on the ground during the earlier disturbance, and followed Seb back to the garden shed. He was half-leaning, half-sitting against the inside wall, breathing heavily but still conscious. "Can you walk?" he asked urgently.

Seb nodded. "Yes, think so."

John looked back over to the wagon. Hale was grovelling in the dust, still shoving the jewelry back into the bag. A man emerged from the dark of the street and Hale turned and thrust the bag at his chest with a grunt that sounded like "Here."

The man took the bag, spat on the ground, and pushed Hale into the wagon ahead of the bundled-up driver. Then he sprang to the reins and started the horses moving. As the wagon turned in a circle and headed back out the way it had come, Sebastian slumped into a dead faint.

The dawn was breaking as John fumbled at the door of his suite. He could barely see to get the key in the lock, he was so bone-weary. Seb was resting at Doc Alexander's, his wound cleaned up and bandaged. He was weak from blood loss, but the doctor said he had good prospects of recovery as long as the wound didn't become infected. For the third night in a row he'd barely had any sleep. He groggily pushed open the door. Getting cleaned up would have to wait for later — he just wanted to collapse into oblivion.

As he stepped over the threshold he saw that a small night light had been left burning on the cabinet closest to the door. He took a few steps forward and tripped over a chair lying sideways, one leg broken, scraping his shin in the process.

His normally tidy temporary dwelling was trashed. The few items of clothing he'd bought to replace those lost in the fire — underwear, socks, pyjamas — tumbled out of drawers. The mattress hung half off the bed, sheets and blankets dragging along the floor.

He stood with his mouth open, staring. This wasn't a normal burglary. It had the mark of someone looking for something very specific. Something small and beautiful and rare, like the Dragon Seal. The wooden box that had held an older Remington lay open on the sideboard. He preferred the small one he'd taken out with him tonight, but the back up was missing.

As for the seal? Just as well it wasn't here to be stolen. He'd already consigned it to Sing Pak's safe hands for a special purpose. He stumbled over to his bed, hauled the mattress back into position, and then flailed wildly, hauling sheets and blankets around him like a cocoon. He was too exhausted to care about it. Any of it. He just had to sleep. He curled up his body like a sea shell, clasped at a soft blanket for comfort, and fell into dark dreams.

Forty-Two

Seb was going to be fine but he wasn't going to be up to deputy duties today, and John couldn't afford to wait. For Lily, every minute was precious. He had to get answers fast, and the only one he knew who could give them was Virgil Hale.

No one answered the door at Hale's house when he returned, and he wasn't at the jail or the deputies' office. John had trawled several of Grass Valley's most popular workingmen's bars when he caught sight of the paunchy lawman in a plaid shirt and fringed jacket in the doorway of a low dive on Cemetery Road. He caught up with him as he was about to ride off on a big, feisty-looking roan.

"Hey, Hale. I've got some questions." He stepped into the street ahead of Hale's horse and caught the roan's bridle under the animal's jaw. The horse pulled back in alarm. Hale glared. "What the hell are you doing?"

"You're not going anywhere. Not till I get some answers." John stood his ground, maintaining pressure on the horse to control it. "After last night you'd have to be expecting that."

"I don't know what you're talking about." Hale looked defiant, and John guessed he was considering running him down.

"For starters, Mrs Chung has not reported her jewels have been returned."

"I don't know what you're talking about." Hale's face reddened, and his breath came in sharp gasps.

"Come now, Hale. You had them last night. We both saw them."

"You saw no such thing." Hale's voice rose to a whine, his face screwed into an indignant scowl. A small group began to gather as passers-by saw a confrontation was developing. Early-morning drinkers from the dive Hale had exited from tumbled out onto the street and muttered to one another.

"What about Lily Chung, then? You know she's been abducted. She's a defenceless young girl. And you know where she is."

"I have no information on her whereabouts. None at all." Hale stuck out his bottom lip from under his mustache and looked like a mutinous child. "But of course, if you can tell me where she is, I'm happy to help you find her."

"I'm sure. Just like you're ready to return the stolen jewels." The back of John's neck was prickling hot and he swiped at it irritably.

"You be very careful who you're accusing, Sir John." Hale made no attempt to disguise his hostility. "Or you may find you're on the wrong side of the law yourself. Now let the horse go."

"Until last night I wasn't sure if you were corrupt or just plain incompetent, but I'm no longer in any doubt." John was burning up inside. He glared up at Hale, letting him feel the full weight of his contempt. "No doubt at all. You're both corrupt and incompetent."

He let go of the roan's head with a sharp flick, stepped aside abruptly and slapped hard on the horse's rump. It reared up and Hale was momentarily in danger of falling. Then he and the horse were gone, leaving grit and dust in their wake.

John spent the next few hours searching fruitlessly for Sing Pak, who was the only one he could think of apart from Virgil Hale who might have information about Lily. He was apparently lying very low, and no one could give him any indication of where he might be. On his way back to the Holborne for lunch, defeated by another failure, he was met at the door by a big man with a boxer's physique and wearing a deputy's badge. He had a tanned face, chiseled cheekbones beneath a wide brow; his jacket smelled faintly of expensive cigars.

"Sir John Russell?" He pointed to the badge pinned on his suede jacket and raised a dark eyebrow in inquiry.

"Sure. Who's asking?"

"Deputy Sheriff Elias Samson. From Nevada City. Investigating the murder of Deputy Virgil Hale."

"Virgil Hale? Dead? When did that happen?"

"About two hours ago." Samson regarded him warily. "Is there somewhere private we can talk?"

"I think anything we need to say can be said here." John's chest tightened. "How can I help?"

"As you wish." Samson drew a cloth-wrapped bundle from a leather pouch slung across his chest and carefully pulled away the fabric to reveal an ivory-handled Remington.

John recognized the gun immediately. He knew if he looked closer he would see a mountain scene engraved on the cylinder.

"Seen this before?" Samson planted his feet in a confronting stance, as if anticipating he might make a break for it.

"It looks very like one I own that was stolen from my rooms last night."

Samson regarded him coolly. "Is that so?"

John sighed inwardly. No point in mentioning his suspicions about who might have taken it — it would sound too far-fetched. "Yes. Someone turned the place upside down last night when I was out. That was the only thing I could see that was missing." He was slightly fudging the facts, but the detail made no difference to the underlying truth.

Samson threaded his index finger through the revolver's handle and spun it several times. The distinctive ivory handle caught the light as it spun. "Seems folks recognize this gun as yours, Sir John. And folks also tell me you and Virgil Hale had a fight in the street this morning."

"An argument. Not a fight. But yes, we did disagree. And in case you are wondering, no, I didn't kill him."

"I was wondering," said Samson. "And you can understand that you telling me you didn't do it doesn't count for much." He tucked the gun back in his pouch. "I want you to accompany me to the deputy's office to answer further questions."

"Where was Deputy Hale killed?" John had the unpleasant feeling of losing his footing crossing a river.

"I'm not at liberty to say. But your gun — if it is your gun — was found at the scene."

"It might be my gun, but I wasn't the one holding it."

"That's to be determined, Sir John. Now please come along." Samson's hand strayed to his hip.

John raised his hands away from his sides in a gesture of surrender and followed Samson out of the hotel and up the street to the deputies' office. A knot of bystanders was gathered at the door. He recognized several of them as the drinkers who'd been attracted by his argument with Hale earlier in the morning.

The mumbling got louder as they approached. "There he is!"

Samson bundled him through the door into the cool quiet of the office. After the clamor outside it felt eerily silent. The lawman gestured him to sit but remained standing himself, hands draped casually along the top of a straight-backed chair as he leaned forward. "So, Sir John, what exactly led to your dispute with Deputy Hale?"

Where to start? "Well, sir, it's tricky. I believed he was concealing information that could have helped in finding a missing girl."

Samson frowned. "What girl?"

"Lily Chung, my cousin Ollie's daughter. She was abducted three days ago."

"And this has been reported?"

"It didn't need reporting. It happened when Lily was in Hale's custody. She was in the courtyard out there while Deputy Hale was questioning her mother about the theft of some jewels."

Samson moved to perch on the edge of the table, arms folded across his chest. "Jewels? What jewels?"

"Selina Chung's very valuable jewels. I suspect Hale knows, knew, where they are and wasn't saying."

"You're accusing the dead deputy of corruption?"

"I'm suggesting Deputy Hale knew more than he was willing to divulge."

Samson raised an eyebrow. "Is that a crime?"

"It is if he was acting as an intermediary."

Samson stood up abruptly. "Really, Sir John!" His voice had a chiding edge of disapproval. "You are suggesting that Virgil Hale was crooked? Have you any proof of that?"

John had a tight band across the back of his neck, and the room felt as cramped as his muscles. "It depends what you consider proof," he said carefully.

"What do *you* consider proof?" growled Samson. He was growing more irritated by the second.

Telling him he'd stalked Virgil Hale last night would only make things worse. John shook his head. "I believe Deputy Hale has been in recent possession of the gems, but I have no idea where they are now."

There was a scrambling noise from the street and two men pushed through, carrying a litter between them. Virgil Hale lay on his back, his face contorted in a final anguish, the front of his shirt a deep red.

The crowd which had gathered on the street trailed in behind.

"Have you got him?" A surly man with a grizzly black beard and a grimy complexion thrust his head forward pugnaciously. "I saw him this morning. Interfered with the lawman, he did. Stopped him riding away. He should get what's coming to him."

Samson looked up in surprise at the invasion. Blackie St James was well known for organising a miner's strike for better wages; he was a notorious hothead even when sober. Men gave him a wide berth when he'd been drinking. His arrival was clearly a surprise to Samson, but not exactly an unwelcome one. John recognized some of the rugged individuals who were crowding in behind him. Jug Ears O'Callaghan, who spent his time conning and gambling. Scottish Sandy, a miner with a chip on his shoulder because he'd gambled away some promising stakes over the years and blamed others for his folly.

"Yeah. Shouldn't be one law for the rich and one for everyone else. As the preacher man says, 'The wicked can be sure of their wages, sooner or later.' We're just making sure it's sooner. Isn't that right boys?" The Scotsman looked around triumphantly, as the deputies' office continued to fill with malcontents and stirrers, attracted by the disturbance.

Samson was fast losing control, but he stepped up gamely to block the men from coming any further. "All right, all right, I'm in charge here." He pointedly rested his hand on his hip. "Move back and give us room. This ain't mob rule."

The room went quiet. The temperature felt as if it had lifted by ten degrees in as many seconds. Beads of sweat were collecting on Samson's forehead and dripping down his face. He went to a drawer and pulled out a pair of handcuffs, which he waved in front of the crowd. "Sir John Russell, I am arresting you for the murder of Deputy Virgil Hale." He motioned for John to proffer his wrists to the cuffs. The way to the door was blocked by the seething mob, and Samson was in a trigger-happy mood. He really had no choice but to submit.

He cursed silently as he followed Samson into the small holding cell, a sinking feeling in his stomach. A straw-filled mattress with its innards spilling through the ripped cover lay in one corner. Apart from the mattress the only furniture was a straight-backed wooden chair and a bucket. His eye caught the flick of a lizard's darting movement as it chased flies on the ceiling.

He had felt at a dead end in his search for Lily when he woke this morning. He hadn't guessed how much worse it could get. The metal barred door closed with a clang and the lock screeched shut. Samson hung the key on a hook high up on the wall. "Whether you're guilty or not, this is the safest place for you right now," he said. "Townsfolk don't like it when their lawmen get killed, and the fact that you'd argued and your gun was found next to Virgil is enough for them."

He turned to the men who crowded around. "Now you lot, get moving. There's nothing more to concern you here."

Forty-Three

"Nobody's going to lynch you, John. Be grateful for small mercies." Seb's calm, serious face flickered with a wry smile. His rangy frame was perched on a bench outside John's cell, the damaged shoulder dangling in a sling across his chest, his voice soft and low. He leaned forward awkwardly. "We can get a lawyer to spring you tomorrow. Just give it twelve hours for the heat to die down out there. We boys will ensure there's extra security tonight. This is just Samson's way of dealing with a restless town." The Nevada City deputy had gone back to base, leaving Seb in charge.

"I haven't done anything." John's voice was gravelly with boiling frustration. "My revolver was stolen last night while we were out watching Hale. And every minute I sit here Lily or Ollie are in danger. It's intolerable."

Nathan was sitting next to Seb, silently observing. Now he said, "The weekend's coming up. Think we can handle it if some hotheads get tanked up and come looking for trouble?"

"I'm making sure of it, Nathan. We're ready with back up if needed."

John stood abruptly and paced the few feet his cell allowed to the wall and back to the chair. "Seb, I don't think you're recovered enough to be involved in rough play. You should still be at home recovering." He squatted back down on his cramping buttocks. "Virgil Hale was corrupt, and I don't know if Elias Samson is any better. Neither of them has any interest in looking for Ollie and Lily."

Through the gaol's thick adobe walls he could hear the crickets caroling against a background hum of late-afternoon bar noises. The occasional sound of a glass smashing, the raucous shouts from men gathered around gambling tables. He took a deep breath. Even in here he could sniff the lingering odor of dust and sweat interwoven with yeast and charcoal; the Friday night aroma of beer and barbecued meat.

"I'm a fool for not realizing earlier that Ji Zeng's ambition had turned toxic." He looked directly at Nathan as he felt his shoulders slump forward. "I was so wrapped up in my own world I wasn't watching the bigger picture. I thought Ollie had it all under control. I guess he did too."

Nat gave a light shrug. "A reasonable assumption, John. Don't be hard on yourself."

"Not easy to do when the comprador died under my roof. I feel personally responsible." He turned to Seb, who looked pale and drawn. "Seb, old man, you should be resting. You'll damage yourself if things get nasty here. Please, I'll be fine."

Seb shook his head. "No, I want to stay. I'm a deputy. I have some authority. I don't want any disasters on my watch. Now, Nat, didn't you say something about cards? Loser buys the first round when life's back to normal."

Nathan produced a pack, dragged a low table from the office over to the bars so John could reach through to play a hand, and they settled to a subdued game of monte.

They'd chatted and challenged their way through four games when Nathan stood suddenly and stretched. "Think it's time for me to go and get you some grub. A late lunch or an early dinner. I haven't eaten all day." He nodded to John. "How about meat loaf and peas from the Holborne dining room? Won't be long."

He'd not been gone more than a few minutes when they heard loud angry voices and the outside wall shuddered under some heavy blows. Seb awkwardly reached his left hand to his holstered revolver. "What the blazes?"

A knot of men led by Blackie St James burst into the restricted space, bringing with them a smell of horses and bad breath. At St James's heels were the other men who had been clamoring for John's arrest earlier in the day. Scottish Sandy was so drunk he could barely stand, but Blackie was sober. He had the determined, fired up look of a man on a mission.

Seb stood gamely with his back to the locked cell door and faced them head on. "Whoa, hold up there. I'm a deputy. State your business."

St James stood forward confidently. "We know he's your brother, but that don't mean he's innocent. He killed Deputy Hale and we want justice."

The group concurred with surly yells: "Justice! We want justice!"

Seb stood firm, though his shoulders were heaving with the effort. "And you will get justice, when the circuit court judge gets here next week. Meantime, the prisoner is entitled to protection under the law."

St James viewed him with a contemptuous smile. "You think we believe that? One as rich as him will buy his way out and a lawman will have died for nothing."

The men with him jeered in agreement. The cell had suddenly become very hot and airless. John could feel his chest tightening and had to breathe deeply to draw enough air.

Scottish Sandy stepped up beside St James. "Yeah. Give ush the key. We want him out." His words were slurred, but the message was clear. The others joined in, advancing on Seb, chanting. "The key. We want the key."

Seb waved his revolver. "Keep back or I shoot. Keep back."

The men had momentarily paused when there was a shout from Jug Ears: "There it is! On the hook!" He lunged for the big iron key high up on the wall, and within seconds had elbowed his way up to Sebastian and shoved him aside.

Seb went down on one knee with a thump, still attempting to hold his healing wound together with his arm as he fell.

John jumped forward. "Sebastian! There's nothing you can do. Don't risk it." Too drunk to closely follow what was going on, and momentarily shocked by seeing Seb pushed aside, most of the group hung back like sheep, suddenly at a loss for what to do next.

Not so St James, who grabbed the key and unlocked the cell. With the Scotsman in his wake he shouldered his way into the tiny space. They grabbed John, one on each arm, and started dragging him out of the cell. They had wrestled him halfway through the cell door when a flaming hot roar cut through the fracas: "Let him go! Let him go *now*!"

Nathan stood in the entryway, a powerful Winchester rifle levelled at St James's midriff. The man froze, his eyes darting around the room like a frightened rabbit's, and the gaol fell silent except for the sound of heavy breathing. The air stank of whiskey breath.

Nathan stalked the perimeter, circling the unruly men, every step drawing him closer to his two brothers. Seb was hunched against the cell bars, barely conscious, his shirt stained with blood from his wound that had reopened in the violent tussle. John was half-in, half-out of the cell, still held roughly by his attackers.

The lines of Nathan's normally genial face were taut; his eyes shone with a ferocious glow beneath his straight eyebrows. He thrust the rifle barrel to within a few inches of St James' gut. "Three seconds to let him go, or you're dead. One. Two." He spat out the numbers with deadly menace.

As he sounded the first syllable of three, St James lost his nerve. He abruptly let go and stepped aside. Seeing his reaction, the Scotsman did the same, backing away uncertainly into the cell. John went to crouch over Seb.

Nathan brandished the rifle again. "Attacking a deputy when he is exercising his legal duties? That's a punishable offense. Leave quietly right now, or you'll all be locked up."

The core group of leaders exchanged hasty looks and retreated, muttering mutinously, and the rest staggered after them.

Nathan joined John at Seb's side and together they gently raised him from the floor to the bench. "Rest there. I'll go and get the doc." Nathan ran a jerky hand through his sun-bleached hair. "There's a good chance those ruffians will be back before the night's through. Why don't you seek refuge at Stockton House, John? We mightn't be so lucky next time. I'll look after Seb."

John squeezed Seb's good shoulder gently and bent low to speak in his ear. "Take care old boy, and thanks for everything." He turned to Nathan. "You too, Nat. I owe you my life."

Nathan shook his head. "It's nothing. But get out of here before they come back. You don't want the risk of meeting up with those madmen again."

John gave his brothers a silent salute, then pulled his hat hard down over his face and tentatively slipped to the doorway into the street. Family people were mostly at home at this time, preparing for dinner; those who were left in town were mainly menfolk sitting over drinks or card tables.

The air was caressingly gentle, and laughter from happy revellers in Main Street bars carried on the breeze. He paused briefly to smell freedom, a smoky blend of grilled meat and cheap cigarettes, and then melted into the golden afternoon to find his horse.

Forty-Four

"That girl there, second in line, she is definitely worth looking at," Harvey said. "We're having a good day so far. Two possibles for our spring tour. You must be a lucky talisman." He smiled at Pania warmly. "I really enjoy having you along."

They were seated at the back of the What Cheer cabaret, auditioning talent for a show Harvey would take on the road next year. Whether Pania and Grayson would be part of it was still to be determined.

She smiled and relaxed back into her chair. Harvey had the old-fashioned manners of a courteous Southerner. She enjoyed having her opinion considered respectfully, although she was unsure if being cosseted all the time would start to pall. Spending time with him had certainly given her new ideas. One of them was to ask herself why, if she stopped singing, she couldn't become an impresario herself. Already women theater managers were becoming accepted in California, no longer regarded as an oddity.

She dismissed the thought as quickly as it flicked through her mind. She was tired of the non-stop travel, staying in hotels and not having a settled home. If she promoted talent, wouldn't she be expected to travel with them? She wanted to marry again and — God willing — have children before it was too late. Harvey was an ebullient, kindly man who had done well for himself and understood her profession. She was growing more confident every day that he would be delighted at the prospect of marrying her. He'd already hinted as much.

So what was this brake she felt when considering him as a husband? She could imagine being married to John Russell, even though she knew his faults well enough to be realistic about what that would mean. There would be days on end when he'd be preoccupied with some deal or another. Times when he was short-tempered or so distracted he'd hardly notice her. She knew it, and she knew she could live with it. Indeed, she'd jump at the opportunity. Would it be wrong to marry Harvey when she felt that way about John?

She smoothed the skirt of her new day dress. It was one from Cressida's summer season, a gorgeous tangerine with black trim, and she felt like a queen in it. She ran her hand through her hair self-consciously to fluff it up a bit. John would like it. He always complimented her when she wore vibrant colors. He said it suited her exotic temperament and light-chocolate skin.

She felt a gentle touch at her elbow, and glanced up into fearful ebony eyes set in a flawless complexion. A young Chinese woman she didn't recognize stood there, her glossy black hair cut into a shockingly short gamine style that feathered around her face. "Mrs Hayes." She spoke in a trembling whisper. "Mrs Hayes," she said, in a stronger, more urgent tone. "I have an important message." She glanced at Harvey's back and her eyebrows contracted in uncertainty. "For you." She lowered her voice again. "A message for you."

Pania nodded. "I understand." She tapped Harvey on the shoulder and said quietly: "Just excusing myself for a moment. Won't be long."

She followed the young woman to the backstage area where ten days ago she had spoken to Ngo Wai. Her companion sank gracefully into a low chair and gestured for Pania to take a seat beside her.

She had a command of herself, this young woman, a sense of capacity and influence which suggested she'd been raised in privilege. As Pania dropped into the chair beside her she glanced once again at the bizarre haircut. Why someone of her class and station would chop off her tresses like that was a mystery.

The girl's hands were trembling in her lap: despite her carefully cultivated poise she was very frightened. Pania took the initiative. "Please, don't be frightened. You know my name. I want you to know that I will help in any way I can, if you tell me what is wrong."

The dark eyes flickered under sculpted eyebrows. She wore immaculately applied make-up which gave her the look of an expensive courtesan, but when Pania gazed at her slim face and clearly defined cheekbones she realized she was probably a lot younger than she first seemed — maybe no more than sixteen — and an innocent.

"I am Lai Jyu. My sister Beautiful Jade was the comprador's wife."

Pania suppressed a gasp. "Jade? Ting Hon's wife?" Pania's tongue felt fat in her mouth. Of course. What other comprador would she be referring to? "I did not realize Jade had a sister." She paused, uncertain how to continue. "You came to America with the comprador and your sister?"

Lai Jyu nodded. "Yes."

"And that explains the hair? You pretended to be a boy?" Pania knew it was much easier for Chinese men to get past immigration.

Lai gave a smile that for a moment softened the tension in her posture. "Clever you. I did. It made it a whole lot easier. Not so many questions."

"Where have you been staying since your sister and the comprador were . . . Since they so tragically died."

Tears welled in Lai's eyes but she sat perfectly upright and stared straight at Pania. "The comprador's household is still together. I am with them."

"You are quite safe?"

"For the moment."

"You speak excellent English."

"My father was a very unusual man for his time. He believed in educating all his children, not just his sons."

Pania nodded. Her respect for this composed young woman was increasing by the minute. "If there is anything I can do, I would be more than happy. Does Sir John know you're here?"

"No. Everything has happened so suddenly."

"I'm sure he'd be willing to assist." She reached across and gently took hold of the young woman's hands, which were moving restlessly; she drew them into stillness and softly stroked them. "I can only imagine the loss you're suffering."

"Thank you. Everything is still so up in the air. The comprador's household is waiting to speak to Ji Ming . . ." She left the rest hanging.

"I know. We're living in terrible times." She released Lai's hands and shifted back in her chair. "You mentioned a message?"

"Sir John. You know he too is in danger?" The girl's white face set into tense lines. "Since he was arrested?"

"Arrested? For what?" Pania felt as though she'd been struck with a whip. The shock couldn't have been greater.

"You didn't know? He was arrested earlier today for the murder of Deputy Hale."

"Murder? Ridiculous." A buzzing sound in her head made it impossible to think.

"But that's not why I am here." Lai peered at her through long black lashes.

"It's not?" Pania felt nausea rising and she clenched her hands to her sides in an effort to stop herself from slumping.

"No. The comprador's steward Chan Jong Ping believes Ji Zeng intends to marry Lily and get rid of both Ji Ming and Sir John. And now that Sir John is a fugitive, that's a lot easier for him to do."

"A fugitive?" Pania gave up all pretense of remaining calm. She half-rose from her chair with a cry. "Oh my God, no! What's happened?"

"I understand he escaped from a lynch mob a short time ago."

Pania stared at the girl as her mouth dropped open in shock. "Lynched?" The buzzing noise in her head had become a roar. She could barely hear what the girl was saying. She clasped her head in both hands and held on tightly. *Breathe deeply.* Slowly the noise faded and she released her hands, but the nausea in her stomach lingered.

"John will keep trying to find Ollie and Lily. He won't give up."

"That's what the steward thinks too."

"Oh!" She wrapped her hands around her middle, battling to ease the sick feeling. "He's going to get himself killed!" She was wailing, uncontrolled drawn-out cries, like a ship in fog.

Lai sat perfectly still and waited. "Mrs Hayes, that is why the steward sent me."

Pania felt another pulse course through her, another lash of the whip across her shoulders. "The steward? What for?"

"He wants to meet you. He says he has information that will help Sir John find Lily."

Harvey scowled at Pania across the small stuffy room. He was incandescent with anger at the idea of escorting her to meet the steward Jong Ping, but she pleaded with him until he agreed to come, though fury still burned in his eyes. He had already told her coming here was the most ridiculous thing he'd ever hear of.

Now they sat in a small, hot, tumbledown house on the fringes of Nevada City's Chinatown, after having been taken on a wild goose chase to shake off anyone who might have been following them. By the time the elderly steward shuffled into the tiny sitting room Pania was a jangling mess.

Jong Ping was a wiry, wizened-faced man accompanied by a much younger interpreter. After the formal introductions were completed he lost no time in getting to the point. "Mr Miller, Mrs Hayes." The young man bowed to each of them in turn with a respectful nod. "Jong Ping thanks you for coming. The loss of our master is a very great grief, and we seek justice. The household is very concerned."

Pania bowed towards him in acknowledgment, and just as the interpreter took a breath to resume his speech the steward broke in and addressed him again, the Cantonese dialect getting shriller and more agitated as he spoke.

When he finished, the silence seemed magnified, until the interpreter began again: "The comprador's steward says the situation is most urgent. There is no time to waste. It is said that if there is no settlement before Hungry Ghost Night it will be too late. All will be lost."

"Hungry Ghost Night? When is that? Is it tomorrow? The day after tomorrow?" Pania perched on the edge of her seat and gazed at Jong Ping, who was staring at the ground, seemingly lost in thought.

He looked up with a sharp glance. *He understands a lot more English than he's willing to acknowledge.* He spoke again to the interpreter, still insistent, but more measured than he'd been minutes before.

"Jong Ping says Hungry Ghost Night is tomorrow. It will be a very dangerous time for Lily and the others. It appears Ji Zeng plans a big celebration that night. It's essential Sir John attends. If he wants to save Lily and Ji Ming, he will have to be prepared to interrupt the celebrations."

Harvey was shaking his head silently. *Don't get involved.*

"Celebration?" she said. "But where? I don't think Sir John knows where Lily and Ji Ming are."

The interpreter and Jong Ping had a long discussion together. "The steward says Sir John would be wise to visit New Gold Mountain."

Pania asked Harvey. "Do you know a place called New Gold Mountain?"

He shook his head. "I don't."

"Where is it? This New Gold Mountain? Is it a place?"

Jong Ping burst into another passionate tirade — this time, Pania sensed, tinged with indignation. "New Gold Mountain is a mining camp about fifteen miles from here," said the interpreter. "In Chinese it is called New Gum Saan. When the gold ran out ten years ago, the white man abandoned it and the Chinese took over. Men have got scratchings of gold out of there ever since."

Pania's heart sank. John would need a small army to get into a town if it was patrolled by Zeng's guards. And as far as she knew, he didn't even know the place existed. And by tomorrow they were saying he needed to be there all primed up with a force to free Ollie and Lily.

Worse yet, if he was a fugitive, she had no clue where she could reach him to tell him.

Forty-Five

Pania shivered involuntarily. *First John, now Harvey Miller. Funny how you can think you know someone, and then they give you a glimpse of their shadow selves.* Harvey had been livid when she insisted she needed to return to Grass Valley immediately. She discovered that he didn't react well when things didn't go his way.

He lost his temper and issued her with an ultimatum: either she give up on chasing around trying to "save" Sir John or the tour — and, she guessed by implication, their friendly alliance — was over. He expected one hundred percent commitment and if she couldn't give that, she could forget it.

Pania's reached out to try and calm him. "Harvey, please. You've got it all wrong."

He flicked her arm away coldly. "Run after John Russell if you must. But don't come tripping back here when it doesn't work out."

Pania felt her face flush and a protesting growl rose in her throat. "I am not 'running after him'. I've been given information that could save the lives of three people. It would break my heart if I could have helped and I turned my back." She spread her hands wide in appeal. "Harvey, this is something I have to do."

He perched on the edge of his seat, distant and disengaged. "Then do it. Just don't expect me to be there to pick up the pieces afterwards."

She had just made the six o'clock coach that ran between Nevada City and Grass Valley, leaving Harvey standing on the sidewalk, bitterness etched in the deep lines in his cheeks. As she settled back in her seat she told herself he did not understand what was at stake. Or didn't want to. She didn't know which it was, and she had no time to care.

As the vehicle rattled and rolled over the pass she reflected on the blow-up. She had burned her bridges as far as anything personal was concerned, she was sure of that. Maybe he would soften on the idea of work — he always could put a dollar first when he chose to. But she had no regrets.

There was only one other passenger, an elderly gent who snored in the corner. Alone with her thoughts and the soothing rhythm of the carriage, she let out a deep sigh and relaxed. In this private space she could admit this wasn't just about Lily. She cared desperately about Selina's daughter, but she knew that wasn't the whole story. An equally dark shadow was John's predicament. As a fugitive on the lam it was open season. Anyone could shoot him and justify the act as apprehending a renegade. All she could do was alert Nathan and Seb to what Jong Ping had told her and hope they took it seriously.

The coach pulled into the courtyard next to the stables as the shadows were lengthening. Dust motes danced in the sun's slanted rays, and the earthy smell of rotting hay and horse dung hung in the air.

As soon as she alighted she recognized one of John's horses tied up on the stable fence. It was the work of a moment to slip next door and find Nathan. "Thank goodness I found you! You won't believe what I've got to tell you."

She recounted Jong Ping's story as they rode back up the hill to Stockton House, where Selena was in the lounge reading.

"Pania! Aren't you back early?"

"Oh, Selena, I have so much to tell you. Let's get everyone around the table and Nathan will explain."

An hour later they were gathered, Nathan and Graysie, Sebastian and Selena, around the dining table in turbulent discussion. "We have to move before dark." Selena thumped the table, her face screwed up in a determined scowl. "We shouldn't even be sitting here talking."

"I understand your urgency," Pania said, "but Seb, Nathan, I've an idea you're thinking it's best to leave it till dawn, especially with Seb's shoulder still bound up."

Graysie shot her a grateful glance. "I think Nat should slip into the Chinese camp outside of town and get as much information as he can about New Gum Saan tonight. Then they'll be better prepared for tomorrow."

"Great idea." Nathan leaned over and squeezed her hand affectionately. "And Seb, I'm sure you won't agree but do you think you should even be coming? Maybe you would be best here protecting the women and children — or, rather, child."

Seb made a face in response. "There's no way I'm leaving you to go it alone. Nelson can stay here with the household. If we need to we can ask a couple of the other neighbors to keep an eye on things too. I'm going with you."

Nathan sighed. "I knew I wouldn't win that one. But we'll have to take it carefully, protect that wound from reopening." Seb waved the remark aside.

"I suppose what you're saying makes sense." Selena's voice was resigned. "Now that we have some idea of where they might be, I can't bear the thought of a minute's delay. But I guess you're right. Better to go into it as well-prepared as we can be."

Nathan looked around their sombre faces. "I'll see if I can get maps and information from the Chinese camp. Seb, can you help organize supplies and then let's all get a good night's sleep for an early start."

"What about John?" Pania asked. "Is he safe? Is he coming?"

Nathan looked straight past her, his expression vague. "I don't know. Couldn't say."

Seb blinked and looked at the floor. "Me neither."

Liar liar, lick spit. You'd lie as fast as a dog licks a dish.

"How many of you are there going to be?" Her voice was unintentionally sharp, dismay skewing her mouth into a question mark. "Just the two of you? One and a half with Seb the way he is. No offense, Seb."

He shrugged and gave her a forgiving grin. "I know."

The back of her throat was parched and painful. "You're really going to need John."

Nathan patted her arm consolingly. "Don't worry, Pania. We're not giving up on him."

Pania tumbled out of bed in the dark before the dawn, ready to farewell the men who were assembling to leave for New Gum Saan.

Her throat constricted as she prayed they would return alive. Graysie stood alongside Nathan, her arm around him, her face pale and anxious. *I guess she has the same empty feeling.*

The crew they had enlisted to face up to the forces Ji Zeng could recruit looked meager. After much discussion they agreed they wouldn't call in the Nevada City deputy Elias Samson. The brothers had allowed John to escape, and even if they could argue it was to prevent a greater injustice being committed, they doubted he'd understand. And they knew he wouldn't take Jong Ping's information seriously either. Evidence from Chinese witnesses was inadmissible under Californian law. They would have to go it alone.

Seb's wound was raw and painful from the previous night but he insisted he could keep up. He was a sworn lawman, and the only one among them who'd been a soldier.

Would Nelson's boss join them somewhere? No one was saying, but Pania was pretty sure he would. He must, surely?

Saddlebags bulging, guns stowed, their horses huffing and snorting as if they sensed the significance of the occasion, the men said their farewells and rode out under a violet pre-dawn sky. Graysie turned towards the house. "I'm going back to bed for an hour, to snooze before Minette insists on getting up." She gave Pania a worried smile. "Nothing we can do now except pray."

"I'll just rest out here and listen to the birds waking." Pania couldn't face the confinement of four walls right now. Her legs trembled with the high-wire energy she felt before a big show. She paced down the rows of trees in the orchard, brushing her fingers through the seed heads of the tall grasses as she passed. The faint smell of night jasmine lingered in the warming, pollen-filled air. Far out on the forest edges she caught the mournful sound of an owl. She pictured the big bird perched, whooping, warning his chicks he was bringing the last mouse home before sunrise, and smiled to herself. Maybe she was loco, as Harvey said.

She wandered on, comfortable in soft cotton trousers, a long hip-hugging shirt and flat boots, the comforting caress of a light silk shawl around her shoulders, thinking about just one thing. John Russell. From the moment she'd heard he was in trouble she'd realized how impossible it was for her to turn away and make a life with someone else. Someone like Harvey Miller.

What a fool! And how unfair to Harvey! Her cheeks warmed at the memory of yesterday's argument. She had let him imagine a future together, but today she recognized how impossible that was for her.

She felt her world come to a grinding halt when confronted with the prospect of John jailed or dead, deprived of his natural term. *How could I ever live without him?* Since her husband's death, and especially in the last six months, their friendship had irrevocably changed to a deep love. Well, she corrected herself, it had on her part. How he saw things she still didn't really know, but she vowed that she wouldn't settle until she'd found out.

The violet sky was fading to eggshell blue and the first birdsong was chiming from the tree tops. She had mindlessly wandered onto a gentle path up the hill away from Stockton House, and paused to look back. Her feet had tracked a faint path in the overnight dew. A thin, blue smoke trail rose from the Stockton House chimney as the cook got breakfast under way.

She sighed and looked around for a log to squat on as she contemplated the peaceful scene. Her trail, the smoke, the floating notes of the waking birds, and further away, other trails — deer perhaps — circling up the hill behind her. She half-rose to look more closely when she heard a twig crack sharply behind her.

Before she had time to turn around, a strong hand came from behind and slapped a damp cloth across her mouth.

I'm suffocating. She worked her elbow in a fierce thrust into her attacker's gut, and heard the man grunt, but he didn't loosen his grip.

I'm going to die. She struggled to open her jaw to scream, but the man's hand locked it shut. Her chest was heaving but she couldn't get air.

I'll never see John again. Her shawl ripped — a tearing, sighing sound that seemed to go on for a long time — and fell away. With one last thrust she wrenched her hip to one side, desperately trying to break free, and a boot slipped off. She had nowhere to turn, and no air left to breathe.

Blackness. That's all there is.

Forty-Six

Selena and Graysie were sitting on a bench seat on the Stockton House veranda with Pania's lost shoe and ripped scarf lying on the table in front of them when a man rode up in a cloud of dust. He hitched his roan to the orchard fence and came towards them across the dewy lawn with long, determined strides.

Selena rose in sharp alarm and in a flash was down the steps and across the damp grass, her hand held up in an arresting gesture.

He didn't take the hint or sense her agitation but gave Selena a genial nod. "Good morning! Sorry for the early visit, but a word if you please. It's urgent." His strong confident bass voice matched his physique — tall, broad shouldered, and well-muscled.

Good morning? There's nothing good about it. She rounded on him. "Unless you've come to offer help, sir, then urgent or not this is not a good time." The words rang around the garden, strident and definitive, and the lawman finally detected their sombre mood.

He flicked his attention to Graysie, who sat with a rifle across her knees, and registered that additional piece of information with raised eyebrows and an impatient huffing noise.

Handsome all round, truth be known. He had uncompromising dark eyes under a cow's lick of dark brown hair, and an air of calm certainty that Selena itched to unsettle.

He addressed Graysie in mild reproof. "Really, ma'am, I can't see the need for weapons." Graysie glowered at him, but remained silent. He swiveled his body in a full circle, casting around him as he turned, and suddenly seemed unsure how to proceed. "Are any of the men folk at home? I need to talk."

Selena felt the bile rise in her throat; she kept her mouth firmly clamped while she fought back her anger. She lifted her chest and glared at this intruder who still hadn't had the courtesy to say who he was.

"I presume from the star on your chest, sir, that you are some kind of lawman. Enlighten us, please. What kind?" She deliberately laid on a Mayfair accent. *He can have a taste of the grand Englishwoman.*

"What kind?" The question seemed to catch him off-guard. "My apologies. I thought . . ." He shuffled uncomfortably. "Nevada City Deputy Elias Samson, ma'am, at your service. But I admit it. I'm nonplussed. What do you mean by 'what kind' of lawman? Are there more than one kind?"

A deputy with a vocabulary. And a sense of humor. That's novel. The sour taste stuck in her mouth. "What I mean, Deputy Samson, is are you a lawman who's interested in justice? Or are you looking for excuses to line your own pockets, like your colleague who purloined my jewelry?"

He took a shocked step backwards, as though she had spat at him, and his tanned face darkened further. He was struggling to master his offense at the insult, but today, right this minute, she didn't care. He deserved someone being rude to him. *Let him stew.* Having lawmen who were completely uninterested or worse, crooked, was one reason things had got to be as bad as they were. Ollie and Lily, and then John. It was already too much to bear. *And now Pania!* She glared at him coldly.

Samson raised one eyebrow. "I appreciate it must be distressing to have Sir John in his current situation. But going on the run will only aggravate the problem he's in, Mrs . . ." Selena glared.

"I presume you are some kind of Mrs." He stopped and considered them both with a more measured respect. "A Mrs who finds justice wanting? And is prepared to be rude because of it?"

Selena stared at the cheeky sod who was confronting her with the ghost of a wry smile in the shadow of his eyes. *Not just a vocabulary, but an ironic sense of humor as well. This is one damned amazing Yankee.*

Like a dam bursting, she began to laugh, a tinkling merry laugh which deepened into painful gasping that was close to hysteria. Graysie propped the rifle against her chair and came down the veranda steps to comfort her. "Selena, Selena." She patted her back gently, a calming, grounding touch. "Breathe deeply. We'll work it out. We will. You'll have to excuse us, Deputy Samson. We're still in shock." She took Selena's elbow and turned her back to the bench seat. "Sit down, sweet friend. I'll get some water."

Graysie disappeared and Selena quietened herself. She took a handkerchief out of her sleeve and dabbed her eyes.

The deputy stood, slack-jawed. *Frightened to speak in case it sets off another hysterical fit.* She nodded to a spare chair on the veranda. "Excuse me, Deputy. Everything's got so absurd it's hard to believe life will ever be normal again. This morning's events are just the icing on the cake."

Graysie returned with a tray with three glasses and a pitcher of water, picked up her rifle and resumed her seat.

"You think it's crazy a young woman sits outside her house with a rifle across her knees, fearful for what might be coming next?" Selena said. "You want to speak to the menfolk. Well, Deputy Elias Samson, the menfolk are off doing the work you should be doing.

And we're sitting here stunned because a short time ago we discovered our friend Mrs Hayes is missing. Gone. From right under our noses."

Her voice cracked and she shot him a look of desperate appeal. "Deputy Hale made it very plain he wasn't interested in our problems but, Deputy Samson, we need help."

Samson leaned forward, elbows on his knees, a concerned frown creasing his deep brow. "I can see you're in urgent need, ma'am. Forgive my intrusion. And now, if you care to, tell me what's happened. What's gone wrong?"

What's gone wrong? The question was enough to trigger another wave of hysteria in Selena, who broke into a coughing fit. *Where should I start? Shall we report Pania missing to the venal Deputy Hale? Try and chase after our menfolk and locate them before a posse does? Just who do we have to turn to?*

Graysie picked up Pania's boot. "Our house guest Pania Hayes, the celebrated singer, was here and now she's gone — but she left these. She was here at six this morning when she told me she was taking a short, early-dawn stroll to listen to the birds wake up. When we awoke an hour later she was gone. We went looking and we found this." She put down the shoe and picked up the torn shawl. "And this."

Selena chimed in, "Pania has not wandered off and got lost. She's been attacked and overpowered. The shawl had a slight smell of chloroform when we found it."

Samson sprang from his chair and moved to the table. "Do you mind?"

He gestured to the items, and Graysie shook her head. "Help yourself."

He picked up the shawl and buried his nose in it, before pulling back and examining it closely. "She was wearing this?"

They both nodded. "I think you're right. There is still a very faint whiff of something like chloroform on it. Show me where you found it."

Forty-Seven

"Deliverance or destruction. It will bring one or the other."

Sing Pak lifted his bright eyes from the elegant jade object nestled on a black velvet cushion displayed on a small desk in front of them. An anxious jolt pierced the deadening exhaustion that shrouded him as Sing Pak gazed into his face, his brow in worried lines. He'd got a few hours of restless sleep last night, after his pell-mell ride here, but it wasn't enough. He raised and lowered his shoulder blades a few times to ease the tension.

The deep furrows in Sing Pak's brow softened. "But you understand that already. Of course you do."

They were bending over the desk in a tiny room fitted out like an office in one of Nevada City's old Manzanita Ravine villas, a home that had belonged to Jong Ping's forbearers since the earliest days of Chinese immigration. The only furniture apart from the desk and a straight-backed chair was a basket-weave armchair draped with a plaid knee rug. On the desk a series of traditional quills were lined up next to an ink pot; leather-bound ledgers sat in an untidy floor stack and on shelves lining the walls.

"Yes, Sing Pak. No illusions. But I have to do it."

John took a deep breath, and an almost sacred silence filled the space between them. He wondered if he was just fatigued, or still in shock, that the emblem affected him so. Did he smell the comprador's orange-blossom fragrance again? He squeezed his eyes tight, and when he reopened them the heightened sense of reality was gone.

The jade token sat unchanged on its black cushion, a motif with the power to release gold, rivers of it. And only one in a hundred men would recognize the fatal flaw it carried. His heart punched with a sudden charge and alertness penetrated the gray blanket of despair that had so quickly snuffed out the euphoria of escaping the lynch mob. He tapped his foot nervously.

Originally settled by Chinese miners, Manzanita Ravine now housed a small black population as the Chinese had moved to Chinatown. Jong Ping's family had stayed put: because they had operated profitably and peacefully here for close to two decades they were left undisturbed when poorer Chinese were driven out of town in the late Fifties, before inevitably trickling back again. The wooden homestead had been rebuilt more than once after the city's devastatingly frequent fires, but it held on, clinging stubbornly to the hillside.

It was a perfect hideout for the comprador's family connections, and they'd kept their movements discreet in the days since they arrived. An ideal place, too, for a man like himself, a man labeled the killer of a lawman.

After he escaped the lynch mob, John knew Elias Samson would be coming after him, and Jong Ping's was the closest refuge. Hidden among more than a hundred other Chinese homes and businesses, it would be difficult for a lawman who spoke only English to find him. He glanced down at the jade piece. The sinuous lines of the stony green dragon, lit by a small oil lamp, were breathtaking in their simple beauty.

"You'd never guess it's fake, would you?" He flashed Sing Pak a hopeful smile, willing himself to show a confidence and martial spirit he barely felt. "Let's hope it takes Zeng a while to notice."

The plan to proffer Zeng a fake seal to buy time to rescue Ollie had been hatched when they last met, and John had entrusted Sing Pak with the original to take to a jade carver for faithful reproduction in every detail except one. It had been a last resort, a fallback option that he'd hoped he would never have to use. Now the day had come when there was no other choice.

"It's the only thing left, Sing Pak. I'm a fugitive. As I told you last night, you're taking a big risk even talking to me. I've already missed the deadline Zeng set for yesterday. Those hours in that gaol, going over everything — well, it made me realize my options have shrunk to zero. I have to step up and take the gamble."

Sing Pak regarded him steadily, stroking his wispy beard as he considered the situation. "I understand. But given all that, how are you going to guarantee he won't get tricky? You can't go there yourself. He'll be looking for any opportunity to double-cross you."

"I have to. He won't inform on me until he's got the seal. He knows if he does, he'll never see it."

"You're probably right there. But once he's got it? That's another story."

John slumped down in the chair beside the desk and reached over to pick up the seal and begin tucking it into a small black leather bag. "We'll talk about the handover. But before we get to that, has Walls heard any whispers about Deputy Hale's death?"

Walls — otherwise known as Wah Lee — was a faithful Russell & Chung retainer, an elderly clerk who had kept the company records for years. Loyal to Ollie and Ting Hon, he fed intelligence from Zeng's household to Sing Pak. Walls was like a piece of furniture, ever-present and barely noticed — just what you needed for 'walls to have ears'.

"I slipped out to meet him after you went to bed last night," said Sing Pak. "And yes, from what he hears, Hale was getting arrogant. Helping himself to Selina's jewels was his death warrant. He's been in Zeng's pay for months now, and he made the mistake of thinking he was indispensable.

"Of course, it was a touch of brilliance to carry it out with your gun. A case we'd say of good *chenyu*. One action, two targets. Or what you gweilo would call killing two birds." Sing Pak smiled grimly. "We have to find a way to get the Nevada City deputy to see what really happened — but I'm afraid he won't care about anything Walls says."

Sing Pak eased himself into the cane armchair and John sensed he was about to make a suggestion about the handover when there was a loud banging on the front door. He jumped to his feet, fear dictating his movements before he mastered the impulse. His hands were icy.

"You'd better go slip down in the tunnels before I answer that," said Sing Pak. "Just playing safe."

Like much of the town, the house sat over old — and in some cases still operative — mining shafts. The trapdoor Sing Pak opened led down into dimly lit, cobwebby wooden stairs. "Wait here. If you need to run I'll thump on the floor." He turned and left.

John heard the front door scrape across the sloping old floor, a little low on its hinges. Muted voices. Then a heavy male tread pushing into the hallway. He held his breath, straining to catch words. Air from the opened door wafted straight down the hallway, carrying with it the smell of dark plum tobacco.

Cuban cigar. He'd smoked it himself, and he knew where he'd last smelt the rum-tinged aroma. He pulled out a handkerchief and laid it over his mouth and nose to stop him sneezing in the dusty space. Then he sat, breathing in and out, long and slow, talking to himself. *Keep calm, take it easy.* He repeated the phrase like a talisman.

After what seemed like an age, he heard soft footsteps and the trapdoor above him creaked open. Sing Pak's body was framed in an aura of daylight from the upper level.

He slipped down the stairs and pulled the trapdoor behind him, making a silencing gesture with his raised index finger against lips as he descended.

When he got level with John he stopped and placed both hands on his shoulders and gave him a comforting squeeze, whispering, "You must leave by the back way. Go along the right-hand tunnel until you come to a Y junction and take the right fork. It will bring you out at street level on Commercial Street, in the middle of Chinatown."

The old man thrust the plaid rug from the office at him. "Take this. Use it to obscure your face as much as possible. The man I've got upstairs is Deputy Samson, and he's looking for both you and Zeng." He swallowed hard, reluctant to continue. His mouth worked but no sound came out, a sure sign he was agitated.

John jumped in with the first question to come to mind, his voice a hoarse whisper: "How did he know to come here, for God's sake? Hardly a soul, Chinese or gweilo, knows you're here."

Sing Pak's voice wavered. "He went to Jong Ping's family store in Commerce Street and asked where he could find Chung Ji Zeng. It's one of the few places with people who speak English, as you know. They were terrified they'd get into trouble whether they talked or whether they didn't, so they sent him here. I'm going to have to deal with that — we're just getting him some tea. I have to be back there any minute." He cleared his throat and ran his hands down his tunic with a jerky movement. "The fact that he's here. That's not the worst of it, John."

John's stomach cramped. He tried to swallow to ease the

discomfort and his mouth was dry. "What is it, Sing Pak? Out with it. What's the worst news?"

"He's investigating a report that Mrs Hayes is missing. Selena's been talking to him. He says it happened this morning. Just in the last few hours."

John's heart jumped so hard he was surprised it was still caged within his chest. He ran his hands through his hair, tearing at it as if the pain might wake him up to what he must do next. From beating faster, his heart slowed so dramatically if felt like it was in danger of stopping entirely. "What happened?"

"Deputy Samson says he called on Stockton House to check if they'd seen you. None of your brothers were there, but Ollie's wife was upset and very vocal. She told him Mrs Hayes went for an early-morning walk and never returned. I wonder about Nat and Seb. I presume they're looking for you. They might be the next ones to turn up." An ironic smile flickered across his face. "Anyway, Selena found one of Mrs Hayes's boots and a ripped shawl up the hill not far from the house. The grass was all stamped down in one area around her and there were heavy men's bootprints in the dirt.

"Deputy Samson says he's satisfied there has been foul play. And Selena was very persistent about him questioning Zeng. I think she's got him thinking, but you mustn't take risks in the meantime."

John's shoulders sagged. Could things get much worse? He put one hand up to the bridge of his nose and held tight. *Keep calm, take it easy. It will be all right.*

Except he couldn't see any way in the world how it possibly could be.

Forty-Eight

"So do you want the seal or not? It's up to you."

John Russell glared at Ji Zeng and willed himself to betray no weakness. After he'd scrambled out from under Jong Ping's house he'd tried Zeng's home and been turned away. The master wasn't at home, the servant said. So he turned to the Sing Song Club, the only other place he knew where he might flush out Zeng — and his gamble paid off.

At eleven in the morning the place was dimly lit and empty. He wondered why Zeng himself was here. Ollie's half-brother looked as sleek and confident as a bull seal in charge of his harem. Like a man who was certain he held all the winning cards. If he did indeed have Pania, John had to concur. The stakes were high and his own leverage pathetically low.

Zeng shook his head, his mouth set in a derisive curve. "No. You had until yesterday. That was the deal. I said Friday. And you didn't deliver." His eyes gleamed with hidden triumph, a man with a trump card he hadn't yet revealed but couldn't resist secretly gloating over.

John gave a slight shrug. "You've got me there." He tried to look suitably contrite. "But what's twelve hours in the grand scheme of things? I presume you still want it?"

Zeng gave him an amused smirk. "Sorry. Made alternative plans.

I'm not looking to trade — well, not for Ji Ming, anyway."

"Why not? You know you can't do business without it."

"Yes, but I don't need Ji Ming or his trollymog of a daughter. Anyway, why the change of heart?"

John cast his eyes to the floor. "Ah well, things change. You've held Ollie and Lily long enough. We want them home."

Zeng's face hardened. "I told you. Too late. You had your chance and you missed out. Now you've got to pay."

"Oh yes? And what exactly does that mean?"

Zeng picked up a small silver bell at his elbow and rang it vigorously. Within half a minute a man with a wrestler's build — he looked Mongolian — appeared. For a big man he moved with speed and fluidity, his black tunic with golden dragons magnifying the sense that he'd materialized from thin air. Zeng beckoned him close and whispered to him behind a sheltering hand, and the Mongolian withdrew as quickly as he'd arrived.

John felt a chill run up his backbone. Something had changed during the mysterious exchange, reflected in the ice that gripped his vital parts. He sensed he'd lost any initiative he might have had, and yet he was clueless about what had just occurred.

"So you had it all the time." Ji Zeng reared back on his stool, increasing the distance between them, cold eyes mirroring a mocking sneer that held a hint of admiration.

John shifted uncomfortably. "The seal? No, I didn't have it. Ting Hon did."

For a fraction of a second, a flicker of doubt ruffled Zeng's composure. "Ting Hon? Why would he have it?"

"I have no idea. I haven't had any chance to talk to Ollie, and your father didn't mention it. I found it in the ruins after the fire."

Another flicker ruffled Zeng's arrogant equilibrium. Was it irritation? Annoyance?

"You were there, weren't you?" He watched Chung Ji Zeng's face intently, and saw a brief meteor of uncertainty illuminate the mask. "You killed him." It wasn't a question. "So near and yet so far." Despite himself he'd assumed a mocking edge. "See, Ji Zeng, if you'd asked nicely you could have had the seal without killing him. All that trouble for nothing."

Zeng's pallid complexion flushed a light pink. "Nothing?" Zeng spat the word. "Nothing?" Louder this time. "I've had enough of being Second Son. Always having to defer to First Son. When I get the seal, I get the business. And Ji Ming can rot in hell."

The dusky flush drained from his face, leaving his cheeks chalk-white, with darker shadows traced in the lines that ran from the corner of his eyes to his jawline. His irises had deepened from brown to black, the pupils contracted to sharp points of loathing.

"Two lives extinguished, and my home destroyed." John's voice was dangerously quiet, close to a whisper. "And for what? Not to mention the deputy killed. I've no doubt that was your handiwork. By proxy, no doubt. Nice touch to use my gun to do it!"

Ji Zeng reared back and laughed. "It was brilliant! How does it feel to be a wanted man?"

John smiled grimly. "You think you've won, Zeng, but it's not over yet." His voice was hardly more than a croak. He closed his eyes and for a moment was comforted by the spicy sweetness of Ting Hon's orange-blossom oil. He breathed it in, deep into his spirit.

He relaxed into the padded seat. The citrus aroma was emphatic and bright. It tickled his nose, and for a moment he imagined the man himself was by his side. He was whispering that everything was going to be all right. He let out a long sigh, and felt himself back in his father's house on Queen's Road.

Yes, everything was going to be all right. Despite the dark and the blood on the floor. His earliest memory flooded him. He was hiding behind a big urn in the hallway of the house where he'd grown up, mesmerized by the big pool of red on the floor a few feet away. He didn't want to look at it, but he couldn't drag his eyes away. It was going to be all right, despite his mother lying there, very still at his father's feet. Despite the funny sharp smell. She wasn't getting up, and his father was making scary noises that sounded like the horse he'd once seen screaming when it broke its leg.

Everything would be all right, because Ting Hon was suddenly there at his father's side. Ting Hon, who came with flares to chase away the darkness, and with servants to carry his mother to bed and to give him honeyed herbal tea that made him so sleepy he couldn't be afraid any more. Ting Hon made everything all right.

He slowly opened his eyes. He was unsure whether he wanted to come back to this reality — Ting Hon slain at the hand of his second son, with Ji Zeng glaring and unrepentant — or stay huddled in the dark with his dead mother.

"Ting Hon has no rest," he said.

Zeng sneered. "What? Going all Hungry Ghost superstitious are you?"

John shrugged. "Not necessarily. But some outrages cannot be silenced. They cry out for retribution. The orange blossom. Can't you smell it?"

Ji Zeng shook his head vigorously. "You're mad. Your age is getting to you."

John regarded him coldly. "Time will tell." He stood up, flexed his shoulders forward and back to shake off the torpor that had overcome him. "So what's it to be? Do you want the seal or not? It's in a bank deposit box. No one but me can uplift it. No one but me knows where it is. So you'll have to rely on me to provide it. Killing me won't work. And if you turn me in you'll never see it again."

"All right. We'll play your little game. Come by my house at one o'clock. Make sure you're alone and you have the seal."

"And you'll have Ollie and Lily ready to hand over? That's the deal? Or have you got something else in mind?" John waited for him to show his hand, play his trump card.

A cold sneer played across Zeng's face. "I've got the Royal Flush here. You're merely holding a Joker. You'll have to wait and see, won't you? But I can tell you one thing — fail to show up with the Dragon Seal and you'll never see your precious cousin again."

Forty-Nine

Within seconds of John rapping on the front door of Zeng's house on upper Commercial Street it flung open, held by the silent powerhouse of the bodyguard he'd seen at the Sing Song club an hour ago.

Without comment or greeting, the muscleman led him through a narrow hall to the back of the house which was configured in a very similar floor plan to Jong Ping's family home up the valley: a narrow hall, lined with closed doors, leading to a back parlor. John assumed that this house too would have a quick exit into underground tunnels, and fleetingly wondered if any of the people he cared about — Ollie, Lily or Pania — were at that very moment held captive in the darkness beneath.

The thought had barely registered when Zeng slipped into the room, dismissed the Mongolian, and looked at him, his black eyes jittery with excitement. "So you came back." He fixed him with a cold glare and opened his palm facing upwards. "Where is it?"

John returned the steely stare. "Oh no, Zeng. This is an exchange. You know that. So go get Ollie and Lily. I need to see them." He raised his voice a notch. "Get them now or no deal."

He could hear the loud tick of a clock somewhere, and felt mildly reassured by the pressure against his chest from inside his jacket. Sing Pak had last night insisted he take a concealed pocket pistol, no bigger than the one that killed President Lincoln. He said he might need it in an emergency and John sensed that emergency was fast looming.

Zeng stood abruptly, a ghostly smile playing at the corners of his mouth. "You got me there, old boy." The eyes were mocking. "Ollie and Lily? No. You won't be seeing them today."

If he expected to see John start with surprise, he was disappointed. John sat rock-calm, though his blood was racing. *Here it comes. The big revelation — that he's got Pania.* He made as if to get up and leave. "No Ollie? No Lily? I'm wasting my time then. And you are too, because there's no deal."

"Not so fast." Zeng swayed, like a deadly snake positioning for a venomous strike, drawing a pistol from the back of his belt. He motioned to the back left-hand corner of the room. "Raise your hands and get over there."

John moved with slow deliberation, desperately running his options through his mind as he moved. *Overpower him? He's not particularly big.* But the big Mongolian out in the hall could crunch a man's neck with his bare hands.

Pull my gun so we have a Mexican standoff? That might end like a bad duel, with both of them killed to no end.

He turned and gave Zeng his most infuriatingly confident smile. "I hope you're not contemplating robbing me of the seal and leaving me for dead. If you are, I have to tell you I'm not stupid enough to come in here with the thing in my breast pocket. For reasons that I'm sure are obvious. When I'm satisfied you've got the trade, then I'll arrange for the delivery of the emblem, and not a minute before."

The gun momentarily wavered in Zeng's hand. "I said no Ollie, and no Lily. But that doesn't mean I haven't got something you'll want. Oh yes, want very badly."

Here it comes. The outline of Zeng's body, his triumphant stance with gun raised, clouded momentarily as blood pounded at his temples. He swallowed to moisten his throat. *Slow down. Don't let him see he's got you hooked.*

He made a show of perching on the arm of a chair that sat in the corner, then slumped forward, hands on his thighs, within tantalizing reach of the gun. "Something I'll want? I can't imagine that you'd have anything I'd want, apart from Ollie and Lily. Do tell." His voice was oily, and Zeng's face twisted in dislike. The needling was getting to him. "I can hardly wait."

Zeng rapped out a sharp order in Cantonese — plainly intended for the invisible bodyguard, and spoken so quickly it was indecipherable. A pre-arranged signal. John looked to the door expectantly. It stayed shut. With a thudding creak, the floor next to his foot vibrated, the rug slipped awry, and damp musty underground air gusted into the room from an opening trapdoor.

He jumped back as the bodyguard thumped up the dusty wooden stairs, his huge shoulders barely scraping through the gap. In front of him he held a woman, his beefy hand clasped at the neck of her clothing as she dangled like a rag doll, her head lolling to one side. She was unconscious, her arms dangling. Something peculiar had been done to her head, the hair shaved high off her forehead and around her ears.

John took an involuntary step forward. Even though he'd been warned, been expecting it, his mind would not fully comprehend that the woman dumped like a bag of flour on the floor at his feet was Pania Hayes, the Queen of the Concert Stage.

Her glorious mane of black hair had been shaved at the front and sides in a parody of a Chinaman's queue. Her clothes were ripped and stained and her left cheek — the only part of her face he could see — was bruised purple. The larger-than-life spirit was completely quenched; without it she seemed much smaller, more fragile.

He swung to face Zeng. "What the hell is this? What are you playing at?" Fury flowed white-hot through him. "You've abducted her like a common criminal, rendered her unconscious, beaten and abused her. To what purpose?" His words were hard, cold and staccato.

Zeng shrugged, unapologetic. "She's my insurance policy. A back-up piece to be played when the time is right. And the time is right now. I've swapped bargaining chips." His insolence hardened into contempt, thighs spread, pelvis thrust forward, a gun slinger's stance. "You needed an incentive. Obviously saving saintly Ollie wasn't good enough bait. I needed a sweetener." His eyes narrowed. "The Dragon Seal. I want it now."

He lowered the gun to Pania's inert form. His eyes were flat. Dead. "When I get the seal you can take her wherever you like. Until I get the seal, she stays."

John glanced down and saw Pania's lashes flutter. Her mouth trembled, and a thin moan escaped.

"Okay. Okay. Don't shoot. I'm moving." His hands were at his sides, and he made a big display of lifting them slowly upwards.

Zeng's breathing quickened. He motioned to the Mongolian. "Search him."

The enforcer took a step over Pania's body towards him and had just grabbed him roughly by the shoulder when there was a loud knock on the door from the hallway. It opened a few inches and a reedy, elderly voice wavered through the small gap. "Chung Ji Zeng, you have an important visitor."

Zeng snarled, "Not now Wah Lee. I'm not to be disturbed."

The door banged shut, but not before John caught a fruity whiff of Cuban cigar. "Tell your goon to keep his hands off me," he said. "I'm perfectly capable of extracting the Dragon Seal without his help."

Zeng's face lit up in triumph. "Do it."

He slipped his right hand into his side pocket. With his left hand, he slowly pulled out the leather bag and dangled it in the air. "Tell your man to pick up Pania and put her in that chair by the door."

Zeng nodded to the Mongolian. As the man dragged Pania to the chair, she raised her head fleetingly.

John saw in the brief flickering of her eyes that she was aware of what was happening. He stepped silently across the floor and dropped the leather bag onto a small table in front of Zeng, who stared at it as if mesmerized, thrust the pistol into his waistband and reached to pick it up.

It's now or never. John ripped the pistol out of his jacket and yelled, "Stop! Tihng dai!"

He turned to the Mongolian and roared in Cantonese, "Stand next to him or you're dead!"

The man hesitated then, shoulders slumped forward, lumbered to Zeng's side.

"Now both of you kneel. Hands on your heads. Say your prayers if you can remember how."

They gazed at him, incredulous dazed stares, but reluctantly knelt.

"You killed Deputy Hale in cold blood. You or one of your men. Why shouldn't you suffer the same fate?"

The room was unnaturally silent. The heightened sense of reality he'd experienced a few hours ago was here again. Time slowed. All his senses were on high alert.

He could divine without looking at her that Pania was getting stronger; he could hear her steadied breathing. He kept talking, quietly, deliberately, working to keep Zeng's attention focused on him, as he edged across to her. "So why kill Hale, Zeng? Not just so you could implicate me, I wager"

Zeng gave a contemptuous snort. "Of course not. Just my good joss. My man was looking for the seal and found the revolver. Figured if he couldn't get one thing off you, he could at least get the other. The rest just fell into place. Hale was getting too big for his boots. Tried to grab those jewels. He thought he could whip his weight in wild cats. He found out he couldn't. And that's no loss to anybody."

Pania's bare feet made a whispery sound on the wooden floor as she attempted to stand. In a flash John changed the gun from his right to his left hand, and leaned to scoop her onto her feet, eyes still fixed on the two men. Her body was warm against his side, and lighter than he'd expected. She was doing her best to bear her own weight, but she was weak. Without his supporting arm he sensed she would fall. *The main thing is, she's alive, thank God. The rest we can take care of.*

He was painfully aware that the Derringer carried only one bullet. If he had to use it, it would have Zeng's name on it, but he had no intention of killing anyone. Unless it was to save their own lives.

"Put the seal back on the table, Chung Ji Zeng. Your reckoning day is still to come, but it won't be at my hand."

The words were just out of his mouth when the door he was standing by flew open, striking him on the shoulder and jolting the Derringer from his hand. He stumbled, bending to shelter Pania.

Zeng and the Mongolian leapt to their feet, Zeng's pistol already whipped out of his waistband.

Deputy Samson stood in the doorway, a Remington revolver pointed at Zeng and the Mongolian. "Hands up!"

Zeng muttered something low in Cantonese to his man, who stood with his hands raised, eyeing Samson. Then without warning he charged, head down, coming on like a raging bull. Zeng was across the room and through the still open trapdoor before Samson's Remington thundered and the Mongolian's rush was arrested. He faltered and then fell, blood gushing from a stomach wound. Pania screamed and fainted. John caught her in his arms just before her head struck the floor.

Samson stood transfixed, eyes wide with shock, gasping. John settled Pania's limp form into the armchair and she opened confused eyes. He turned to the deputy. "I presume you heard all that. Don't say I didn't deliver the guy who murdered your deputy right to you.

"I trust this means I'm no longer a wanted man?"

Fifty

Pania slumped against the reassuring strength of John's shoulder, his arm braced around her back, holding her steady. Despite her dizziness a sense of warm security washed over her. He'd held her close as a dance partner at the balls when they were younger, but that was different. She'd never before experienced the warm intimacy that trickled up from the soles of her feet to her core as she relaxed against him. It was almost worth pretending to be out of it a while longer to prolong the closeness.

The sun that shafted through a window into the small room made her eyes smart, and she let them flutter closed again while she savored his strength. They were in some kind of gaol. The shadow of cell bars spilled across the floor, and she heard the soft murmur of men's voices. . .

How did I get here? What happened? Then it all came flooding back. The dew sparkling on the grass. The early morning birdsong — and then the stifling, eye-watering cloth jammed over her face. *When was that?* She calculated. *Unbelievable. Only yesterday.*

She jolted fully alert and ran her hand over the top of her head. Her hair! They shaved her hair to humiliate her, to send John a message that nothing in his domain was safe. She uttered an involuntary cry as her hand went to her hairline and felt the high smooth band across the front of her head. John started beside her, readjusting his arm and partially withdrawing his support.

"Pania, it's all right. You're safe here."

Her eyes flew open as she remembered the loud report of the gun, and the man who had abducted her falling bleeding in front of her. Her hand flew to her mouth. "That man! Is Lily . . . ?"

John's eyes glowed with a soft light. "We're still looking for Lily. At least you're safe. I'm so sorry for what you've endured."

She bit her lip hard to hold back tears. "Goodness knows how you knew where to come, but thank you for rescuing me. If you hadn't come I don't know what would have happened."

John patted her arm gently. "Thank Selina for sounding the alarm with Deputy Samson."

The deputy made a demurring gesture. "Just doing my job, Mrs Hayes. Very thankful we got here in time."

"Have you found Zeng?"

"No, 'fraid not. He slipped away into the tunnels and escaped. It's just a matter of time, though."

"Time? But we haven't got time, have we? He'll be furious. He'll probably go straight to Ollie. And what about the seal? Did he take that?"

John's face suddenly looked lined and drawn. He nodded affirmation.

"So it was Ollie's life for mine. Is that what it came down to?" Her voice sounded high and tinny in her ears. "Oh, John. I'm so sorry. I should've listened." She couldn't finish without breaking into tears.

"It's not your fault, Pania." John removed his arm and she felt an immediate sense of loss. "We'll just have to find another way to get him and Lily out. We still don't know where they are, that's the bind of it."

She looked at him in astonishment. "You don't? But I thought your brothers would have told you—"

"My brothers? I don't understand." He was blinking rapidly, mouth open. "I haven't seen my brothers since yesterday. Deputy Samson, you said Selena was deliberately obtuse about where my brothers were. Neither she nor Graysie would say."

Pania put her head in her hands and twisted it from side to side, making distressed sounds as she did. "No! Please God!" She straightened, looking from one man to the other. "That's what I came back for. That's why I was at Stockton House yesterday."

John ran his hands through his thick black hair. "Came back?" he said. "I don't understand."

"I came over here to Nevada City with Harvey. Someone approached me, one of the comprador's family — his wife's sister, in fact — and said they needed to get an urgent message to you that Ollie and Lily were being held at New Gum Saan. The old Dogville Creek mine, fifteen miles out in the mountains. Zeng plans to put Ollie on trial or something on the final night of the Hungry Ghost Festival. I went back to Stockton House to warn Seb and Nathan. I thought they'd be able to get word to you somehow."

She looked apologetically at Samson. "No offense, deputy, but we stick together. We knew John had nothing to do with Virgil Hale's killing. He's just not that sort of man."

Samson grimaced. "I'm sorry to say Deputy Hale let us all down. I've apologized to Sir John about that."

Pania stood up with a rush, and swayed on her feet. John jumped forward and grabbed the tops of her arms to steady her. "Woah. You're still whoozy."

She sat down again with a thump. "Yes, yes, afraid I am. But we can't waste any more time. Because of me, Zeng might get to Ollie and Lily before we do. Now he's got the seal, there's nothing to stop him, is there?"

Fifty-One

Hurry up old man! Ji Zeng took a long sip of tea to quell his rising impatience as he eyed the old man who sat across the table from him. Harry Chow was at least ten years younger than his father, but he gave the impression of being much older. Doddery, even. But Harry was the president of the most powerful of the Six Companies, and had already established himself in the vice business. If Zeng wanted a piece of the action, this was the man who could open the door for him. This was his final hurdle. Pass the test with Harry Chow, and he'd be free to pursue his ambitions.

"Fine piece of work. Your father had it made, is that correct?"

Harry was turning the Dragon Seal over in his fingers, caressing it as he examined every flowing curve.

"His father's father, actually." Zeng had no time for long family histories. Conventional inheritance rules decreed that Ollie was the head of Chung Trading's China side, and he wasn't prepared to live with that.

Harry Chow raised his eyebrows and looked at him over the carved block of jade. He had a round moon face, big yellow teeth, and fleshy jowls that hung under his chin and spilled over his collar. Sitting there in his richly worked emerald brocade robe, he looked as if he had stepped out of an Imperial court.

By contrast Zeng wore a modest tunic in purple silk shot through with tiny flecks of turquoise. He leaned forward, silently gloating over the exquisite carved lines of the seal with its intricate dragon design. It had cost the life of one of his retainers, but what was that in the total sum of things? And that deputy? It would be easy enough to manage him. He tugged at his tunic cuffs, rousing himself for the next challenge. It had been easy to slip away from the deputy into the darknesss, and wait him out. His focus returned to the quiet room, and the business at hand. He imagined a river of gold flowing from the writhing form. It was said the dragon brought power and riches to those worthy of it. *Those not afraid to go after it, like my older brother.*

A narrow-faced, full-bellied man sat at Harry's side, watching but not speaking. His bodily amplitude might lead an observer to think he was a jolly, easygoing bon vivant who put pleasure before duty. The hawkish, piercing cold eyes which sat above the sharp cheeks and thin mouth quickly dispelled that impression.

If Harry Chow was the figurehead, Lai Choi was the power behind the throne. *I need to treat him very carefully. Offend him and I'll regret it.* Ji Zeng snapped his fingers to signal to Wah Lee, who hovered anxiously in the hall.

"I'm sure Lai Choi would like more tea and mooncake." He nodded towards the dignitary. Lai Choi's chilly manner thawed and he proffered his cup to Wah Lee. "Very kind, thank you." The coal-black eyes that bored into Zeng were still icy.

"Where is your brother Ji Ming? He hasn't been seen for some time, I understand?"

"Traveling, I presume. I haven't heard from him."

Another penetrating stare. "And he doesn't worry that the business is being left to Second Son to run?"

"Apparently not."

"He is in favor of the things you are planning, however? You've discussed it?"

"In broad terms. He leaves the detail to me."

Lai Choi responded with a stare void of emotion.

Harry leaned towards Lai Choi and handed him the seal. Lai glanced down at it, and ran his index finger over the stamp face. "Something very special about a dragon chop," he said as he fingered the stone. "Holds tremendous power."

Zeng thought of the cascade of wealth it would bring him and nodded in agreement.

"Very bad joss, the comprador dying as he did,' Lai Choi continued. "My sincere condolences for your loss." His darting, calculating eyes did not convey sympathy. "Have you found out what caused the fire? Very strange that. Very bad joss again. And with such a lovely young wife too."

"I believe the law is still investigating," Ji Zeng lied. "But enough of this. Tell me, have you got the documents ready? That's why we're here, isn't it — to finalise our arrangements for the *White Cloud* shipment?"

Lai Choi was still peering at the Dragon Seal. He glanced up with a dark expression and eyed Zeng keenly. "It's most odd to have the two top men in the Black Dragon Benevolent Society both unavailable. Most unusual. Who gave you this chop?"

Ji Zeng bristled at the presumption of the question, but he reined in his annoyance. If he had to curry favor by being obsequious, he would. "My father left it with Sir John Russell for safekeeping and he passed it on."

Lai Choi's eyes lit with surprise, but he remained silent. He leaned towards Harry. "Call in the clerk. We need the papers."

Wah Lee materialized as if by magic rather than eavesdropping. "You called, sir?"

"Get Lai Choi's clerk from the staff quarters and join us here," said Zeng. "Quickly."

A few minutes later Wah Lee shuffled in holding one parchment roll, while a lanky, much younger man held the other. "Your agreement, sir," Harry Chow's man said, handing over the manuscript.

Harry read over it slowly, then handed it to Zeng. "If you are satisfied with this we can affix the seals and complete our business."

Zeng quickly read through. It was as they had discussed. The Black Dragon Benevolent Society was investing in a quarter share of a $200,000 shipment, to be delivered in five-tael tins selling for $8 each — a good sum when Chinese workers building the Central Pacific railway line over the mountains were being paid $30 a month.

Zeng smiled as he handed the documents back to Harry to affix the seals. The trade into the Bay was rumoured to be worth $2 million a year, and he was about to get a share of it. Lai Choi had been checking the second document, which he now passed to Zeng. He took several minutes to give it a thorough reading while the two older men sipped their tea in silence. The only sound in the room was the chink of china teacups and the soft rhythm of Lai Choi's wheezy breathing.

Time for the ritual of exchanging seals — the climax of their formal business. The principals handled the seals as though they were treasures, passing them and the accompanying ink blocks to the clerks, who each stamped both documents with the relevant seal and waited a few seconds for the ink to dry.

Zeng felt his shoulders relax and let out a long sigh that he masked with his hand in front of his mouth. No point in letting Lai Choi see he'd been tense and anxious. It was finally done. He was on his way as an independent merchant.

He was settling back into his chair with a satisfied glow when he saw Lai Choi's bushy eyebrows gully into a sour V shape across his forehead. He had two documents alongside each other and was comparing the chops.

He reverted to Cantonese with a sharp querulous exclamation, followed by a stream of invective.

Zeng rose out of his chair and pulled at the edge of the documents to see what the problem was.

Lai Choi had also risen from his seat and was stabbing at the pages with his finger angrily. "What is this fake? It's a counterfeit chop!" A red flush infused his angular cheeks. "Never have I seen such a thing. Your father would never—" He broke into a coughing fit that stopped him completing the sentence.

Zeng had stopped breathing. His throat was bone-dry, and he had to take a deep breath to get air into his lungs. "What is wrong? That is the dragon chop of the House of Chung. The Dragon Seal from my father's own hand!"

How could they challenge him? There must be some mistake. He moved around the table so he was standing next to Lai Choi, who was still stabbing his finger at the red ink pattern, the sinuous dragon. "See here; a five-toed dragon. An outrage! A dangerous jest! You know as well as I do, no one but the Emperor is entitled to display five toes. Now compare it with this agreement I made with the comprador last year, with the Dragon Seal he was using then."

He stabbed at the alternative page in triumph. Zeng bent over the design, and could see it clearly. A four-toed dragon. He heard a thundering noise in his head. His great-grandfather had enjoyed high ranking as a trusted court retainer — high enough to qualify for nobility status and a dragon seal with four toes. Four, but not the imperial five. Anyone attempting to use five risked execution for treachery.

Lai Choi rose, his bulky frame looming over him. He was bug-eyed and breathing hard. He took hold of the agreement they had just signed, his surprisingly long, slim fingers holding it delicately on opposing edges of the page. Then he ceremoniously began tearing it apart, first in one direction, then in another, until paper confetti showered the table like small white petals. He glared at Zeng and without another word he stormed out.

Fifty-Two

They rode out of Nevada City with the two o'clock sun burning at their backs, a fool time to be on the trail but they couldn't afford any more delay. John smiled. It was probably the oddest quartet he'd ever been a part of.

He glanced behind him, to the end of the group, where Deputy Samson sat in his saddle as if it was a second home, well-shaded in a broad-brimmed hat, hips loaded with visible firepower. Sing Pak was alongside him, looking like a mild-mannered traveling apothecary in an anonymous dark-blue tunic and head-hugging black cap. And Pania. He cast a sly admiring glance her way. Visit a ladies' store and she could assemble an outfit in minutes. She rode astride her hired mount in an amethyst riding skirt and blouse, a matching turban wrapped around her head to mask her brutal hairline.

There was nothing remarkable about their appearance, and that was the way they wanted it. But in their saddle bags they carried the props that might come in handy for the challenge ahead — ambassadorial brocade for Sing Pak, for starters.

The fifteen-mile ride to New Gum Saan would take them several hours, and they had agreed they should ideally steal into the one-time ghost town at dusk. When they got closer, Pania and Sing Pak would find somewhere out of sight to rest up while John and Samson reconnoitred the area. They needed to get a better sense of the lie of the land, and what sort of reception awaited them.

Around them, the surrounding hills had been reduced to barren pale rock. The first wave of miners had stripped them of trees for timber for houses and mine props. Now the sterile mountain faces were being flushed away by high-powered hydraulic water guns which laid bare everything.

There was no foliage, and few birds. The only sound was the occasional squeak of saddle leather and the snuffling of their mounts. They slackened their pace as the route flattened and widened, riding abreast as Sing Pak filled them in on the history of the town they were heading for.

John already knew that New Gum Saan had seen its first heyday in the 1850s, when placer gold was found. Several hundred miners flooded in to work Dogville Creek, as it was then called, but after they exhausted the easiest gold sources they moved on to the 'next big thing', as happened all over Gold Country.

A German consortium built a stamper with ambitions to mine deeper, but when that too disappointed, the discarded diggings were left to the Chinese. Dogville became New Gum Saan as the Guongdong men happily took over, and the name proved prophetic. The relentless work ethic of the new citizens unearthed ore drifts that yielded good returns. It was rumored that a substantial number had made enough to fulfill their dream of returning home wealthy men, but in time the Chinese too had moved on, leaving New Gum Saan a ghost town again.

They saw no one else on the road and were making good progress so when they came across a scrubby oasis — a muddy circular pool ringed by wiry-leaved bushes a short ride off the main road — John suggested they pull aside and water the horses and themselves.

Sprawled on a clump of long, dry grass, his back up against a warm rock, he closed his eyes, sipped water from his canteen, and was tempted to forget what lay ahead. Sing Pak wasn't about to let him do that. He squatted down beside him, took a sharp stick and began to sketch lines in the sandy gravel. "Here's what I've been able to pick up listening in keyholes," he said with a wolfish grin. "Your father would be pleased."

John smiled broadly. Russell & Chung's early success was partly founded on Sir Robert's seemingly uncanny ability to be first with the news of developments that could make or break their business. Being first, and being willing to act without hesitation, had confounded the competition and made him rich. "I'm all ears," John said.

"New Gum Saan is nestled in a natural crater, not unlike this one but much bigger. The miners camp in stone houses and shelters that were left behind by the first wave — just abandoned, rough, doss housing. And I understand there are a couple of stamper mills left behind. The defunct first one, and then one the Germans built that was discarded before the Chinese moved in. I believe there's even an old Catholic church. That doesn't get much use either, these days," he said with a grin.

As he talked, Sing Pak scratched a diagram on the ground. "No deep tunnels, but some smaller ones like coyote holes. Those, and big ditches dug by the Chinese for the water for the hydraulic guns. The most likely places to hold Ollie and Lily if they are here would be somewhere in the buildings, rather than outside. That's my guess, anyway.

"As you'll know, the workers mainly belong to the same villages back in China. They'd pretty well all be beneficiaries of Black Dragon benevolence. Whether that makes them automatic supporters of Zeng or not, I don't know. But they are more likely to feel a loyalty to him over an outsider."

John nodded. "And to Ollie? What about loyalty to Ollie?"

'Ollie is well respected. Very well respected. But if Zeng slung them a plausible line promising great wealth and riches — who knows?"

John and Samson left the old man and the beautiful woman resting in the flickering shade and went out to take a look around. He guessed they must be only a short ride from New Gum Saan, where Ollie and Lily were being held — if they were still alive.

And so it proved to be. Not far up the track they came to a weathered signpost. It had once shown a primitive stick drawing of a dog with an arrow pointing to a right-hand fork that wended its way down a gentle curving corner that disappeared into scrubby sage. The gritty surface showed signs of recent traffic but gave no other hint of human habitation. John looked closer and saw that the dog drawing had been scored with an X which had faded to near invisibility in the sun. Dogville no longer. Alongside it someone had painted a sign in Chinese script. Now it was New Gum Saan. New Gold Mountain.

There was a sudden crunch of wheels behind them. John brought his horse around quickly and his jaw dropped.

A tall, thin merchant, staff in hand, loped along beside a small covered cart pulled by a wild-eyed mule. The canvas awning that stretched over the main frame was rolled up on the side away from the sun, revealing a cornucopia of imported and local food items. At the back, legs draped over the tail gate, two small children and a woman sat jammed in next to a bamboo coop containing live chickens.

John had seen before the amazing network of provisioning that kept miners who were hundreds of miles away from San Francisco's exotic suppliers stocked with practically anything they could wish for. Dried cuttlefish or shark fin, pickled vegetables and candied fruits, there was no shortage of exotic items like these in Grass Valley, and all along the Pacific Rail Construction route, anywhere where Chinese workers gathered. He expected to find it there. But out here in the backside of Nevada County?

The smells stirred memories of his Hong Kong childhood — of star anise and turmeric, of pickled eggs and duck, flattened like cod fish and preserved in a paste to keep it fresh. He was ten years old again and back on Queen's Road.

He slipped from his horse and waited for the caravan to draw up to him, then said, "Ni hao."

The familiar greeting took the merchant by surprise. He raised his hand to his forehead in a semi-salute and replied: "Ni hao."

John pointed at himself by way of introduction: "Hon." Chinese for John.

The merchant bowed respectfully. "Moon Ting."

"You've got a very full load there. Where are you off to, Moon Ting?" John continued in Cantonese, moving closer. Pretty blue-and-white ceramic jars of pickled vegetables, dried shrimp which almost certainly had been fished from San Francisco Bay, salted melon seeds, pickled ducks' eggs. Locally grown, elongated Asian radishes, foot-long beans, and bitter melons. Sweet-tasting imported wines and brandies in little crockery jugs, small neat sausages, preserved snow lichen, dwarf oranges and ginger. He leaned against the cart and breathed in the fragrance.

At the front, away from the food and the chickens were gew-gaws and gifts: fringed squares of Chinese silks (the Californians called them "Spanish shawls"), finely wrought combs, Chow Chow fireworks, Canton shoes, striped pants, cooking pots and bowls . . . The merchant had enough here to supply a village. "You're going to New Gum Saan? Is that right?"

Moon Ting broke into a broad toothless smile. "Hungry Ghost

Festival. A day before full moon. Big celebration. Lots of Chinese people. They will want to eat."

John's heart lurched at the merchant's words. If he'd heard the crash of cymbals overhead he couldn't have been more surprised. *How have I been so blind?* He'd missed all the clues.

"Of course," he said. "Chung Ji Zeng and the Black Dragons are marking Hungry Ghost night. What have you heard he has planned?"

Moon Ting glowed with importance. "My friends say very important night. Zeng's father's spirit roaming. Very bad joss. And his wife. Very bad." He shook his head. "They say Zeng is going to settle their roaming spirits and bring new success and riches to all families. Everyone is very excited."

John hoped Moon Ting didn't notice his sharp intake of breath. "I see." He tried to inject the two short words with all the enthusiasm he could muster, but his insides were quivering like jelly. He reached out and shook Moon Ting's hand. "May it be a most propitious visit for you and your family."

He stood aside and watched as the merchant's cart swayed on. The world receded to one urgent drumbeat in his brain.

Ollie. What has Zeng planned for him? Surely he'll have to account for his absence at the gathering in some way? And how in the name of Jove, among hordes of adoring followers, can I pull off a successful rescue for both him and Lily?

As he and Samson rode back to the oasis, he explained to the deputy what Moon Ting had said. "There could be a couple of hundred people out here. I'm not sure if that's to our advantage or disadvantage."

Samson shrugged. "I'm sure we can make it work in our favour."

Sing Pak had agreed to play look out for his brothers and when John got back they were there, watering their horses and brewing coffee over a glowing fire.

"Am I so glad to see you." John let his horse drink as he squatted on his haunches with Nat and Seb by the fire. "Got a lot to tell you, but first, I'm a fugitive no longer." He gestured to Samson. "Elias will fill you in on that. He's now just as interested as we are in finding Zeng."

Fifty-Three

From his cover in the dark corners of the derelict stamper battery, John could see a long, narrow dais set up in front of the skeletal rusted pillars of the abandoned gold crushers. The flat surface was laden with platters of food, and the guests of honor dipped and licked and ate with relish, an unruly Upper House facing down the brawling crowd below.

He loitered in the shadows on a side wall, obscured from view by a big iron basin set in a frame, a bit like a bucket over a wishing well — the rust-red remains of a berdan, the big iron dish where gold particles were crushed to the consistency of flour and then extracted in a slurry of mercury.

Zeng had set up in the area at one end of the derelict mill. The space around him had the magnitude of a soaring cathedral nave, but instead of marble columns the perpendicular supports were solid timber, and instead of an altar the ochre-red stamper battery loomed, its ten ore crushers reared up like two-storey battering rams. Forever silenced, they stood a mute witness to the night's proceedings. On the right-hand side of the crusher columns, a wide wooden stair rose on three levels to the top platform, where a conveyor had once disgorged gold-bearing quartz into ore bins, ready to be smashed in the stampers.

Like some weird version of the Old Master he had copied for fun when he was younger, John had the uncanny sense he was viewing a deranged version of Tintoretto's *Last Supper*, with Chung Ji Zeng a delusional Jesus, surrounded not by disciples but by a ratty pack of envoys, influential merchants and enforcers.

The dais was illuminated by a string of rainbow-colored Chinese lanterns slung overhead, and John could clearly make out the faces of the seated men. He didn't have to look any further to grasp the significance — the top men in all of the Six Societies were represented, Harry Chow among them, though he couldn't see Lai Choi.

His gut clenched at the sight, and his knees momentarily sagged. Zeng had bribed or pressured practically everyone who was anyone in the Societies to be here, that was clear, and their presence as guests validated his authority, with or without the Dragon Seal.

In his mind's eye he caught a flashing glimpse of himself, a minute figure dwarfed by a towering wall of water, about to be swept away. *How can we do this? We don't even know where Ollie is. And we have nothing to match the numbers of armed men Zeng commands.*

He pinched himself on the bridge of his nose to bring himself back to reality. *I will run this race to the end, no matter where it leads me. I will finish strong. Ollie and Lily deserve it. Ting Hon and Beautiful Jade too. I will finish strong.*

He noted the row of empty, red-varnished chairs facing the high table. Folk tradition dictated they were left vacant for the ghosts to use while viewing the musical entertainment that would come later, and no one was game to challenge a ghost for a seat.

He felt a creeping admiration settle like a damp blanket across his shoulders. Ji Zeng appeared to have thought of everything. It was a pity that he was goodness inverted, a murderer and a jerk. The image of the Tintoretto flashed upon him again: the artist had painted an audience of angels, clamouring above, witness to the scene below.

Immanent, ever-present and watching, maybe even influencing events. He shot a prayer heavenwards: *Please send your delivering angels. Nothing else will do, here and now.*

Down one side of the battery space he could see Moon Ting's caravan parked with several others of similar design. They were doing a roaring trade, and he didn't have to taste the food to know they were serving up minced-pork cakes, preserved oranges, water-lily seeds, oyster pie, sweet rice, and Chinese cigarettes. He could smell the mixed aromas of fried meat, sugary dumplings, and jasmine tea.

Underlying it all was the heightened awareness that flooded the senses on a night like this, a night when even the most stoic of men could feel dwarfed by supernatural forces. The cavernous space vibrated with an intense energy that flowed back on itself, ramping up the subtle subterranean levels of hysteria, layer on layer.

A starlit sky leaked through great gaping holes in the roof, but no cooling draft reached the roiling crowd of men who ate, smoked, dug one another in the ribs with laughter at ribald jokes, and waited with twitchy anticipation for the show they sensed was coming.

The Hungry Ghost smell so familiar from John's childhood filled his nose and caught in his throat, making him cough. It was the saccharine sweetness of spoiled fruit mingled with the acrid tang of burnt paper money, patchouli hair tonic, and incense. There was nothing else like it.

"They say Chung Ji Zeng is boss now."

"So where's Ji Ming?"

"No one knows."

Snatches of conversation. Many of those present understood there was more at stake here than a Hungry Ghost festival. Suddenly the conversation died away. An eerie silence fell in the dark void where John estimated five hundred expectant men waited, with a thin trail of latecomers still filing in.

Then there was a thunderous drum roll and a gay swag of instrumentalists, singers and acrobats filed in, led in by a clutch of drummers and a towering man in red-and-gold priest's robes who rang a bell as he strode at the head of the band. Their part was to rouse this world and the next with the sound of raucous merry-making, the beat of the drums, clang of the cymbals and shrieking of horns and human voice producing a wall of sound which was believed to both please and frighten away any ghosts who might be hovering. They were loud and vital, the rising fluid notes of the horns and flutes contrasting with the deep underpinning of bass and chorus, while the acrobats tumbled back and forth in a nimble display. The crowd's silent approval was soon replaced by enthusiastic cheering every time the priest rang his bell, calling the spirits in.

The din went on for five or ten minutes, an effusive interlude signaling proceedings were moving into a new phase. As the music faded, the priest stepped up and took Ji Zeng's wrist and raised his arm above his head, presenting him to the onlookers like a newly crowned king. "Chung Ji Zeng, Black Dragon master," he crowed, and the crowd roared its approval.

Zeng looked pleased, bowed, and stepped up to speak. "My people, the men of New Gunn Saan," he began. "We came to this place of California seeking our fortunes, and some of us found them. Some. But not all. I'm here today to tell you there is no going back from here, for we have a brilliant future opening up before us. If you will put your trust in me, you will see rejoicing."

He clenched his hands into fists and raised them above his head in a victory salute. "That is my promise, worth a thousand pieces of gold," he shouted louder, quoting a popular proverb.

The crowd responded with a thunderous affirmation and the stamper battery thundered with the drumming of feet and clapping of hands and the echoing cry from a hundred voices: "Yi nuo gian jin!" *Promises worth a thousand pieces of gold.*

John felt his stomach dropping to his knees. The men closest to him stood with their eyes transfixed on the scene being acted out, wanting to believe in Ji Zeng, the new savior.

"We have unfinished business this day my people, and we now must make it right." Zeng looked back along the dais, eying the solemn, oddly compliant line-up. "My father, the Venerable Ting Hon, came to a terrible end, as you all know. It is a great shame to my house that his unhappy spirit still wanders, seeking justice. There are two people responsible for this travesty, and they are both here tonight."

He paused theatrically and gazed out over his audience. John's hollow feeling intensified, as the man he'd always just known as Second Son demonstrated with each new breath he was a gifted and dangerous demagogue. He wondered distractedly if the others were having any success at finding Ollie and Lily, or whether they were watching the unfolding drama from somewhere in the shadows.

Zeng had his audience captivated. With impeccable timing he whirled back to the men on the dais and gave a sharp command. Two retainers, big men clad in the black robes of the Black Dragon house, stepped out of hiding in the stamper ruins, and dragged forward a white-robed figure, his arms pinned either side of his body, held between them in a prisoner's grip.

A furious buzzing sounded in John's ears. He braced himself against the berdan frame, breathing deeply, waiting for the dizziness to pass. *He has Ollie here, and is going to make a public display of him.*

Panic rose in his gut as he tried to put himself in Zeng's head. *What is his next move, and how can I be ready to meet it?*

Ollie looked fragile. He was bent over, his head bobbing downward, but there was no mistaking his identity.

Zeng addressed the crowd with angry fervor. "Here is one of the men responsible. Chung Ji Ming. Ting Hon's own son."

Around him men gasped; some cried out. John felt as if he might be sick, and clasped his hand over his mouth, holding himself in rigid check as he watched.

"You will confess to this crime, will you not, Ji Ming, curse of the house of Chung."

Ollie could barely stand or speak. Under the white robe, his frame was skeletal; it wasn't hard to see he was a broken man. He remained mute, collapsed against the side of one of his guards, who shook him violently by the shoulder.

"You will confess to patricide, the death of the beloved father, curse of the House of Chung!" Zeng demanded again, more loudly.

Ollie nodded weakly and said in a papery whisper, "I confess."

They might not have heard the words, but the crowd saw the moving lips, understood he was confessing, and John's ears rang as a vehement wave of howls and catcalls erupted all around him. No one wanted to be guilty by association of such a heinous crime. Everyone wanted to appease the rightfully angry ghosts. The wave of protest swelled and then died in a silent horror as the crowd gazed on. Ollie's face was shining wet in the lamplight.

John didn't hesitate a moment longer. He pulled himself up to full height, stepped out from behind the berdan frame, and addressed the line up on the dais in his strongest voice, "No! No, that is lies! All lies!" His cry was loud, determined, spoken out in clear Cantonese, understood by all the men around him.

He stepped out of the shadows and strode to the stage, to Ollie, his hands swinging in determined arcs as he covered the distance to his cousin in seconds. Ignoring the guards, he stood in front of Ollie and took his face in his hands, caressing the chiseled cheekbones with his thumbs, whispering, "No, Ollie. No." Over and over. He felt a searing pain in his ribcage, so strong his breath caught in his throat, and then his breathing restarted, coming in quick and short puffs, his normal inhale-exhale pattern cut short in the burn of grief.

"He ambushed you with Lily, didn't he?" he said in a low, urgent whisper. "You've agreed to this to save her? Don't you understand? You've made a pact with the devil. And he won't honor it."

Ollie's eyes widened in acquiescence, but he shook his head weakly in denial. "He's got her here somewhere. I have to do what I can to save her." Tears rolled down his cheeks.

Zeng roared, "Seize him!" His urgency galvanized two of his black-clad enforcers, who rushed up and grabbed John by his shoulders and arms. They held him in a tight grip as Zeng paced back and forth along the dais while the crowd watched, spellbound.

"This is the second man responsible. Sir John Russell. This cur, this dog, Sir John, the host who offered my father his house and then failed to protect him. The man was supposed to show Chung Ting Hon the respect, protection and honor of a venerated father."

Zeng spat into John's face, a looping stream of spittle that hit him right between the eyes. "These are the two men guilty of my father's death, Ji Ming and John Russell. Both must pay the price so my father's spirit can rest. They must die!"

Zeng's eyes were wild and glittering. He had a strange, exultant smile on his lips, the ghoulish stiff grimace of a man who had risked everything and won.

The crowd began chanting, "Pay the price! Pay the price!"

John's ears rang with the chant. He shook his head to cast off the spittle on his face. *How in the hell did I get myself into this?* He gave Ollie a quick wink. The momentary shock that crossed his cousin's face showed that he understood.

Ollie was close to collapse, his chalk-white face gouged with deep anxiety lines, his eyes red rimmed with fatigue. His poet's face with its intelligent wry smile had disappeared, replaced by the visage of a frail old rag-and-bone man. But he was holding it together by his indomitable will.

Ollie's own fate would be the thing that bothered him least, John knew. He had no clue where Lily was, what she was suffering, even if she were still alive. But he knew that his daughter would be the biggest burden on her father's shoulders.

Yes, he had to be here. Even though things looked grim for them both, he had to do whatever he could to get Ollie out of Zeng's murderous grasp. Sure, right this second, he had no idea what exactly was coming next or where it was taking them. His stomach churned with a bilious wave as he admitted to himself he was out of ideas. But as long as there was the smallest chance of freedom for Ollie and Lily, it had to be worth the risk. He and Ollie had spent six years — pretty much all of their later childhood and early adolescence — at school together in England. More time than he'd spent with his brothers by blood. They'd backed one another against the other boys' midnight taunts and dormitory bullying. Ollie was picked on because he was Eurasian and John simply because was 'different', born and raised in Hong Kong and ignorant of English ways. He was the elder by three years, and he'd always been stronger physically, the brawler defending them both from pinches and punches, but Ollie was always ready to back him with a steely resolution of spirit. Having each other had been the only thing that had made it bearable for either of them.

The chant rose to a scream. "Pay the price!" A wave of warm air, loaded with the odor of pork dumplings and jasmine tea, wafted up. Miner's work boots drummed the ground in a stamping rhythm.

Nausea rose in John's gullet. He swallowed hard, his throat sandpaper-dry, a bitter taste penetrating his mouth. *What a run I'm having — escaping one lynch mob only to fall into the hands of another.*

It was a dark private joke and he allowed himself a grim grin. He had a dizzy sensation of being catapulted into space. He was flying, had no clue how far, or how heavy his landing would be. He'd never felt so exposed, stripped of the protections of money and status he had taken for granted.

If the bastard is afraid he isn't showing it, Zeng thought. Saliva dripped from the tip of John's nose and he shook his head violently to rid himself of the drool, like a water dog exiting a duck pond. He seemed impervious to the hostile chants and cat calls, staring right back at him with a glare that said, "Come on, then. Just try it."

His dark eyebrows were set below deep forehead trenches, his lips pulled back, baring straight white teeth. His naturally olive complexion was dark with rage. Despite the guards pressing in on his right and his left, he did not cede one ounce of authority to their restraint. "You will not prevail." John leaned forward out of the guards' grip. Zeng could feel the gust of hot breath on his cheek as the bigger man inclined his face so close they were almost touching noses. "You will not!"

Zeng's pulse surged. He took a small step away from that intense stare and laughed. His chest lifted and lightened, his shoulders loosened. "And who is going to stop me? Huh? Who?"

He laughed again and rolled his shoulders to further relieve the tension that had formed like a tight band across the back of his neck. "One thing I like about you — you never give up."

"And nor will I. You got that right."

"Such a waste. Together we could do such great things. It could be just like before, when the comprador ruled. John and Chung. You and me. Nothing needs to change, really. We're just moving on to bigger and brighter things. Besides, your other option is not nearly as attractive."

"I'll take it. The other option." He was fast on the draw, exuded an iron will, and a feral cunning.

Zeng's scalp tingled. The man's intransigence was starting to irritate him. "Come, come. Without even knowing what it is? Even if it means others may die? Ji Ming? Or his beautiful virgin daughter?"

John's glance flickered to Ollie. Zeng saw his prisoners' eyes meet in silent communication, and his half-brother give John a barely perceptible shake of the head.

John let out a long sigh. "Whatever you're selling, Zeng, I'm not buying. And where's Lily?"

He braced himself to straighten up to his full height, hard to do with men holding him down on either side, and in Cantonese spoke over Zeng's head to the line-up of dignitaries. "What possible justification do you have for keeping an innocent girl — your very own niece — a prisoner? Is that just?" His voice sounded out like a trumpet call to battle.

Behind them, the Hungry Ghost crowd was becoming restless. Zeng could hear the rustle of shuffling feet, and a rising murmur of confusion. He was suddenly aware that the initiative was slipping from his grasp.

He turned to the top table, to Harry Chow and the other Society masters. For a moment his gut clenched at the one obvious absence — no Lai Choi. He had refused point-blank to come after the debacle with the fake seal. Luckily Harry didn't have the same strict scruples when it came to profits. He needed more Harry Chows — and he needed to grab control back again, stamp his mark.

He jumped forward and brandished a crowbar, detritus from the mine's past, like a standard bearer. "Respected brothers of Black Dragon, you have seen it with your own eyes. Ji Ming confessed to the murder of his father. And this man refuses to honor the comprador's house. He sympathizes with the patricide. No clemency can be offered to such a man."

Harry Chow's eyes shifted nervously from his face to the men who sat with him. Zeng sensed the conversation with John had unsettled him. He wasn't going to be acquiescent for too much longer.

"We shall waste no further time on this. Midnight is approaching. We know this is the hour of greatest power for the wandering spirits. We must appease them now.' He glared at Chow. "Pronounce sentence!"

The big envoy grasped the dais edge and used it to brace his weight as he lumbered to his feet with a noisy sigh. His rolling extra chin wobbled as he swallowed. He looked down at his hands, still resting on the dais, and then looked up and cleared his throat in a series of barking coughs. "Men of New Gunn Saan—"

There was a disturbance at the back of the hall. Zeng could see men's heads bobbing in the dim lantern light. A strange whirlpool was forming: men at the hub scrambling away, as if frightened of what they were seeing, while others further removed stood frozen, staring. Those closest scuttled crab-like sideways, bumping and banging into the men next to them. A wail of moaning rose and spread until that corner of the mill resounded with a rising howl of protest.

And at the center of it all, Zeng could make out a curtained sedan chair, carried by uniformed attendants, swaying unerringly towards the stage, the crowd wheeling like flocks of birds to make way and then circle back in to feast on the sight. Hanging down the closed sides were embroidered panels of five-toed dragons, the claws of each toe finished with sparkly crystals in red, green and topaz.

As the chair reached the dais, a sacrosanct hush fell over the gathering, as if the people feared a representative of Empress Dowager Cixi was truly in their midst. The musicians, who had faded out to stunned silence as the chair approached, struck up an imperial marching tune. Chow pursed his rubbery lips and stood in undisguised astonishment as the conveyance drew up at the foot of the dais.

The men carrying the chair set it gently to rest and turned in a formal sweep to stand by the closed curtains. With a flourish of one arm they bowed low and then placed their hands on the curtain edge and slowly drew it open.

The music played on and no one stepped out until the final notes died away. Then the trumpets blew a fanfare and a richly robed old man stepped out, his head crowned in a satin-covered pillbox hat from which his dark-plaited queue hung down his back. In one hand he held a gold curved staff stamped with an intricate cross-hatch design. A ruyi, the imperial rod which gave whoever held it the right to speak and rule.

"What is going on here?" He spoke in the stilted accent of the Imperial Court, but Zeng recognized with a start that the face belonged to someone much closer to home — Sing Pak. The comprador's one-time right-hand man. He'd played second fiddle to his father, Ting Hon, but he came from an aristocratic line of court servants. His father and grandfather had famously served the Qing dynasty, and it was Sing Pak's family connections that had helped establish Chung Trading in its early days.

Quick as a flash, John fell on his knees at Sing Pak's feet, dragging his unsuspecting guards with him. "I appeal to the emperor!" he called. Seconds later Chung Ji Ming found his voice and followed suit: "I too appeal to the emperor!"

The great hall fell deathly silent as Sing Pak brandished the ruyi like a sword over John's head. "Under what authority are you held? On whose orders?"

From the back of the hall a loud voice demanded, "Yes! Whose orders? Darkness or light? Darkness or light?" The lone voice was joined by other voices, setting up a chant of "Darkness or light?" and all hell broke loose.

Harry Chow had slumped back in his seat but he now half-rose and pointed an accusing finger at Zeng. "The Black Dragon master, Ji Zeng, he pronounced death on these men. He demanded the death sentence."

"On what grounds?" Sing Pak's face was impassive, his expression distant, but that worked to reinforce his authority. His voice demanded a response. A long minute of silence dragged out in the spellbound hall. "Well? What grounds?"

Zeng pointed at his half-brother who had risen from his prone position and was once again standing between the guards, erect and defiant, no longer a man in abject defeat. Zeng roared, "Murder! That's the charge. He killed my father!" He swung and pointed at Russell. "And *he* abetted him."

"That's lies! All lies! And you know it." John stood his ground, his voice loud, certain and calm. From the way the crowd rustled and shifted Zeng knew it had penetrated to the back of the gathering.

Then without warning John spun inwards, turning towards the shoulder of the man holding his right arm, then ducking low and fast, pulling him with the momentum in a crashing roll over his back. There came the crack of a wrist bone followed by a high-pitched howl.

John spun in the other direction, attacking his second guard. Zeng knew he had to act fast. He whipped out the curved knife he carried in a scabbard on his hip and sprang forward. Within seconds he had Sing Pak pinned against him, the flat-bladed dao knife poised against his throat. "Stop! Stop or he dies."

His second attacker lay crumpled at his feet and John was springing towards the men who held Ollie, but at the sound of Zeng's roar he froze. The chant from the floor had resumed, "Who do you serve, darkness or light, darkness or light?" and men were beginning to rush forward in a melee of discontent as they chanted.

Zeng faced the crowd, his knife stretched across Sing Pak's throat. *What now? I've killed twice already. A third time will be no problem, but will a third body get me what I want?*

He dragged Sing Pak backwards off the back of the platform and yelled to the guards holding Ollie. They responded by wrenching his arm up his back and hustling off the platform in the opposite direction. *I'm not finished yet.*

Within seconds they had all melted into the dark, hauling their hostages behind them, headed to opposite ends of the mill.

I'll have to finish this off in a dirty little secret corner, with no cheering crowds, no public affirmation. But it will still be done.

Fifty-Four

John stood dazed by the sudden turn of events, momentarily unsure who to follow first, Zeng and Sing Pak, or Ollie and the guards. He swung about wildly and looked out over the crowd, desperately hoping to see Samson or one of his brothers emerging from the seething mass, but if they were out there it was impossible to spot them. He whirled back to the space where seconds before Ollie had stood. It took just seconds to make the decision. Ollie. It had to be Ollie.

He took a few quick steps towards the top table. The Six Societies headmen and their associates looked dumbfounded. He was about to address them to try and rally someone to go after Zeng and Sing Pak when he heard a disturbance behind him. He spun around, hand on the revolver he'd retrieved from his captors, and saw Samson, Seb and Nat lunging up the steps to meet him.

"You go after Ollie. Samson and I will take Zeng." Seb's voice was rasping and urgent. He gestured to the dazed hatchetmen who were still sprawled at John's feet, and Samson sprang forward with handcuffs at the ready. "Nathan, give me a hand to handcuff these turkeys to the stamper struts and then go after John." Nathan sprang to do it, yelling, "We've disabled all the muscle men we could find, inside and out."

"Good to see you were doing something." John deliberately adopted a laconic tone, but flashed them a relieved grin that told them how glad he was to see them. "See you soon."

He plunged off the dais, dodging around rusting stampers, thrusting the gun into his belt as he ran. Away from the strings of Chinese lanterns he was swallowed up in a gloomy darkness. He looked up. The shreds of a ruined canvas belt that had once driven the crusher wheel hung eerily over his head, like a giant hovering moth uncertain of where to go. Over the fading noise of the Hungry Ghost crowd he could just make out the slap of running boots on gravel away to his left.

He knew Zeng had headed right, climbing the stairs to the top of the stamper. Noise on the left made it a good gamble these were the men who held Ollie.

He drew out the revolver and ran after the sound, trying for stealth without compromising speed. His biggest danger was breaking his ankle in a blind fall or over-running his quarry and being taken prisoner again himself. *I've got to be careful that doesn't happen.*

They were moving towards the area where the crushed ore was fed out in rushing water onto ribbed separator tables, where the heavier minerals such as gold and silver were caught and the lighter quartz washed away.

The roof in this section had totally caved in and the night sky, stars washed out to invisibility by a luminous near-full moon, bathed the area with light. John drew up fast, skulking back in the shadows, his eyes ranging over the bright void ahead. At first glance it looked empty, but as his breath steadied and his eyes adjusted to the unexpected brightness, he saw that the men holding Ollie had split up.

Ollie was held by one of them, with a machete like an iron band across his throat, backed into the farthest corner of the room. The other was crouched beneath the edge of the gold-washing table, betrayed by a long shadow which spilled across the earthen floor in the moonlight.

He had to take the croucher out before he had any chance of rescuing Ollie, and he had to do it in such a way that Ollie would not be hurt while he was doing it. He was back in Hong Kong, rampaging through the island jungle, playing pretend war with Ollie and the others. He took a deep breath and he could imagine the green woody undergrowth smell of his adolescence.

He thrust his revolver into his belt and picked up a chunk of quartz that lay in a waste pile to one side of the table, which had drop-down sides that screened him from general view. He dropped to his haunches and very slowly made his way around the back of the gold table, hidden by the superstructure that carried the crushed ore in the rushing water from the stampers to the table. It wasn't hard for a man familiar with mining equipment to take cover and not be seen. He knew that somewhere near there would be another gold-treatment station, and in the darkest back corner he spotted it.

The dark, round shape of a rusting berdan pan stood silhouetted in the moon's light. He squatted by the amalgamation table, and considered his position.

The Black Dragon guard was still crouched expectantly behind the table edge, raising his head over the table at intervals to peer into the darkness, awaiting his approach. The thug's companion was holed up with his back tucked into the corner, the comfortable slouch of his shoulders signaling his semi-relaxed state. *Basking in a mistaken sense of security.* John allowed himself a wolfish grin.

There was a gap of eight or ten feet from the gold-washing table to the berdan pan where he would have no cover. He gauged the distances cautiously, still clutching the quartz rock. *Which one to take out first? The guy in the corner or the one hiding behind the table? It has to be the guy by the table.*

With lightning speed John stood and flung the quartz rock at the back of the crouching man's head, then made for the berdan in a crouching run he hoped would not show up in the moonlight. He was into his first couple of steps when he heard the satisfying soft thud of rock against skull and the whooshing noise of lungs emptying of air. The man in the corner gave a sharp exclamation.

John took cover behind the berdan and concentrated on quieting his breathing. After what seemed like an interminable wait but was probably no more than a minute, the corner guard called again, "Sau wong?" What's wrong?

From his hiding place six or eight feet away, John could see the man slumped face down on the earthen floor. He was groaning softly, and a dark flow of blood ran down his back from his head wound. He'd be groggy for a while, but would come round eventually. John had to move fast to capitalize on what Ollie's custodian would choose to do next.

The man thrust the machete into a leather belt at the waist of his black tunic and frog-marched Ollie across the floor towards the prone figure. He stopped a couple of feet away and stared down, disbelieving.

He loosened his grip on Ollie, restraining him by holding a handful of his robe in a fist at the back of his neck, the ugly blade dangling on his left side. The way he held Ollie meant he was staring straight into John's line of sight. *This is it. Now or never.*

He drew the revolver out from his waistband and rose slowly into the pale moonlight. As he unfolded his six-foot frame Ollie's eyes widened to big gleaming orbs. Across the gap John mouthed a word they'd used as a secret code right through their childhood:

"Charge!" It was what they'd said at boarding school when some bully had one or the other of them by the hair, cornered. What they said when they played pirates with the gang of brothers and hangers-on and had to break through an attacking cordon back to their home port. And it was what they used now, twenty years later, in a life-and-death situation.

As John stepped forward with his gun raised, Ollie whirled in towards his captor and violently kneed him in the groin. The man grabbed for his machete as he collapsed like a sack of potatoes, taking Ollie with him.

John was upon him, grabbing for the hand that was grasping for the machete. He found it and held it in an iron grip, bending it back with grim determination until the bone snapped and the man fell back with a scream.

Ollie rolled to the side and found his feet. The cousins stood panting and sweating, covered in streaks of dust and grinned stupidly at one another.

"Jolly good show, old chap," John said with an accent that mimicked the snooty intonation of the public-school bullies who'd made their lives hell. "Now we go help the brothers rescue Sing Pak, and Lily, eh what?"

Ollie threw back his head and laughed with the release of a man who has just escaped the noose. Then he fell on John's neck gasping and laughing and sobbing. "My God, thank you, John. Thank you — it's totally inadequate for what I'm feeling, but it'll have to do for now."

John shrugged him off. "It's nothing, Ollie. You'd do the same for me. Now let's tie up these goons and go get Lily and Sing Pak."

Ji Zeng leaned over the barricade at the very top of the stamper battery, his arm wrapped securely around old man Leong, the ruyi sceptre still held at his throat, and considered his options. Below him the men in the hall gathered in scattered groups, some pointing up at them and talking in excited, high-pitched voices, while others stared around them in silence. Uncertainty cloaked everyone, as they milled around, reluctant to leave but at a loss over what to do next. Stay or go? They'd been expecting a big show, and it was coming up to midnight, when the supernatural world went crazy.

Behind him was the tramway from outside where the ore arrived to be unloaded onto the conveyor belt. He could see John Russell, Nathan and Ji Ming three flights down, staring up at him with anxious faces. So Russell had done what he'd planned and managed to free Ji Ming. But he could see no woman. Apparently they hadn't found Lily. And there was no sign of the other brother.

"A trade!" he screamed. "I want a trade. Leong Sing Pak in return for free passage out of here."

What did he have to lose now? He'd done with any chance of taking over Russell & Chung Trading, but he still saw endless possibilities for a man who was willing to grab a tiger and swing it by its tail. He could still get rich. And having Ji Ming's precious daughter in his thrall would be a sweet way to show his brother he might have lost one battle but he, Chung Ji Zeng, had won the war.

"Leong Sing Pak for free passage!" he screamed down to Russell again, and saw Ollie's head jerk. He dropped the curved dao knife, drew a revolver from his belt and leaned over to take a shot, pressing Sing Pak's spine hard against the wooden railing. Someone screamed a warning and men scattered in all directions. Sing Pak struggled and his shot flew wild, splintering the dais and leaving a faint whiff of cordite in the air.

Someone dropped the string that threaded the Chinese lanterns and the forum space fizzled into darkness. He could hear feet stamping, and smell the dust rising as the prudent snuffed out flames from some of the still-burning lamps. He felt the reverberation in the soles of his feet as the ore loader trapdoor slammed shut, and he swung around to face it, holding Sing Pak in front as a shield.

Damn. Must be Sebastian trying to jump him from behind. He caught a glimpse of a black hat, the glint of moonlight on a revolver barrel and fired off two more shots.

His hand was slippery, his tunic glued across his back, the sleeves sticking against his sides as he moved. Okay, he was in a tight corner, but he could keep them at bay and he still had some trump cards. Lily, for one.

He felt the thump of feet on the stairs below him, and shuffled backwards to the top barrier to lean out and check who was coming. Without the light from the lanterns it was hard to see anything beyond vague dusky shapes, so he held his fire. He couldn't afford to keep shooting wildly at shadows. He only had a couple of bullets left before he'd have to reload, facing who knows how many adversaries.

A flicker of lights on the far side of the battery floor below caught his attention. There seemed to be some sort of procession forming, but in the candlelight it was hard to make out any detail.

He felt Sing Pak stiffen against him. His voice was husky but unmistakeable: "They're coming for you."

Before he could tell the old man he was going loco, the quiet hum of voices below was broken by the silvery notes of flutes, underpinned by a deep, throbbing bass drum. All over the battery floor men gasped and cried out. Dark masses surged towards the disturbance, as well as away from it, whirlpools of movement in the gloom.

A woman's voice strong and lyrical, rose above the flutes, launching a haunting lament. Holding a candle, she led the procession, with two big bodyguards beside her, each with a lantern in his hand and a machete over his shoulder. Zeng felt an eerie sense of the supernatural, and for a second imagined they were surrounded by ghosts. He shook his head to clear it and tightened his hold on his gun.

The singer called the songlines in English, and the mixed chorus of men and women following behind sang them in Cantonese:

> Streams of light flow over the mountains
> As I look for you, my beloved Grandfather,
> Fated to wander these foreign peaks,
> Beyond my embrace but not at peace.

The singer was statuesque and commanding, dark hair falling from a violet turban to her shoulders, the deep lavender of her gown shimmering faintly in the candlelight. Zeng's stomach clenched at the sight. It was the opera singer, Russell's woman, the one he detained for a little chat just a day ago.

What the hell she was doing here he had no idea, but she'd clearly not learned her lesson about not sticking her nose in where she wasn't needed. His eyes swiveled to what came behind Pania and the chorus. Sing Pak's sedan chair, held aloft by four of the acrobats who'd entertained the masses earlier, the poles at each corner holding a lantern which threw light onto a woman in a gauzy white dress that made her look like a ghost.

The curtains of the sedan had been stripped clear and the chair hoisted higher, so that it now resembled a bier-like platform. The new arrival sat erect, one hand raised in salute as she was conveyed through the crowd which melted before her.

> Streams of light flow over the mountains
> As I look for you, my beloved Grandfather,
> Fated to wander these foreign peaks,
> Beyond my embrace but not at peace,
> Your life cruelly ended by a traitorous son.
> Cruelly ended by a traitorous son.

Lily! Somehow they found Lily!

Zeng loosened his hold on Sing Pak as he stood transfixed by the sight of Lily's sudden appearance. The old patriarch took a step away from him.

Zeng's jaw dropped as the group slowly wended its way across the stamper-battery floor to the dais where some envoys still sat, goggle-eyed. The crowd swooped like starlings settling to rest at dusk, black-winged, diving in close, then wheeling away in overlapping circles as the procession moved through the human mass.

> Streams of light flow over the mountains,
> As I look for you, my beloved Grandfather,
> Beyond my embrace but not at peace.

The singers were drawing their song to a conclusion, and now stood in a semi-circle around the sedan chair as Lily was helped out to stand in front of everyone.

The hall burst into loud conversation and then stilled as she raised her hand like a queen who could expect unquestioning obedience from her subjects. In a clear strong voice she began, in perfect Cantonese, "Hello all people gathered here tonight to appease the Hungry Ghosts. It is close to midnight, and we have work to do. I am Lily Pakenham Chung, only daughter of Chung Ji Ming. Until a very short time ago I too was a prisoner of Chung Ji Zeng, destined like my father to be food for the fishes. This man, my Uncle Chung, my father's brother, has done unspeakable things in pursuit of ambition and riches. The worst of these by far is murdering my grandfather — his father — and his father's young wife, Beautiful Jade.

He has an appointment with fate on this Hungry Ghost night, and I plead with you to see it is fulfilled."

Her voice rang out with unearthly clarity, and the men seemed spellbound by its purity and power. She drew a small scroll from the folds of her skirt. The sedan man closest to her leaned in to shine a lantern on the wording, and she began her recitation:

"My grandfather's spirit cries out to us standing here tonight. He mourns for the many lost days of joy he should have shared with his young wife, and he seeks rest for them both. I beg you, do not fail him, the venerable Lord merchant you knew and loved. What follows is a lament for my murdered grandfather, with thanks to the ancient poets."

She then began, in a rhythmic, musical cadence.

> For you I would hover at the end of the nine heavens,
> And clutching the reins gallop away:
> I would go east to watch the shimmering Fusang Tree, where the sun rises,
> And venture west to where the Ruo River runs at land's end, where the sun sets,
> Northwards I would go, to attain the isle in Dark Sky,
> Soaring to the south I would ascend the Red Hill, where the immortals live,
> But I do not find you, beloved Grandfather,
> Fated to wander these foreign peaks,
> Beyond my embrace, but not at peace,
> Murdered by a traitorous son.

She looked up from her scroll, as if piercing the gloom to the farthest corners of the stamper expanse, and said with chilling finality, "Tonight, Grandpapa, you will find peace."

For five, perhaps ten seconds, total silence prevailed. It was as if no one dared to breathe. And then the place erupted into stamping and cheering, the men showing her as words alone could not that they accepted the justice of her cause.

Some of them raised their heads and looked up, checking to see if Zeng still occupied his position alongside the stamper feeder. Others stampeded for the stairs without any further hesitation.

The floor beneath his feet shuddered. The thought flashed through him that the old timber might not stand the strain of dozens of stamping feet, but it was swept away by a footfall much closer to him. He wheeled around to see John Russell standing a few feet away, gun trained on him.

"Step away from him, Sing Pak."

Russell stared coldly into his eyes, his gun hand unwavering, as he nodded towards the older man to move further away.

Zeng pulled out the knife he kept stowed in his boot and assumed a crouched, defensive stance, weaving from side to side like a snake. *Let him come for me, I'm not giving up.*

"It's over, Zeng. The game is over." John's voice was soft but menacing, barely audible over the roar of men's voices and feet coming closer up the stairs. Behind him Zeng could see bobbing heads as the vanguard reached the top level.

Then with an almighty crack of timber the stair struts gave way, and the whole structure broke away from the upper platform. Part of it hung drunkenly in mid-air, still attached, men clinging to it in terror. The air was thick with dust and splinters, making his eyes water.

A great keening wail rose, drowning out the lament of the chorus below, which had resumed. Within seconds the superstructure broke free and plunged men, loose planks, and sections of boxed-in stair onto the crowd below.

Zeng leapt over the barrier behind him and onto the giant wheel that bordered this side of the upper deck. When the stamper battery had been in operation, this steam-driven belt drove the crushers. He grasped at the rotting canvas which hung in shreds from the structure, gambling on getting a free ride to the ground and escaping into the chaos below. John was now trapped up here, able to exit only around the back through the ore galley onto the mountainside.

If he could make it to the ground, it would be easy to escape while the crowd was intent on rescuing others. He hung onto the canvas, his fingers grappling furiously to get a strong hold on the flimsy material. Several times it gave way and he dropped precariously, but each time he managed to grab a new strip and hang on.

With a wild swing of his legs, he gained momentum and wrapped them around one of the wooden spokes that came out from the wheel center, further stabilizing him. Now he just needed to exert some weight to get the wheel moving downwards to the ground. He looked up and saw that John had been joined by the deputy. Samson was peering over the top of the barrier, yelling something to him, but the noise from the collapsed stair drowned out his voice. He looked upwards with a jeering grin. "An di geen!" See you around.

Then the wheel spoke he was entwined around trembled, and slowly began to peel away from the upper rim of the wheel. He looked up just in time to see it separating from the central base and, as if in slow motion, it collapsed outwards. He flailed towards the canvas drapes that hung like ungodly shrouds around him. He got his fingers latched around one, then again sensed movement above him. Russell was leaning out, a long blade in hand, hacking at any shreds of canvas belt he could reach. Hacking with Sing Pak's imperial sceptre, the totem of upright authority.

Zeng felt the tautness of the belt suddenly slacken. There was nothing there but air! And then he was free-falling, spinning at violent speed to the rushing earth. Hot air, the odor of sweat and fear, hit his nose as he plummeted towards the seething bodies. One of this father's favorite sayings trailed like a shooting star across his mind as he fell: *No matter how big your hands may be, they can't cover the whole sky.*

And then there was darkness.

Fifty-Five

The five candles on the white-iced birthday cake glowed amid the flowers and the pink and white streamers that graced the table centerpiece for this happy family occasion, Minette's fifth birthday. Graysie's — and soon to be Nathan's — adopted daughter took a big breath, pursed her little wet lips, ballooned out cheeks that were shining with happiness, and in one big huff blew out the flames.

"Out in one blow! Now make a wish." Graysie drew her arm affectionately around the child's back as they all broke into a round of 'Happy Birthday' followed by three cheers and dissolved into laughter and chatter.

Everyone who was precious to John was here, safe and accounted for. His half-brothers Nathan and Seb sat next to one another at one end of the table, while he and his cousin Ollie sat opposite them at the other end. Spread between them over plates that bore the gnawed-over chicken bones and cake crumbs of a well-consumed feast, was almost everyone he loved, in a happy disarray of relaxed attitudes — elbows resting on the table, chairs pulled back to allow room for a laid-back sprawl. Selina and Lily, Pania and Graysie, Huldah and Isabella. And of course sweet little Minette, who was bubbling over with happiness. Basil and Alycia had long ago returned to New York and Leong Sing Pak was on his way back to China, but otherwise . . . he allowed himself a huge sigh of satisfaction.

Before Leong Sing Pak had departed he and John got together for a remarkable post-mortem on the Hungry Ghost night events, where Sing Pak explained he'd anticipated he might have to pull rank and draw on his imperial ancestry to exert a final authority over proceedings, so he'd come prepared with the ruyi sword.

John picked up his coffee and sipped the warm brew. They had made Minette's birthday the excuse for lunch, but it was also the first time they'd all been together since the horror of Zeng's rampage three days ago. They'd all needed time to rest and recover, so it was their first chance, too, to give thanks for the miracle of being alive and the family business being back on the road to restoration in prominence and stability.

They'd gone over the audacious role Lily and Pania had played with their little show in the stamper battery. Pania had already been coaching some of the Chinese singers in a traditional lament; Lily composed the poem for her grandfather in her head to stop herself from going crazy when she'd been held prisoner — it all just fell into place. The sedan chair Sing Pak rustled up was assembled from debris left around the battery, along with some Spanish shawls from Moon Ting's merchant caravan.

Yes, all was right with the world. Ollie and Lily seemed to be recovering well after getting the doctor's all-clear. They were pale, bruised and sore, but starting to feel better.

So why did he not feel over the moon with relief? Instead of being charged up and raring to go, he had woken every morning since the Hungry Ghost showdown with a heavy heart, his body a leaden weight in the pearly dawn light, with no desire to raise himself from the mattress, not even to go and see the latest developments at Gold House, which was progressing well.

He felt it now, a sinking feeling in the pit of his stomach, as a tense contraction in his chest increased the rapidity of his breathing. He had replayed the moments before he cut Zeng loose to fall to his death over and over, and asked himself the question he didn't want to answer. Was he simply a pallid version of Zeng? Guilty of putting business interests before anything else, just like Zeng. Was it just a difference in degree? He would stop at murder. But not, when it came to Elanora, at being an accessory to wilful death.

He remembered Zeng's contempt, and his face tingled hot. He'd never been as close to Chung Ji Zeng as he had been to Ollie, not by a long shot, but he still mourned for what might have been. He sensed the shame, rising like a hot tide of self-loathing inside, as he told himself he should have anticipated, could have stopped, Zeng's deadly assault. If only he'd taken the time to observe, to register Zeng's toxic ambition.

Zeng was right. He had thought he knew everything, and he'd been so far off the mark that the lives of two precious people had been snuffed out.

He glanced up, sensing someone was addressing him, and saw a plate held close to his nose. He breathed in a light fruity smell.

"Have some peach cake." Graysie was proffering a piece of birthday cake with a candle on top with a concerned smile. "Are you all right?" she asked quietly. "You don't seem your usual ebullient self."

Startled at her concern, he took the plate with studied cordiality. "I'm fine. Just a lot to process."

Minette was watching him with a grave expression. He lifted the plate in a toast. "Happy birthday, Minette! Here's to Starlight." The little girl broke into a wide smile at the mention of the pony he had given her.

"Thank you so much, Sir John."

He smiled in spite of his gloomy mood. The child was learning some manners.

Feet scuffed, chair legs scraped as the family members pulled back from the table. They had eaten well and were getting restless. Minette was wriggling in her seat; Lily and Isabella were standing and asking permission to be excused. "Can we go for a little stroll in the orchard? We could take Minette with us — maybe even give her a ride if she wants one." Lily's voice was light and carefree, and she smiled at Graysie as she spoke.

"I'm sure she'd love that!" Graysie beamed, then turned to the other women. "We could move out to the pergola to finish our coffee if you like. It's a lovely afternoon."

Pania, seated the other side of Graysie, rose reluctantly, catching John's eye as she straightened. They had barely exchanged more than a few off-hand sentences since the showdown with Zeng. His heart thumped loudly in his ribcage, urging him to speak, but he remained silent.

He recalled the days before New Gum Saan, when he had imagined Pania as his wife, had thought they could share a future together. His pulse still quickened when he looked at her, but along with that excitement was a deep pain, as if he already knew deep down he'd missed the boat. He'd lost her trust with his deception over Elanora's death, and he wasn't sure he could win it back again.

From what he'd heard, Pania was intent on new plans for a concert tour to Australia and New Zealand. Selina said she planned to reconnect with her whanau, her Maori family, in Rotorua after twenty years away.

They exchanged a wordless look, then Pania turned towards Graysie's bright chatter: "The sun's not too hot, it will be lovely in the gazebo. And autumn will be here soon."

Autumn. Then winter. Another year passed. Life was racing by, and he was growing old alone. One of Ting Hon's proverbs came to mind: *No flower stays red for a hundred days.* The old man had certainly lived every minute of his life in that understanding. John wanted so much to believe he had it in himself to do the same.

"So you're going to New Zealand?"

Pania's hand jolted at the sound of John's deep voice and warm tea sloshed from the cup she'd been raising to her lips into the saucer she'd daintily poised under it. "Oh John, don't do that to me. I nearly spilled tea on my dress."

Desolation. That's what she saw when she looked into his penetrating dark eyes. Eyes that shadowed to almost black when he was upset, and today they were inky orbs. He had been wrapped in despondency for days, and she just didn't understand it.

She had anticipated that freeing Ollie and Lily and restoring the family business to a sound basis would give her old friend dozens of reasons to be ecstatic about life, but it was not so. Even the news that Deputy Samson had broadcast all over town that John hadn't killed Virgil Hale barely drew a response.

It was the day after Minette's birthday lunch. A lazy afternoon, and she was quietly relaxing in solitude in the Stockton House drawing room, patiently threading cross stitch in a needlework sampler she'd had on the go for months and was keen to get finished. She cherished these rare private moments when she could push a needle through linen and reflect, while everyone else in the household was off doing other things.

"New Zealand?" She narrowly missed pricking her finger. "Where did you get that idea?"

"It's not correct, then?"

"I didn't say that. I asked where you'd heard it."

He sank down into an armchair opposite her. "Sorry. May I

disturb you for a moment? You look very comfortably settled."

She had on a modestly styled day dress in a green silk which set off her caramel skin to glowing perfection. Her head was wrapped in a matching turban which made her feel queenly, though her insides contracted at the memory of what it concealed.

"I am relishing some quiet. It's been so turbulent around here."

John's legs were stretched out in front of him with a slackness that looked more like dejection than relaxation.

She gave him a quick smile. "But please do feel free to interrupt. We haven't had a chance to talk in ages."

He looked at her then, but said nothing.

"Would you like some tea?"

He shook his head. "No. I'm fine, thanks. I have to be up at Gold House soon."

She took up her own cup again and sipped. "New Zealand was my home for the first sixteen, seventeen years of my life. I've been finding myself wondering lately what's happened to them all. Wondering if my mother is still alive. While Henry's brother was still alive I got occasional news through him. But now they are both gone I've had no word for the last year. I suppose it's a sign of growing older, that I'm thinking this way."

She gave a wry grin, and he responded with a fleeting upturn of the corners of his lips. "Don't tell me. I've been having the same thoughts of mortality myself." He screwed up his face in a self-mocking grimace. "That whole business with Zeng, knowing I was the one who killed him, it's affected me in ways I'd never had imagined. He was a total bastard, and yet . . ."

He gave a big sigh and then, as if steeling himself for interrogation, said, "I can't help wondering if we were all that different, Zeng and I."

Pania gazed at him in amazement. "You can't seriously think . . .

Oh, John, you have no need to worry on that score. Really?" Before she could stop it she'd given a breathless laugh.

John sat like a stone.

"I'm not laughing at you," she scrambled to explain. "The idea that you're anything like Zeng is ridiculous."

He shook his head and said very softly, "Not so far-fetched. I sat on a terrible secret for sixteen years. I share responsibility for the death of a young mother and the abduction of her children. One of those children . . . Well, we have no idea if he's alive, or what conditions he's living in. And I kept quiet. Why? Out of fear for my own reputation. And for Eustace's, I suppose. And because it suited my business interests. Not admirable, was it. I thought you of all people might find that untenable."

"Untenable." She turned the word over in her mouth. "Do me a favor." She gestured to the bookcase. "Pass me that dictionary, will you?"

With the air of a sleepwalker John drifted to the bookcase and drew out a tattered dictionary. He carried it across the room and placed it in her outstretched hand.

Pania made a show of looking up the word. "Untenable. Meaning 'indefensible'. Now let's see, was what you both did 'indefensible'? Well now, I believe you when you say it was a boyish jape that got out of hand — as much of a nightmare for you as for those involved. I accept that the stagecoach driver's spur-of-the-moment decision to run Eustace down, and the shying of the horses, contributed to the disaster. So, indefensible? Unwise, stupid, ridiculous, certainly. All of those, yes. But indefensible? At least debatable.

"What else? Oh yes, here we are. 'Unsustainable'. Well, that definition is correct, for so it's proved to be. Sixteen years later, it's come back to haunt you. You've had to confess to some of the people most affected by your folly. Face up to them. Put things to rights as best you can. And so far as I can tell, you've done all that."

John's head was cocked on one side, and his eyes were opened wide. He shook his head, as if trying to wake up from a bad dream. "You're making excuses for me, Pania." He spoke slowly, shaping each word carefully, as if he wanted to digest its meaning. He shook his head again. "I would never have believed it."

"Not making excuses, John," she said. "Just accepting that we're not all perfect and we have to pick ourselves up from our mess ups and move right on."

They stared at each other across the low table that separated them. Pania sensed something huge had shifted in their personal geography. The mountain that had somehow loomed between them, blocking their passage to one another, had revolved on its axis, showing another perspective. There had been a clear-cut pass through to the other side all the time, she just hadn't seen it before.

Sir John Russell settled himself back into his chair, the familiar alertness of old she knew so well shining from his deep brown eyes. He smiled, and she caught a twinkle of the boyish mischief that had always been there under the mantle of the serious businessman.

"So, New Zealand. What's the story? When are we leaving? Must say, I've always wanted to go there."

THE END

Thank you very much.

GET A FREE PREVIEW of the FIRST FOUR CHAPTERS of DOUBLE JEOPARDY, Book Three in Of Gold & Blood.

He's haunted by war. She's searching for her twin. When a mysterious murder brings them together, can solving the case heal their broken hearts? If you like shocking twists and turns, emotional journeys of the heart, and romance that defies the odds, then you'll love this third installment in a pulse-pounding story.

Building a relationship with my readers in one of the nicest things about writing. Of Gold & Blood is planned as a multi book series and in future volumes we'll trace the fortunes of key characters like Alex and Rosie, travel back in time to learn more of Elanora's ill-fated first love, as well as meet some exciting newcomers – like Nathan's sisters and Pania's brother.

If you would like to join my non-spam updates to keep in touch, sign up at this link and you'll receive the first four chapters of Book Three in the series, Double Jeopardy for FREE within minutes. This also signs you up for my email list, where you can expect to receive monthly updates on new books and free giveaways. I'll never sell, rent, or misuse your information.

http://www.jennywheeler.biz/free-book/

MAKE A DIFFERENCE

Enjoy this book? You can make a big difference.

Reviews are the most powerful means for an author like me to get attention for my books. Much as I'd like to, I don't have the reach of a New York publisher, and bill boards and full-page advertising are way beyond my budget.

But I do have something much more powerful and effective than that, and it's something those publishers would kill for:

A committed and loyal bunch of readers.

Honest reviews of my books help bring them to the attention of other readers.

If you enjoyed this book I would be grateful if you could spend just five minutes leaving a review on the book's Amazon page.

Thank you very much.

ACKNOWLEDGMENTS

So many people have given me help and guidance with this second book in the Of Gold & Blood trilogy, and some of them – research librarians for example – I don't know by name to thank personally. Never mind, be assured of my gratitude, especially for access to the wonderful Interloan facility which allowed me to wander into some weird and wonderful, little-visited corners.

In particular, I want to thank Gold Country historian Wallace R Hagaman for his warm and helpful response to my inquiries about Chinese customs and experiences in nineteenth century California. Wally was a delight to correspond with, and provided me with copies of two of his publications, Chinese Temples of Nevada City and Grass Valley, 1868–1939 and The Chinese Cemetery at Nevada City, California, and a variety of historical clippings, which were especially helpful.

I greatly enjoyed my visits to the Thames School of Mines – thanks to John Isdale - and the fantastic people at the Thames Goldmine Experience, where the functioning stamper battery gives a good idea of what such a beast would have looked like in 1868. Their passion for goldmining history was contagious.

For invaluable advice and guidance on Chinese names in this place and time I am beholden to Auckland historian Lily Lee, who has done many years of research into Cantonese emigration throughout the Pacific in the nineteenth century. And Denise Yong kindly answered midnight emails with urgent pleas for help on the finer points of Chinese vernacular.

Editor Stephen Stratford improved the book in dozens of ways that went far beyond questions of correct punctuation — though of course I relied on him for that too — and proof reader Nikki Crutchley once again helped catch errors and oversights the rest of us had missed.

Sadly I'm sure there still will be some (hopefully small) gaffes and anomalies that stubbornly remain, and for these I accept one hundred per cent responsibility. The time has come, however, to stop combing through the commas and let this second instalment take its place on the shelf. Book Three — Double Jeopardy — is not far behind!

ABOUT THE AUTHOR

Jenny Wheeler is the author of the Of Gold & Blood historical mystery series. Her online writing home can be found at www.jennywheeler.biz and she loves helping readers find fantastic books to read with her podcast, https://thejoysofbingereading.com/

She is on Facebook at www.facebook.com/JennyWheeler.Biz/ and you can email her at jenny@jennywheeler.biz

www.ingramcontent.com/pod-product-compliance
Lightning Source LLC
Chambersburg PA
CBHW021056110726
47900CB00007B/1906